GONE
TOO LONG

———

GONE
TOO LONG

A Novel

Lori Roy

DUTTON

DUTTON

An imprint of Penguin Random House LLC
penguinrandomhouse.com

Copyright © 2019 by Lori Roy

LIBRARY OF CONGRESS CATALOGING-IN-PUBLICATION DATA
Names: Roy, Lori, author.
Title: Gone too long: a novel / Lori Roy.
Description: First edition. | New York: Dutton, [2019]
Identifiers: LCCN 2018053742 (print) | LCCN 2018056027 (ebook) |
ISBN 9781524741976 (ebook) | ISBN 9781524741969 (hardcover)
Subjects: | BISAC: FICTION / Suspense. | FICTION / Literary. |
GSAFD: Suspense fiction.
Classification: LCC PS3618.O89265 (ebook) |
LCC PS3618.O89265 G66 2019
(print) | DDC 813/.6—dc23
LC record available at https://lccn.loc.gov/2018053742

Printed in the United States of America
3 5 7 9 10 8 6 4 2

Book design by Francesca Belanger

For Savanna

Part I

Chapter 1

BETH

March 2010 — 7 years before

The truck driving toward our house is black. Lots of cars drive past our house because there's a good turnaround spot just down the road and the interstate is the other way. Most every car driving past wants to go the other way, and usually they're in a hurry, but not this truck. It drives slow and it glitters where the sun hits it and the tailgate rattles like pennies in a mason jar. I hear it even though all the windows and doors are closed and locked, have to be. That's the rule when Mama's at work and I'm home alone.

The driver, he is a man. One of his arms hangs out the window, and something dangles from his hand. I don't know what it is, but then he keeps slowing down, almost rolls to a stop, and as soon as he flings that something, I know. It has happened before. If Mama comes home and finds it, she'll be angry and maybe even cancel her going-out plans for tonight. And if going-out plans get canceled, Julie Anna won't come.

I wait until the truck rolls past before I slide off the sofa. Making sure no one will hear, I touch my feet down real soft, don't jump like I sometimes do, and tiptoe to the front door. The lock is stiff and I have to use both hands to turn it. Mama's big enough, it only takes her one hand to open the door, and someday, that'll be me. The lock makes a loud click and I freeze. I try to be quiet because I'm doing wrong and I know it. Someone is always watching, that's what Mama likes to say, so I guess I'm sneaking so the someone, whoever that someone is, won't see.

Once on the porch, I keep tiptoeing because the boards here are

soft and creak every time I take a step. Before walking on, I stop
and pretend I'm having a look at the blooms on Mama's magnolias
so whoever is watching, maybe God or Jesus or the Virgin Mary,
won't catch on to what I'm really up to. Then I walk on down the
three porch steps, not so scared anymore because the sidewalk
doesn't creak and won't give me away. I'm also not so scared when
I finally walk outside the shadows and the sun hits me full on.
It's warm on my head and the air is sweet because someone cut
grass today, and high up in the oak growing near the road, the
leaves crackle and the stringy gray moss hanging from its branches
floats on the breeze. Here in the outside, it's easier to breathe and
it makes me feel like Mama and I won't live in this little house with
the soft floorboards forever.

I shuffle my feet as I walk through the thick grass because it's
quieter that way and try not to step on any pecans. Mama calls
what that man threw garbage and says it's nasty and dirty and we
shouldn't even touch it with our hands. She was especially angry
when I studied the state of Georgia this year in school and we
didn't learn one thing about the garbage that gets thrown in our
yard. She even went down to my school to talk to the principal, Mr.
Marshall, but when she got there, he told her she should be figuring on how to get me a decent pair of sneakers for PE instead of
complaining about the history class. I look up when I hear pennies
rattling in a mason jar again.

A hedge of pink oleanders grows along the side of our house
and up to the road. Mama always makes a fuss about my not putting them in my mouth—not the branches or leaves and especially
not the flowers. Mama almost did it one time, brewed up the leaves
in a cup of tea and sat down at the kitchen table like she was going
to drink it. I sat on the floor, my arms wrapped around her ankles,
and cried. After that, I had to live with another family for a while.
When I finally got to come home, my two best friends, Ellie and
Fran, weren't allowed to play at my house anymore, but a new

strange woman started to come. She visited once a month to make sure Mama didn't brew that tea again. On her fifth visit, the woman asked where my daddy was; Mama said I didn't have no daddy and was damn lucky for it. Then the woman scribbled something in a small notebook and told Mama she should cut out those oleanders. But Mama said she'd always know they were out there, growing somewhere, so why not in our yard. Besides, she said, the frost will get them soon enough. It's from behind those pink flowery bushes that the truck's black nose reappears.

It's crawling now, the truck, but it doesn't look like a truck anymore. It has turned into a monster, something with a hide and a heartbeat. I want to move my feet, first one and then the other, and run to the front door, but I can't. It's like the grass has sprung up and knotted itself tight around my toes and ankles and is keeping me right in this spot. The man inside the truck is holding the steering wheel with one hand. With the other, he stretches out across the passenger seat and I think he might wave at me through the open window. But he doesn't. The truck stops all the way and he takes a good long look at me. He looks at me like that woman looked at Mama after she made the oleander tea. Folks look at Mama and me like we're blocking out the thing they'd rather be seeing.

"You be sure your mama gets a look at that," the man says. "You hear?"

His face is covered over by dark whiskers, and his voice makes the tiny hairs on my arms go stiff.

"You hear me, little girl?" he hollers louder when I don't answer. I stumble backward because his voice is like a two-handed shove. "We know what all goes on here. You tell your mama that. You tell her we know plenty."

I'm still standing in the middle of the yard when I hear those leaves crackling overhead again and smell the sweet air. One string of gray moss hangs so low, I could tug it from the tree. I don't know how long it's been since I slid off the sofa and sneaked outside. The black truck is gone. Maybe it's almost time for Mama to come home. I worry I forgot to do my homework, because I have homework this year for the first time. In fourth grade, I have my own books I bring home in a backpack and have to carry to school the next day.

I swallow, and that's what finally gets me to look down at the bag lying at my feet. I poke at it with the toe of my shoe just like Mama did the first time one of them landed in our yard. She poked at it like she was afraid whatever was inside might rear up and take a snap at her. After staring at the bag for a good long while, Mama had pulled a limp piece of paper from inside, called it a flyer, and said I was never, never ever, to read such filth.

So as I squat to the ground, trying to stop my chin from quivering because that man looked at me like I'm worse than nothing and because my shirt is too big since we bought it secondhand at the thrift store and because I'm afraid Mama will one day sprinkle pink oleanders in a pot of boiling water again, I already know what's inside the bag. It's a flyer and it's from the Knights of the Southern Georgia Order. It's from the Ku Klux Klan.

Chapter 2

IMOGENE

March 2017 — Today

Stopping in front of Tillie's place, Simmonsville's only thrift shop, Imogene Coulter pauses, turns away from the smell of fried eggs and sausage gravy rising out of the café on the corner, and closes her eyes until her nausea passes. On the street behind her, the antiques shoppers are just starting to arrive, all of them drawn on a Saturday morning to the part of town where quaint hasn't yet morphed into dilapidated. Most will pass Tillie's place by because there's no striped awning to invite them in. Drawing in one last breath of fresh air, Imogene grabs the door handle and pulls. Overhead, a small bell rings. It's not the weight of the door she struggles with, but instead it's the weight of yet another hangover and another one-night stand.

"Didn't mean for you to come in today," Tillie says, smiling to see Imogene. "Mrs. Tillie'll have my hide for bringing you down here."

Tillie, the shop's owner for going on fifty years, sits at his worktable. He wears a banded magnifying lens over his eyes, and his thinning white hair is tussled. He'll be repairing a cell phone because that's mostly what keeps the lights on these days.

"I was out and about," Imogene says. "Figured I might as well stop by."

Tillie will know she's lying. She came because he sounded worried in the message he left, and he has been more like a father to her than Edison Coulter ever was. The fact that Edison is getting buried today doesn't change that.

"They in the safe?" she asks.

"The cabinet," Tillie says, sliding the single lens up onto his forehead.

Tillie has surely noticed that Imogene's voice is pitched too high, making her sound like her sister, Jo Lynne. The only thing Imogene and Jo Lynne share, besides a mama, is a similar voice, but only when Imogene is compensating. Compensating for drinking too much or sleeping with too many men.

She never asks the names of the men she sleeps with, and they don't need to ask hers. Some, she already knows. Small town and all. Others seek her out because they've traveled to Simmonsville, Georgia, to meet the great Edison Coulter, head of the Knights of the Southern Georgia Order, and they believe his blood flows through her veins. She never tells them otherwise until she's walking out the door, and then she shakes out her long red hair and asks . . . you think this mess come from Ed Coulter? But now Ed Coulter will be buried by day's end, a fact she wishes would bring her some relief, hope even, but doesn't because everything he believed will live on in all the others who followed him. She wonders if all those men who came from across the country will still come now that he's dead, and she wonders why she ever slept with them in the first place. But she knows why. It's been the perfect way to punish herself while simultaneously punishing Edison Coulter. Anyone whose people go a generation or two deep in the South will have a story about a grandpa or a great-uncle who was in the Ku Klux Klan. Imogene's family dates all the way back to the Klan's beginning, but she also has to sit across from it at the supper table every Sunday night.

"We're closing up at noon," Tillie says, and hollers for Mrs. Tillie to come on out and say hello. "We both want to be there today for you and your mama too."

Imogene stretches over Tillie's worktable to give him a hug. Some days, coming here and seeing these two has gotten easier.

Other days, walking through that door is as hard as walking through a brick wall. Today, hugging Tillie is like grabbing on to the one thing that'll keep her afloat.

"Well, look who it is," Mrs. Tillie says, walking out from the back room. She smiles at first, but as she gathers Imogene's hands and explains she's just leaving to get her hair done, her smile softens and droops. "You're looking too thin. Are you taking care of yourself?" And then turning to Tillie, she says, "Doesn't she look too thin?"

"Quit fussing at the child," Tillie says, waving her out the door.

"I'm sure real sorry to be dashing off, sweetheart," Mrs. Tillie says, ignoring Tillie and laying a warm hand on Imogene's cheek. "I know today is going to test you."

Mrs. Tillie doesn't say anything about Edison Coulter being a good man, because it isn't true, and also because his passing isn't what Mrs. Tillie is sorry about.

Imogene tries to say something, but a smile is the best she can do. The hardest part about coming to the shop is looking down into Mrs. Tillie's face—her round cheeks, which shine when she's happy, her watery blue eyes, her tiny nose—because it's like looking into Vaughn's face. From the day he was born, Vaughn favored his grandma.

Still holding tight to Imogene's hand, Mrs. Tillie says, "We'd like to sit with you at the service, if that's okay. If you think your mama won't mind."

Imogene nods, but again can't answer. The last time the three of them were inside Riverside Baptist, five years ago, they'd been burying Russell and Vaughn—husband and one-year-old son to Imogene, and son and grandson to Tillie and Mrs. Tillie. Imogene's first thought upon hearing Ed Coulter had died wasn't any sort of sadness that the only man she'd ever called "Daddy" was gone. It was fear that she'd have to go back inside that church. It was another first. There had been the first Christmas without

Russell and Vaughn. The first birthday. The first family picture. And now, when she thought all the firsts were behind her—the first funeral. The spicy, musky smell of the church, the colored slivers of light that filtered through the stained glass, the hollowed-out organ music, all had come crashing in on her at news of Daddy's death. And she fears the pain of losing Russell and Vaughn would come crashing in too, just as tall and broad as it did the day they died.

Once Mrs. Tillie has left the shop, Tillie tosses Imogene a set of keys. "Not a word of this to Mrs. Tillie," he says.

Snagging the keys from the air, Imogene nods and walks toward the cabinet where Tillie keeps his most valuable merchandise. She's been coming to this shop since she was a kid, and the dusty smell of water-stained mahogany and tung oil is the same now as it was back then.

"Any idea who they belong to?" she says, looking down on the two watches Tillie called her about. They're locked under glass and pinned to a white velvet backing.

"Patek Philippe's the brand, 1957. White gold," Tillie says. "Belong to Robert Robithan. They was a wedding gift from Robert's daddy. Sixty years ago, I figure."

Imogene backs away from the cabinet at hearing the Robithan name. "And I'm guessing Mr. Robithan isn't the one who came here trying to sell them," she says.

Two dozen or so men have been murdered in Griffith County alone over the past hundred years. The story goes that they were all discovered strung up between two pine trees in a clearing near the river someplace south of town, their feet bound and a knife driven through their hearts. No one has ever been arrested, not in a single one of those deaths, and yet everyone knows, has always known. They were Klan killings, and a Robithan man had done the killing. All her life, Imogene's heard the stories, sometimes in the classroom or at the post office or in line at the grocery store. And sometimes in her own home. Like the men of some families follow one another into studying to become lawyers or teachers, Robithan men follow one another into killing for the Klan.

"Haven't heard a word out of any of the Robithans," Tillie says. "Hell, Robert probably doesn't even know the watches are missing, let alone someone tried to sell them."

"So who brought them in?" Imogene unlocks the case and slowly opens the glass cover.

"Natalie Sharon," Tillie says. "Said they was hers. Knew straight-away that weren't true."

A dozen insurance claims have brought Imogene to Tillie's shop over the past few years. Harder times for the town have meant more folks trying to one-up the insurance companies. First the mills shut down; then a good number of jobs were lost to the closing of a nearby prison. Without jobs, folks have taken to pawning their valuables and then turning in insurance claims. Over the past few years, Imogene has cobbled together a career of investigating such scams and disability claims too.

"Here's the thing," Tillie says. "Natalie dates the Robithans' oldest boy. Tim Robithan. You know him, yes? I'm figuring maybe they're in on it together."

Yes, Imogene knows Tim Robithan. Everyone knows him. Whenever Daddy and his men gathered on the courthouse steps, Tim Robithan usually did all the talking. While the rest of Daddy's men would shout and rant, Tim Robithan was soft-spoken and had a way of cozying up to a camera. He could talk into one as if he were chatting with you across the kitchen table. Over the past fifteen years, ever since coming back home from a failed try at making it in Atlanta, Tim has become the son Daddy always wanted but never had in Eddie, Imogene's only brother. And the son Garland never managed to become either, something that gnaws at Jo Lynne most every day, because she always figured if Eddie got passed over, her husband would be next in line. But now that Daddy's dead, it'll be Tim Robithan—not Eddie and not Garland— who takes over. Probably already has.

"Ain't you taking them watches with you?" Tillie says as Imogene closes the cabinet without taking a picture.

Even if the work comes her way, Imogene won't take it. She shakes her head as she snaps the lock back in place, and with her shirtsleeve, she rubs out a smudge her fingers left on the pane of glass. It's the thought of Tim Robithan that's making her want to leave behind no sign she was ever here. Imogene grew up not fearing monsters in her closet but instead fearing a Robithan was hiding in there. Her father represented the Klan of the past, a past that dates all the way back to 1915 and Stone Mountain. Or rather Mama's past dates back that far, her granddaddy's daddy having been one of the sixteen men who marched up that mountain and breathed life back into the Klan after it first withered. All her life, Mama has shunned her family's historic ties and all that the Klan stands for, but Daddy gladly shouldered the fame and carried on the family tradition. Tim Robithan, however, is the cleaned-up, sweet-talking, media-savvy Klan of the future.

"Haven't been contacted about a claim," she says, starting toward the front door. "You really think the Robithans will bother with insurance?"

Imogene's phone buzzes. It'll be Jo Lynne again, reminding Imogene they're all driving to the funeral together. It's Jo Lynne's way of trying to keep Imogene sober, and Eddie too. Whereas Imogene and Jo Lynne share a voice, Imogene and Eddie share a love of whiskey.

"Would you bother with seventy thousand dollars?"

Imogene stops at the door. "They really worth that much?"

"I'm guessing there's not another two like them in the whole of the South."

"My advice?" Imogene says. "You need to call the police. You do not want the Robithans thinking you had a part in whatever is going on here."

"I can't call the police," Tillie says. "I known Robert and Edith Robithan most all my life. And I ain't going to be the one to tell them their son is a thief."

"Why didn't you just send Natalie away, refuse to buy from her?"

"And have them Robithans find out I let her walk off with their watches?" he asks. "What if Tim isn't involved? You really need to ask me that?"

"No," Imogene says. "I get it. How much you give Natalie for them?"

"Nothing," Tillie says. "Told her I needed some time to look into them and asked could I keep them here. Got her on film too." Tillie nods toward a camera mounted on the ceiling behind Imogene. "Told her come back in a few days and then called you."

"That's called receiving stolen property, Tillie."

"With no intent to sell it. Planned to call Robert straightaway until I pieced together Natalie goes with his son. Might mean my word against Tim's, and I know how that ends."

"All the more reason to call the police," Imogene says, pulling open the door.

This is new, Tillie asking Imogene's advice. Ever since she was about twelve years old and realized she would never be a real Coulter, not in name or any other way, he's been the one Imogene has turned to. Eddie is seventeen years older than Imogene, and while he could have been a father figure to her, he was too busy living a young man's life by then. Jo Lynne, ten years older, was too busy with Garland. And Mama would have done anything for Imogene, but asking Mama for help was too close to asking Daddy, and by the time she was a teenager, Imogene wanted nothing from Edison Coulter.

As a little girl, Imogene had been afraid of the Klan and their white hoods with the black, empty eyes, but by the time she accepted that she'd never be a real Coulter, she was old enough to feel, not fear, but instead all the shame and anger that went along with her family's history. She worried what people would think of her once they learned her last name. She worried they would assume she was like Eddie and Jo Lynne. She worried they would think she should be able to stop it or change it and think her cowardly that she wouldn't or couldn't. It was a shame so heavy she didn't even want to carry the Coulter name anymore, and she begged Mama to tell the name of Imogene's real father so she could take his instead. But Mama refused. Even if she had ever told, Imogene would still be known as a Coulter. She is technically a Tillerson, having happily taken her married name, but in this town, she'll always be known as a Coulter.

"Tell Mrs. Tillie I'll look for you both at the church," she says, hoping Eddie has a bottle for the drive over. "And promise me, please, as soon as this door closes behind me, you lock up and call the police. The sooner those watches are gone, the better."

Chapter 3

BETH

Before

Even though Julie Anna left my closet light on and didn't shut my bedroom door all the way, things she always does when she comes to stay with me, I'm not going to go to sleep. I'm going to stay awake until Mama gets home so I can tell her about the terrible thing I've done. After I picked up the flyer that man threw in our yard because I didn't want it to ruin Mama's going-out plans, I stuffed it under my mattress, and now I can feel it under me like a hard lump, a rock digging into my back and reminding me I did bad and that I have to tell Mama the truth. That's what a lie is like, a hard stone cutting into your backside that won't let you sleep.

Lots of those flyers have landed in our yard. Sometimes there is a picture of a man wearing a white, pointed hat who has black holes where his eyes should be and he's pointing right at Mama and me. JOIN BEFORE IT'S TOO LATE, they sometimes read. RALLY THIS SATURDAY. BRING THE KIDS. LEARN TO LIVE AS GOD INTENDED. Mama works with lots of old folks, and some of those folks are black. She takes in their mail, gives them their medicines, and changes their bandages and sheets. She figures her taking care of black folks is why we get those flyers.

Just last month, Mama and I went downtown to buy me an Easter dress, and a group of men were standing on the concrete steps outside the courthouse. One of them wore a blue shirt and tan pants and he talked into a microphone. "That's a rally," Mama said as we stopped on the sidewalk to watch the man and the small group that stood around him, hollering and cheering. The man who held the microphone talked about Simmonsville not needing anybody but white folks to teach its children. Not needing anybody but white folks anywhere. It's only right, he said. You pay good money for that college education. Real Americans should be teaching your children.

As we stood there, other people stopping alongside us to watch and listen too, Mama's hand closed tight around mine, so tight I almost hollered out. "Don't you say nothing about this to Julie Anna," she said. "It'll just scare her." Then Mama looked down at me, tugged on my hand to make sure I was listening. "You understand me? Pretend it's a secret you can't never tell." I nodded like I understood even though I didn't and promised to never tell Julie Anna.

At first I'm not sure what I'm hearing. And then I hear it again. It's someone knocking. Rolling out of bed in a way that won't make any noise, I crawl across the floor, slowly stand, and peek out into the living room. Julie Anna has opened the front door and is talking to someone. With one finger, I push on my door, opening it a bit more. A man stands on the porch. His voice is gravelly, and he holds a square, flat box in both hands. Even all the way in my bedroom, I smell pizza, greasy and salty, the kind that drips runny red sauce down my hand and all the way to my elbow. Mama and I never order takeout because it's too expensive, and frozen from the Piggly Wiggly is just as good. As the man and Julie Anna keep talking, the toes of his two black boots stick over the threshold and almost touch the linoleum in the entryway. He is teetering there, not quite inside. Not quite out. I hear Julie Anna say she didn't order pizza.

"Maybe someone else did," the man says, talking louder than he needs to. "Your mama? A friend? A boyfriend, maybe?"

"Just me here." The light from the living room lamp makes Julie Anna's black hair shine. "House-sitting. Not even my house.

Must have been a neighbor. I'd call them, ask if one of them ordered it, but I'm afraid I don't know the area."

We don't call it babysitting when Julie Anna comes over because I'm too old. We call it house-sitting instead, so she's only part lying to the man. She isn't really alone, because I'm here, but it's true that she doesn't much know our neighbors. She only moved to town a short time ago. She lives in a real nice house with a big green lawn, and her daddy took a job teaching at a college. Mama says it's an important job where he's the boss of lots of people.

Ever since Julie Anna and her parents moved to town, Mama has been saying Julie Anna is the right kind of influence. Her hair is always freshly combed and she doesn't ruin her precious face with makeup like so many of the girls. Mama says that's putting brains over bosoms and she wants the same for me. She wants me to be smart and clean and sweet smelling just like Julie Anna, and she wants me to go to college too because she never did and neither did anyone else in our family. She doesn't want me wearing God-awful white granny shoes—Mama's nickname for the white shoes she has to wear every day—and working a job where I'm on my feet a full eight hours and still can't pay the cable bill.

"Tell you what," the man says. The toes of his boots shuffle forward. "Seeing as you're all alone, ten bucks and it's yours. Will just go to waste otherwise."

Julie Anna glances at my door. Maybe she winks. Maybe not.

"Come on, pretty lady," the man says in that deep voice. "Five bucks. Comes out of my pocket otherwise."

The man's voice flows out of him like warm gravy. That's what Mama says about a Southern man's voice. Like warm, peppery gravy that'll leave you craving more and give you heartburn all the same.

"You got a deal," Julie Anna says. "Let me grab my purse."

Leaving the door open, Julie Anna walks toward the kitchen, where she always drops her books and purse. I watch, and when I can't see her anymore, I look back at the front door. First one black boot steps into our house, then the other. Then all of the man is standing inside. I see mostly the back of him because he is leaning around the door so he can see into the kitchen. I wish Julie Anna would come back and give him five dollars and that he would leave. I wish it more than anything I've ever wished. The man slides the box onto the small cardboard table where Mama and I eat our meals, and in three long steps he crosses the living room, his feet quiet on the carpet, and disappears down the hallway that leads to Mama's room.

The tops of my legs go numb as I sink to the floor, and my heart starts beating fast like it does when Mama turns on her favorite music and gets me to dancing with her. When Julie Anna walks back into the room, I try to speak, even just to whisper, but I can't. With her head down, Julie Anna picks through her wallet and pulls out a bill.

"Here you . . ."

She drops the arm that is holding out the money and, with one hand, touches the top of the square box. She stands still, like maybe she's listening for the man, like maybe she feels something is wrong. But then she shoves the money in her front pocket, steps into the open doorway, and looks outside. I try again to speak, but my tongue won't move and my mouth has gone dry. The woman who used to come once a month to check on me and Mama would ask if strange men ever came to the house. I always told her no. And now there is a strange man here, and I wish I would have told the woman the truth because maybe this is what happens when you lie.

Julie Anna closes the door, and as she takes a step toward my room, she smiles because she is coming to tell me we are going to eat delivery pizza. She's happy and she doesn't hear him or see him, and before she takes a second step, the man is on her.

Part of the man is blue, his shirt maybe. Part is darker, almost black, his pants. Mostly, he is a blur. He is on Julie Anna like they are cars crashing out on our road. It will be a quiet Saturday afternoon, Mama's wind chime ringing, a lawn mower humming somewhere far off in the neighbor's yard, and then a screech and a crash, metal crumpling, glass breaking, and then quiet again. That's how fast he is on Julie Anna.

From where I sit, huddled at the bottom of my door, my lungs burn because I can't take in a single breath. I try to call out to Julie Anna, but I have no air.

"Quiet, girl." The man stands behind Julie Anna, one arm wrapped around her body. She dangles like my sock doll in his arms. "That's a good girl," he says. "Now tell me your name."

"Julie Anna," she says.

"That ain't your name. Tell me your given name."

His back is to me, but I hear every word like he's whispering them in my ear. My neck tingles like his hot breath is washing over it.

"Julia Marianna," she says in a clear and strong voice that makes me straighten my back. "My name is Julia Marianna Perez."

Julie Anna doesn't sound like Julie Anna when she says the name I've never heard. It scares me, makes me pull my knees to my chest and squeeze my eyes tight.

Even though I can't see Julie Anna and the man anymore, I can't stop my ears from hearing. The room was silent after Julie Anna said her new name, but now they're breathing heavy again and stumbling through the room. The air is rushing in and out of their mouths and noses. Something knocks against a wall, maybe the back of the sofa. Something rips. There is more shuffling and knocking, and then something shatters, maybe the glass top of the table where Mama sets her drinks and always uses a coaster. There is more banging about, and the man hollers.

He'll tell me later it was Julie Anna's own fault. She got ahold of a piece of broken glass and sliced him good in the arm. Don't you never make the same mistake, he'll tell me soon enough. She'd have been just fine. She'd have gotten the message, whole damn family would have gotten the message, but she'd have been fine. God damn it all, I didn't mean to do it. But she was high and mighty, the all of them were. Her daddy teaching over there at the college, teaching God only knows what to all them good kids.

After the man hollers, Julie Anna screams. It is a single scream, one that I'll hear in the middle of the night for years to come. It will wake me, cause me to sit straight up and hold my breath, waiting to hear another, wondering if somehow Julie Anna is just there in the other room even though in the years to come, there will be no other room.

And after the single scream comes silence. I lift my head and look out my open door. The sight of him makes my stomach screw itself up into a ball, and I press a hand over my mouth. He is on top of Julie Anna. I can see only her feet and legs, and they aren't moving. He is talking, mumbling really. Something about good people being on his side and God's will and a storm that's coming and does she understand. When Julie Anna doesn't answer, he begins to shake her and yell at her to wake up. When she still says nothing, he pulls back a hand and slaps her face.

I scream. Just like Julie Anna, loud and clear. One single scream. The man swings around, that hand pulled back into the air like he's ready to use it again. He pushes himself off Julie Anna, who still doesn't move, and before I can close my eyes, he is walking toward my doorway.

Chapter 4

IMOGENE

Today

Standing at the door where Mama asked her to wait, after the last of the mourners left Mama's house, Imogene braces herself for the things Mama will say when she walks out of her bedroom. She'll sit Imogene down, gather her hands, and tell her how much she loves her little girl and that it breaks her heart to see Imogene treating herself so unkindly. It's always toughest when Mama cries. Imogene never intends to hurt Mama, but her acting up at her own daddy's funeral, whatever that might have involved because Imogene doesn't much remember anything after they left the cemetery, might be the thing that forces Mama to finally give up. Imogene's single goal these days has been to spare Mama, and Tillie and Mrs. Tillie too, as best she can. But all too often the grief is bigger than Imogene, and she long ago grew tired of trying to make it behave. It's the misbehaving that makes her feel better, at least for a short time. Another person's grief must be exhausting. It has to be, because Imogene is exhausted by her own.

She's exhausted too from a day spent burying Daddy, but instead of feeling like she was seeing Edison Coulter into the ground, it felt like burying Russell and Vaughn all over again. Just as it had five years ago, a pressure settled in her head, right behind her eyes, pressing so hard it barely left her room to breathe. When a bit of food at the reception and a few shots from Eddie jump-started her thinking, she began to wonder if this day restarted the clock on grieving, because if she had to relive the last five years, she was done. She couldn't, wouldn't, go through it again.

"You sure we need to do this tonight?" Imogene asks when Mama walks from her bedroom, her gardening jacket draped over her shoulders. "It's getting awful late."

"It won't take long." Mama cups Imogene's face; pokes her in the side so she'll stop slouching, a bad habit that settled in when Imogene sprouted to six foot tall; and motions for her to follow Mama outside. "And mind you, not a whisper of this to Jo Lynne or Eddie."

Pressing her shoulders back, Imogene crosses her heart and promises to say not a word and can't stop the sigh of relief she lets out. Mama having a secret to share is better than her wanting to have yet another talk. Truth is, Imogene probably wouldn't have overdone it today if Jo Lynne hadn't kept eyeing Imogene's plastic highball every time their paths crossed at the reception. By the end of the day, Imogene was looking her sister straight on and draining her whiskey in one long swallow. Imogene's overdoing it also made her forget to ask Tillie if he'd called the police about Tim Robithan and those watches. As soon as she finishes with Mama, she'll give Tillie a call.

Following Mama outside, Imogene stumbles as she tries to keep up. The wind out of the north has shifted from cool to cold with the setting sun, but none of it slows Mama. Imogene's never been one to stomp around outside after dark, not since she was a little girl. The farmhouse that's been in Mama's family for more than 150 years is a modest enough place, not the grand plantation home people imagine. It has white clapboard siding, a screened-in porch, and six-over-six windows flanked by dark green shutters, and is framed by massive oaks. It also has a heavy history that clings like a fog and blurs what might otherwise be a charming picture.

She'd see them, the men who shaped that history, as a child when peeking through the house's front windows. They were carved into the dark night—the white, ghostly figures with pointed hoods—and carried torches that glowed orange against the pecan trees, trailed smoke, and smelled of kerosene-soaked burlap. She'd hide behind the living room drapes and hold her breath for being so afraid and wanting to be so quiet. Clutching the window ledge, she'd hang there until Mama caught her peeking and chased her away.

And as a teenager, she'd see the men down at the lake. All those same ghostly figures would gather in a circle, arms stretched wide, black eyes tipped toward the sky. First just one man would step forward—it was Daddy, the only one to wear a red robe as leader of the Knights—and touch a torch to the cross and then another and another, all the while shouting about God and country and Klan. In the beginning, Imogene would blame Mama, shouting at her for letting the men march past their house and down to their lake, because there was no one else in the house to blame. And then Imogene realized Eddie and Jo Lynne were both among the ghostly figures, right alongside Daddy, and she never blamed Mama again. That was also when Imogene realized that her having a different daddy was the thing that saved her from the same hate-filled fate as Jo Lynne and Eddie. If Edison had wanted Imogene, not even Mama could have protected her.

"Right up here," Mama calls out as she rounds the side of the house where Imogene grew up.

"What's right up here?"

"That there," Mama says, jabbing at the house with her pointer finger.

A single wire appears from a hole drilled in one of the garage's window casings, runs down the clapboard siding, and disappears into the ground. It's an electrical wire that's been beaten up by time and the weather.

"You talking about the wire?" Imogene says.

"I ain't told no one else about it," Mama says, turning her back on the house and looking out toward the lake that lies in the valley to the east. Then she waves Imogene to her, gathers her hands, and squeezes them tight. "Only you. You're the only one I *can* tell."

The lake is an easy walk from the house and is the spot where

Daddy and his men would gather. On those nights when Mama would scold Imogene for peeking out the front window to watch the hooded men walk past, long before she was old enough to sneak out and follow them to the lake, Imogene would crawl into bed, pull the quilt up to her chin, and listen for the crackling and popping of the burning cross.

"Only one spot that wire could be going," Mama says.

"You think it goes to Grandpa's old place?" Imogene says.

The old house where Grandpa Simmons last lived but that's been empty ever since he died sits a quarter mile on beyond the main house.

"And I'd like you to take care of it for me," Mama says, dropping Imogene's hands and cupping her face again. "Yank it out."

Mama smells of her stiff white face cream, and her gray, wiry hair hangs loose down to her lower back. And even with the wind whipping around the house, Imogene can hear the quiet ticking of Mama's heart. It's the reason Mama spent the whole of the reception in her room, where the few folks who weren't troubled by her condition could pay their respects. Brought on by a surgery soon after Imogene's birth, the beating of Mama's heart, loud enough to hear across a room, is so unfamiliar, folks don't generally realize what they're hearing. There's something entirely unnatural about hearing another person's beating heart, and folks will be feeling queasy or coming up faint without ever knowing the reason. Imogene is one of the few who isn't troubled by the never-ending pulse.

"Yank it out?" Imogene says. "I don't know anything about . . ."

Mama steps away from Imogene and presses her face into the wind. It catches stray strands of her gray hair and blows them across her bright blue eyes. Mama's shrunk in recent years and grown rounder, but she has always carried herself with good posture and pride. She has had to hold her head up through a good bit during her life, and this wire seems to be another one of those things.

"You know what this means, don't you?" Mama says.

"No, Mama," Imogene says, leaning against the house to steady herself because the alcohol is still working on her. It's that last shot Eddie poured as he was leaving. "It's a wire. That's all I see."

"Now that your father is gone, I want it out. Might not have been able to tend it while he was living, but I sure enough can now. I'm done putting up with his nonsense."

"We can do that," Imogene says, stumbling as she pats her pockets for her phone but not finding it. It's Jo Lynne's rule for all family gatherings—cell phones go in the basket by the sink. "Let's get ourselves back inside and I'll call Eddie. He'll know what to do about it."

"No," Mama says.

Her voice is sharp as if she's angry, but then she ruffles Imogene's stocking cap and smiles. Mama has never much minded the black stocking cap Imogene likes to wear or her wild red curls that are never quite contained, but Jo Lynne, with her smooth blond hair, clear blue eyes, and perfectly powdered skin, hates nothing more than that cap, except maybe the leather work boots Imogene wears most days. How'll you ever find another husband, Jo Lynne started asking a few years ago, if you insist on dressing like a lumberjack?

"I'm not trying to upset you, Mama," Imogene says. "But I still don't understand. Do you think Daddy ran this wire?"

At Imogene asking this question, Mama straightens her back and lifts her chin. She wakes every morning to a day of tending her garden, a day she'll spend alone because Imogene is one of a few people who can be in her company without falling ill. But still Mama sees to her hair every day and puts on a sheer pink gloss. She's kept her pride, and even now with Imogene, she isn't willing to let it go. If Imogene had Mama's toughness and dignity, she'd have become a better person after losing Russell and Vaughn. Hardship would have made her stronger, but that hasn't happened.

"I don't want Eddie knowing," Mama says. "Jo Lynne neither.

It'll hurt the both of them. I hate to put this on you just now, but you're all I got. I need you to do this, Imogene."

"It gave him privacy," Imogene says, because she finally understands. "That's why Daddy was using the old house."

Mama nods. "I'd be happy if that wire were gone tonight."

There's no doubt Daddy had reason to want privacy. There were plenty of other women over the years. You can't hardly blame the man, Jo Lynne would say, what with Mama's heart being what it is. And then there was his Klan business. Mama never allowed Daddy's nonsense in her house, so maybe Daddy was meeting with the Knights down at the old place. That's what Mama called Daddy's Klan business . . . nonsense, likely because she couldn't bring herself to say her husband, the man from Missouri who once whispered to her about gabled roofs and longleaf pine and whom she loved in their early years, had become a member of the Klan. She must have thought things would be different for her and the children she'd eventually have when she married Edison Coulter. He'd had no part in the history Mama had been born under. She must have been happy for a time and thought she had finally escaped, but then her husband, like her father and his before him and his before him, joined the Ku Klux Klan. He became one of its leaders.

"I'll take care of it," Imogene says, trying to shake off that last shot and promising herself yet again she'll do better tomorrow. In the meantime, she can at least do this one thing right. This wire is a leftover of all the things Daddy did to hurt Mama, and Imogene will see to getting rid of it. "Tonight, right now, while I still have light. Whatever it is, I'll take care of it."

As much as Mama has always railed against any suggestion Imogene isn't a real Coulter, she's never been able to change what's true. And she's never told Imogene who her real daddy is, or was. He had been an evil man who attacked Mama and left her in an indecent way. Nine months later, Imogene was born, and her being born is what broke Mama's heart, literally. That was the story in the beginning. You are what comes from an unholy union, Edison Coulter once said to Imogene, and then he flicked her long, wiry hair and pointed out her ridiculous height. That's why Mama can ask Imogene to cut out the wire that leads to Edison Coulter's indiscretions. She's not a real Coulter, and so it won't hurt her to hear about his lying, cheating ways like it would hurt Jo Lynne and Eddie. They loved Edison Coulter. Imogene did not. This is also Mama's way of making Imogene believe she is still needed and of giving Imogene a reason to keep waking up in the morning.

The Origins

On or about December 1865, six Confederate veterans met in a law office in Pulaski, Tennessee, and founded the Ku Klux Klan. Derived from the Greek *kuklos,* meaning "circle," the Ku Klux Klan, which was formed as a secret organization, committed violent and deadly attacks aimed at, among other things, intimidating black voters during the Reconstruction era. In 1871, following congressional hearings, a law passed with the intent to stamp out Klan activity. That law, in combination with white Southerners having successfully regained control of Southern state governments—a primary goal of the KKK and one that originally incited the surge in membership—led to a significant reduction in Klan activity.

Chapter 5

TILLIE

Today

Tillie parks in back of his shop and turns off the engine. It's darker back here for the oaks growing alongside the alley and blocking out the last of daylight. Pushing himself out of the car, he glances toward the end of the alley where the narrow dirt road gives way to the bricked street. It's empty. Same on the other end. Mrs. Tillie will know he lied when he dropped her at home after the reception and said he was running down to the shop to check he'd turned off all the lights. She always knows.

Earlier in the day, when Tillie and Mrs. Tillie walked into Riverside Baptist for Edison Coulter's funeral, Mrs. Tillie didn't know anything about the watches, and so she hadn't been scared of running into Robert Robithan. She hadn't been scared of Robert trying to draw Tillie back into the Klan after forty years either. Instead, she'd been scared of the memories that would surely be waiting for them inside the church. It had been five years since they stepped into Riverside Baptist, and only then because they were burying their son and grandson, husband and baby to Imogene.

Forty years ago, Tillie had indeed been a member of the Klan, but he got out, is likely the only fellow who ever did. And since that day, Mrs. Tillie has refused to walk into a house of the Lord in the company of any of them fellows. Riverside Baptist was their place, always had been. It'd be like telling the good Lord that we're just fine with the things them fellows do. I won't be saying any such thing to my Lord. Will you, Jean Tillerson? And Tillie told her no. Five years ago, the day they buried their Russell and Vaughn, a day he and Mrs. Tillie still cry about some nights when they've set their books aside and turned out the lights, was the only time in all those years they stepped into Riverside Baptist. And they'd only done it then so their boys could be near family.

"Don't make a fuss," Tillie whispered when they both saw Imogene standing in the church's front aisle. She stumbled, righted herself by grabbing on to the back of the pew. It was the whiskey, no doubt, and he couldn't hardly blame her. He couldn't hardly blame her for any of it—the drinking, the late nights, not even the random men. Grief was a heavy load, and he couldn't blame Imogene for doing whatever she had to in order to bear it.

"If ever there was a day that child needed someone to fuss over her," Mrs. Tillie said, "today is that day."

Even though that awful first pew had been where they all sat together five years ago, Mrs. Tillie walked straight to it and wrapped Imogene in a hug. They stood like that, rocking to and fro, Imogene with a hand pressed over her eyes, her red hair mostly pulled back, for a good long time. Imogene was a foot taller than Mrs. Tillie, and yet somehow looked small in her arms. Tillie often thought he and Mrs. Tillie were no good for Imogene. They were a bitter reminder, a crutch even. Imogene was a young woman and needed to move on. She even—and with this thought, Tillie choked on a sob—had time to start a new family. But she might never do any of those things, be it out of compassion or shame, as long as Tillie and Mrs. Tillie are near enough to watch it all unfold.

"Pretty near your daughter, ain't she?" It was Robert Robithan. Tillie had been so all consumed with keeping his grief at bay, he hadn't noticed Robert walk up.

Back when the Klan was last in its heyday, Robert had been a feared man. Robithans were Klan killers, and everyone knew it. But age and a membership that had been dying off, literally, for years generally silenced Robert and all the Knights of the Southern Georgia Order. They kept up with lighting their crosses down at the Coulters' lake, occasionally gathered on the courthouse steps, and spread flyers now and again. But mostly, they communed among themselves, quietly, as they tried not to get dragged into court, a tactic that had effectively destroyed many Klan chapters. They were biding time until they could rise again, because always there was another rising. And in the past year or so, all their waiting had started to pay off. Young men were joining again and propping up the old ways. Timmy Robithan in particular had a gift for spreading their word, and Robert could again be seen cruising through town in his red pickup, just like the old days, one arm slung out an open window. He was making sure folks knew he was back and that the old Klan ways were still alive.

"And don't your Mrs. Tillie look fine too?" Robert said. He wore boots and black trousers, smelled of a sweet cigar, and his hair, while gray, was thick as ever. "How about you, Tillie? Things good down to the shop?"

"Real fine," Tillie said, wondering what Robert did or did not know about his son trying to sell his daddy's most prized possession.

Whatever fading might have happened to Robert in years past, he was back to being a big man with a deep, clear voice. His size had always been his way of making folks take notice. Tim, his son, had the gift for drawing attention too, but he did it with smooth yellow hair and a knack for stoking fears in one sentence while offering up how to soothe them in the next. As Tim slid up alongside his father and rested one hand on Tillie's shoulder, Tillie wasn't sure who scared him more—the father or the son.

"Such a sad occasion, Mr. Tillerson," Tim said, holding tight to Tillie's shoulder.

"Indeed," Tillie said, his heart pumping hard and fast in his chest. "God rest."

Tillie was flanked by Robert on one side and Timmy on the other. Maybe they both knew those watches were laid out in Tillie's shop, or maybe neither of them did. Maybe Natalie Sharon was fooling the both of them. And just as Tillie thought Natalie's name, she grabbed on to Tim and whisked him away. As she led him across the aisle, she looked back at Tillie and ever so slightly shook her head.

"Ain't she a lovely girl, Tillie?" Robert said.

"Pardon?" Tillie said, trying to figure why Natalie shook her head at him.

"The Coulter girl," Robert said. "I think she and Tim would get on good together."

Tillie shook his head, slow at first and then faster. "Imogene ain't a real Coulter."

He didn't say it with any mind toward disrespecting the dead. Everyone knew Edison Coulter wasn't Imogene's real daddy, though folks mostly didn't talk about it. Tillie said it because he knew Robert was really after the Simmons bloodline, which came from Imogene's mama, and that he was tempted by the idea of Tim being father to the next generation. Not only was the Simmons name the last remaining tie to the rebirth of something that was sacred to men like Tim and Robert Robithan, but their very town was named for a Simmons.

"Besides," Tillie said, "Timmy is too old for Imogene, don't you think? And he goes with Natalie Sharon, don't he?"

Robert made a face as if Natalie's name tasted sour to him. "I know Imogene ain't a Coulter, but Coulter ain't the name that counts. Lottie Rose, she's Imogene's real mama, yes? That's the Simmons side of the family, and the Simmons name is what matters. Thought you might like the idea, knowing a good man was looking after her."

Tillie spent the rest of the funeral trying to figure why Natalie had shaken her head at him and how in God's name he was going to convince Robert Robithan that Imogene was no good for his son. Dang it all, nothing had gone right since Tillie let those watches into his store, likely because letting those watches in was like letting the Klan back in. The fear Tillie felt when he first left the Knights of the Southern Georgia Order had faded over the years, just as the Klan had faded. But recent days were feeling more and more like days from long ago, and Tillie's fear had returned. First thing tomorrow, he would get rid of them watches one way or another, but for tonight, he'd make sure they were locked up tight.

Taking one last look to make sure no one has followed him from his car to the shop's back door, Tillie makes his way inside. In the dark showroom, he takes long, slow steps so he won't bump a shin or knock Mrs. Tillie's favorite milk glass from the shelves. He could take the watches home with him or put them in the safe right here in the shop. At the cabinet, he feels for the small lock, squints, and leans close so he can see. The lock pops open. He lifts the glass top, and as he leans in again so he can get a good look, he drops his key. The velvet-lined display case is empty.

Chapter 6

BETH

Before

My eyes are closed. If I can't see him, he isn't real. But I can't stop the sound of him or the smell of him. One big boot hits the floor and then another, and each time one lands, it's louder than the last. He's getting closer. He is real. The floor shakes, and I close my eyes tighter, pinch them hard until silver specks swim in the darkness behind my lids. The smell of him grows stronger too. Spicy and thick and greasy because he was carrying pizza, and that smell presses down on me. I curl myself up, make myself as small as I can, so small I'll disappear into nothing, maybe float out into the dark solar system we're learning about in school.

The footsteps stop. No more heavy boots rattling the floors. It's quiet like before he came. Only the sound of the TV. A commercial is playing. I hold my breath so my ears will work better, but I still hear air rushing in and out. It's his air, not mine, but I won't take another breath, not until the sound stops. There is the smell of him too. It's still here, hanging right over me. Something wraps around my arms and I suck in a breath and I scream. My arms and legs take off on their own. I'm kicking and hitting and squirming, but then his arms wrap all the way around me. His smell burns my throat and nose. He squeezes so I can't kick. I can't move at all. And he carries me out the door.

Chapter 7

IMOGENE

Today

After first pushing open the iron cattle gate that Eddie and Daddy had kept up with even though they hadn't had cattle in years, Imogene drives a quarter mile over a gutted dirt road that leads from Mama's place to the old caretaker's house. Mama's favorite strategy for dealing with Imogene these past few years has been to keep her busy with chores or favors, and this is another one of those times. Imogene's latest career was partly Mama's idea too. After her favorite necklace, a family heirloom, was stolen a few years back and never recovered, Mama suggested Imogene take up insurance investigation. It was a little like being a lawyer, Mama said, the thing Imogene had hoped to be before her world collapsed.

As Imogene nears the old house, she has to guess where the drive is because the weeds have run it over. She rolls to a stop, the car lurching when she brakes too hard, throws it into park, and stares up at the front door where Grandpa Simmons lived after Mama married Edison Coulter. Like the main house, the old care-taker's house has clapboard siding, but its slats bow and buckle from lack of care. The narrow porch that runs the length of the house is sinking, along with the pitched roof above it, and while all the lower windows have been boarded over, the second-story windows have not and the glass in them looks almost black.

It's just dark enough that the headlights throw a soft glow on the oaks that have taken over since she was last down here. She'd been in high school, nearly ten years ago, and had come here with Russell, sat on those steps, and talked about becoming a lawyer one day and moving off to Atlanta. Russell, a few years older, had already graduated and was rehabbing houses. There were plenty of old homes to be saved in Atlanta, so they could go together, he said, but that wasn't really what he wanted. He loved the old homes only found in small towns like Simmonsville, homes that hadn't been touched in fifty years, that still had original tile, and doors that hung from rusty hardware. Despite the dreams they shared on those steps, they'd both always known they'd say good-bye as soon as Imogene graduated from college. While Russell's life was in Simmonsville, the history that hung over Imogene's house and family and even the town was too heavy for her.

But one year into college, long before Imogene could graduate and go off to law school, she turned up pregnant. Edison Coulter would have gladly let her move away, but he wouldn't have her giving birth to a bastard child under the name of Coulter. She wasn't happy about it in the beginning, being pregnant, but then Russell proposed, swore he wanted to. He said there wasn't another person on earth he could love like he loved Imogene, and whoever was growing inside of her, well, Russell loved him or her too. He had a house already picked out for them. Original woodwork. Hard pine floors. He'd fix it up, he said. Spend his nights and weekends doing it. Imogene had always loved Russell, in truth since she was just a girl, yet she'd feared and hated her family's history and its present more. But Russell's passion and excitement proved contagious, and they gave Imogene faith. They gave her room enough to breathe and to love Russell in a way he deserved. She began to believe she could build a life in Simmonsville out from under Ed Coulter and the Knights of the Southern Georgia Order. She said yes to Russell, and they were married.

Mama says Imogene has to forgive herself for not being happy like Russell was in the beginning. She was, after all, happy soon enough, well before Vaughn was born. When she wasn't in class or studying, she helped with renovating their home—a hundred-year-old three-bedroom craftsman with a fenced backyard. After the accident that killed Russell and Vaughn, Jo Lynne moved Imogene out of the house she shared with them and into an apartment she'd had freshly painted and fully furnished. Imogene has never been back to the house she lived in with Russell and Vaughn, has never even driven past, and she never will. Another young family moved in, which is as much as Imogene ever wanted to know about the new owners. Mama says if Imogene can't forgive herself for how she felt in the beginning, she'll never be right again.

Shaking her head in hopes of knocking loose the memories, Imogene throws open the car door and grabs her flashlight from the glove box, something she finds handy when running down her disability cases, leaves on the headlights, and steps outside. Giant reeds, thick clumps of them, grow like wheat along the front of the house and around the west side as far as the headlights reach. They rattle like the wooden chimes hanging on Mama's front porch.

If Daddy did run that wire down here, it'll likely come up out of the ground west of the house. Not quite needing the flashlight yet, though the orange sky is slowly melting into gray and she'll need it soon, she tucks it in her back pocket. Then, holding her arms crossed over her chest like a cattle guard, she shoulders a path through the hollow reeds that tower over her. Kicking and stomping, mostly to scare off whatever might be slithering underfoot, she cuts a path all the way to the far end of the house, and on her way back, she stumbles, falls forward onto her knees and then onto her bare hands.

Digging through the broken, mushy reeds that drip slime, she feels around until she finds the wire and then follows it to the house. Standing, she tugs back on the stocking cap one of the broken reeds snatched from her head, switches on her flashlight, and runs it along the stacked-stone foundation. The white stones are edged at their grout lines in mold and moss. Every few feet, the wire is anchored to the stones by a metal bracket. Running her fingers over them, one after another, she can feel that some are old and rusted and others are smooth still, newer. Imogene's hopes that Edison Coulter's indiscretions were solidly in the distant past dwindle. Whatever he'd been up to down here, he'd been keeping up on the maintenance of it.

Her daddy, the only daddy she's ever known, likely hadn't considered who would clean up his mess after he died. He'd have had to consider his own mortality to do that, and men like Edison Coulter, men who are worshipped, idolized, revered even, don't bother with thoughts of mortality.

After clearing away a few feet of reeds from the foundation, Imogene reaches the first of the narrow basement windows. She'd been looking for the wire to snake its way up the house and disappear into a first-story window. But instead, it disappears into the basement. Bracing herself with one hand to the side of the house, the loose paint flaking as she leans there, Imogene squats to the window. It sits just above ground level and has been boarded over with a sheet of plywood. She runs her flashlight along its edges, trailing the yellow spot of light with one hand. Feeling for any sort of give, she tries to work her fingers under the plywood, but it won't budge. Next she pulls her jacket sleeve down over her thumb and scrubs at a few of the screws that have been driven into the wood.

They had a problem in the early 2000s with folks trying to settle in the old places around town. The hospital over near Milledgeville started letting folks go, and some of the newly released patients started to wander. Some wandered north, and still to this day, a few of those fellows regularly sleep on the benches along Simmonsville's Main Street. That's when Daddy and Eddie first boarded up the old house. Seventeen years ago or so. Grandpa had just died, and no one was living there anymore. But the screws in this window, they still have a smooth finish.

She's about to lose the last of daylight and soon it'll be too dark to do anything else, and much as she knows it's only childish fears that have come back to haunt her, she'd just as soon get home. And she'd just as soon spend no more time remembering Russell and her sitting on those steps, or remembering the way he trailed his fingers along the insides of her arms or talked about dovetail joints and hard hickory or how the first time they slept together, he used his arms to hold himself above her so he could look straight into her eyes, not letting her turn away because she was shy about it. She'd rather not remember dreaming of a future they both knew they'd never have, and then that very thing coming true.

Tomorrow, she'll call someone to come out and cut the wire on this end and up at the house so no one will ever know Daddy had been up to anything. Tucking the flashlight away, she starts back to the car, when something inside the old house kicks on. Pressing an ear against the siding, she listens. It's definitely coming from the house. A motor perhaps or a fan.

She was down to this old place dozens of times as a child, especially before Grandpa Simmons died. She was too young during those years to understand his doings with the Knights. He was Mama's father and Imogene's protector; that's all she knew. When Imogene's own daddy would flick her hair, call her unholy, say she wasn't a real Coulter, Grandpa Simmons would stop him. Sometimes, it only took Grandpa standing from a chair or maybe dipping his chin in Daddy's direction to stop Daddy saying those things. Other times, a few times, Grandpa Simmons grabbed Daddy by his shirt collar and dragged him from the room, saying nobody talked that way about his daughter and grandchild. Nobody. Once Grandpa died, there was no one left to silence Daddy when he took to saying those things.

If Imogene was brave enough to walk into the old house back then, she should be brave enough now. First checking that her flashlight is still burning strong, she pushes her way through the rest of the reeds until she reaches the back of the house. Imogene won't do this to spare Jo Lynne or Eddie like Mama wanted.

Already, Imogene's anger at Daddy has bled all over those two. So many years, they've told Imogene not to stir up trouble about Daddy and his other women. Boys will be boys, they'd said. A seventy-year-old boy? Imogene had said. When do boys finally become men?

And Eddie, like Daddy, is one of the Klan, and so is Garland, Jo Lynne's husband, though nobody is meant to know that. He never attends the rallies or spreads flyers. He can go to the lightings down at the lake because under a hood and robe, no one would know it's him. Garland holds deed to all the Knights' property and manages all the membership money, and as long as he has no ties to the organization, no matter what damage the Knights might inflict, the courts can't seize their assets. Or so Daddy and the other Knights hope. No, Imogene won't tend to this wire and whatever she finds inside for her sister and brother or to cover up whatever it might imply. This one time, at least, she'll sidestep being a disappointment and do it for Mama.

When Imogene was a kid, before the hospital started letting patients go, the door off the kitchen was always unlocked. Coming around the back corner of the old house, she sees that same door hasn't been boarded over, and when she turns the knob, it opens. Stepping inside, she sweeps her flashlight around the kitchen and tugs on the small chain hanging from an overhead light, but nothing happens. Crossing into the entryway, she pauses and listens but hears no more of the humming sound.

"Hello," she hollers, and coughs because the air is stale and dusty.

Calling out a second time and still hearing nothing, she takes a few more steps and reaches the staircase that leads to the second story. Underfoot, the pine floors are soft, and fearing her weight might be too much for them, she slides her feet, testing the next step before she takes it. Beyond the staircase that leads up to two bedrooms, she crosses into the small dining room. Daylight is mostly gone now, and because the windows are boarded up, the house would be totally dark without her flashlight. She tries another light switch. Still nothing, but things are exactly as she remembers them. No Confederate flags hang from the wall, no gun racks in the living room, no flyers stacked on the kitchen counter. She can report back to Mama that Daddy wasn't up to anything after all.

She walks around the large dining room table, trailing a finger over its dusty top, and as she passes the door that leads down to the basement, the hum she heard from outside grows louder again. Something down in the basement is running. No mistaking that, but there's also no mistaking that she isn't going down there tonight, another fear left over from her childhood. She never went into the basement, not even on a dare. Besides, whatever she's hearing, it'll have been running for days, weeks maybe, so one more night won't matter. It's another thing she'll see to tomorrow. For now, she'll go home and tell Mama it's all taken care of. She turns to leave, thinking she can almost feel the hum of whatever is running down there in the basement, and the sound disappears. The house falls silent.

She takes another step toward the basement door, the floorboards creaking with each movement, but instead of reaching for the doorknob, she only stares down at it. Her flashlight is beginning to lose its power, and the light has faded from bright yellow to a cloudy orange. There is just enough left to let Imogene make out two bolt latches that have been installed—one at about eye level and one near the bottom of the door. A keyed padlock has been installed just above the doorknob.

With one finger, Imogene touches the top bolt latch. What was once smooth metal is now pitted with rough patches, most certainly rust, though she can't make it out. The lock will be stiff with age and lack of use, but when she pushes, it slides easily to the left. She does the same with the bolt near the floor. Lastly, she runs her

fingers over the lock that has been installed just above the doorknob. It is a keyed lock, and while the lock has been snapped closed,
the key dangles from it. She slips the lock free and opens the latch.

As a child, when Grandpa Simmons was still alive and living in
the house, Imogene sometimes stood at the top of those stairs and
stared down. Eddie would give her a little shove as if to push her
down, and Jo Lynne would holler at him to leave well enough
alone. Even before rumors began of the patients from Milledgeville
taking up in the old house and even before Grandpa died, leaving
the house empty, Eddie would tell stories of anchors drilled into
the basement's stone walls where people were once chained by the
caretaker and kept for days until they learned their lessons. Learn
your lessons, Imogene, Eddie would say, less you be chained in
Grandpa's basement too. Imogene reaches into the stairwell and
pats the wall to her right until she feels it. A switch. With one finger, she flips it.

A single bulb at the bottom of the stairs lights up. It hangs from
the ceiling, a bare bulb dangling from a wire. The light shifts, as if
her opening the door has caused the bulb to sway. Her eyes are
drawn to it first, that single bulb that cuts a yellow cone into the
darkness below. And then there is a movement. She lowers her eyes
to the floor beneath the bulb. It's a person. A small person. A child.
He, maybe she, looks up at Imogene. The child leans left and right,
tips forward as if squinting to see who is standing at the top of the
stairs, looking down. Yes, it's a child.

Chapter 8

BETH

Before

Mama and I have fallen asleep on the sofa. We do that sometimes on Saturday nights. Mama always does her going out on Fridays, so Saturday night is family time and that means only Mama and me. Mama never stays up late on Saturdays because Sunday is church and church is an early morning. We always go because it keeps the lady who started coming after Mama almost drank oleander tea off our backs; that's how Mama says it. But we also go because Mama can sing there, and Mama is about the best singer ever. People are nice to us there too, and we always see Julie Anna and her parents. Ever since they came to town, Mama likes to tell Mr. and Mrs. Perez all about how good I do in school and how I'm going to go to college just like their Julie Anna.

I know I'm on the sofa because I can't unfold my legs and that makes my knees ache. We're all tangled up, Mama and me. And I'm cold. I want Mama's white blanket, the fuzzy one that reaches all the way around the both of us. I shove at Mama so she'll scoot over and wrap her one arm around me, let me wiggle up alongside her and rest my head on her shoulder. I say her name, think I say her name, but my mouth is dry and maybe nothing comes out.

It's loud too. I want quiet so I can sleep, but my hands are stuck and I can't press them over my ears. My one hip and shoulder throb because I am rolled over on my side. I'm not lying on the soft sofa with pillows stacked all around. I am lying on something hard, and my body is shaking because I'm cold and shaking because something is rattling beneath me. My teeth knock against each other.

It's dark in here, wet and filled with a roar. It's like lying in the back of Mama's car when we drive home from Madison, where we go every year to see the houses lit up for Christmas. It's always late and Mama lets me sleep in the back seat on that one special night only.

The sound changes. I open my eyes but opening them doesn't work because it's still dark. The rattle slows. There it is again . . . the slowing of tires on a dirt road. Just like the black truck on our dirt road. I'm in a car, or a truck maybe. It slows some more, and then my teeth stop knocking up against each other, my head stops bouncing. I am still and I remember Mama. Her hair was like fluffed silk before she left the house and her skin sparkled because she polished herself with glittery lotion. She always does that on karaoke nights because a lady needs a little help after a certain age.

Footsteps are growing louder, but not Mama's footsteps. She walks on the cement sidewalk when she comes home from work and she takes care of old folks so her shoes have rubbery soles and make no noise. These footsteps are loud and growing louder. They come from shoes walking on dirt and gravel. I try to believe they are Mama's, and I almost do until I remember Julie Anna and the man with the fists. I screamed and he heard me and in a few long steps, he was in my room and now I'm gone.

I know the sound of keys in a lock too, Mama pulling hers from her purse, standing on the porch and sifting through them, and then the rattling as she slides her key into the lock. Except, this time, the keys don't rattle outside the front door and the sound of the lock popping, those tiny gears lining up perfect so the door will open, is loud because it's right here near my head. I pinch my eyes closed as something above lifts and cold air washes over me. I suck in a deep breath, cough because it's too much air.

Something orange glows on the other side of my closed eyes. I hope it's the Sunday morning sun, waking us up for church. I open my eyes but have to squint. It's a single stream of light and all around it is darkness. I blink, try to shield my eyes, but my arms won't move. The light shifts and hands appear. I hope for Mama's hands. She has tiny wrists and closely clipped nails so she doesn't snag the old people's thin skin. But they aren't Mama's hands. The fingers are thick. I stare at those hands as they lift me up and out, my head bouncing off a sharp corner. Mostly, I see thumbs, two. And yellow, crooked fingernails.

I'm standing now, and the bright yellow light has slipped off to the side. The thumbs with split yellow nails aren't denting my arms anymore. Something shakes me. My head is heavy and hangs off to the side. Everything is tilted. I stumble. Those hands grab hold of me again.

"Jesus," a voice says. "Are you even in there?"

He's a dark shadow. I see only parts of him. A gold metal circle on his pocket. A rivet, that's what Mama calls them and gets angry when I dig at them. Yellow stitching on dark denim. The tail of a blue flannel shirt. Black laces, frayed at the end, no plastic tip. I want to say something but can't. Mama sometimes has dreams like that, where she wants to talk or shout or scream but no matter how deep she inhales or how wide she opens her mouth, nothing comes out. Terrible, she always says when she sees me the next morning, and then she hugs me like I am the reason she was trying to scream. Mama saying that makes me worry that maybe one day those dreams of hers will leak out into the daytime.

"Jesus," the man says over and over. He shakes me. "Jesus Christ. Are you okay?"

He keeps muttering to himself, and he's walking now, back and forth, so I must be standing on my own. We're in the back of a pickup and it moves under my feet as he pounds three steps this way, three that way. I'm like Julie Anna now, like the sock doll I keep on my dresser. Its arms and legs are stuffed with old sheets Mama and I tore into strips. Its hair is made of red yarn. I am a nude-colored stocking doll stuffed with old torn-up sheets, yellowed from too many washings.

"We drove all night," the man says, grabbing hold of me. I think it's the man with the pizza who hurt Julie Anna. "And all the next day too. You hear me?"

He shakes me. My head bounces, hangs off to one side and won't straighten.

"Hey, you hear me? That's how far we come."

The man sounds like he's far away on the other side of something. I want to say I can hardly hear him, but I can't. I can't say anything.

"You understand me?" he says, knocking one of his knuckles on the top of my head. His voice is loud again, right next to me. "We're nowhere near your house. Long ways away. So don't even think you can run off and find your way home."

He drops me over the truck's edge to the ground. And then he's pulling me so I walk. His boots are loud, and I follow the sound. There are other sounds too. Leaves rustling like they do in the oak tree by the road. Something is buzzing. I smell wet ground and slippery leaves and mossy rocks in a river. When I step onto something hard like the sidewalk outside our house, from somewhere far away on the other side of something, he tells me to stay put. Keys rattle, a door opens, and a light pops on.

"Just for now," he says.

I'm lifted again, and then I'm sitting on more hard ground. I pull my knees to my chest and rest my head there. The flashlight shines on my legs. Five pecans lay by my feet. They are covered over with a dusty spiderweb. Pecans, brownish red, smooth, just like we have in the trees at home. He hasn't driven me so far away after all.

"You be good," he says. The light switches off. His voice floats to me through the dark.

On Sunday, Mama is making baked chicken and pineapple casserole. It's my favorite. Julie Anna said just tonight she might come over special when Mama is cooking so she can learn how to make it.

The door squeals and closes. And the lock snaps into place.

Chapter 9

IMOGENE

Today

Imogene learned to swim in the lake that runs between the old caretaker's house and Mama's house, or tried to learn. The lake was once the lifeblood of the farm because just south of it, near the fall line, the land turns sandy and drops steadily until it reaches the river and continues beyond. That piece of land, which Mama's family once owned, is prone to flooding, being wedged like it is between the lake and the river. It's what made for good rice-growing land in a place where not much rice was grown, but once slave labor was lost, the economies collapsed. In the wake of the war, much of the acreage, including all the land beyond the lake, was sold off to pay taxes, and Mama's family took up dairy farming for a time. And now they're in the business of rental properties. Daddy finds the houses and decides which ones to buy. Eddie cleans them, repaints them, and maintains them best he can without investing any real money, and collects the rents. He isn't allowed to do any plumbing or electrical work, because he ends up costing more money than he saves. Garland does the accounting and banking and works out the financing.

On the day Imogene learned to swim, the lake was twenty feet at its deepest, likely still is, and even though it had been July, the water was cold enough to shock the air from her lungs. Eddie and Jo Lynne were supposed to be watching over her that day. But Jo Lynne was mostly busy with Garland, the both of them huddled together under the shade of the pines that lined the lake. Even back then, long before they married, Garland was doing Jo Lynne's bidding. He had been ever since they were kids, growing up together. They both came from suitable families, and their getting married had long been assumed.

Imogene had been hearing the story of the lake from Eddie for as long as she could remember. They'd sit together, she and Eddie, on the sandy patch at the lake's northern end, on an early foggy morning when he'd maybe taken her fishing or on a late dusky afternoon when they'd been tossing stones, and he'd point to the other end, so far away a person couldn't hardly see it, and say, your real daddy lives a way over there. A way on the other side. Not your pretend daddy. Your *real* daddy. You learn to swim, you can see him, if you dare. You'll finally know who he is. Know where you come from. Can't you almost see him? Can't you, Imogene? Are you brave enough? And he'd tell her that the lake, this lake right here on their own property, was magical. It lay nearer to heaven than any other place on earth. That was why Daddy and the other men gathered on that sandy patch, had been for years, even men who came long before Daddy. Just look how the clouds settle here and don't settle no place else. You dare to find your real daddy, this lake'll get you to him, and sometimes he'd laugh a little and if Jo Lynne was along, she'd holler at him to quiet himself down.

When Imogene was real young, she'd cry and say she had a real daddy, same daddy as Eddie and Jo Lynne, and Mama would holler at Eddie for telling such stories. Sure, Mama, he'd say, and then to Imogene he'd say, you got the same Daddy as me and Jo Lynne. But once the story was told, it couldn't be untold, and Imogene always knew her real daddy was out there, maybe across the magical lake that lay nearer to heaven than any other place on earth.

It was her twelfth birthday the day she decided to swim all the way across, and she figured twelve was old enough. The next year she'd be thirteen, and thirteen was near an adult. Wading out toward the middle until she was standing on her tiptoes, she stretched her chin to keep her head above water, all the while keeping her eyes on the farthest southern shore.

"That's it," Jo Lynne was hollering from the sandy bank. She was twenty-one and almost done with her studies to become a social worker. She wanted to do something helpful to the community until the day she had children of her own, and then she'd quit working to stay home with them. "You're doing it. You're almost doing it."

Jo Lynne wore a pink dress that day, and her smooth yellow hair was held from her face with a matching pink band. All together, it made her look like she'd just been peeled off a postcard. All her life, Jo Lynne had had that snapshot-ready look about her. Next to her, Garland was on his hands and knees as he brushed the pine needles from the blanket so Jo Lynne didn't snag her dress. Imogene waved at them both and then went back to drawing her hands forward and back through the water to steady herself, just like Jo Lynne taught her.

"Now swim on back this way," Jo Lynne said. "No more touching bottom. Swim, Imogene. Swim on back this way. Reach and kick. Reach and kick."

Jo Lynne didn't know that was the day Imogene planned to find her real daddy all the way over on the other side.

"Come on back this way," Jo Lynne shouted. "Reach with your arms. Kick hard now."

Jo Lynne's cheering made Imogene want to swim so bad, made her want to draw her arms through the water, smooth like Jo Lynne did when she slipped into her tiny bikini with ties on the bottom and took to the lake. She'd glide through the water with beauty and elegance, her long limbs working together as smooth as if she were dancing on waxed pine. Jo Lynne swam like no other person Imogene had ever seen, and that's what Imogene wanted to do because that would make her like a real sister to Jo Lynne even if they didn't have the same real daddy. Them being real sisters would carry Imogene as far as she needed to go.

But as hard as she tried, Imogene couldn't get her feet to let go of the bottom. With her toes, she clung to it, tiptoeing over the silky-soft mud, and the harder she tried to steady herself by pulling and pushing at the water with her arms, the deeper she drifted. She stretched her legs, wiggled her toes, and then the bottom was gone and there was nothing to hold on to anymore. Her long curls floated like red twine on the water, some of them drifting into her mouth so she had to spit and cough them out. Her red hair, the thing that reminded everyone she wasn't a real Coulter and that she'd never belong and that she was the unholy one.

And then there was Eddie. Imogene didn't see him, but she heard him. He was weaving his way along the rocky bank and in among the pines, somewhere out there, watching her slip closer and closer to the middle, where she couldn't touch. Eddie was seventeen years older than Imogene, and he came and went from Mama and Daddy's house as he pleased.

"It's getting dark, little girly," he shouted, his voice rising and falling like he was singing a song. "It's getting dark and the earwigs is coming."

There was no tide, no stream tugging, but still the water was pushing Imogene and pulling her and she was fighting to keep her head above it.

"You got to start swimming now."

It was Jo Lynne's voice. And then Eddie again. He was laughing.

"Them earwigs going to get you. Going to claw their way inside your brains."

Imogene dreamed about the earwigs sometimes, crawling over her white pillowcase, climbing her mountain of red curls. She'd wake some nights, wondering if one of those earwigs had crawled inside her ear, burrowed into her brains, and laid its eggs, because Eddie said they liked young girls' brains best for egg laying. And she felt them now. One brushed past an earlobe; another knocked up against a shoulder. Or maybe that was her hair, floating with the water that was carrying her deeper into the lake.

"Little earwigs burrowing into your brain."

Imogene began to swat at the bugs, to swing left and right. She kicked her feet, searching for the bottom, but it was gone. She coughed, choked. The water swamped her, dragged her under. She wasn't going to make it across. Her lungs ached. She fought the weight of her arms, fought to make her legs move. The day had turned suddenly dark. She was sinking. The world above was slipping away.

And then something clamped on, a hand that grabbed her by the arm and pulled at her. The light overhead grew brighter. When her face broke through the surface of the lake, she gasped, drew in a breath of air. Once back on land, Imogene collapsed on the warm sand and looked up at Jo Lynne. Her pink dress hung limp with water, her blond hair stuck to her face and shoulders, her matching pink headband was gone, and she was hollering at Garland, telling him he was no man of any kind because he was still safe and dry. But that one breath Imogene took after going so long without, that's what she remembers most from that day, and that's the breath she takes when she sees a child there at the bottom of the stairs leading down to the basement in the old house where Grandpa Simmons once lived. It's the breath that starts her going again, shakes loose the panic, and brings the world back into focus. And as quick as she inhales, the child is gone.

Chapter 10

BETH

Before

I know it's daytime by the slivers of light that leak through the roof. Long-handled tools lean in the corners and the concrete floor is spotted with something black. I shift from one hip to the other and dust lifts into the air and sparkles in those tiny slivers of sunshine. I sleep and wake. It's dark and then light. In school this year, we learned all about the universe, and overhead, the planets are spinning around the sun, making it day and night and day again. I had wanted to invite Ellie and Fran for a sleepover so we could camp in the backyard and lay our sleeping bags in the grass and stare up at the night sky to see those planets, but Mama said don't bother because they wouldn't be allowed.

When the door opens, I think I'm still alive. It's dark again. Mama, I think I say, but maybe not. A bright light pops on and shines in my face. A flashlight. And a man is moving toward me, slowly, sideways like Mama when she sneaks up on the black racers that like the cool rocks our house sits on. The floor bounces each time his boots hit.

"Good God almighty," he says. "Stinks to high heaven in here."

I can't get my eyes to latch on to him. Instead, I try to see the lawn mower that sits in the corner, but really I want to see its rubbery red button. I know it's there because I saw it when the sun shined through the ceiling. It's just like the mower Mama borrows from Mr. Lawson every other Sunday. Mama always says renters shouldn't have to mow but she liked a nice lawn so she did it anyways. She first showed me how to start the mower when I turned ten and said when I was responsible enough to mow by myself, she'd pay me five dollars. More than anything, I wanted to be responsible enough. That would make me like Julie Anna, and I'd have my own money to spend when Mama and I went to the thrift store. Flip this switch, Mama had said, showing me the lever. And push this button, this red, rubbery button, three times. I bet Ellie and Fran aren't allowed to do this, she said. I nodded and pushed the button. It was spongy like a rubber ball. She called it priming the mower and told me to use my pointer finger. Just like this, she said, and poked me three times in the belly.

"Is something wrong with you?" he says, snapping his fingers in my face, but I don't stop looking at that button.

"Hey, come on. I ain't been gone that long. We're going to get you food now, something to drink. It just took me a little time to get it all set up. I got everything you need now. Got everything ready."

But I can't stop looking for the rubbery button. Something inside has unhitched. I've come apart, like the sandwich baggies Mama puts my PBJs in for lunch. My two halves won't catch. One part of me is here in the shed. But another part is gone, or maybe it stayed behind and is clinging to my house and Mama and the red, rubbery button.

"Come on, now," he says. "We'll get you cleaned up, something good to eat. Wake up. Come on, this ain't my fault. Sure as hell didn't plan on this happening."

Even when two hands hook me under my armpits and lift me, I stare at the mower. And as we walk out into the dark, I cry because leaving that mower all alone in the corner of the empty shed means I'll never see Mama again.

Chapter 11

IMOGENE

Today

With a finger still on the light switch at the top of the basement stairs, Imogene thinks to flip it off, slam the door, and run. The child is gone. The spot at the bottom of the stairs is empty. Instead, she presses her hand over the switch and forces herself to breathe slow and steady and to listen. She listens for something that comes from down below, that comes from behind, from overhead. There are two bedrooms upstairs, and the floors are at least 150 years old. If someone is here in the house, she will hear footsteps. She *will* hear footsteps.

A child is down there. She's certain. A small child. She thinks he was small, or maybe she was small. Slender shoulders, dark hair, bare feet. But Imogene only got a glimpse. Someone else must be here too. A child wouldn't be left alone. Not a child so small. Someone else might be down there in the basement too.

She lets her eyes drift over her left shoulder, slowly, as if someone, probably a man, is near, maybe standing close beside her. And then she looks right, moving no part of her body, only her head and eyes. If she moves, makes any noise, he'll know she's here, whoever he is. She takes another deep, quick breath because she is trying too hard to be quiet and is forgetting to inhale and exhale. She swallows, and that's the thing that startles her. The muscles in her throat tightening and loosening, the click of her tongue popping off the roof of her mouth. She closes her eyes, turns to face the basement, and opens them. And the child is there again, creeping into sight.

"Are you Imogene?"

The sound of her name bleeds the feeling from Imogene's legs and arms, and her mouth turns dry. She should speak but can't. Setting her flashlight on the floor, she grabs hold of the banister and slides one foot forward until it drops to the next tread, all the while keeping the child in sight. It's a boy, she thinks. He stands beneath the yellow light, exactly at its center, like he's been waiting for her. Making her way down three stairs, she holds on as if something might otherwise drag her down.

"Who are you?" she says.

She whispers, and something makes her look behind, at the top of the stairs. Up on the main level, the house is dark. Still clinging to the banister, she sinks to the stairs, and from there, studies the boy. He is, indeed, dark-haired. His pants are too large and he has rolled them up to his ankles. He wears a white undershirt with a neckline stretched so that it droops low on his sunken chest and hangs off one thin shoulder. He buckles his toes as if they are cold and stares up at Imogene. His skin is pale against his dark hair. She asks him again who he is, but he says nothing. He's waiting for an answer from her.

"I am Imogene," she says.

"I know because your hair is red," the boy says. He is smiling. "Red and fuzzy. Imogene has red, fuzzy hair."

To hear the boy talk makes him somehow more real; it sharpens his edges whereas before he was cloudy, and Imogene's chest begins to pump too fast. Her hands ache from squeezing the banister. She forces her knees to unfold, uses her hands to pull herself to her feet, and while she manages to stand, she doesn't straighten all the way but stays crouched. She unwraps one hand from the railing and reaches out toward the boy with it. She balances there, her stretched-out hand reaching for him. The blood drains from her fingertips, and her elbow begins to burn. The boy's smile fades and he tips to one side as if trying to see beyond Imogene to someone who might be coming up behind. She jerks around but the staircase leading upstairs is empty, the doorway still dark. She listens for those foot-steps overhead, for footsteps stomping through the pile of reeds she knocked down, for the slap of the screen door off the kitchen.

She begins to wave faster; maybe she says please to him. Please, come. Hurry and come. Her thinking mind has caught up with instinct and, with it, fear. As she forces herself to breathe, she pieces together the boarded-up windows and the three locks on the out-side of the door and the electricity run to the basement. Someone is keeping the boy here. They've locked him in. And then the boy shifts, places one bare foot on top of the other, wobbles. Imogene's stare drops from the boy to the floor beneath his feet. It's covered by mismatched carpet squares.

As far as the light from the single bulb reaches, the floor is lined with scrap carpet. There are carpet squares, sea-grass welcome mats, and long, narrow runners. They are all different colors and sizes and are pieced together with silver duct tape. The boy is bare-footed and buckles his toes and stretches them. He hops from one foot to the other. Even through the mismatched carpeting, the floor must be cold on his bare feet. She forces her legs to move, lifts one and then the other, creeps down two more steps to where the walls on either side of her open up and give way to a greater view of the basement. A sofa sits off to the left. Only the arm is visible. Just ahead and to the right is a card table. Three chairs sit around it.

"Come," she says, whispers. Her mouth is still dry, and her tongue doesn't move like it ought to. The boy hasn't heard. Or if he did hear and said something in response, she doesn't hear him because her heart is pounding in her ears. "Come."

This time, the boy shakes his head and is gone.

"No, don't." Imogene lunges for him. She slides the rest of the way down the stairs, cracking her back on the bottom step.

She sits there at the end of the long staircase, knowing her back should hurt but not feeling the pain. It's coming to her quickly, the things to be frightened of, what might lie here in wait. It's solid in her mind now. She closes her eyes to block out everything else and listens. It's all she has. But the house is quiet. She pushes off the stair, rocks forward, and stands, and as quickly as she does, she falls backward again. A small bed sits directly in front of her. A twin bed like she slept on through sixth grade. A patchwork quilt lays over it, and as if a child has made the bed, one side of the quilt rides too high and exposes the wooden footboard. Someone has laid out two dolls, one a life-sized infant and one much smaller. Both rest with their heads on the single pillow, and at the foot of the bed sits a large wooden cradle, empty. A wooden cradle for a baby. Something about the sight of that bed, the dolls, something about the sight of the cradle makes her turn her head and cough. Dry heaves, that's what they called them in college.

Once her stomach settles on itself, Imogene lifts onto her hands and knees, pauses there, her head hanging, her eyes closed. She's suddenly cold, and her body begins to tremble. She stands though her legs are still numb.

"You have to come with me," she says.

Her voice echoes in her head. She turns her back on the cradle, and without looking left or right because she's afraid of what she'll next see, she takes a few steps in the direction the boy went when he disappeared. She doesn't have air enough to force her words any louder, and probably the boy didn't hear her.

"We have to go. I'm Imogene. Remember? Red and fuzzy. You can come on with me."

She doesn't see him until he finally speaks. He has crawled into a dark space under the staircase. Only his small feet poke out where she can see them. The rest of him is hidden by the darkness and behind the wooden supports.

"I can't go," he says.

His voice is high-pitched and soft. She reaches to pull the stocking cap from her head, but it's gone. She lost it somewhere between knocking down the reeds along the house and falling down the stairs. It's one more way he, whoever might be upstairs or outside, will know she is here. It's also how the boy was able to see her red, fuzzy hair. Smoothing her hands over it, she creeps closer and tries to match her voice to his.

"You *can* go," she says, nodding at a pair of white sneakers near the bottom stair. "I'll show you how. I see you have shoes here."

Before the boy can say anything more, a motor kicks on, and again, Imogene startles. She ducks and turns a shoulder toward the sound. It's instinct, only instinct. Nothing is coming for her. She has to keep telling herself that. She'll hear him, whoever he might be, first. She'll hear him, and she doesn't, so she has to keep on. Still she's taking in too much oxygen, not letting off enough. It will get away from her if she lets it. It happens to Mama sometimes, though not as often now as when Imogene was younger. Panic attacks, the doctor had said. Have her breathe into a paper bag. It'll right the oxygen. Or have her blow out hard, like she's blowing out a candle. That'll do in a pinch. Imogene does that now. She lifts her index finger, holds it like it's a candle on a cake, and blows hard as if she's blowing it out. Again.

"Then let's put those shoes on those feet," she says, when the darkness stops closing in from both sides. Her voice cracks. She forces herself to lean and look toward the top of the stairs. The doorway there is black. Maybe it's still open, or maybe it's been closed, or will be soon and she'll be trapped like the boy. She was wrong. She won't hear anyone who might be coming, not now, not with that motor running. The thought of it, of what she can't hear or see, makes her chest begin to move too quickly again, and she can't stop the trembling that has reached her shoulders. She tucks her hands up under her arms to hide the shaking from the boy.

"Is it just you here?" she asks, trying to keep the fear from her voice. Like the darkness that was trying to close in, her imagination is closing in too. She imagines the door slamming shut, the slide bolts sliding into place, the keyed lock snapping closed. "Is it just you?" She pauses, swallows, forces herself to ask. "Is there a baby, too?"

There are three chairs. A twin-sized bed. The locks had been on the outside of the door. And a cradle for a baby.

"He'll bring Mama back," the boy says. His feet slip out of sight, and then his hands appear, followed by the rest of him as he untangles himself from the underworkings of the staircase.

Imogene takes a step toward him, can't stop herself because she doesn't understand what she heard. The boy stands and hugs himself with both arms, his narrow shoulders collapsing.

"If I'm good, if I'm quiet," the boy says, lifting his eyes to look at Imogene, "he always brings Mama back."

The First Rising

On Thanksgiving eve in 1915, following a massive immigration from countries such as Great Britain, Italy, and Germany, a growing distrust of US allies during World War I, and the release of a film titled *The Birth of a Nation* that glorified the KKK, William J. Simmons led fifteen men up Stone Mountain near Atlanta, Georgia, set a cross on fire, and reignited the Klan. Through the use of a publicity firm and the establishment of an enemies list that included, among others, blacks, Catholics, Jews, immigrants, bootleggers, those who didn't attend church, and those who engaged in premarital or extramarital sex, Ku Klux Klan membership swelled to four to six million by the 1920s.

Chapter 12

TILLIE

Today

From the shop's phone, Tillie calls Mrs. Tillie and tells her he's going to do a bit of cleaning, another lie, and not to wait up for him. Then he walks around the shop turning on every light so a passerby will know he's here and not at the house. If Tim or Robert Robithan is wanting to find Tillie, he wants them to find him at the shop, a good ways from home and Mrs. Tillie, because when they find him, they're also going to find out that their watches are gone. They won't care that Tillie tried to do the right thing by locking them up in the cabinet. They'll assume he betrayed them and stole from them, and there's nothing worse in the minds of men like Robert and Tim Robithan.

As Tillie waits, he whittles away the time by dusting his antique scales and giving their brass pans a good scrubbing. The scales are his favorites, especially the counterbalance sort. Mrs. Tillie says he prices them too high and they'll never sell, and she knows, rightly so, that is his intention. As he works, he thinks over all the things he could do. He could call the police, but then Robert would know Tillie lost his watches. He'll want seventy thousand dollars, and Tillie doesn't have it. Or he could deny Natalie ever brought them in, but that would leave her to take the brunt of whatever Robert and Tim Robithan might dole out, and Tillie knows exactly what the Robithans dole out because he once stood alongside Robert Robithan as he did it. Tillie keeps scrubbing and thinking until his fingers are wrinkled and chapped, and when still no Robithan has come looking for Tillie, he drives himself home.

It's clear he has to tell Mrs. Tillie about the watches and that someone has stolen them because this will be the thing that makes them finally leave Simmonsville. And maybe they should even take Imogene with them because Robert Robithan has set his sights on her. They'll have to pack up and be gone by morning. Tillie thought the memories had faded so thin they could no longer dredge up fear in him like they once did, but they're as strong and clear to him now as they were some forty years ago when he held tight to a man's arm while Robert Robithan drove a knife through his beating heart.

Thinking about leaving Simmonsville makes Tillie see his house differently as he sits in his driveway and looks up at it from his car. He sees it like a new family might, one with a baby on the way and maybe a youngster just out of diapers. They'll notice that the front shutters are real wood—board-and-batten cedar that Tillie made himself. They'll say the house has good bones and that it'll look bigger once all Mrs. Tillie's trinkets, knickknacks, and whatnots are gone. The old place will be young again, and whoever buys it will always wonder why two old folks left their home of so many years and almost everything in it without a word to anyone.

Mrs. Tillie has left on the light in the living room. The soft glow is the same one he came home to that night forty years ago. Mrs. Tillie had been awake to greet him when he walked through the door, and in all the years since, Tillie has wondered what roused her from bed. She'd known straightaway to hold her arms out to him because he was crying and shaking in a way he didn't know a man could. She had already known. Somehow Mrs. Tillie always already knows.

Once inside the house, Tillie takes care setting his keys on the entryway table. As he's pulling the door closed, quiet as he can, the smell of cherry blossoms chases in behind him. It's the lightest of scents, roselike with a hint of almond. The trees, and the surprising pink show they put on come every spring, are one of the things

Tillie will miss most, and he hopes in their next house, a single lamp shining in a dark living room will be nothing more than a light in the dark.

"You ready to tell me now, are you?"

It's Mrs. Tillie, sitting right there in the glow of that table lamp, a bundle of her knitting resting in her lap. Her long gray hair has been let down, and it hangs over one shoulder.

"I'm ready," Tillie says.

He tells about Robert Robithan's watches first and how he had to take them from Natalie Sharon lest Robert Robithan find out he let them watches walk out the shop's front door. Seventy thousand dollars' worth of watches, he says. And he tells how Natalie goes with Robert's son and that she and Robert's boy likely stole them watches so they could sell them for good money and how Tillie couldn't never tell Robert Robithan a thing like that about his own son. And if he did tell Robert, Tim Robithan might somehow turn the mess around on Tillie to save his own hide. And last he tells how Robert Robithan has got it in his mind Imogene is a good match for his son. But now them watches are gone and Imogene is likely more broken than ever and nothing will ever bring back their Russell and Vaughn and Tillie surely doesn't have seventy thousand dollars.

When Tillie is done telling his troubles to Mrs. Tillie, she sets her knitting on the side table and leans forward as if to whisper. She understands the kind of being scared that Tillie is feeling, the kind that has made his fingers go stiff. And probably it's his fault for telling her things too good. He'd let every detail of what he'd seen and done spill out to Mrs. Tillie as he was crying and shaking in her arms forty years ago, and while he didn't know it then, he knows it now. He was crying and shaking because he'd never be able to take back knowing better but not doing better.

"I didn't know them watches was special," Mrs. Tillie says. "I locked them up in the safe. You know, like we always do. You check in there?"

First, Tillie laughs, and Mrs. Tillie smiles and laughs too. But then he stops, and she stops at the same time because she's figured the same as Tillie.

"That don't solve my problem of how to tell Robert his son stole from him," Tillie says. "I'm still wedged smack between the two of them. They wouldn't think twice about destroying everything we got. And that don't solve what Imogene's up against."

"Well, I know one thing for certain," Mrs. Tillie says after the two of them have sat quiet a good long time. "We ain't got to worry about Imogene. She won't have no part of Timmy Robithan. And as for the rest, well, you listen to me, Jean Tillerson. This here is what we're going to do."

Chapter 13

IMOGENE

Today

Imogene stares at the boy. The single light shining at the bottom of the stairs makes him blink in steady sets of three. The stone floors and walls and the low-hanging ceiling trap the sound of his voice and keep it from ringing clear. He said something to her. She knows he did, but it's as if he spoke in a different language. She is staring and wants to speak but can't. He's waiting for her to say something. He's tilted his head and is leaning toward her. It's her turn. She can see it in the way his eyes have grown wider. He's waiting.

"What did you say?"

"If I'm good," the boy says, buckling his toes again, "he always brings Mama back."

The boy is growing smaller, the distance between them growing larger. It's because of Imogene. She's backing away from him. The boy takes a step toward her. She stumbles, shakes her head at him.

"He brings me special things," the boy says. "When I'm good. And he always brings Mama home."

Imogene backs away until something stops her. She swings around, her arms rising, but it's only the sofa. She leans against the back of it, and with her head turned away from the boy, she closes her eyes. A moment is all she needs. One quiet moment to think on this. She tries to make sense of what he said, but no matter how hard she tries, she can't grab hold of a single thought. They're vanishing like puffs of smoke. Squeezing her eyes tight and pressing her lips into a hard line, she tries harder, but that motor is still humming, and it won't let her make sense of what the boy has told her.

She can't grab for the boy because that will frighten him back under the staircase. Instead, she digs her hands into the coarse upholstery covering the sofa. She already knew there was someone else. She already knew it was a man. And he's coming back. The boy has told her what her instincts had already warned her about. She opens her eyes and turns back to him. He's close enough now to touch.

"Where is it?" she asks.

The boy shrugs.

"What's making the noise?"

He points with one small finger to the other side of the staircase. Imogene nods.

"Wait here," she says, holding up a hand to signal the boy should stay put. "Everything's going to be fine." And as she says it, she thinks of her car parked outside and of her cell phone sitting in the basket by the sink up at Mama's. She has no idea how long she's been in the house, can barely remember walking through the back door, standing in front of those three locks. She left the headlights on, and maybe the engine is running, maybe not. She tries to remember how much gas is in the tank.

On the other side of the stairs, past the table and three chairs, the piecemeal carpet stops and the floors become bare stone. A large crack appears from under the carpet, travels the length of the room, and disappears into the back of the basement. A small refrigerator stands against the far wall, and a cast-iron sink, white paint chipping from its edges, hangs next to it. A coffee maker and a hot plate with two burners sit on a piece of plywood, but it's the sight of a white tea towel that stops Imogene. It's embroidered with a single magnolia and hangs perfectly and evenly over a slender silver bar. Like the sight of the bed, something about a tea towel, something she might see in any home, maybe even Mama's home, makes her fingers grow stiff. She gives them a good shake and turns away.

It's darker on this side of the basement, but the sound of the motor is instantly louder. It must be some sort of heater or dehumidifier—an old one judging by how loudly it's running—because the air is light and the room doesn't smell of mold like a basement normally would.

Forcing herself not to look at the embroidered towel again just as she forced herself not to look at the cradle, Imogene takes a few more steps and she sees it—a small window unit. It's mounted high in one of the slender windows and rattles as warm air blows out of it. She yanks its cord from an outlet that dangles loose. Again, the house falls silent.

Imogene thought she wanted the silence so she could hear, but instead of comforting her, it frightens her. She walks toward the foot of the stairs, sliding her feet rather than picking them up. She could leave the boy and run to the car alone. But she left the lights on, and she doesn't know how long it's been or how long a car can sit like that and still start. She could take the boy with her, and if the car's battery is dead, she could lock him inside and run home. She could tell the boy to hide on the floorboards, don't look up, even if someone comes banging on the windows. Mama's house isn't so far. If she has to leave him, it will only be for a few minutes, fifteen at most.

"He said someday I might live in the house where you used to live."

Imogene swings around. The boy stands in front of the staircase.

"Is that why you're here?" he says. "Are we going to go live in that house?"

"Who told you that?"

The boy doesn't answer and instead squats to the carpet squares and begins picking at the duct tape that pieces them together. Imogene drops down beside him and grabs him by both shoulders.

"Tell me," she says, looking from the boy's face to the top of the dark stairwell.

The boy's shoulders cave, and as he tries to pull away from her, he shakes his head.

"Why? Why won't you tell me?"

"If I tell, he won't bring Mama back."

The house is full of silence now that the window unit is off, and it's choking her, muddling her thoughts instead of clearing them. She drops her hands from his shoulders, grabs one of his wrists, and pulls him to his feet.

"We're leaving."

When the boy makes no move to follow her, she drags him toward the stairs. His body goes limp. She grabs that same wrist with her other hand. He begins to scream. She reaches the bottom step, but the boy is kicking now and rolling his body from side to side as he tries to break free. He screams again. Not just once. He screams over and over, shouting that he won't go, can't go. Whatever else he is saying, she doesn't know because she can only see the next stair and then the next and all the stairs between him and her and the door at the top.

Imogene has made it to the third stair when the boy's screams change and he begins to cry instead. It is the switch from fear to pain. He's hit his head on one of the wooden steps. She drops his wrist and slides down the stairs where he lies in a ball, both hands pressed to his forehead. At first, there is no blood, and then only a single stream trickles from between two fingers. It dribbles over one knuckle. He must feel it because he pulls his hands away and looks down at them. Then he holds them up so Imogene will see they're smeared with blood. His cries turn back into screams again as he tries to scramble away from her. This time, she grabs one of his ankles.

"Stop," she says, looking back at the stairs because she's certain they'll have been heard. "You have to be quiet. Please." Dropping his leg, she holds her hands out to the side to show she won't grab him again. "I won't make you go, okay? But please, you have to be quiet."

Not knowing what to do next, she sits back on her knees.

"When he takes your mama," she says, "how long until he comes back?"

"Not long," the boy says, his chest shuddering as he slowly stops crying. "Mama is never gone for long. But this time, I think she's been gone too long."

Chapter 14

BETH

Before

We walk up three outside steps and into a house, the man leading me by one hand. The house is wooden and white paint is peeling and flaking near the door. I hear my feet hitting the ground but don't feel anything. Still, they keep moving me forward. Then we're inside a dark kitchen and it smells like the underneath side of our house where a man crawled when our toilet stopped flushing right. He flashed his flashlight under there so I could see the guts of where I lived. There were thick pieces of wood under there and pipes and cobwebs draped between them. Look at here, he said, digging his hand down into the thick red dirt. He lifted a handful, opened his fingers, and let it drain through. This here is good Georgia clay. I could see only as far as his flashlight reached and always wondered what else was under there. I'd fall asleep some nights, thinking about the dark corners I couldn't see. Sometimes I'd hear things down there and would stay still and quiet, hoping whatever it was didn't crawl up to the surface.

Just inside the kitchen, I stop my feet and lean back because it feels like I'm walking into the guts, all the way in, even where the light doesn't reach, and I know this place is bad. With one yank, the man pulls me forward. My legs give way and I crumble. I press my hands to the floor. I want to melt into the darkness. I know I shouldn't be here, and if I close my eyes, this place will be gone and I'll be home again with Mama.

Those same hands hook me under my arms. He wants me to stand, but my legs won't hold me. And then he's dragging me. My feet bounce across the floor. My head sags. The farther he drags me, the darker the house becomes even though it should be getting lighter. The sun was just beginning to rise when we drove up to this new place, and the air was wet and heavy. Mama calls it the seam between day and night, and if a person is going to fall through the cracks, Mama always said, it will happen at the seam—during that cold, wet, orange time of day when no one is looking. But the house isn't getting brighter. It's getting darker and I'm going deeper too. Deeper like once I go in, I'll slip between the seam and never dig my way out.

At a closed door, he wraps one hand around the back of my neck, pinches tight, and holds me upright as he reaches for the knob. I dangle, kicking my legs and stretching my toes until I feel the floor. I can't turn my head any which way because he's holding too tight. I'm like one of the giant catfish the men catch down at the river and hold high with one hand while someone takes a picture of their trophy. Keeping a tight grip, the man opens the door, and I close my eyes, and if I weren't a giant catfish dangling by its neck, I'd turn my head away. Then a light switches on. I hear it and I see the glow through my closed lids. He shakes the hand still holding me so I'll walk ahead of him, but I don't because the stairs go down, and even though I can see the bottom, I can't see what else is down there. This is the deeper part I felt coming. I'm afraid there is something down there, but I'm also afraid there is nothing.

When my legs let go again and I start to sink to the floor, he scoops me up. I cough and cry as the man takes one stair at a time. We go deeper and deeper. At the bottom, he sets me down, holding on while he tests to see if my legs are working yet. He's staring at me, shaking me because of the coughing and crying. When I get enough air and I can stand again, he begins to lead me around the room. I walk slow because the floor is hard and uneven. The ceiling hangs low, making the room small and dark. This is a basement, the underground part of the house.

"I want to go back to Mama," I say.

Mama will come home and be sad I'm not there, and she'll worry that a stranger has taken me away.

"Your mama is long gone." He walks back and forth in front of me as he talks. "Forget about your mama."

This place is cold. I try to run back up the stairs, but my legs are heavy and I stumble. He grabs a handful of my hair and I fall backward. Taking hold of me by the neck again, he makes me walk ahead of him. The air is thick and sticky, like I have to wipe it away to see ahead, and it's wet like fog. It settles on my skin, making me wet too. There is a sofa, one chair, one small table. And there is a bed and a pillow and a pink blanket with satin trim that is torn and hangs loose. The same happened to one of our blankets and Mama stitched it back together with a needle and thread.

"What do I call you?" he asks, stopping in front of the stairs.

I don't say anything because I don't know if I'm still Beth down here. Mama is gone and Ellie and Fran will never call me for a sleepover and Julie Anna will never babysit me again. When I think of all of them being gone, the ceiling drops lower and the wet, sticky room starts to swallow me up. Everything that made me real is gone. I don't know what to say.

"Hey, I asked you a question."

"Beth," I say.

"Okay, then, Beth it is." He doesn't tell me his name and instead points at square pieces of wood hanging from the walls. With one of his fingers, he lifts my chin so I have to look. "You see there?"

They are boarded-over windows, he tells me. Boarded over on the outside and the inside, and that means there ain't no way out. Did it himself, he says, so it's a job well done. He didn't have time to find me more clothes, but he would soon. Just give him time. I nod, but even though my eyes are pointed at the boarded-over windows, I don't really see them. Mama is gone and Julie Anna is lying still on the floor and now everything around me is just outside my reach, as if no matter how far I stretch my hand, I will never touch anything solid ever again. Mama once took me to a 3-D movie in Atlanta. Fish of all sizes swam across the screen. As they darted past us, we stretched out our hands, thinking for certain their smooth, slimy skins would slip through our fingers. But no matter how far we leaned or how high we stretched, they were always just beyond our reach.

Next he shows me a small room with a toilet. He crosses his fingers and says we'd both better hope it's held up. After the bathroom, he shows me a blue box with a lid. He opens it, and the inside is filled with ice. He shoves in a hand and pulls out a small bottle of orange juice. He shakes it, shoves it back down into the ice, and tells me there is plenty of food in there to last me a few days.

"You know how to feed yourself?" he asks, rubbing his hand on top of my head. "Three squares a day? Got sandwich makings in there. Tuna too. You use a can opener? You drink milk, brush your teeth?"

He keeps asking questions and I keep nodding until he shows me the toaster oven.

"I'm not allowed," I say, staring at it. I want to pinch my nose so I can't smell. Sometimes Mama leaves our laundry in the washer and never hangs it on the line, and then my shirts smell like this basement.

"Yeah," he says. "Yeah, I guess not." Then he reaches under a white sink that hangs from the wall and pulls out a large bottle with a handle on it. "You know what this is?"

I can't look at him because seeing hands or eyebrows or the collar of his shirt would make him real, and that would make me being here real. I know he wears black boots and his fingers are rough. I know he's big but only because of the shadow that hung over me when he first pulled me from the metal box. I don't know if he is young like Mama or old like a grandpa. He asks again if I know what the bottle is, and I shake my head.

"This is what you use if there's a fire," he says. "You pull this here and point this here."

He unravels my pointer finger from my wadded-up fist, pokes it through a plastic ring. When his hand touches mine, blackness starts to close in around me. It starts to swallow me up.

"Can I go home?"

"This is your home."

I shake my head.

"Only home you got, little girl, little Beth. Better take it."

"No," I say, but my voice doesn't sound like my voice. It sounds like somebody else's coming out of somebody else's mouth. The fish are still swimming past, just out of reach, and I'm sinking deeper.

He grabs me by the arm, drags me to the wall in the back where the light doesn't reach. I fall on both knees, and he presses on my head with one hand so I have to look.

"See that there?" he asks, pointing to three fat metal rings stuck onto a wall made of large, bumpy stones.

I try to nod but can't move my head. The stone floor is hard against my knees. I want to sit back to stop them from hurting so bad, but he won't let me.

"You better figure out right here and now that this is where you'll stay put or you'll find yourself chained up to them rings."

I don't know what he means, but I think someone else was once here and maybe they were chained to the wall. Maybe I will be too.

"I didn't figure on this happening," he says after a time, and he starts pacing back and forth again, his head passing near the light bulb that hangs from a wire in the ceiling. "Damn it all, I knew she'd be trouble. Knew it the moment I seen her. She was the house sitter, you know? You know what that means? Means sitting for the house. Not sitting for you."

Every time he walks under the bulb, the light twists and swirls. The shadows slipping across the floor make me dizzy. I curl myself up as tight as I can and hug my knees.

"Didn't go there intending nothing," he says, still pacing. "Folks want them gone, is all. Her daddy, he shouldn't be teaching no kids. This ain't my fault."

Still hugging myself tight, I say nothing. His voice is deep and too loud. It fills the room, and I want to cover my ears over. I want to scream at him to stop talking, but I'm emptied out inside because there is no one to hear me. I squeeze myself tighter, tuck my head into my knees, make myself as small as I can.

"Hey," he says, one of his boots nudging my hip. "You there?"

The lace on that boot is untied. I point so he'll tie it.

"I done the best I could for you here," he says. "You see them stairs? Don't you set foot on them stairs. Hear me?"

I touch the black lace that lies on the floor, but he jerks the boot away. In school, we've started talking about being almost fifth graders and all the things we'll study next year. We'll do fractions some more and learn about how plants live and how people eat and digest their food. I don't think I'll learn any of those things.

"I cleaned up down here for you," he says. "So you keep it clean."

I nod but don't say anything. It isn't clean here. The floors are like hard dirt and it's dark here and the walls are slimy and already my clothes are wet and soon they'll smell like Mama left them in the washer too long. And because he's asking can I feed myself and telling me to keep things clean, I know now he's going to leave me here alone. I'm sinking and the water is slipping over my head and the light is almost gone. I'm seeping between the cracks, falling through the seam. I'll be alone like when I come home after school and Mama is still at work, except I think I'll be alone here forever.

"At least tell me you understand about the fire," he says.

I nod, must nod, because he doesn't ask again. If there is ever a fire, I think I'll let it burn.

Chapter 15

IMOGENE

Today

Taking care to keep her hands out wide so she won't frighten the boy again, and so she won't frighten herself any more than she already is, Imogene stands and leaves him to sit on the floor. Blood is still leaking through his fingers from where his forehead bounced off one of the stair treads. He said his mama never stays away for long and that a man always brings her back, except this time, she's been gone too long.

"The kitchen," she says, trying not to look at the blood he's left on her forearm and motioning for him to follow. Her body is stiff, and she has to force it to move, first her feet and then her arms. "We'll get you cleaned up at the sink."

The boy stands, but only when Imogene walks toward the kitchen instead of up the stairs, and he follows. At the sink, she reaches for the embroidered towel, but he tells her no, not that one, in a tiny voice that reminds her how young he is. With a hand she can't stop from shaking, she grabs a roll of paper towels instead and pulls off several.

"Only one," the boy says. "You only get to use one or we'll be out too soon."

Imogene nods but still wads up the handful and presses them to his forehead. Once she has covered over the spot that's bleeding, she takes another few towels, dampens them in the sink, and wipes his face. As she cleans him, he stares up at her with pale blue eyes that should be brown to go along with his dark hair, and his breathing slows. Hers slows too. Tossing the damp towels aside, she wraps one arm around him and with her free hand takes over holding the wadded towels to his head.

"Let's sit," she says, still in a whisper, because she doesn't want anyone to hear and because she doesn't know what to do next and because the shaking has exhausted her or maybe it's the whiskey still working its way through. The strength in her hands, legs, and arms is gone. "Let's just sit awhile."

At the small card table, she sits first, pulls the boy into her lap, and lifts the towel to see the cut beneath.

"It's not bad," she says, setting the towel on the table. "Not even bleeding anymore. Are you dizzy? Does it hurt?"

The boy shakes his head.

Again, Imogene forces herself to ask the question. "I see a cradle there," she says, nodding off toward the bed. "Does a baby sleep there? Is there a baby who lives here with you?"

"That's my bed," the boy says, resting his head on Imogene's shoulder. "Except I'm too big for it now."

Carrying the boy's weight in her arms, Imogene rests one hand lightly on his head. He smells clean, like the lotion she put on Vaughn when he was a baby, and he'll feel that Imogene is trembling. When he starts to speak again, she quiets him. He draws in a deep breath, shudders, and the last of his crying fades. She can't understand what all of this means—the boy knowing her name, his thinking he'll live in Mama's house, his saying the man always brings his mama back, the cradle that he says belongs to him. Her thoughts spin around each question, but no answers take hold. All she can figure for certain is that she must get the both of them to the top of the stairs, and later, when they're safe, she'll sort it all out. Waiting for the boy to fall asleep, she listens for footsteps overhead.

Soon enough, her elbows begin to ache. Her thighs go numb, and she's beginning to sweat where their bodies are pressed together, but still she holds the boy tight. No matter how her arms or legs or neck aches, no matter how long it takes, she'll stay still until the boy falls asleep, and once he has, she'll try again. She'll carry him up the stairs and hope he doesn't wake until they reach the car. After a time, the boy stops shifting about. To give the muscles in her arms a rest, she leans back in the chair, just a fraction of an inch, and when he doesn't stir, another fraction, and then she stares at the wooden beams overhead.

As they sit together in the chair, Imogene and the boy, she notices his slender pink fingers are wrapped up in the black fleece fabric of her jacket. At some point, he grabbed on, and even as he nears sleep, he won't let go. Without moving, she studies the room around them. Clothes hang from a line strung near the stairs where the boy first hid. He went there straightaway, knew just where to squat so she could barely see him. He's hidden there before. On either side of a small television, slender wooden bookshelves have been built, unfinished lengths of pine hung with metal brackets. The sofa has been mended with the same silver duct tape that was used to stitch together the carpet squares. And she sees it again, the cradle pushed up against the footboard. In her arms, the boy twitches and then is still. When his hand loosens where he was holding on to her jacket, Imogene lowers it to his lap so it won't fall and startle him when she stands.

The boy is easier to carry up the stairs than she feared. As she begins the climb, she moves steadily toward the dark door at the top, hoping with every step that it is still open. Between stairs, she pauses only long enough to listen, and once she is sure she hears nothing overhead, she takes another step. The light from below only reaches so far. She moves slowly, letting her eyes adjust to the dark as she climbs. In a few steps, she can make out the door. It's open, and she climbs faster, with greater ease. At the top, she leaves the light on and the door open so she'll have some light as she makes her way through the rest of the house. After taking a few steps through the dining room, she stops and wonders if she's made the wrong choice. With the door open and the light on, he—whoever he is—will know straightaway someone has been here. But it's too late. She won't go back, not even a few steps.

Passing through the dining room, she shuffles sideways around the table so the boy's feet don't hit the edge. She can't help that her heart is beating faster. It's the effort of the climb and fear. At the back door, she struggles to turn the knob, and once the door is unlatched, she uses her foot to open it, shoulders through the screen door, and they slip through.

Outside, the night air against her damp skin startles her. She draws in a sudden breath and muffles a cough by pressing her mouth to her shoulder. Afraid she'll have woken the boy and that he'll cry out and alert someone to their escape, she stops walking, fights the urge to readjust his weight to ease the burn in her elbows and shoulders, and stands still until the steady rhythm of his breathing starts up again. Whatever has happened here, even knowing all that she knows about Edison Coulter, it couldn't be his doing. And if it wasn't him, it was someone else. She'll get the two of them to Mama's house quick as she can, and once there, she'll lock the doors and call the police.

It's fully dark outside the house, dark like in the country. The air is tinted with smoke, which means Mama has started a fire up at the house in the fireplace in her room. She does it most nights when the weather is cool enough. A few feet beyond the back door, the field of pampas grass is quiet. Imogene listens for a rustling or for twigs snapping underfoot. Afraid someone, he, might be looking down on them from the second story, she doesn't look back at the house. She tries to make her stride smooth as she begins to walk again, but the smell of Mama's fire and the dark that has settled over her like a weight and the quiet that looms out in the field and the safety of her car make her begin to move faster and faster. The boy bounces in her arms. That little hand grabs for her jacket again, and he begins to scream.

If twigs are snapping or leaves are rustling somewhere behind her, she doesn't hear them. She tries to quiet the boy as she runs, his head bouncing under her chin, but he continues to scream and kick and try to twist his way out of her arms. She turns her face away, but still one of his nails scratches her on the cheek and something hits the bridge of her nose. Her eyes water. She blinks, holds her head back and away from the boy's flailing arms. As she nears the front corner of the house, the glow coming from the car's headlights shows her the way. Fewer canes grow along this side of the house, but as she runs, they still slap her in the shoulders and the boy turns his face into her chest. She stumbles. The ground is rocky near the drive and uneven, but she keeps on.

At the car, she tries to push the boy inside, but he grabs the door and kicks against her. Over and over, she tells him to be quiet. He'll hear us, she says. Stop. He'll hear us. He throws his head back, his whole body arching in her arms as she shoves him across the seat and into the passenger's side. Once behind the wheel, she pulls the door closed and hits the lock button.

Crossing her arms over the steering wheel, Imogene rests her head there. Her breath is coming fast, and her chin and mouth are wet. Next to her, the boy continues to scream and cry, louder now that they're inside the small space. With his palms, he beats on the window in his door, and when he tries to climb into the back seat, Imogene grabs him at the waist. An elbow swings around, and this time catches her top lip and then her eye. She tastes blood.

"Ed'll be mad," the boy cries, slapping at Imogene as he makes his way over the seat. "He'll be mad."

"Stop." This time, Imogene is the one to scream. She wipes her sleeve across the eye the boy struck with his elbow. It won't stop watering. "Stop it now."

The boy goes silent, even presses a hand over his mouth as he slides down to the floorboards in the back seat. He pulls his knees up and buries his head. Still holding her forearm to that one eye, she reaches to touch the top of his head but stops because her hand is shaking. Instead of comforting the boy, she lowers her hand to her lap and stares back at him.

"What did you just say?" she asks.

The boy doesn't answer and instead pulls his knees tighter to his chest. The air in the car has turned thick. Imogene pushes her wiry hair from her face and asks again.

"You said a name just now," she says, softly. "What name did you say?"

The boy's shoulders shudder, but he makes no more sounds of crying. Someone has taught him how to stay quiet.

"How long has your mama been gone?" Imogene says. Her heart races as if she's stepped to the edge of a tall building. Something is going to pull her over, and she can't force herself to step away. "You have to tell me. You know me. I'm Imogene. Red and fuzzy. How long has your mama been gone?"

He still says nothing.

"What do you eat for breakfast?"

"Bread with peanut butter." His mouth is pressed against his forearm and his words are muffled. In the dark, only his forehead and cheeks are visible and the whites of both eyes.

"That's good." Imogene smooths her hair from her face. Her skin is damp and her curls are hot on her neck. "Did your mama make that for you today?"

He shakes his head.

"Yesterday?"

Again, he shakes his head.

"You made it yourself?"

This time he nods.

"And how many times have you made your own breakfast?"

He says nothing and buries his face again.

"Two times?" she asks.

Again, nothing.

"Was it more than two?" she asks.

"The bread's almost gone."

"But how many days?" Imogene says. The boy's mama could have been gone for days, weeks even, since before Daddy died. If this was Daddy's doing, what did he do with her?

The boy says nothing else. He doesn't nod or shake his head, doesn't lift his eyes to look at Imogene. He has slipped away, someplace inside himself, and he isn't going to say the name again.

A few days ago, Edison James Coulter died. Today they buried him. Most folks called him Ed. Imogene is certain, almost certain, that's the name the boy called out.

Part II

Chapter 16

IMOGENE

Today

The boy is asleep again by the time Imogene parks in front of the main house, and he stays asleep as she opens the car's back door, slips her hands under his shoulders, and pulls him out. It's as if he's run himself dry, either by fighting Imogene or by missing his mama or both.

Imogene could have driven the boy straight to the police or to the hospital in town or even down to Jo Lynne's office. It's what Jo Lynne does. She cares for children pulled from their homes in the middle of the night for whatever reason. Without children of her own—one of the many ways in which Garland has disappointed her, because his sperm count is to blame—Jo Lynne's job gives her someone to fix other than Imogene. More than once, over a Sunday dinner, Jo Lynne has shaken her head and said it's unimaginable, the things those people do to their children. It's always *those* people. Unimaginable how broken people can be and yet they still carry on. Sometimes she looks at Imogene as she says these things, as if Imogene is one of those broken people who, despite it all, has managed to carry on. Jo Lynne would be able to find the boy a home to stay in, a bed for the night. She'd take control, and right now, Imogene would welcome it. But something stops her from doing any of those things. It's the smallest of itches, and even though she can't sort through the possibilities just now, she can't ignore that itch.

If the boy did say Daddy's name, it might mean Edison Coulter did the unimaginable. It shouldn't be surprising. The unimaginable has been happening in this house for more than a hundred years. W. J. Simmons—whose grandfather was the man after whom the town of Simmonsville was named—led the climb up Stone Mountain in 1915 to reignite the Ku Klux Klan after the government squelched the original uprising in earlier years. He sold the new Klan not as a group that hanged, bombed, and burned people but as a defender of law and order and morality. And the organization he peddled grew to more than four million members.

W. J. Simmons lived in this house, walked across this screened porch, took his coffee in this kitchen. He coddled his hatred and passed it on to his son and he to his. The wives of these men instead passed on a prayer that they give birth to no sons and that the Simmons name would die. Mama says their prayers were strong but not strong enough, not until Mama's generation. Every Simmons man fathered one son to carry on the name until Dale Simmons. He fathered only a daughter—Lottie Rose—and the Simmons name, as it traces back to that night on Stone Mountain, died because Mama had no brothers.

Once outside the car, Imogene muffles another cough. It's the smell of smoke catching in her throat. She tells Mama not to start the fire herself. Sometimes she forgets the flue and the house fills with smoke. Leaving the car door ajar so as not to wake the boy by shutting it, Imogene rearranges him in her arms until she has a good grip. His head is heavy on her shoulder and his breath warms the side of her neck. One small hand rests on her sleeve, his fingers clutching the black fleece as if even in sleep, he's holding on.

Imogene hasn't held a child like this since she held Vaughn. But that had been for such a short time and so very long ago. That's the thing she spent all day remembering, Vaughn in her arms, even feeling the weight and warmth of him against her chest a few times as she sat with Tillie and Mrs. Tillie during Daddy's service, the organ music, so familiar, crushing her to the point she wanted to scream out for it to stop. After five years, Russell has mostly let go. Imogene doesn't wake anymore expecting to see him next to her in bed, one arm slung across her waist, doesn't see him in strangers walking down the street, doesn't hope to hear his voice on the other end of her phone. She's mostly forgotten how it felt to be happy like she was during that short time with Russell and Vaughn, how comforted she had been to think she knew what her future looked like, and now she's mostly grown accustomed to the emptiness.

But Vaughn is still holding on, or rather she's still holding on to him. This new boy, too, is holding on to Imogene, and there's a permanence to how he's doing it, a vigor, as if he knows Imogene can't do much to keep him safe. He's been alone, possibly for several days, and he hasn't just fallen asleep. It's more than that. Something in him has shut down. His head and arms hang loose. He's limp, as if he'll slip through her arms if she doesn't hold tight.

The steps leading onto the porch, though there are only three of them, are harder to manage than the dozen she climbed to get them out of the basement. Imogene pauses after one step, the tops of her legs burning, her back straining to keep her upright. The adrenaline has worn off, the whiskey too, and her body is getting ready to give up altogether. At the screen door, she shifts the boy's weight to her left side and, with her free hand, fumbles with the latch, and after passing over the threshold, she balances on one foot so she can keep the screen from slamming closed with the other. At the door leading into the kitchen, she repeats the same thing.

The house is dark except for the light that shines under Mama's door, and the muffled sounds of voices from her television seep into the living room. She'll have surely fallen asleep by now. Tomorrow, Mama will ask Imogene if the wire is gone and did it lead to the old house and what was your father up to. And while Imogene could have stripped out the wire and emptied the old house of any proof of Daddy and his women or his Klan cohorts, she won't be able to hide a child.

Not able to face another set of stairs, Imogene lays the boy in her old bedroom instead of the guest room on the second story. She lowers him onto her bed, the frame creaking as it takes his weight, slides her hands out from under him, and then straightens and stretches her lower back. After she and Russell married, she boxed up all signs of her childhood—the trophies and medals from sports she'll never play again, yearbooks she never looks at, notebooks, binders, and textbooks. Now the room is where Mama stores extra blankets and pillows, and her gardening magazines are stacked along the wall under the window. Mama also moved her reading chair in here so she could get some peace and quiet from Daddy, and he from her. Though they still call it Imogene's room, it isn't hers anymore.

With only the light from the hallway spilling into the room, Imogene can look at the boy now, really look at him. His hair is dark and too long, leaving the ends to curl. His face is slender, and where his cheeks should be soft and round, they're instead sunken. His arms and legs are bony and pale, making them look longer than they are, and even in the dark room, she can see that thick black lashes line his eyes. Pushing aside his hair, she checks the cut on his forehead. There's no swelling and she thinks that's a good thing. She presses one hand to her chest, tries to catch her breathing as it starts to run away from her. Again, her mind is catching up with something her body knew straightaway.

This boy is the same age Vaughn would have been if he'd lived. Imogene sees them in town sometimes, children who are the age Vaughn should've been. They get older every year. She stares at the mothers too, wondering if she would have become as good at mothering as they have. Mama said in the early days after Vaughn was born that Imogene needed to remember he wouldn't be a baby forever. The crying would eventually stop. He would eventually sleep through the night, and so would she. It was okay that Imogene disliked being a mama some days, that she hated being tired and never sleeping and not getting a shower or a decent meal. But what Imogene hated most was not knowing what to do or how to do it or if she'd done it right. She hated feeling like her life was over. Remember, Mama had said, he'll grow up. It'll get easier and everything you're feeling is part of loving him.

And it did get easier. Imogene stopped being so tired. She figured out how to keep Vaughn awake during his feedings so he slept better, and he started to smile and squeeze their fingers. She studied for classes while he slept, and Russell began to help by getting up during the night. Later, Imogene hated that she wasted so much time missing her old life when she could have been loving her new one. Draping a blanket over the boy, Imogene backs out of her room, one slow step after another, and once outside pulls the door closed.

Out in the hallway, Imogene bends forward and rests her hands on her thighs. Her chest rises and lowers faster when it should be slowing down. It's panic, first lighting on top of her skin, then slowly sinking in. It grows brighter as it does, and hotter. Letting her head hang loose, she forces herself to exhale through her mouth and inhale through her nose, and when that doesn't slow the terror racing through her body and settling in her chest, she drops to her knees, closes her eyes, and tries to replay it in her head. The boy thrashing about, angry and frightened. Someone taught him the rules—never say the man's name, never ever, the boy said—but in that moment, he forgot.

Still kneeling, the pine floors hard beneath her, Imogene lets her back round and her arms hang loose. An old house is somehow quieter and lonelier, both things amplified by its past. She didn't know that until she moved out and got an apartment of her own after Russell and Vaughn died, and even though she hasn't lived in this house for several years, she's ready for the ache that comes with its history.

The giving in has worked, and her breathing has slowed. She's coached Mama to do it so many times. It's the only thing Imogene does well these days. She can comfort Mama like the others can't, mostly because the beating of Mama's heart—the ticking that never ever stops, that makes some bend over the nearest trash can—has never troubled her. It's the one thing that's special about Imogene, though Mama would scold her for thinking such a thing. But it's true. Eddie is the son, and though Daddy never touted it, others may still defer to him now that Daddy's gone, at least the ones who don't know Eddie well. Jo Lynne has a husband and a career where she saves children's lives. Imogene has nothing, except a stomach for Mama's beating heart.

As air moves freely through her lungs again, she starts to think more clearly. Daddy was seventy-five years old, and old men don't keep boys and their mothers locked in a basement. Edison Coulter had plenty to be ashamed of, though he'd never suffered a moment's shame his entire life, but not this. She has time and the room to think like she didn't when panic was crowding out every clear thought, but time enough to think also means time enough for the things she saw to continue to take form in a way they hadn't before, not even when she was looking right at them.

It's as if in the quiet, the whisper of all the evil that's passed through this house can almost be heard. If Daddy wasn't the person keeping the boy down in that basement, then it's someone who's still out there, maybe right now, watching the house. Maybe someone who's hiding among the pecan trees, someone who saw Imogene bring the boy inside. As quickly as she thinks it, she imagines a shadowy figure slipping across the drive and up onto the porch. She can feel eyes peeking in at her through the blinds and fingers landing gently on a doorknob, turning, pushing.

Keeping low to the ground, she scrambles toward the back door and, once there, looks out the sidelight. The porch is lit up, but the yard beyond is too black even for shadows. The simple square columns are not thick enough to hide a person, and she'd hear if someone had walked onto the porch. Whoever was living there in the basement had dug in. It's a horrible thought, and yet it's true. Someone had made a home down there—embroidered tea towels, books stacked smallest to tallest, chairs pushed under the table, squarely, evenly. Whoever loved enough to do those things had been there a long time. And there were locks on the outside of the basement door. The outside. That's the sight more than any other that makes Imogene's throat tighten. She's spinning, stumbling, doesn't know how to find her footing. The only thing she knows is that a strange boy is asleep in her bedroom, his mama is missing, and Imogene can't be the one to know what to do next.

The whiskey has burned off entirely, and Imogene is left with a headache. Over in the kitchen, she opens the freezer and pulls out the bottle of vodka Mama hides behind the frozen vegetables. She drinks two quick swallows, just enough to fend off the rest of a hangover, slides the bottle back in place, closes the door, and leans there until the burn fades. The counters have all been cleared and cleaned and the silver serving trays they borrowed from the church are stacked near the door, a slip of tissue paper tucked between each one and the next. Even the old cabinets, which should have long ago been replaced, shine from having been scrubbed down. The entire house smells of pine cleaner. All of it is Jo Lynne's doing. Sadness never slows her down. Neither does anger or fear. They ignite her, set her to work with her carefully drawn face, smooth hair, and dresses cinched tightly at her perfectly narrow waist. She likes having people depend on her, because that means she is making the decisions, charting the course. It means she is in control, and it's why she's so good at her job.

If Imogene calls Eddie and tells him what's happened, he'll pace in the kitchen and shout about the state of the world, and he'll use words like "repercussion" and "oppression." He'll string them together in ways that make no sense and he'll want to ask Daddy what to do and then he'll remember Daddy is dead. But not Jo Lynne. She'll tuck away whatever shock she may feel and know exactly what to do. Grabbing her phone from the basket on the counter, the only phone remaining after everyone left the house, Imogene sends Eddie and Jo Lynne each a text. It's too late for a phone call. COME TO THE HOUSE ASAP. MAMA'S FINE. EMERGENCY.

Chapter 17

BETH

Before

The light that hangs from the ceiling at the bottom of the stairs never goes out. It's on when I close my eyes and on when I open them. I have a small clock. The bright orange numbers tell me the time, but I only know day from night because a sliver of sunlight slips around one of the boards in the shadowy part of the basement. In the beginning, it was the only thing I knew, but now I know more. I know he comes on Sundays and Wednesdays, but I don't know how long since he left me or when he'll come again. I watch the sliver of light come and go so I can keep track of the days, but I sleep and wake and sometimes I don't know if it's the next day or the same day. It's daytime now. Tuesday. I think it's Tuesday. I hope. And the clock reads 3:22. It's 3:22 on a Tuesday afternoon when I walk to the bottom of the stairs.

Standing in the center of the light that hangs from the ceiling, I count twelve steps leading to the door at the top. I've made it halfway up three other times, but no farther. Upstairs is where he goes when he leaves. It has to be because there is no place else. I'm breathing fast like I've been running except I haven't. Here in the basement, there's no room for running. And I wear nothing on my feet, so they're always dirty. Even when I wash them in the sink and dry them, they're never clean. I curl my toes because the stone is cold. Mama always says, no running in bare feet. She would fuss at me too because the shirt I'm wearing hangs too long, so I stuff the shirttail into the elastic band of my pants. They're not mine. He must have brought them to me, but I don't remember.

Squeezing my hands into fists, I hold my arms stiff at my sides and force one foot to lift off the ground. My foot shouldn't feel so heavy as I try to hold it there, just above the wooden step, but it does. It feels like I'm lifting someone else's foot, a bigger foot, a heavier foot, and I'm waiting for something bad to happen. Mama says someone is forever watching. I always thought it was God or Jesus or maybe even Mama, but I don't think that anymore. I think it's him. He told me so once, said he's always watching. He also said I might hear voices sometimes and that they're the voices of bad people and I'd better not cry for help. He said I damn sure didn't want those people knowing I'm down here. He promised to keep me safe, he said, but only if I followed every rule. One of the rules . . . I'm never allowed on the stairs.

I don't know how long since he brought me here. I'm better now, but for a long time, I don't know how long, I would wake and sleep and wake again, and always I'd be lying on the sofa and always the light at the bottom of the stairs was shining. I'd stare into it until black spots danced across my eyes. Sometimes, I would wake and a blanket was laid over me. Other times, I'd have socks on my feet and someone had clipped my fingernails and cleaned under them so the narrow tips were shiny and white. Sometimes I'd hear Mama's voice, a sweet voice telling me to drink up and take a small bite and I would wonder if it was real. I wanted her to come closer so I could see her, and just as I wished it, a soft hand would cup my chin, brush the hair from my eyes. I cried because this world was muddy and I couldn't see through it. I couldn't see Mama. And sometimes it was him again. He would shake me, tell me to wake up, get myself going. He'd pour cold water into my mouth. It would dribble down my chin and onto my neck.

I couldn't tell him then, but I know now. I had been living underwater. The light didn't reach me, and what I could see was wobbly like waves were passing through it, ripples of water that went on and on. And sound didn't reach me either, no matter how hard I listened, and the weight of the water pressed down and every breath was hard to take. I was wrong about thinking Mama had been here with me. She was only a part of a dream, and no matter how hard I fought against it, I was sinking. I think I was sinking for missing Mama so bad and wanting so bad to go home.

I began to float back to the surface the day I opened my eyes and saw a stack of books on the floor next to the sofa. I rolled onto one side, stretched out a hand, and rested it on top of the stack. I stared at it until the ripples cleared and I was certain the books were real, and then I pushed myself up, reached down, and gathered them. There were six, all different colors, and all had hard covers. They were warm in my hands and smelled like another place, not like here. They were dusty, and when I opened the cover of the top book, it creaked. I counted them twice, hugged them to my chest, slid back down on the sofa, and when I woke again, still holding the books, I walked across the cold stone floor to the shadowy side of the basement and reached into the cooler for the first time.

As I ate and drank that day—two cheese sticks and a box of apple juice but not the milk because I like chocolate not plain—I first saw the orange slice of light around one of the windows and cried because that slice brought the outside in. I kept the books next to me so they wouldn't slip away and be lost like everything else. The next day he came, and I knew it was a day later because the sliver came and went and came again, and he smiled to see my eyes open. He smelled of spicy cologne and wore a white shirt and shiny shoes. Church clothes, he said. I hugged my books, nodded when he asked if I wanted more. But when I asked if I could show them to Mama, he said no and that I'd better damn sure quit asking for Mama and be happy for what I had. You should be thanking me, he said as he jammed more juice boxes down into the cooler and poured in more ice. You understand? He stared at me until I nodded and then said he'd be back on Wednesday. That's when I learned one more thing. He comes on Sundays and Wednesdays.

And today, I think, is Tuesday. He doesn't come on Tuesday, so I lower my foot onto the stair and lift the other to meet it.

I have to move off the first step because I have eleven more to go, and this time, I'm going to make it all the way to the top. I've been too scared the other times I stood at the bottom of the stairs and looked up at the dark door above me. I didn't know what he'd do if he opened that door and found me breaking a rule. But today is Tuesday. He isn't coming, and I want to make it to the top, where I'll see farther than I've ever seen, so I imagine I'm a mountain climber. Twice, Mama and me went to Stone Mountain. It isn't a real mountain, but it's tall, and we puffed and panted our way toward the top even though we never got close. And that's what I'm doing as I walk my hands up the railing to help my feet along. I've reached the tenth stair. The fronts of my legs don't have much push left in them, and my throat aches because I'm sucking in too much air too fast.

In two more steps, I'll be to the top. I'm dizzy like when we climbed toward the top of Stone Mountain. Mama said the air was thinner and we Georgians didn't take to thin air. I imagine the sun is shining, but really it's just the light that hangs from the ceiling, and I imagine Mama is there behind me. Taking up the rear, she called it. And I pretend I'm seeing tiny yellow daisies like we saw on the mountain and gray squirrels and a red fox like the one that scared Mama and then made her laugh. Just wait until you see the view, Mama had said. It'll stretch on forever, farther than you've ever seen. And I think it'll be like that when I reach the top step. I'll see everything then, farther than I've ever seen. Maybe I'll even see a way out.

I have to sit down. Just for a minute, and then I'll be able to make it. Mama and me never made it to the top before, but I'm going to make it now. Still holding the railing with one hand because I feel dizzy like the air is too thin, I sit on the edge of a step and lean against the wall. I close my eyes, and when I open them again, I don't know how long it's been. Maybe I fell asleep. My neck hurts because my head was bent off to one side. I remember Mama was taking up the rear, following me up Stone Mountain. I can hear her footsteps, the creaking as she steps on a fallen branch. Yes, those are footsteps. I push myself up, grab on to the railing again, and straight ahead, the door opens.

He is a shadow at first that doesn't move. I don't move either, can't move. I'm holding the railing with both hands so I don't fall because the stairs seem to tilt and sway. The height'll make you dizzy. Careful there, Mama had said. I hang on. His hands are full of something. He drops it, whatever it is, and grabs for my arm. I'm only two steps away. The outside is only two steps away. I have to let go of the railing so he won't get hold of me, but when I do, I fall. At the bottom of the stairs, he stands over me again just like that night when he opened the silver box.

"Can you move?" He's squatting next to me, close enough I could touch his face.

I close my eyes, and when I open them again, he's still there, looking down on me. He doesn't look angry; he looks afraid, like when Mama drank too many whiskeys, fell down the porch steps, and pulled me down with her. When the doctor was wrapping a hard cast around my wrist, Mama looked scared like he looks scared. Slipping his hands under my knees and around my shoulders, he lifts. My body feels long in his arms. I've grown since I've been here. All of me is bigger, taller anyway. And I wonder again how long I've been in the basement. I rest my head against his chest. Together we look down at my left ankle. It's too big and it throbs like it has a heartbeat.

"I just wanted to see the outside," I say as he lowers me back onto the sofa. "Can't you take me? Just for a look?"

He grabs the pillow from the small bed I've never slept on and rests my ankle on it. And still without answering, he climbs back up the stairs, limping as he goes, as if one of his knees is hurting him. It takes him two trips to bring down what he dropped. He empties the bags and fills one of them with ice.

"Just for a few minutes," I say, as he walks toward me with the bag of ice. "I just want to see it."

Setting the bag on my leg, he stands over me as if watching to see if it will stay put. He nods as he backs away, looking just like Mama as she backed away from the doctor who asked how my wrist got hurt. When the door at the top of the stairs shuts, I close my eyes and listen. Three locks. I will hear three locks being locked. Sometimes, after he has left me, I make myself say out loud all the names of every kid in the fourth grade. Already I've forgotten the girl who sat in the last desk on the front row, and I don't remember Mrs. Wilton's name before she got married. I say everything I remember about Ellie and Fran and Julie Anna too. And mostly, I say everything about Mama—her yellow hair that shimmered like a silky curtain and the flowery smell of her skin and her lips that she outlined with a glossy red pencil—because I'm most afraid of her slipping away. I'm already so alone, and if I forget her too, I don't know what will happen to me next.

When the last lock snaps into place, the clock reads 4:28, and it's Wednesday. He comes here at four o'clock on Wednesday. Next time he comes, I'll ask for a pencil because I know more and more things and I want to write them all down so they won't slip away.

Chapter 18

IMOGENE

Today

Jo Lynne is the first to text Imogene back. REALLY? her message reads. Imogene replies, PLEASE. It will take Jo Lynne twenty minutes to dress, tie up her hair, and at least do her eyes and lips. And because she and Garland recently moved into a new home, one they had built on the west side of town, it'll take her another fifteen to drive to Mama's place. For the past year, Jo Lynne has spent every free moment picking out finishes, floor trim, and window treatments.

Setting aside her phone, Imogene checks that the boy is still asleep, turns off the TV in Mama's room, and closes the door. The kitchen still smells of the jar of fire-and-ice pickles someone dropped during the reception. Out in the living room, Imogene closes all the drapes and lowers all the blinds. Not knowing what else to do, she thinks to pull out the vodka again but instead drinks a glass of water and then takes a seat on the sofa to wait for Jo Lynne and Eddie. Scooting to the edge, she sits with a straight back, her feet squarely on the ground and her hands resting in her lap, because those are the things that make Jo Lynne happy, and if Jo Lynne is happy, she'll take care of the boy and anything else that needs taking care of.

Startling at the sound of ice dropping in the freezer, Imogene wishes she'd left Mama's TV on. In the silence, she can hear the wind catch in the roof vents and the pop of the house settling, and every sound makes her squeeze her hands tight and hold her breath, afraid a knock at the door will follow or a window will break or footsteps will begin circling the house. Letting her posture go, she drops back on the sofa. On the mahogany table directly in front of her is a picture of Daddy and Mama. Jo Lynne set out as many as she could find for the reception. In mismatched frames, another two dozen have been displayed all around the room. The picture sitting on the coffee table was taken many years ago, because Mama is smiling and Daddy is standing next to her, one arm draped around her shoulders. It was taken before Grandpa Simmons died. Daddy had yet to take over for him, and Mama's heart trouble had yet to begin. All before Imogene was born.

Standing from the sofa, quietly though she isn't certain why, Imogene moves around the room and gathers up all the pictures. Most are of Daddy with the family, but there are a few of him wearing a white robe and holding his hood—the color he wore before ascending. The faces of all the other Klansmen he stands with have been blacked out with ink. Once her arms are full, Imogene dumps the pictures in a laundry basket in the washroom and closes the door on them.

She thought she'd convinced herself it couldn't have been Daddy who kept the boy locked away, but some part of her hasn't been persuaded. She's gathering the pictures so they can't frighten the boy or maybe so he won't be able to identify Daddy as the man who kept him in the basement, but only because it'll devastate Mama if that turns out to be true. And when the sheers over the window finally glow yellow for a moment and fall dark again, she turns the first picture she noticed upside down on the coffee table, the only one she didn't pick up, and drops onto the sofa again.

Normally the slap of the screen door would have been followed by Jo Lynne's slender heels clicking across the pine floors, but tonight those footsteps are softened by slippers. Hopefully, she won't wake the boy, and there's no chance of Mama waking. She takes pills these days to help her sleep. Up until about a year ago, Jo Lynne counted those pills at least once a week to make sure Imogene wasn't stealing them again. And she wasn't. Isn't.

"So, is it every day now?" Jo Lynne drops her purse on the coffee table. "Or did you just start drinking special for Daddy's funeral?"

Shifting her weight to one foot, Jo Lynne stares down on Imogene. Instead of heels and a belted dress, she wears slippers and a terry-cloth robe.

Imogene gathers her hair at the nape of her neck and, with the tip of her tongue, touches her top lip. It's swollen, though probably not enough that Jo Lynne will notice. But she might notice the scratch the boy gave Imogene on her cheek.

"I didn't start anything up again," Imogene says. She never promised to stop drinking, just to stop drinking so much.

"Is it Vaughn and Russell?" Jo Lynne asks. "I'd understand if—"

"No," Imogene says, not wanting their memory to get tangled up in this mess.

"Then what in God's name is going on?" Jo Lynne says, and that toe starts tapping. It means Jo Lynne has compassion, God knows she has compassion and patience too, but enough is enough. "Is it Mama?"

"Mama's fine," Imogene says. "I want to wait for Eddie."

Just as she says her brother's name, another set of tires rolls to a stop outside the front porch. Imogene rocks forward from her seat on the sofa, stands, and she and Jo Lynne walk into the kitchen as a car door opens and closes. Jo Lynne flips on an overhead light, crosses her arms, and leans against the counter. All her life, she's had a look for every occasion, even this one, whatever it turns out to be. Her blond hair is pulled over one shoulder and tied off loosely with a pale blue ribbon. A single long curl sweeps around her jawline, framing it softly. The sight makes Imogene run both hands over her hair, smoothing it as best she can, and she wishes she had brushed her teeth and washed her face.

Normally, Eddie would throw open the screen door and then the kitchen door and ask first thing for someone to put on the radio so he couldn't hear Mama's ticking. Big as he is, what with a squared-off jaw and every bit of Daddy's height, Eddie can't abide that ticking, though he doesn't like to let on. He's always one to help Mama when something needs fixing but never stays for supper or sits down for a cup of coffee. Mama always says she understands and even seems relieved, because sitting across from her son and hearing him talk like all the other men in her family must strain even a mother's love. Jo Lynne gets on all right with Mama's heart if she keeps herself busy doing something else and doesn't look Mama straight on, which is why Mama's kitchen is always cleanest after Jo Lynne's been to visit. But when Eddie's feet hit the porch, heavy as usual because he always wears black steel-toed work boots, there is silence. And Eddie is never silent. Probably because he has never been quite the man Daddy had hoped he'd be and so is always trying to remind people, convince them, he is someone to contend with. The worst came when Daddy would close his eyes and shake his head at something Eddie had done wrong. Those quiet shows of disapproval seemed to weigh heavier on Eddie than when Daddy hollered at him.

About the time Eddie turned twenty-five, Daddy stopped hollering. He seemed to give up hope. That's when Eddie started trying to fill up as much space as he could, whether it was with his heavy stride or his loud voice or the weight he had been putting on ever since. All of it was his attempt to make up for every other way he fell short. So as the silence on the porch stretches out, it's unusual, and Jo Lynne and Imogene look at each other. As Jo Lynne sets aside the rag she has been using to wipe down the counters, the door flies open.

"Jesus, Immy," Eddie says, not asking about the radio. His brown hair is damp because he sweats when he drinks, and he wears a heavy flannel shirt left untucked, loose-fitting jeans, and those black boots. "What in the hell is going on down at the old house?" His eyes settle on Imogene as he draws a hand over his squared-off jaw.

Jo Lynne grabs Imogene's arm, pulls her close. She smells like the lavender water she sprays on her pillow every night. "What on earth is the matter?" she says.

Eddie doesn't answer but instead picks up the house phone and jabs a thumb toward the driveway as he dials.

Out on the porch, the bright light of the kitchen behind them, Jo Lynne walks toward the corner of the house while Imogene stands at the top of the steps leading down to the drive. Both are searching for what has upset Eddie. It's too dark beyond the porch to see anything. The smell of smoke is stronger now, stronger even than when Imogene first got home. Sometimes Mama uses wet wood and it smokes real bad.

"Here," Jo Lynne shouts. Standing at the edge of the porch light's reach, she is little more than a faint outline.

In the few steps it takes Imogene to reach Jo Lynne, she already knows what is happening. A faint orange glow rises over the ridge to the east. It's fire. Something is burning on the other side of the lake. The old house likely or the field just beyond the rise. It's all on fire.

It Falls Again

During the 1920s, under the leadership of a Texas dentist, the KKK began to make unprecedented political gains. In August 1925, forty thousand Klansmen paraded down Pennsylvania Avenue in Washington, DC. By the mid-1920s, the Klan was regularly terrorizing communities with whippings, shootings, and lynchings. Additionally, women deemed immoral became targets. However, lawsuits, internal power struggles and scandals, and increasing coverage by the press of Klan violence began to take a toll on its membership. The Great Depression led to a continued decline, and in 1945, the Internal Revenue Service filed a lien of 685,000 dollars against the Ku Klux Klan for back taxes on income earned during the 1920s. These factors combined to cripple the KKK for the second time.

Chapter 19

TILLIE

Today

As Mrs. Tillie begins to talk, every so often smoothing her nightdress, Tillie nods along. She says they won't be leaving Simmonsville because of stolen watches, and Tillie is glad of that because leaving behind their home would've been like leaving behind Russell and Vaughn. Russell is there in the shop, behind the counter where he stood on a stool as a little boy so he could reach the register and punch at its keys. He's out on the porch, where he'd sit to tinker with his fishing poles. And Vaughn is there too, right in those same spots alongside his daddy, because he didn't grow up enough to make memories of his own. Relieved to be staying, Tillie leans back in his chair, and his aching joints finally loosen. Mrs. Tillie always knows what to do. It was the same all those years ago when Tillie came home crying and shaking and knowing he had to get out of the Klan but not knowing how he could do it. Once he had quieted down, Mrs. Tillie leaned back and said . . . this here is what we're going to do.

Nearly forty years ago, the Kmart had been scheduled to open the day after Tillie came home, crying and shaking. That had been the thing keeping Mrs. Tillie awake every night since the *Simmonsville Herald* first started writing about it coming to town. Our little shop won't never be the same after that ribbon is cut, she'd been saying for weeks. So that's likely why she'd been awake and sitting under the glow of that same lamp. Her hair, smooth and brown in those years, hung loose to near the center of her back when she stood.

"There's only one way Robert Robithan will let you out," she said, and as she began to pace, her white nightdress brushed her calves with every step. "Family."

Tillie nodded, though he didn't understand, nor was he entirely paying attention. The crying and shaking had stopped, and the house smelled of the cinnamon, cloves, and honey Mrs. Tillie used to spice her grape jam. And because he was feeling better, he couldn't help noticing the way Mrs. Tillie's curves were being back-lit by the lamp and how he was seeing them through her nightdress right here in the living room. Seeing her soft, round parts out in the wide open made something hum inside Tillie in a way that it didn't generally hum.

"You'll tell folks I'm sick," Mrs. Tillie said. "You'll go to that godforsaken ribbon cutting tomorrow and tell folks I'm ill. Tell them I'm proud and been hiding it for weeks.

"I'll skip church a few times too," she continued, sitting in her chair again. "And stay in the back room down to the shop so folks won't see me working. And then in a month's time, you'll tell Robert Robithan I'm sick and ask him what you should do. He'll tell you a man tends his family and then you'll ask his permission—his permission, I'm saying—to leave the Knights so you can tend your wife. When I'm better, you'll return."

"I'll return?" Tillie said, wanting never to go back again after what he'd seen that night.

"You'll just say that," Mrs. Tillie said. "You won't really mean it. We'll drive once a week to Macon and make like we're going to a finer doctor over there. Even close the shop for a few hours so folks take notice. And we'll start attending services in Macon too. Say my only niece lives there. I damn sure ain't going to pray with that bunch no more."

Tillie nodded but knew he was going to have to ask Mrs. Tillie to explain it all again.

"And we'll keep it up a good long time?" Mrs. Tillie said.

"Yes," Tillie said.

And they have kept it up a good long time. It's been forty years now. They don't make like they're going to the doctor anymore, and when Mrs. Tillie got pregnant with Russell, they made out like it was a miracle and folks mostly stopped asking after her health. Tillie thought it was all far behind them, but now they got a whole new mess and Mrs. Tillie has a whole new plan.

"We have fourteen thousand two hundred seventy-four dollars tucked away," Mrs. Tillie says. "And we're going to give five thousand of that money to Natalie Sharon for them watches."

Tillie starts to stand because he damn sure isn't giving away his money, but then he understands.

"And she'll give it to Tim," he says. "That'll make Tim happy, and Robert will never know Timmy stole from him."

Mrs. Tillie nods. "Then you'll drive them watches over to Robert Robithan and say a fellow you don't know brung them into the shop. Say you knew they was stolen the moment you seen them. Say you give that man money out of your own pocket to keep them watches safe." She pauses then as if thinking some more. "And you'll tell him you didn't call the police because you know Robert likes his business kept private."

"Tomorrow is Sunday," Tillie says. "So come Monday, I'll head into the bank, get that money, and call Natalie back down to the shop."

Mrs. Tillie holds up a finger at the sound of the phone ringing. She keeps her eyes pinned on Tillie as she mostly nods to whoever is talking on the other end.

"The Coulter place is on fire," she says after hanging up.

"Was that Imogene?" Tillie asks.

Mrs. Tillie shakes her head. "One of the fellows over to the police station. Anything you need to tell me?"

Tillie shakes his head. "Is anyone hurt?"

"Tillie, is Imogene Coulter mixed up in all this?" Mrs. Tillie asks. "Is that why she was at the shop this morning to see you? Because the Coulter place is on fire and Robert Robithan is missing seventy thousand dollars' worth of watches and something don't seem right."

Chapter 20

IMOGENE

Today

At the sound of the door off the kitchen flying open, both Imogene and Jo Lynne turn. Eddie walks out of the house and onto the porch, takes two long steps, and pushes through the screen door. Once across the drive, he disappears into the dark. Before Jo Lynne can pull Imogene back into the house, he reappears.

"The gate's already open," he says, yanking on the screen door and holding it as he stands in the threshold. His face is damp even though it's nearly cold enough to turn their warm breath to clouds of fog. "Was it you, Immy?"

Imogene pulls back, crossing her arms over her chest. She looks to Jo Lynne, who is looking at her just like Eddie, both of them waiting for her to say something.

"Was what me?" she says. The way Eddie is staring down on her, his eyes wide, not blinking, is making her want to back away from him.

"Gate's open. Means someone's been down to the old house," Eddie says. "What the hell did you do?"

"Imogene?" Jo Lynne says.

Imogene takes a few steps toward the end of the porch closest to the fire and points. "I did not do that. That's not why I told you both to come."

"The whole damn place is up in flames, Immy," Eddie says.

"I didn't start any fire."

Imogene is a child again, twelve years old, and it's the day Jo Lynne hauled her from the lake before she could drown. Don't you

dare tell, Jo Lynne and Eddie said once Jo Lynne had dumped
Imogene on the banks and wrapped her in a towel. It was the two
of them against Imogene, and they knew for certain Imogene would
tattle on them because she had a way of ruining everything. She
even ruined Mama by being born. But Imogene didn't tell. She
didn't tell about Garland bringing beer or Jo Lynne and him kiss-
ing under the pines or Eddie teasing her about the earwigs, and she
mostly didn't tell how she wanted to swim all the way across so she
could finally see her real daddy and know his name and see if
he had red hair too, how she wanted all those things because she
had stopped believing he was evil like everyone always said.

Imogene didn't tell Mama or Daddy what happened that day,
but someone did. Eddie had to move out for almost making Imogene drown, and even though she was mostly a grown woman, Jo
Lynne wasn't allowed to leave the house for a month except to go
to classes over in Milledgeville because she had been drinking beer
with Garland instead of keeping a close eye on her little sister. Imogene first imagined her real daddy told, but in the end, she knew it
was Russell Tillerson. She already loved him even then, in a childish twelve-year-old sort of way. The day after it happened, Imogene
told Russell, the only person she ever told, about coughing and
spitting up water and about her real daddy maybe not being bad
like everyone said. Russell was angry, stomped around, trying his
best to puff up his chest, which was still scrawny and sunken in,
and hollered about Eddie being a Goddamned fool. Though Imogene never asked him, she knew Russell told Mama because he
loved Imogene even then too and didn't want Eddie to get away
with what he had done, and he didn't want Imogene trying to swim
to her real daddy ever again.

"Jesus, Immy," Eddie says, letting the screen door slap closed
and starting down the stairs toward the drive. "You hate Daddy
and this family so much you burned the place down?"

"I didn't," Imogene says. "I don't, I mean. I don't hate Daddy or this family, and I didn't start that fire. Why would you say that?"

"Ain't none of it a secret," Eddie says.

He doesn't have to say anything more. It's never been a secret that Imogene would have left the family long ago if not for Tillie and Mrs. Tillie. Being near them was the closest Imogene would ever get to being near Russell and Vaughn. Not even Mama would have been enough to make Imogene stay. And it's never been a secret that Imogene isn't a real Coulter and that Daddy, at best, tolerated her and she him. Her hate for what the Knights believe and the things they do has never softened. What has shifted is her fear. She feared the robes and hoods when she was a child. Those men were monsters sprung to life, but as she reached her teenage years, she began to think of them as pitiful and cowardly, ridiculous even. And these last several years, grief left her fearing only one thing—another day alive while Russell and Vaughn were dead. But over these most recent months, she's beginning to fear the Knights again because they're becoming louder, stronger, and pushing their way back into everyday life.

"What should we do?" Jo Lynne says, grabbing Imogene's hand to stop her from saying anything more. "Do we need to leave?"

"Fire ain't going to jump that lake," Eddie says as a set of headlights hits the trunks of the pecan trees growing on the other side of the drive. "You all will be fine up here."

"I don't think we should stay," Jo Lynne says, holding Imogene's hand with both of hers, maybe because of nerves or maybe to keep Imogene from following Eddie. "What if you're wrong?"

"Suit yourself," he calls back as he walks toward the approaching car.

A sheriff's car parks in the drive, and a man Imogene recognizes from town steps out, but she doesn't know his name. She knows most of the deputies because of her work. They copy burglary reports for her and sometimes let her take a peek at a particular person's record when really they shouldn't. Eddie motions for Jo Lynne and Imogene to get back inside as he and the sheriff's deputy walk toward the top of the ridge where they'll be able to look down on the lake and old house beyond. A fire truck comes next, the small one they keep downtown. If there's real trouble, the fellows from Milledgeville will come and use the back road into the old place because it's wider and flatter. Everyone in Griffith County has lived through enough high winds and dry, hot springs to take care they have a good firebreak carved around their house or a well-fed spring.

"How much have you had?" Jo Lynne asks as the fire truck rattles past.

She stares at Imogene and shakes her head in that same way Daddy did when his fellow Knights of the Southern Georgia Order insisted that new succession plans be discussed. Much as it pained them to say it, Eddie just didn't have the brains to lead them in their modern-day battles and asked did Daddy ever think to get Eddie tested for hookworm. It makes fellows look to be lazy, they said. Makes them out to be not so bright. That's how Jo Lynne is looking at Imogene now, as if she's a hookworm-infested embarrassment.

"It's not the drinking," Imogene says.

Except it is the drinking. Her head aches, throbs really, because she's sobered up too quickly, even with the vodka she drank, and the pain is tangling her thoughts and making her fear run off in all different directions.

"Go on and get Mama's things pulled together," Jo Lynne says.

"But Eddie said we don't need to go."

"And when is the last time you took Eddie's word for anything?"

"I can't go," Imogene says, knowing this is the moment she has to tell. Except now, she doesn't know what to say.

"What do you mean, you can't go?"

"Mama showed me something," Imogene says. "Outside. Earlier tonight, after you and Eddie left."

"And?"

When Imogene doesn't say anything else, Jo Lynne tips her head and cocks her brows in that way she always does when waiting for Imogene to admit she'd been drinking when she cracked her shin on the coffee table or lost the spare house key so instead broke a window to get inside.

"It was a wire."

"This is going to have to wait," Jo Lynne says, walking past Imogene toward the kitchen door.

"An electrical wire," Imogene says, grabbing Jo Lynne by the arm. "I followed it to the basement at the old place."

"What basement?" Jo Lynne says, trying to tug her arm free, but Imogene won't let go. "What are you talking about?"

"The wire," Imogene says. She lets her hand slide down Jo Lynne's arm to her hand and holds it. "It went underground, all the way to the old house. All the way to the basement there."

"What have you done, Imogene?" Jo Lynne says it slowly, pausing after each word.

The sound of that question is too familiar, so familiar Imogene has to grab at her stomach with both hands. Even amid everything else—the basement, the fire, the boy asleep in her bedroom—that question takes Imogene back five years. The pain is fresh again, an open wound that has yet to spend five years trying its best to heal and made all the more raw today by Imogene having sat in that church again and walked through that cemetery. Imogene had been holding a phone to her ear but then dropped it because Warren Nowling, a detective relatively new to town at the time, was on the other end, not wanting to tell her over the phone but her screaming until he did. Vaughn and Russell, both, an accident, they were gone. Just like that. What have you done, Jo Lynne asked, because Imogene dropped her cell phone and it shattered when it hit the ground. Hearing those words again, in that same way of Jo Lynne's, has knocked the wind from Imogene's lungs, and she stands motionless, waiting for them to open up again.

"I didn't do anything," Imogene says. It's little more than a whisper but all she can manage. "I went there. To the old house. I found a boy."

Jo Lynne yanks her hands free this time and stares up at Imogene.

"You found a what?" Jo Lynne says.

"He's in my room." It's passing, the pain from that punch in her gut. "Right now. Sleeping. And there's a mother somewhere. He was living down in the basement. His mama too, I think."

Jo Lynne tries to push past, but Imogene grabs her by the wrist again.

"Listen to me."

Jo Lynne twists and pulls, but Imogene won't let go.

"For the love of God, Imogene, let loose of me."

"Someone was keeping them down there. And the mother, she might still be there. In the house. Maybe somewhere nearby." And then she has to say it. Even though she'd been trying to convince herself she was wrong ever since she laid the boy in her bed, because if she's right, it will devastate Mama. "I think Daddy was the one keeping them down there."

Chapter 21

BETH

Before

I know today is Wednesday. Wednesday, March 16, 2011, and I've been in the basement for one year. I'd be in fifth grade if I still went to school. Fifth graders get to make crystal snowflakes with borax, pipe cleaners, and wide-mouth mason jars and go on a field trip to the museum in Macon. When I think about Ellie and Fran going to Macon without me, and the two of them sitting together on the bus instead of all three of us squeezing into one seat, it makes me angry. But then I can't remember what color Ellie's hair was or which one of us was tallest, and I start wondering if me not remembering anymore is the same as parts of me not living anymore.

I know for sure today is a Wednesday—not like before, when I thought it was a Tuesday and was wrong—because I keep a calendar now. It's on the inside cover of a high school chemistry book where I think he'll never look. My calendar starts with November because he came special on Halloween and brought me candy. I knew Halloween was October 31, and the next day I started my calendar with November. I have forty-two books now, and one of them, a workbook for second graders, helped me remember the order of all the months and how many days are in each, and because today is Wednesday, I push my one chair under the bulb that hangs from the ceiling, stack three of the other textbooks also meant for high schoolers on it so I can reach, and holding a small flashlight between my teeth, I get ready to climb on top.

Each time he comes, he brings me books, but my favorites are the ones about Laura. She lives in a small house in the Big Woods.

There are only trees as far as she can see, and I think she's alone like me except she has a family. I have four books about Laura now, and if I'm good, he'll bring me more. He asked me once if I wanted to call him Pa like Laura called her daddy Pa. It was Christmas. I knew because he brought me a present wrapped in newspaper and because my calendar told me it was December 25. I shook my head, and he said that was all right. I never had a dad, but if I did, I think he would have been like Pa in my books. He would have taken me for walks in the Big Woods and set traps for bears to keep me safe like Laura's pa did for her. And because maybe him asking me to call him Pa meant he was a little bit like Pa in my books, I made myself ask him a question too.

"If I promise not to tell about Julie Anna," I said, "will you take me home?"

Knowing it was Christmastime made me miss Mama so bad my chest ached like the basement was running out of air and soon I'd suffocate. I wanted to be sitting under our small Christmas tree, its white lights glittering on my face and making my eyelids flutter, while Mama told stories about where each ornament came from and why it was special.

"What happened to that girl was her own damn fault," he said. His lips always turned into a hard, straight line when I said Julie Anna's name. "She and her whole damn family should have stayed where they come from."

I stared at him but didn't answer because he was talking in a quiet way that meant a louder voice was simmering inside. The same happened to Mama when the woman came to our house for her monthly visits. Mama would try to use her quiet voice, but a loud voice was always waiting to explode.

"But her daddy ain't teaching no one now. He sure as hell ain't."

"Are Julie Anna's mama and daddy dead too?" I could hardly make myself say the words.

We saw the men one Saturday, Mama and me. We'd been going to buy me an Easter dress and they were standing on the steps at the courthouse. A man in tan pants and yellow hair was angry about someone who was teaching over at the college. Mama said that was a rally and those were the Ku Klux Klan.

"If it weren't for me," he said, jabbing a finger at me, "you might be dead too. Could have been a whole lot worse for you. A whole lot worse."

I didn't know what could be a whole lot worse, because Julie Anna was dead and maybe her mama and daddy were dead too. But I did know him saying what he said meant he would never take me home. It also meant he was part of the Ku Klux Klan. I waited until he had left and I couldn't hear his footsteps anymore before I started to cry and then scream because I missed Mama so bad. I didn't even care if bad people outside might hear me. Mama was the only mama I would ever get to have, and Pa in my books was the only daddy I was ever going to have. He was a great man, and he set traps for bears to keep his family safe. But Pa wasn't going to keep me safe, so when my calendar read "Jan. 1" and I had to write a new year, 2011, I started to plan my own trap.

First, I began doing chores like Laura did in her stories. I set an alarm to wake me up every morning, brushed my teeth after every meal, and scrubbed my clothes in the kitchen sink every Saturday. I made myself eat three meals every day, even when the food made my stomach ache, because he was always telling me I was too thin, and I started climbing the stairs too. In the beginning, my lungs burned for my breathing so hard and heavy. I climbed them until I knew where to step to miss every spot that creaked. I didn't know what I'd find on the other side of the door at the top of the stairs, but I knew the locks were on the outside and sometimes he left the door standing open when he carried things down to me. I also knew the outside was on the other side of the door. He sometimes tracked things in on the bottoms of his shoes—clumps of red clay I rubbed between my fingers and breathed in and touched to the tip of my tongue or scraps of yellow dandelions that hadn't turned fuzzy yet. And I knew what happened when the light bulb at the bottom of the stairs went dark.

Before I started keeping my calendar, when I was still afraid of the stairs, he came one Sunday and said it was time to change the bulb. Handing me a small flashlight, he told me to point it at his head so he could see what he was doing and that I'd better not get smart. When he unscrewed the bulb, the basement went suddenly dark, darker even than when I close my eyes. With both thumbs, I pushed the button on the flashlight. A small stream of light broke the darkness and shined on his face. It was as if the flashlight cut a small hole in the blackness and only he could peek through. He held a new bulb to his ear and lightly shook it. No good, he said and handed the bulb to me. I reached into the darkness, took it, and gave it a shake like he did. Something inside rattled. Filament's broke, he said. He took a third bulb from the box, screwed it in, and the basement lit up again. I switched off the flashlight and felt sad because him changing the bulb made the basement somehow deeper underground and it meant I was staying.

"You keep it," he said when I stretched out a hand to give him back his flashlight. He looked like he felt shame, which is what Mama said I should feel when she caught me sticking a candy bar in my pocket without paying for it. "Turn the big light off when you're ready for bed. Switch is there at the top of the stairs. And use the flashlight to make your way back down and up again in the morning. Sleep in the bed too. It's a good bed. It was Imogene's. When she was your age."

"Imogene?" I said.

"Yes, Imogene," he said. "Books were hers too."

Three visits later he brought Halloween candy and I started my calendar with November. I made mistakes at first and sometimes I thought Wednesday had come and gone without him bringing more food and I started to think no one would ever come again, and then he came the next day. Yes, it was Wednesday, he said, and I knew I'd made a mistake. Mostly, the mistakes happened because I slept all the way through some days. I would lie on the sofa, because I still didn't sleep in the bed, and because sometimes my body wouldn't move, couldn't move. After a few days passed like that, he would find me lying on the sofa and make me eat bread and butter that wouldn't upset my stomach and drink white milk even though I didn't like it. Something was broken inside me, like the tiny wire that broke in the bulb.

But I've been right about my days ever since I started setting a trap like Pa and climbing the stairs and doing chores like Laura. I don't sleep so much and I've read more books and I try to eat good, but eating is the hardest because I can't stop my stomach from not wanting the food. I've filled out every workbook, even the seventh-grade math book, and I've read all four Laura books twice. I do different voices for Pa and Ma and use my own voice for Laura, and as I read those stories, I want to feel strong like Laura and Pa too. I'm not so alone when I read aloud, pretending all those characters are here with me.

I also give myself spelling tests now. Every Tuesday and Thursday is spelling test day. So I know today is March 16, 2011. A Wednesday, I think, for sure. I also know March is warmer than November. He said we drove for a whole day and night to get here, but I found the pecans and Mama and me had pecans at our house, so I think I'm still in Georgia. Mama's magnolias always bloomed in March, so that means March is warmer. Warm enough to run.

Making sure the biggest textbook is on the bottom of the pile, I straighten them good before I step on top. I sometimes had to stack things at home when I wanted cereal and Mama couldn't get out of bed to reach it for me. I fell once, and a doctor said I sprained my ankle and another woman came to visit, but she only came once because Mama had already moved the cereal to the cabinet under the sink. Before reaching up to the light bulb, I look quick at the clock with the orange numbers. It reads 3:27.

He'll be here in thirty-three minutes.

Chapter 22

IMOGENE

Today

Imogene stands behind Jo Lynne, both of them peeking through the bedroom door they've opened a crack. The boy still lies as he did when Imogene first lowered him onto the bed. The room is dark except for the light from the kitchen that travels down the narrow hallway and throws a faint glow over the small body. Even though they're upwind of the fire, the smell of that broken jar of pickles has been pushed aside by the smell of smoke. It must be midnight, or maybe not. Imogene has no idea how long she sat down in the basement and cradled the boy. Or how long she kneeled outside her bedroom door until she mustered the courage to text Jo Lynne and Eddie.

It's a relief to see the boy unmoved because that means Imogene has more time to think. It's never been so hard, the thinking. But it's also a concern seeing the boy so still. He seems not to have moved at all. Something could be wrong. He could be dehydrated or have not eaten a decent meal in days, maybe weeks. Or he could have a concussion. Imogene turns away from the open doorway and lowers her head because the boy looks smaller than he did before and already the room smells of him, like powder that his mama maybe rubbed on his skin to keep it from chafing in the damp basement. The thought of that makes Imogene pinch her eyes closed, and the little bit of thinking she had been able to manage is gone. She's suddenly back in that dark basement, her body stiff from fear, her heart pounding in her ears. It all really happened, and the sweet smell of baby powder is proof of it. Imogene pulls at Jo Lynne, nearly knocking her off her feet, and quietly closes the door.

"We can't wake him," Imogene says, turning away from Jo Lynne so she won't see the deep breaths Imogene is taking to calm herself. She can't let the fear grab hold again here in the hallway, not like it did in the moments after she first brought the boy home. Jo Lynne will think it's pills for certain if Imogene collapses.

"What is going on?" Jo Lynne says, stepping around Imogene to get a look at her face. She leans in as if checking Imogene's eyes. "We're going to have to go in there eventually so we can carry him to the car."

"He won't go," Imogene says. "He won't leave his mama."

"Leave her where?" Jo Lynne says. She speaks slowly and quietly, has slipped into the calm, measured person she has to be when coaxing a hysterical mother to let Jo Lynne take her child.

"She might still be down there in Grandpa's house," Imogene says, starting down the hallway, but Jo Lynne grabs her arm and stops her. "I need to go tell Eddie. They need to know she might be in the house somewhere, upstairs maybe."

Keeping hold of Imogene's arm, Jo Lynne pulls her down the hallway, out into the living room, and to the sofa. Once seated, Jo Lynne pauses, eyes down. She'll be counting to three and composing herself. Then she takes hold of both Imogene's hands. It's a certain way Jo Lynne has with people. By taking hold of their hands and speaking in a soft, hushed way, she takes hold of their worries.

"Very clearly, now," she says, looking Imogene straight on. It's a familiar pattern, Jo Lynne staring at the whites of Imogene's eyes, sniffing her breath, moving from side to side as she talks to see if Imogene can follow her. "Who is he? Where did he come from? And where is his mother?"

"I told you," Imogene says, trying to pull her hands free, but Jo

Lynne holds tight. "And I need to tell Eddie now so they'll be looking for her."

"You've told me nothing." Jo Lynne's voice is pitched lower than normal, and though her jaw is set firm, she still speaks slowly and quietly.

"The basement. I found him in the basement at the old house."

"So you found this boy in the basement and now the house is on fire. Where is his mother, how did the fire start, and what does any of that have to do with Daddy?"

"I don't know," Imogene says. "The boy was living there. He didn't want to come with me because he said a man took his mama and would bring her back so long as he was good. His mama, I think she's still down there. Jo Lynne, the boy, he said Daddy's name. I'm sure of it."

"What does that mean? Did he say Daddy took his mother?"

Imogene shakes her head. "No, when he was fighting me, not wanting to leave, he said it. Said he wasn't allowed to, but he said Daddy's name. That means something, right?"

Finally letting go of Imogene, Jo Lynne slides to the edge of the sofa, sits with a straight back, and rests her hands in her lap. In a moment, she'll rest one of those hands on Imogene's shoulder, rub it there lightly, and tell her everything will be okay. This is how it's always gone. Jo Lynne lectures Imogene about giving up the drinking and the ridiculous parade of men and the dead-end career she's chosen, and then when Imogene caves under the shame of it, which she never really feels but does a good job of pretending to do, Jo Lynne rests a hand on her shoulder and says it'll be all right. As much as Jo Lynne fusses about the mess Imogene's made of her life, she loves picking Imogene up. Better than anyone, even Mama, Jo Lynne cleans things up, puts things away, starts things over. She has a softness and beauty that she uses to reel people in and a sweetness to her voice to make them trust her and to make them forget she is a part of the Klan. But Jo Lynne doesn't do any of those things now.

"Get up," she says instead, again grabbing Imogene by the upper arm. The soft, sweet tone is gone. "You get Mama's bag together and then you get whoever that is sleeping in your room up and in your car."

"And take him where?"

"Downtown," Jo Lynne says. "To my offices. We cannot have this boy here, fire or no fire. You have any idea what kind of trouble you could get me in? And don't you dare say another word about Daddy. I will not let you do this."

"I'm not doing anything," Imogene says. "And Eddie said we're safe here. We don't need to leave. I have to go down there. They need to know about this boy's mama."

Jo Lynne shakes her head. "First of all, when is the last time Eddie had one damn idea what he was doing? And you're not going anywhere except to gather that child up and get Mama's bag. Mama and I are leaving, and you and that child are coming with us."

Chapter 23

IMOGENE

Today

Imogene and Jo Lynne stop talking at the sound of another car rolling across the gravel drive outside the house. This one doesn't drive on through the gate but stops, and a car door slams. Footsteps hit the stairs leading to the porch and Garland walks through the door, bringing with him the smell of more smoke. He pulls off his hat and smooths his dark hair.

"You all okay in here?" he says, glancing at Mama's door to make sure it's closed, because like most men, Garland has a hard time with Mama's heart. It likely gets to men more because they are inclined to fixing things and there's no fixing Mama. He switches on the radio even though there's nothing to drown out. Already his face has started to shine.

"You should have a jacket on, for goodness' sake," Jo Lynne says, meeting him at the door. She kisses his cheek and tugs the tip of his dark beard. Silver streaks, nearly the same color as his eyes, cut through the closely cropped beard that Jo Lynne has been nagging him to shave since he first grew it a few months ago.

Not standing from the sofa, Imogene does her best not to look at them because she doesn't like seeing Jo Lynne pick at Garland. Maybe it's his beard or the belt he's wearing or the way he cuts his steak. Even though Garland and Russell were never really friends, in part because Russell was five years younger, seeing Jo Lynne pick at Garland is still like seeing her pick at Russell. Your husband is alive, she's said to Jo Lynne more than once. Quit nagging him all the time.

"You all should get Mama around," Imogene says. "Take her to your house, and I'll stay and hope we don't have to leave. At the very least, this smoke won't be good for her."

"Wind's carrying the smoke," Garland says. "Eddie tell you all you should leave?"

Sitting at one of the chairs at the kitchen table, Garland leans back on its metal legs and lets his knees fall out wide. There's a lag to everything he does, because he's always waiting to get Jo Lynne's approval before making his next move.

"He said to get Mama ready," Jo Lynne says. "Said we should take her and go."

"No, he didn't," Imogene says. "*You* said we should leave. He said, suit yourself."

"No reason for waking your mama," Garland says. "Fog's thickening up."

Jo Lynne swings around to face Garland and cocks her head in a scolding way.

"Dampness in the air," he says, lifting a hand as if he can feel it. "Got plenty of men down there too. Any idea how it started?"

Jo Lynne crosses her arms and looks to Imogene.

"I did not start that fire," she says.

Wiping his face with one of Mama's tea towels, Garland studies Imogene and Jo Lynne. "What's going on, ladies?"

"Tell him," Jo Lynne says to Imogene.

It's only been a few hours since Imogene sat in the first pew and held Mrs. Tilley's hand on one side and Mama's on the other and every so often leaned over Mrs. Tillie to squeeze Tillie's hand, but it feels like days have passed and now there is a boy who is scaring Imogene almost as much as being in that basement. The thing she hasn't told anyone is that he said her name and knew about her red hair. She doesn't tell Jo Lynne and Garland because they'll see it as more proof that Imogene is somehow at fault. She doesn't want to be special to the boy either or someone he believes in or maybe even, though she couldn't imagine why, loves. She doesn't want any of it, never again. There is too much hurt on the other side of someone needing her. Today of all days won't let her forget that.

And it isn't just him knowing her name or about her red hair that she can't bring herself to tell. There were those books, organized smallest to tallest. They were hers, she's sure of it. The boy had her books and he knew her name and it's all really happening, this thing that is only supposed to play out on the news. A girl rescued from a backyard prison. Three girls trapped for years in the second story of a house with neighbors on all sides. Strangers crawling through bedroom windows to steal girls in the middle of the night. It's supposed to be news. Not life.

Without looking at Garland, Imogene tells him what happened. She starts with the wire Mama showed her. She tells every detail, except for the books and the boy knowing her name and the color of her hair, doing it as much for herself as for Garland and Jo Lynne. She needs to secure what happened in her mind, because the details are thin and wispy and will vanish if she doesn't do something to give them some weight. The entire story is surprising, shocking, unimaginable. But none of those words are big enough. As she talks, blinking under the glare of the kitchen light so bright against the white cabinets and linoleum floor, she's careful not to let her eyes drift off to Jo Lynne, who's leaning against the sink, arms crossed, staring at Imogene as if trying to decipher, based on the absurdity of her story, exactly how many drinks she had at the reception.

"And then he said Daddy's name," she tells Garland. "He didn't mean to. I think he wasn't supposed to. But he said it. And you need to go down there and tell Eddie, tell whoever, so they know to look for his mama."

"There is a boy, here in this house?" Garland says, ignoring everything else Imogene said. He stares hard at her, his gray eyes bright under the kitchen lights.

Imogene nods.

"White boy?"

"Jesus Christ," Imogene says. "Really? That's what you're going to ask me?"

"Just want to know who I'm sharing a roof with," Garland says. "Anything wrong with that?"

Imogene forgets sometimes who Garland is because he keeps a safe distance from the Knights so he can protect their assets. He's most often kind too, and Imogene finds herself feeling sorry for him because he's up against a life of being a never-ending disappointment to Jo Lynne. But he's one of Daddy's, or rather he *was* one of Daddy's. Now he'll be one of Tim Robithan's. All of them believe—Garland, Eddie, and Jo Lynne—though they've all learned to do as Tim Robithan does and talk like they're only trying to do as their Lord intended. Jo Lynne is especially quick to quote a scripture as if trying not only to convince Imogene but also to convince herself that she isn't the same as all the Klan who came before her. You can't take the stink out of shit, is usually Imogene's reply.

"Don't you start, Imogene," Jo Lynne says, starting to scrub at one of the windowsills in the kitchen. The smoke will settle on everything and leave a black layer of soot. "Yes, Garland, he's a white boy."

"And where is this mother?" Garland asks. "Did you see her too?"

"That's what I'm trying to tell you." Imogene lowers her voice. Waving her outrage just now isn't going to help that boy or his mama. "She wasn't there."

"So she abandoned her son?" Jo Lynne says, still scrubbing. The house is starting to smell of lemon-scented cleaner. "Why on earth would that have anything to do with Daddy? Course, we'll see to the boy, but this has nothing to do with Daddy."

"But I think it does. She didn't abandon him. A man took her."

"You don't know that," Jo Lynne says, her hips moving as she stretches across the countertops. The cleaning and keeping busy is what she does to avoid Mama's heart, and it's what she's doing now to avoid what may have happened.

"I do know that," Imogene says. She remembers that part clearly, the boy looking up at her and saying . . . if I'm good, he always brings Mama back.

"And you think Daddy was the man who took this boy's mama?" Garland says, mopping his face again. The skin around his eyes has taken on a blue cast, the first thing that happens to him before Mama's ticking heart chases him from the house.

Imogene nods.

"And that's why you started the fire?" he asks.

"I already told you," Imogene says, "I didn't start any fire."

"They were squatters, then?" Garland says, looking over his shoulder at Jo Lynne. When she nods in agreement, he says it again. "Yes, squatters. Hell, the mother probably started the fire." Again, he glances at Jo Lynne. And again she nods.

"Squatters don't put locks on the outside of the door," Imogene says.

"But mothers do," Jo Lynne says, jabbing the bottle of cleaner at Imogene to emphasize her point. "Heaven knows why she's living there, but I see it all the time."

"You see mothers locking up their babies?" she asks Jo Lynne.

"Sweetie," Jo Lynne says, and damn it all but Imogene hates when her sister calls her sweetie. "I seen a whole lot worse than that."

"Town's full of crazy people," Garland says, pushing out of his chair and tugging at both shirtsleeves. "I'll give Warren a quick call, make sure he knows about the boy."

"You think it's wise to call the police just yet?" Jo Lynne says.

"Can't hurt," Garland says. "Warren'll know this wasn't Daddy's doing."

"He needs to see to finding the boy's mama too," Imogene says.

Warren Nowling, detective with the Simmonsville police department, has tried to be a lot of things to Imogene since the day he had to notify her that Russell and Vaughn were dead. Brother, cousin, best friend, in the beginning. The past year, something more. But nothing has ever fit. Mostly, Warren is just a reminder and not one she needs right now.

"Did the boy actually see Daddy?" Garland says, holding open the door while he stands on the threshold. "Did he say that? He seen Daddy take the boy's mama away?"

"Maybe. I don't know," Imogene says, leaning forward and burying her face in her hands. "It all happened so fast."

"You should know by now, Imogene," Garland says. "Plenty of folks have tried to cause your daddy grief." As he speaks, Jo Lynne nods. "Who knows what that boy's mama told him to say. Can't imagine why she'd burn the place down, but some folks is beyond imagination."

"Garland is right, sweetheart," Jo Lynne says, stepping up to Imogene and smoothing her hair. "We'll see to the boy tonight, and I'll call into the office in the morning. Maybe someone down there knows his mama. They'll see to it the boy is safe."

Jo Lynne always has a way of smelling sweet through and through, even in the middle of the night in a house that's leaking smoke. If anything were to make Imogene cry after all that's happened, it would be the warm touch of her sister and her sweet smell, all of it reminding Imogene of being a child and wanting to be so like Jo Lynne. But that didn't happen. The girl Jo Lynne once was is gone, and Imogene has ended up like this.

"That'll be good," Imogene says, relieved that Jo Lynne knows what to do for the boy and that Garland is calling Warren. "That'll be real good."

Even if they don't believe her, Garland and Jo Lynne are doing the right thing. Imogene drops back in the sofa and closes her eyes. She never thought she'd feel this kind of tired again. It kept her from getting out of bed in the days and weeks after Russell and Vaughn died. She wasn't there for her own son when he most needed her, and he died, and all these years later, she can't be here for this child either. She, like Eddie, is the disappointment, the one who never gets it right. The one who never will.

Chapter 24

BETH

Before

Every day since I first started planning my trap, I've practiced climbing on the textbooks. One of the first times I tried, the books fell and I fell with them. I had a lump on my head that lasted for two days. Now I know to hold on to the back of the chair until the books are steady. I do that now, and holding the flashlight between my teeth, I start to unfold my legs. I move slowly, my thighs aching for carrying all my weight. The books wobble. I stop, wait for them to quit shaking. Already, my jaw is tired from holding the flashlight. I never exercised that part of me.

When my legs are all the way straight, I reach for the bulb, and as soon as I touch it, I jerk my hand away. That's another thing I wasn't ready for, the burning-hot bulb, but the clock reads 3:30 and he usually comes at four and I'm already up on the chair and I have to do it now. I take the flashlight from my mouth so I can stretch my jaw, lick my fingers, and give the bulb one quick turn. I give another turn. The light goes out and the basement turns black. The smell of damp things that never dry is suddenly stronger. And the air is colder.

Flipping on the flashlight, I stick it between my teeth again and tilt my head back so the yellow stream of light shines on the bulb that still hasn't come loose. One more turn and it's free. I toss the bulb from hand to hand until it's cool enough to hold. Then I bang the bulb once in the palm of my hand, lift it to my ear, give it a good hard shake, and listen. It rattles. Taking care to hold on again,

I screw the bulb back in the socket. It doesn't light up. The basement is black.

I practiced another thing as I got ready to set my trap like Laura's pa set traps. Day after day, I sat on the arm of the sofa nearest the stairs, closed my eyes, and walked to the bottom step. I did it until I could make it the whole way without opening my eyes or making a sound. I knew about walking quiet because sometimes Mama would sleep late on a Saturday and she'd yell if I woke her and say her Goddamn head was killing her and couldn't I manage to keep myself quiet. I practiced walking from the sofa to the staircase until I landed at the spot where I could start up the steps in the way I'd practiced, quickly and so none of them creaked. I practiced because he'd never let me out. I practiced so when he walked down the stairs into the dark basement, he'd think I was sitting on the sofa where I'm supposed to go when the door opens. Mostly, I practiced so he wouldn't know I was gone until I was up the stairs and had closed and locked the door on him. Mostly, I practiced so I could see Mama again.

Climbing off the chair, the books wobbling under me but not falling away, I slide the three textbooks back in their spot on the bookshelf I have now, using my small flashlight to guide me, push the chair under the table where it belongs, and take my seat on the end of the sofa. Then I change out one good battery in my small flashlight for an old battery that stopped working and stuff the good battery down in the cushions of the sofa. I have left the flashlight burning all night for three nights and used up every new battery he brought me except these last two. Sitting in the dark, because not even my little flashlight works now that I've changed out a good battery for a bad one, I screw the top back on. Only the orange numbers on my clock still shine. It's 3:52. And it's Wednesday. I'm sure.

Then 4:00 flips up on the clock. I stare at the orange numbers until they turn watery and listen for the house's creaks that should come from overhead when he gets here. As I wait, I try to think about cooking with Mama on a Sunday afternoon and think maybe we'll do that again soon. All month we would save up money so we could make one special meal. I liked it best when Mama made fried chicken and greens. She would drizzle vinegar on the greens, and I would taste its tangy flavor on my lips all the way until the next day.

And then it's five o'clock. At six o'clock, I dig down in the cushions until I find the good battery, drop it back in my flashlight, and eat a piece of the fried chicken he brought on Sunday. I chew every bit of meat from the bone and lick my fingers and try not to cry because it's nothing like Mama's, but really I can hardly remember what Mama's tastes like. Fried chicken was supposed to be a special treat, and when he brought it, he said it was because I'm so God-awful skinny that he can't hardly stand looking at me.

I chew on the big end of the chicken bone until it's smooth under my teeth. I'm crying now because across the room, the orange numbers read 7:26 and I think I'll never cook with Mama again. Sometimes I forget to mark off a day in my calendar, but I thought I had done better. Now that I have chores to do and books to read and voices to make up, I sometimes forget to do my marking off first thing and then when later in the day comes, I can't remember if I did it. I mark off two days on my calendar some days, and others, I don't mark off any. Maybe I marked off two and that's why he isn't here or maybe he brought the fried chicken because he was never coming again and that made him feel bad and so he thought he'd do one last kind thing.

I read the Laura book with my flashlight. I read out loud, and as if there's someone else in the room, I explain about the cow that was really a bear and how Laura saved herself and her mama because she did as she was told. As the flashlight's stream turns from white to yellow to orange and begins to flicker, I shake it and think about all the dark corners here in the basement. The flashlight flutters. I start crying again and the flashlight goes black. Those dark corners were dark even when the light at the bottom of the stairs was burning all day and all night. I would hear things rustle, sometimes whisper to me from back there. But now the whole basement is a dark corner and I wonder if the whole world is dark too. And I know now what he meant when he said things could have been a whole lot worse for me. He meant I could be dead like Julie Anna and maybe I will be soon because maybe he's never coming back.

A light wakes me. It's shining in my eyes and I squint when I open them. He's leaning over me, shaking me.

"How long's it been?" he says.

My eyes are two slits. They'll barely open. It's all the crying. They're swollen, and when I try to speak, my voice is like a whisper. I screamed for him. I don't know when or how long I've been alone here in the dark, but I know I screamed, and now he's finally come. The air is soggy and sour, like without the big light, things started to grow in the corners. I rub my nose and press it to my shoulder so I won't smell it anymore.

"How long you been in the dark?"

He touches a cup of water to my lips and tells me he's sorry. He thought there were enough extra batteries. He had tax day to contend with yesterday. He was late with a few things and had to see the accountant. That's what he tells me, but I don't know what tax day means. Businessmen like him have important forms they have to mail and he forgot and had to fix it. He's sorry, he says. I want to ask him if tax day will happen again and when because I should add it to my calendar, but I can't figure what words to say. One Sunday he didn't come because there was a wedding and three Wednesdays he didn't come because things broke in a house and he had to tend them because that's his job. Things happen, he has told me before. He's doing his best. I did my best too, but my plan didn't work. He'll replace the bulb and never let it happen again. I don't have another plan.

"God damn," he says. "I didn't mean to leave you in the dark. We'll do something nice for you. How about that? What can we do? What can we do nice for you?"

"Can you let me go home?'

"You know that ain't going to happen," he says. "There ain't no undoing what you seen. What's something else?"

"Will you take me outside? For just a visit?"

It isn't a new plan, but it makes my old plan work out in a different way. Outside may not be home, but it's closer to Mama than inside.

He lowers his flashlight so my eyes don't have to squint and hands it to me as he stands. "Be back shortly," he says. "I'll bring extra bulbs."

I hold the flashlight in both hands, let it shine on the underside of my face and slide low on the cushions.

"Sunday," he says. He's over near the stairs, though I can't see him. He's only a voice.

I know now that I would have run right into him when I made my way from the sofa to the bottom of the stairs. He'd have grabbed me up and known I was doing a bad thing. My stomach tightens up, and my throat gets small so I can hardly breathe. He'd have caught me if he would have come like he was supposed to. He's told me I don't want to know what happens if I break a rule, and I think that means something really bad will happen.

"On Sunday, we'll take you outside. Mind you, only for a bit. Okay?"

"Okay," I say, and when I open my eyes again, the light at the bottom of the stairs is on and he is gone. He came one day late because he had things to mail and sign and couldn't manage it all. He sure was sorry. That was yesterday, so today is Thursday, and that means Sunday, the day I get to see outside again, is three days away.

The Kludd

The role of the Klan Kludd, the KKK's term for "chaplain," is in part to speak at Klan rallies, incite enthusiasm, and further the Klan's message of white supremacy through a mixture of Christian principals, humor, and hatred. One such Kludd was a former bricklayer from North Carolina. Speaking at a rally during the 1960s, he illustrated these tactics by berating the media in attendance and accusing them of telling half-truths and being lazy. He further taunted and criticized the Federal Bureau of Investigation, which was investigating the Ku Klux Klan organization at that time. In October 1965, having since resigned his position with the Klan, the former bricklayer testified at the hearings before the Committee on Un-American Activities, which was investigating Klan activity.

Chapter 25

TILLIE

Today

First thing out of bed, Tillie goes looking for a Phillips screwdriver, and as he's rattling around in his toolbox, he smells Mrs. Tillie's cheese grits. She'll be adding cheddar to be sure, and maybe even baking up some biscuits with a little syrup for dipping. He'll need a full stomach when he goes by Imogene's later to give a hand with cleaning up, and no matter what Mrs. Tillie might say, he's going to give her a warning about that Timmy Robithan.

All morning, the phone has been ringing, and folks are saying vagrants started the fire at the Coulters' place. Someone was living down there at the old caretaker's house, likely one of them fellows let loose from the Milledgeville hospital. And vagrants setting the fire meant the Klan didn't. That had been Mrs. Tillie's fear, and Tillie's too. The Coulter place going up in flames on the same day Robert Robithan was robbed and the same day he went snooping around Imogene was too strong a coincidence to ignore, and no coincidence involving the Klan could be ignored.

Tillie's gotten rusty, that's the problem. After those lawsuits started upending Klan chapters across the country, membership dwindled, at least in Simmonsville, but nobody much missed them. What they did, they mostly did in private. Tillie should have been more aware. Where there's an ebb, there's a flow.

It started again with one fellow down to the post office shouldering his way past another fellow who was black. He didn't have to shoulder the fellow out of the way, could have taken one step to the right and walked around him. And then there was the fellow what reached right in front of a young girl at the grocery store, didn't say excuse me or nothing, and nearly knocked her over to get at a box of cereal. She had long black hair, so maybe she'd come from Cuba, or maybe she'd just come from Indiana. Or it could have started up again before that. Seven, maybe eight years ago, Timmy Robithan and the others gathered on the courthouse steps to holler about a Puerto Rican fellow teaching over to the college. Poor fellow's daughter was killed. Tillie always figured it was Klan doing because they didn't want to believe Puerto Ricans were real Americans, but the police said the killer was likely the estranged father of the little girl she'd been babysitting. Didn't have nothing to do with the sitter being a Puerto Rican, they said, but Tillie never believed that. He knew how the Klan thought and how they hated, and making sense or being right never had anything to do with either.

Regardless of when it first began, Tillie didn't see it coming, this rising of the Klan yet again, because he had let himself get rusty. For too many years, those sorts had been out of sight, and so they were out of mind too. For too many years, he's been gone too long from paying attention. A lot of folks have been gone too long.

Grabbing hold of the first Phillips he finds so he can tighten up that sagging shutter, he walks through the house and out the front door. Cheese grits are something a young man eats, and this morning, Tillie is feeling like a young man. He and Mrs. Tillie won't be moving anywhere. They still have a good many years of living here, and no sense letting things go to shambles. All that good thinking stops when the phone in the kitchen rings again.

By the time Tillie gets back inside the house, Mrs. Tillie has already hung up.

"Someone's broke into the shop," she says.

Her hair is wound up tight, and like it does every day, it sits on top of her head and is covered over with a sheer yellow scarf.

"It wasn't more news about the Coulter place?"

"No, Tillie. It's the shop. Someone's broke in."

"But we ain't got the money yet," Tillie says.

"You're talking gibberish. The café called. Window's broke there in the back room. You got to go check and see that them watches ain't gone."

Tillie nods and pats at his pockets. Mrs. Tillie grabs one of his hands, drops his set of keys in it, and wraps his fingers up into a fist so he won't drop them.

"Probably just kids," she says, smiling for Tillie. "But you see anything, or if them watches are gone, you get down to the café and call the police."

Chapter 26

IMOGENE

Today

Trying not to groan, Imogene slowly unfolds her legs from the chair she did her best to sleep in and shivers from the dampness in the air. Her body aches, not just from too much whiskey the day before and not just from a lack of sleep, but it's the ache to get back to something normal. And then it's the ache that this life she's been living for the last few years would seem normal to her. Across the room, the boy is still sleeping, though he has shifted about during the night. The quiet in and out of his breathing stirs the otherwise silent room.

After Garland left last night, promising to call the police about the boy, he was in and out of the house and then returned for good with word that he'd talked to Warren and that the men were letting the southern field burn. All that Goddamned pampas grass was doing nobody no good anyway. And nobody cared to save the old house. Don't go waking your mama, Garland said to Jo Lynne, and to Imogene he said Warren Nowling would be along first thing to contend with her and the boy. When Imogene asked if they'd found a woman in the house, Garland shook his head, and quietly he said that no one would survive a fire like that. Truth is, they ain't going to send no one into that mess on a hunch. Just ain't going to happen.

Though the sun has barely risen, enough light is streaming through the window to let Imogene get a good look at the boy. He seems not so thin as he did last night and his skin has a warm glow, and she's relieved, or maybe the morning light is fooling her. But still that small thing might mean she's done something right. By sitting here in this chair, she's helped him make it to the morning. A half dozen times during the night, she crept to the bed's edge and listened at the boy's chest to make sure he was breathing. It was a silly fear, but she couldn't fight it off, and she crept once more, just once more she promised herself each time, to his bedside, where she leaned down to listen for signs of life. She'd done the same when Vaughn was a baby. Of course he was alive, but the stillness of a sleeping child had frightened her, made her worry the very worst could happen. And then it did happen and she has struggled to find a way to live in its wake. One last time, she creeps to the edge of the bed, braces herself with one hand to the headboard, and leans over him.

As the boy exhales, his warm breath tickles her ear. It's a familiar feeling on her skin, one she shared with Vaughn. It conjures a pain that makes her pinch her eyes closed but a joy, too, from something so sweet that she can't tear herself from it. The warm breath punishes her and soothes her all at the same time. But no matter, she knows the boy is alive. That's something. Really, that's everything. Knowing he's alive and that she had some small part in that changes the days ahead in a way her days ahead haven't been changed in five long years. The last time she'd felt such a thing, Russell had been alive. The two of them had been looking at each other across the front seat of his truck and were on their way to the hospital, smiling, almost crying, because they knew they'd be returning home with a newborn. That one moment had been the sweetest of her life because everything was on the horizon. And she feels a glimmer of that same thing now as she looks down on the boy. It's hope, though she barely recognizes it, or at least it's akin to hope, and it's something to live for.

Taking slow backward steps, she keeps her eyes on the boy as she makes her way to the door. She should have enough time to run back to her apartment, grab a quick shower and clean clothes, and be back before he wakes. Then wherever they take him later today, Imogene will go with him. She's been a disappointment to so many people over the past five years in so many ways, but she can't afford to fail this child. Doing that would be too much like failing Vaughn and Russell again. She didn't realize until now how hope has fed her all her life and how starved she's been without it. She had started with the hope that she'd be a real Coulter one day, and then that she'd find her real daddy and that he'd love her, and then she had hoped for a future away from this family and this town, and lastly for a future with Russell and Vaughn. None of those things have come to pass.

In the hallway, she pulls the door closed behind, and with her ear pressed to it, she listens for any sound from the boy. The boy. She doesn't even know his name.

"Imogene?"

Swinging around, Imogene falls against the door. "Jesus, Warren," she says. "You scared the shit out of me."

She holds up a finger to silence him as she listens again for any sign she woke the boy. It's quiet inside her room, but now that she's on this side of the door, she can hear voices out in the kitchen and living room.

"Already with the language?" Warren says.

"Keep your voice down," Imogene says in a whisper. She leans around Warren, hoping for a glimpse of who has come to the house so early, but she can't see beyond the end of the hallway. "Did Garland tell you about the boy's mama? You need to get men here. You need to find her."

"And you need to slow down," Warren says, running his hands along Imogene's arms and taking a long, slow breath so she'll do the same.

Warren only moved to town about ten years ago, something not many people can say, because not many people move to Simmonsville, Georgia. Mills and prisons once fed the town, but they both dried up, and about the only jobs left are the ones that keep the town running, jobs like being a detective. Warren wears his light brown hair a little too long for most people's taste around here, and he's thickened up over the years for liking Southern cooking too much.

"Had men looking all night," he says, nodding his approval as Imogene's breathing slows. "No sign of anyone at the house, or what's left of it. Checking hospitals too. Got to tell you, it's going to be pretty tough drumming up any sign of her or anybody else down there."

Imogene takes a few steps down the hall so they don't wake the boy.

Warren follows. "Boy still in there?" he says, nodding back toward the closed bedroom door.

"Sleeping." Out in the kitchen, the voices have grown louder. "Who's that I'm hearing?"

"Fellows here helping with the fire," Warren says. "Jo Lynne's feeding them."

"What fellows?" she says. When Warren doesn't answer, she asks again. "What fellows, Warren?"

Warren didn't grow up with men like Daddy or Tim Robithan. He knows them from history books and case files, but he doesn't know what they are or what they can do, not really. Truth is, Imogene barely knows. She's heard their dangerous talk all her life, heard the calls for white pride, the warnings of a country overrun, the threats of a new day coming. She has stood in line next to it, sat beside it on a church pew, heard it spewed from the courthouse steps, but hearing it and seeing it, even living with it, aren't the same as being the object of it. She can't possibly know. Not really. And neither can Warren.

There was a time when some folks in town figured the Knights would cease to exist. Ten years ago, they were limping along with nothing more than stragglers. But then things started to change.

Imogene was so lost in her own grief, she may have missed when it began, but over the past year, they've come to stand taller. Membership has grown, many of them younger men to replace the ones who've died off. They've been propped up, emboldened, and they're proud.

"Don't get upset. They just come to see to the fire, Immy."

"Don't call me that."

Warren probably once overheard Mama call her that nickname, but him using it is too familiar. Him using it shows that he believes, or at least hopes, they mean something more to each other than just the few hours in bed they occasionally spend together.

Warren raises a hand in apology. "They just come to help. Nobody's causing any trouble."

"They sure as hell better be gone before Mama wakes up."

"I'm sure they will be," Warren says, placing a hand on Imogene's lower back to guide her down the hall and lifting his hands in another apology when she jerks away. "Come on out to the living room and talk with me. The fellows won't trouble us."

Mostly, Imogene sleeps with Warren to torture Jo Lynne, because in her estimation he's Imogene's best chance at marriage. But Imogene has no intention of marrying him or anyone, or at least that's what she tells herself because it's easier than admitting Warren is the one man of all the men whom she could care for, already does care for. He's thick through the chest and has dark eyes that have a way of looking sad, though he generally seems happy with life. Imogene especially likes how those eyes settle on her when she's peeling off her clothes for him. And while she might seek him out on a Friday night after she's had three rounds to fortify herself, the next morning, the caring for him is what leaves her feeling guilty and makes her promise herself to never see him again. The caring for him is what feels like a betrayal to Russell and Vaughn.

"So," Warren says when they've sat in the living room, him on the lounger, Imogene on the sofa. It's exactly what he says when he sees her at a bar. There's a question in that single word. So, you coming home with me? So, you going to stop hanging out in bars? So, you ever going to stop running away from me? "Tell me your story, then."

"It's not a story," she says. "I didn't imagine what happened to me."

"Didn't mean to imply otherwise. Go on, then."

As Imogene tells Warren about the boy, she takes in the men sipping coffee in Mama's kitchen as they eat platefuls of Jo Lynne's buttermilk biscuits and sausage gravy. There aren't as many gathered as she feared when she was standing in the hallway and hearing only their voices. The men all know Imogene's not real family. She's not the product of a marriage. Not the product of love. Not even the product of consent. Poor woman, poor Lottie Rose, gave birth to a child forced on her against her will. No wonder her poor heart got broke. Everyone knows the story. And the way they look at Imogene, even now in her own home, is like she's made of something less than they are, something that stinks and is rotting at its edges.

While Imogene only knows a few of the men, they're all familiar, and they're all members of the Knights. Most have closely cropped hair, sideburns that cup their jowls, and a few have tattoos growing out of their collars. Soot covers their sleeves and most have black rings around their eyes from having worn goggles, and they've all tracked black ash through the kitchen. There's a smell to them too. It's smoke, soggy socks, and cigarette-stained fingers. There will be no hiding that they were here from Mama. It's always been the rule, ever since Imogene can remember. Daddy's men are never allowed inside.

When it was Mama's time to marry, she chose Edison Coulter, a man from Missouri who knew construction. He had no interest in the Klan or what its members believed, had never even met a Klansman before coming to Georgia. But when Grandpa Simmons finally accepted that he'd die one day and realized plans had to be made, he told Daddy he would carry on with the rental properties and with leading the Knights. It wasn't so much the Klan's message that attracted Daddy, not in the beginning. It was the promise of notoriety. That's how Mama explained it. And then the camaraderie and the power he could garner in no other part of his life seduced him, and the Klan's hatred soaked in until he believed. But Mama's rules, the ones she learned from her mama, never changed, no matter what became of Daddy. She never let Klan business in the house. Jo Lynne and Eddie were still drawn in, but Imogene wasn't a real Coulter. Daddy didn't make a robe and hood for Imogene when she turned eight like he did for Eddie and Jo Lynne. He never hoisted Imogene onto his shoulders and took her to a lighting or a rally. Somehow, it never occurred to him that, even though Imogene wasn't a Coulter, she was a Simmons.

Holding up a finger to silence Warren, Imogene starts to stand so she can tell the men it's time for them to get going. Mama will be out for breakfast anytime now, and Imogene doesn't want her to see these men sitting in her kitchen and eating her food, and she doesn't want them taking time away from Warren helping the boy and his mama. But instead of standing, Imogene stiffens and slides back into the cushions. Tim Robithan is leaning against the wall near the door, his arms crossed and one foot draped over the other as if he's comfortable enough to stay a good long while. He meets Imogene's eyes when he catches her staring at him. He smiles and tips his head in her direction.

As it is every time she sees him, a numbness spreads from her fingers up her arms and settles in her chest. She's thought on it, from time to time, the reason Tim sends such a shiver through her every time she sees him. He is nothing special. He's average through the shoulders and chest, slightly slender through the neck, freshly shaved. It's what's in Tim's blood. Even if, as far as Imogene knows, a man has yet to turn up strung between two pines, feet bound and a knife driven through his heart, in the years Tim's been at Daddy's side, it's coming. It's what Tim was born into, what he's chosen to become. And the stench of it, that thing in Tim's blood that is sure to make him one day string a man up and plant a knife in his heart, is enough to make Imogene always back away. Ever since she saw those watches in Tillie's place, she's been worrying what Tim Robithan might be up to, and now he's right here in Mama's kitchen and there's a boy without a mama in Imogene's bedroom.

Chapter 27

IMOGENE

Today

"What is it?" Warren says, shifting around to see what Imogene is looking at.

Keeping her eyes on Tim Robithan, Imogene leans toward Warren so she can whisper. "Any of you get a call from Tillie yesterday? About some watches."

"Not that I know of," Warren says, shaking his head. "What's going on at Tillie's?"

"Later," Imogene says.

"Okay, then," Warren says, leaning forward as if to touch the scratch on Imogene's face. "The boy?"

Imogene pulls away, signaling that she's fine, and shifts slightly in her chair so she can still see Tim. At the sound of the door onto the front porch opening, she startles. It's Garland. He walks in, looking surprised to see so many people in the house. Dropping his jacket on one of the hooks just inside, he takes a seat at the table. And then, beginning with the wire and ending with her laying the boy in her bed, Imogene tells Warren everything.

"Locks on the outside of the door?" Warren asks. "You're sure?"

Imogene nods as she glances up to see that Tim Robithan is still looking at her. He has a ring around his light hair where a hat was sitting, something he also took off before coming inside, and he's wearing a collared shirt with both sleeves rolled up.

"How can you be certain?" Warren asks. "About the locks, I mean."

"Because I unlocked them."

"And the kitchen door? There a lock on that too?"

"Don't know. It was open when I got there."

"Go on."

"The boy, he knew me by name."

Warren pulls back in his chair.

"When he saw me. He knew my name. Said it to me. Knew I had red hair too."

"How is that possible?"

"I'm guessing Daddy told him."

Imogene leans forward in her seat to signal Jo Lynne it's time for everyone to leave, but she doesn't notice because she's leaned over a man Imogene doesn't recognize. With a tape measure, Jo Lynne is measuring the distance between his eyes. Shaking her head, Imogene falls back in her seat. They can go weeks, months even, without having the facts of Klan life flare up. Everyone gets busy with work, errands, cleaning house, and keeping up with the lawn. Long spans of time pass with no reminder, and Imogene, probably Mama too, is lulled into thinking, hoping, maybe it's all going to go away. And then something like this happens. Jo Lynne is measuring that man for a hood.

"I need you to focus, Imogene," Warren says. "This is serious. We got a boy seems to have appeared out of nowhere."

"I'm plenty focused," she says as a man who works at Larson's Hardware near Tillie's shop steps up to Tim Robithan and whispers in his ear. "And he didn't appear out of nowhere. He appeared out of a locked basement. And he wasn't living down there alone."

As the man continues whispering in Tim's ear, Tim keeps on staring at Imogene in a way that makes her wonder now if one of those nights he sat down next to her at a bar, which happened more than once, she took him home with her and doesn't remember. There were a few times when she woke in her own bed and was certain a man had been there beside her at some point but was gone by morning.

"How do you know he wasn't alone?" Warren asks.

"A clothesline," she says, shifting so she can't see Tim, but his eyes on her are like a weight pressing on her neck and shoulders. "Clothes were hanging from it."

Warren scribbles something in his notepad and looks up when Imogene says nothing more.

"The line was too tall for him. And the clothes were carefully hung."

"A woman's doing," Warren says, and Imogene nods.

The man who was whispering to Tim rejoins the others at the table, but Tim doesn't move. He's not leaning against the wall anymore, one foot draped over the other. Instead, he's standing straight, feet shoulder-width apart, hips forward in that way men stand when they're bracing themselves.

"And?" Warren says. "Imogene, what else did you see?"

Instead of answering Warren, Imogene calls out to Jo Lynne. She's finished measuring the man's eyes and is popping corn muffins from a tin. When she looks up, Imogene taps at an imaginary watch on her wrist so Jo Lynne will know it's time to get these men going. Jo Lynne nods and whispers in Garland's ear.

"You were saying?" Warren asks.

"There were books," Imogene says as a few men begin to push back their chairs to leave. "There was order to them. And carpet pieced together on the floor and a blanket draped over the back of a sofa and a tea towel. An embroidered tea towel. I know what I saw, Warren, am certain of it, and we need to be doing something."

"And you're sure the boy said it was Edison keeping him down there?"

"No." It's Jo Lynne, standing at the threshold where the kitchen meets the living room, an oven mitt in hand. "She is certain of no such thing."

Her voice is loud enough to make the men in the kitchen go silent, and even the ones already headed for the door stop and turn toward her.

"That true?" Warren asks.

"You asked me what I saw," Imogene says, sliding forward to the edge of the sofa, her way of letting Warren know this conversation is about to end. "And I told you. That should be enough."

"What are you all up to in there?" one of the men still sitting at the table asks. Imogene's seen him before. He's one of the old-timers. That's what Daddy would have called him. Someone who remembers how the world ought to be. "You set that fire, Immy Coulter? That why you're here, Warren?"

"Nothing for you to worry yourselves about," Warren says.

"Garland, you want to tell us what's going on?"

It's Tim Robithan. Not moving from his spot, Tim is talking to Garland, who still sits at the kitchen table, but he's staring at Imogene.

"Just a little trouble Imogene got herself into," Garland says, his chair legs squealing on the linoleum as he pushes away from the table. "Nothing to do with nothing."

"Police don't come out at dawn to deal with nothing about nothing," Tim says.

"You ought to be worrying about yourself," Imogene says to Tim, knowing as she says it she should be keeping her mouth closed.

Mama's always said to keep clear of Daddy's men and their doings. You ain't going to change nothing by spouting off. Just steer clear. But Imogene is tired and hungry and thirsty to the point she's struggling to swallow and she can't stop herself.

"Warren, go on down and talk to Tillie at his shop," Imogene says, standing from the sofa. "He'll show you a couple watches he's got down there what belong to Tim's mama and daddy. Real expensive watches. Tens of thousands of dollars' worth of watches, and he'll tell you how Tim's girlfriend come in there trying to sell them off as her own. Maybe you want to talk about that. Because what goes on at my mama's house, it ain't any of Tim Robithan's concern."

In four steps, Tim is standing within arm's reach of Imogene. His spicy cologne reaches her first and then the heat off his body. Warren jumps from his chair, stumbles as he goes to step in front of Tim, and Imogene stops him with a hand to his chest.

"Garland, you hear me?" Tim says, staring at Imogene. His eyes start down near her waist and slide up to meet hers. "You think what goes on in this house is none of our concern?"

"It ain't for Garland to say," Imogene says. She tries not to swallow because that'll let on how much fear she's feeling, but she can't stop herself. The smell of Tim's cologne is familiar. She's smelled it on her pillows and sheets before, on one of those mornings she woke to an empty bed, certain a man had been there. "This is Mama's house. Not Garland's."

"Back up, Tim," Warren says, sliding a shoulder between Tim and Imogene. "Back up now."

"Warren's being here's got nothing to do with the property, fellows," Garland says, coming up behind Tim and resting a hand on his shoulder. He's smiling and trying to laugh off the tension. "Come on, now, let's not have any trouble. Ain't got nothing at all to do with the property."

"Garland? Jo Lynne?" Imogene says, as Tim holds up two hands to Warren and starts to back away. "You want to tell me why these men are in our mama's house talking about our mama's property?"

Jo Lynne shakes her head the tiniest bit, most certainly telling Imogene she ought not be asking that question.

"You all get on," Warren says, corralling the men and walking them toward the door. Instead, they line up next to Tim.

Imogene turns back to Jo Lynne, uncertain what to say next, when the kitchen door opens and Eddie stomps inside. As if they're carrying on Daddy's disappointment in Eddie, a few of the men shake their heads at the sight of him.

Eddie scans the room, and when his eyes settle on the men sliding up alongside Tim Robithan, he must realize the trouble brewing is Klan business. He drops his jacket, crosses his arms, and leads with his chest, his way of trying to take over the room and Daddy's position as head of the Knights.

"Somebody care to tell me what's going on here?" Eddie says.

The room is silent. No one answers because no one cares what Eddie wants. They're all waiting for Tim Robithan to speak.

"They're all just leaving," Warren says.

Eddie steps toward Warren. "Don't think I asked you."

While Jo Lynne would be happy enough to see Imogene end up with Warren, Eddie doesn't care for any sort of law enforcement, unless the law enforcement is a Knight.

"I'll be happy to tell you, Eddie," Imogene says before Warren can respond. "But first, you tell me. Why are these men so intent on concerning themselves with our mama's property?"

"Warren's right, let's save this for another time," Garland says as he wraps an arm around Jo Lynne's shoulders. "What do you say, Tim? These kids just buried their daddy. Another time, don't you think?"

"Tell me, Eddie," Imogene says, looking at Eddie but still feeling that Tim Robithan is staring at her. "Tell me why this garbage is in Mama's house."

"Jesus Christ, Imogene," Warren says, grabbing her by the arm and dragging her toward the hallway. He glances over his shoulder and nods off toward the group of men, a reminder that there is one of him and many of them. Warren would have learned about the Knights of the Southern Georgia Order during his first days on the job. Ten years in, he knows enough to see trouble coming.

"Surprised to hear you calling me garbage, Imogene," Tim says, staring and smiling at Imogene across the room and letting her know she's right about him leaving his cologne behind in her sheets. He keeps on staring, the silence between them giving everyone else in the room time to understand the same.

"I think Garland is right," Tim finally says, keeping his eyes on Imogene. "Place ain't going nowhere. Am I safe in assuming that, Garland? Place ain't going nowhere?"

Tim doesn't have to cross his arms or lead with his chest for men to follow him. It's what Daddy knew, what everyone knows, and what Eddie just doesn't have.

"Get out," Imogene says, trying to force her way past Warren and jabbing a finger at Tim Robithan. "All of you, get out of my mama's house right now."

Chapter 28

BETH

Before

He ties a dark cloth around my head to cover my eyes, and he jerks me by the wrist as he leads me up the stairs toward the outside. I stumble, hold tight to the railing so I don't fall. We stop, and when the door at the top opens, I feel the change.

"If you know what's good for you," he says, "you'll behave."

There is a house on the other side of the door. The floors underfoot are wood and softer than the stone in the basement, warmer too, something I feel even through the rubber soles of the shoes he brought for me. They give way, the wooden floors, when I step on them. I nod so he'll know I'm going to behave. Even though I can't see anything, I can feel the open space around me. The air is different. There's more of it. It's stronger, sweeter, heavier.

"Stop," I say. "I need to stop."

"The hell you mean?" He jerks me again.

"I can't breathe."

He drops my wrist, the same one he always leads me by. I bend forward, brace myself on my knees. My lungs burn, my thighs ache. My hands, arms, shoulders, even my head shake. It's the ache for being so close to somewhere else and still being so far away.

"Jesus Christ, then," he says. "Forget it. We'll get you back downstairs."

The floors creak and shift as he steps toward me. I startle, maybe jerk, because his hands grab me as if he's afraid I'll try to run. I kick and twist as he tries to lift me. He never makes me be close to him in the basement. He always sits on the one chair at the small table while I sit on the sofa, and he talks to me about what books I like best and lately he tells me about Imogene. She has wild red hair, wild because she's wild, but she's married now and has a sweet baby boy. She goes to college and wants to be a lawyer, but she has a different daddy than him and his other sister, Jo Lynne. Jo Lynne has a good husband so she doesn't need him like Imogene does. Imogene was a mistake and her real daddy was a nobody, and her husband is a nobody too. He says that's why Imogene needs him. She needs at least one good man in her life, and that'll be him. He tells me his family is special and his daddy is a great man. He asks me if I know who his daddy is. I don't answer because just thinking about it makes me afraid his daddy might come here to the basement one day.

Sometimes he tells me he is sorry it turned out this way for me. I just wish you didn't see, he says over and over, and I know he means he wishes I didn't see what he did to Julie Anna. I still don't know if Julie Anna's mama and daddy are dead too or if they just moved away. I asked him once, and he said it didn't matter if they were dead or alive because they didn't matter and I'd better damn well get used to it.

At the top of the stairs, as I choke on the new air, he grabs me and pulls me into his body. I smell him and feel him and inhale him like I never have before and I scream. I scream like I should have screamed the day he took me away. I scream like I should have when the black truck rolled out from behind the pink oleanders. I scream like part of me is breaking away from the rest of me that has been trapped. I scream like someone will hear and like I'll never get another chance and like this is the last moment of all moments. I scream until a rough hand covers my mouth and nose and I can't breathe and my lungs burn for trying so hard to suck air.

And then we are going down, step by step. He holds me tight, that hand still pressed over my face, and at the bottom, he drops me on the stone floor. I gasp, take in the sour air that is worse now because I got a taste of the sweet air from outside. I cough and cry and pull my knees to my chest.

"Goddamn it," he says. "I told you to behave."

I grab at his pant leg, try to push past him by jamming a shoulder into his shins. I throw my arms and kick my legs. With a hand to the top of my head, he shoves me away. I fall backward on my hind end. Heavy boots pound the wooden stairs, and the door at the top slams closed.

Chapter 29

IMOGENE

Today

As the last of the men leaves the house, Eddie closing the door behind them and asking for someone to please tell him what the hell is going on, Imogene drops back onto the sofa. Eddie is giving her the same look he gave her the day Jo Lynne fished her out of the lake, like she never quite gets anything right, so it's clear somebody has told him about Imogene finding a boy in the basement. Squeezing her hands into fists, Imogene shakes them out and stretches her arms to release the energy trapped there. Her whole body is quivering and she's breathing too quickly. Closing her eyes, she doesn't answer when Warren asks if she's okay because her mind has settled on two questions, and every thought is aimed at sorting out the answers to them. Why are the Knights so interested in Mama's property, and why are they here at the same time she found the boy?

"That was a stupid thing you just did," Warren says, talking in a quiet voice and resting a hand on Imogene's knee. "I'm guessing you know how bad that could have gone and how quick it could have gone that way."

Opening her eyes, Imogene stares at Warren's hand. It's like a stranger's hand on a stranger's knee. She leans forward, and as she pulls her legs from beyond his reach, she knocks one knee against the coffee table. The one photo of Daddy she didn't pick up and hide in the laundry room rattles as it falls over on the glass tabletop.

"Leave it," she says when Warren reaches to right the photo, and she presses one hand flat on top, cementing it upside down where the boy won't have to see Daddy's face.

"Take it easy," Warren says, glancing at Jo Lynne as if for help.

"I want to know right now," Imogene says, picking up the picture and pressing it to her chest as she stands. Her throat has gone dry from taking in too much air too fast. "Why were those men here, and why were they talking about Mama's property?"

Shaking his head at Imogene, Garland walks toward the door, maybe because he wants to leave or maybe to get farther away from Mama's room. Now that the house has cleared out, he and Eddie both will be worried about her ticking heart getting the better of them. Warren won't have been around it enough to be worried, though it still might get hold of him.

"Sweetie," Jo Lynne says. "Let's focus on the boy. We have enough to contend with without—"

"We'll contend with it right now," Imogene says.

One of Imogene's first thoughts, as she sat in that basement and cradled the boy, was that even in death, Daddy was causing Mama more pain. And those men standing in Mama's kitchen and talking about her property like it meant something to them was another sign of trouble and hurt for her. Imogene was right. Trouble is sneaking up on Mama, and it has something to do with Tim Robithan standing in the corner of the kitchen and staring at Imogene.

"Those men were concerning themselves with Mama's property," Imogene says. "And we have a boy who was locked in a basement and a missing woman, and I want to know why that is and what those men have to do with it."

"They ain't got nothing to do with that boy or his mama," Garland says. "You know we already figured they was squatters down there."

"And Mama's house?" Imogene says.

"Daddy has debts," Eddie says, dropping his coat over the back of a kitchen chair. "No one kept that secret from you."

"Still doesn't explain why those men have an interest in Mama's property," Imogene says, still clutching the photo of Daddy and Mama to her chest.

"Daddy owes them." It's Garland. He glances at Jo Lynne and says it again.

"You mean he *owed* them," Imogene says. The smell of it, the nastiness of what Garland is about to tell her, reaches her first, just like Tim Robithan's cologne. "Owed. Past tense. Dead men don't have debts."

"They want the property, Immy," Eddie says.

Imogene is looking to Warren even before Eddie says it. She's looking to Warren because he'll be the one to say that's not possible.

"It's Mama's property," she says to him. "Don't matter what they think or what they want. Right?"

"Immy," Warren says.

"I told you, don't call me that."

"Not for me to get involved in something like this. No way I can know the details."

"Garland, do you know the details?" Imogene says. "Do you know why these men think they got some right to Mama's property?"

Garland is the one who runs Daddy's business from the inside. He meets with the bankers and the accountant and all the things Daddy always said Eddie wasn't up to.

"Daddy promised them," Jo Lynne says, stepping up to Imogene and trying to rest a hand on her shoulder. "Collateral. That's what they call it. Don't you know about collateral?"

"Yes, I know about collateral," Imogene says. "But I also know this house is in Mama's name, and Daddy couldn't put up an asset he didn't own." Again, she turns to Warren. "Is that something you can speak to?" When he doesn't answer, she says, "I guess not. How about this? All these years, what . . . a hundred, the police have let this go on, let these men keep doing whatever they want to do. Did you talk to all of them like you're talking to me? Ask if any of them started the fire? Is that among your duties?"

"No one thinks you started the fire," Warren says, first looking out the window onto the drive and then slowly turning to Imogene. "And as to the rest, I'm not looking to you to tell me how to do my job. That's one thing I can damn sure speak to."

"Well, if you're so certain of what you're doing," she says, scanning the room, "I'd guess you know that one way or another, that pathetic group is somehow responsible for all of this. They're all so loyal to Daddy, they'd do anything for him. Maybe they were cleaning up after him. Maybe that's why they started the fire. Maybe that's why Tim Robithan was needing money so bad. Covering up for a boy locked in a basement likely isn't cheap. Those watches, Tillie said they're worth seventy thousand dollars."

"That's enough," Warren says, stepping up to Imogene.

"Warren's right," Jo Lynne says, taking hold of Warren's forearm and trying to soothe him. "You're being ridiculous, sweetie."

Either the room is getting smaller or everyone is creeping toward Imogene. Still holding the photo, she begins to back toward the hallway that will lead to her bedroom. Her body is still trying to shake loose all that adrenaline. It's swirling in her stomach and making her joints ache, and the spot between her eyes pulses like Mama's heart.

"So you all are expecting Mama to move?" Imogene says, working it out in her head as she pulls farther away. "After everything she's done for you two, you would throw her out of her own house."

Jo Lynne tries to follow, but Imogene holds out a hand to stop her.

"That's not fair, Imogene," Jo Lynne says. "Eddie and me have always been good to Mama. And we'll see to it she gets enough to take care of herself. She'll live just fine. We'll all see to that."

"You tell those men, Garland," Imogene says, certain now that the men mean trouble for Mama and the boy and his mama too.

"You too, Eddie. Tell all of them, they're not to come back to this house. Never. And Mama is not leaving."

"He was stealing," Garland says, causing Jo Lynne to swing around and tell him to quiet himself. "He was stealing from them, Immy. From the Knights. For years."

Imogene shakes her head as she looks to Warren. He's never been so angry at her, not even on the nights he watched her leave the bar with another man. She'd done it intentionally, a message to let him know he was nothing special and she wasn't ever going to be his. Either he didn't believe what she was trying to say on those nights or he didn't care, and looking at him now, she's hoping he didn't believe her.

"Mama'll be just fine right here," Imogene says. "I'll move in. I'll pay the bills, whatever needs doing."

"Goddamn it, Imogene," Garland says. He takes three long steps that carry him across the kitchen and up to Imogene, where he leans in and whispers. "Your daddy was stealing their money, their membership." His breath is hot on the side of her face. He glances over his shoulder as if checking on Warren's whereabouts to be sure he can't hear. "These last few years, we got more money coming in than we could have ever imagined. All because of who your daddy was, and he was planning big things, like being national again. Folks know we don't got to take it anymore, all the shit we been taking all these years, and when I say your daddy stole Knights' money, it was money that's been coming in from people all over the country. And, Immy, I covered it up for him. Covered up for your daddy. And now we got to pay them back. You understand that? I got to pay them."

Continuing to back away, Imogene slowly tests the ground with each step before letting her weight settle. Jo Lynne is floating in her direction again, slipping in and out of focus as she tells Imogene she doesn't look well and maybe she should sit for a moment. Imogene just needs a little sleep so she can straighten out her thoughts and work through what needs doing. When she bumps up against the wall, she leans there, rolls from one shoulder to the other until she's headed down the hallway. Directly to her left is Mama's door. It's open. It had been closed before. She's sure of it.

From the moment Imogene saw that wire, she worried it would lead to something that might hurt Mama. And it has, and now Imogene will have to tell her about the boy and the wire to the basement and the boy's missing mother. They sure can't hide the fire from her. And in addition to Daddy's other women and his loyalty to the Klan, Mama will have to find out Daddy left her with nothing and that a dozen men are coming for her family's property—property her family has held for more than 150 years.

Imogene leans into Mama's room, but the bed is empty and so is the chair where Mama sits to tie the laces on her green gardening sneakers. Imogene hears it then, the quiet murmur of voices. They're coming from Imogene's room, and at the far end of the hallway, her door stands open. In four steps she stands in front of it. Mama sits on Imogene's bed, and next to her sits the boy.

Chapter 30

BETH

Before

Eight months after he first tried taking me outside and instead had to carry me back downstairs, he brings squares of carpet, all different sizes and colors. He spreads them over the cold floor and tapes them together with silver tape. It's the kindest thing he's done for me, and I think that means he's finally forgotten how I kicked and screamed when we tried to go outside. He's brought me other new things too—a hairbrush, bands to hold my hair back, fuzzy socks to wear when my feet are cold—but none as nice as the carpet squares. When he's done spreading them out, I say thank you and that I know it isn't his fault I'm here. I know he's only trying to do good and that he didn't mean for this to happen. I think I should say I understand about Julie Anna too, but I can't make myself say those words.

"Can we try again?" I say when I'm certain I've made him happy. "Going outside, I mean? Can we try again on Sunday?"

"You know there ain't no one looking for you no more," he says as he lays a loaf of bread on the counter and holds up a jar of peanut butter to show me he remembered to bring more this time. His dark hair is trimmed shorter and combed straight back, and his jaw is smooth and clean instead of covered with dark whiskers. "They think your daddy made off with you. You even know you had a daddy? Poor fellow, probably living a quiet life off somewhere, not even knowing they've been hunting for him."

We have a rhythm now. He asks me what I need on Wednesdays and makes a list. Don't bring so many bananas, I've told him, because they spoil too fast. Apples last longer. And bring canned vegetables, all different colors. Canned doesn't go bad.

"I know no one's looking," I say, because that's what he'll want to hear. Saying what Mama wanted to hear always kept her happy, and it'll keep him happy too. I don't tell that I never knew my daddy or even that I had one.

"And you know I got friends, important friends like in the police. Ain't none of them going to help you if it means getting me in trouble. You understand that?"

I don't understand, but I nod like I do.

"Lots of important friends," he says. "Lived here all my life. My daddy's real important too. I told you that, right? Ain't no one going to hurt our family to help someone like you. Ain't nowhere for you to go."

Again, I nod.

"You and me," he says. He stands too close to the light at the bottom of the stairs, and he squints because it's too bright. "That's all there is. Your mama, she was a drinker, you know? Alcoholic is what they call it. You know that, right?"

"Yes, I know," I say, feeling sad for Mama because not one thing in Mama's life was easy for her. "I know she's a drinker."

"No," he says. "She *was* a drinker. Ain't no more." He pauses and looks around the basement as if he's forgotten what it looks like or maybe as if wondering what else I might need down here. "She's gone, dead. Drank herself to death."

I stare at him but must not answer, because he says it again.

"She's dead. Do you understand?"

I nod and drop down into my one chair at my one table and press my hands there to steady myself.

"I ain't no bad person," he says. His voice is thin. He's slipping away, and the sound of him can hardly reach me.

"Yes, I know you ain't a bad person."

There have been times I thought I might tell him about the trap

I once tried to set for him because I think he might be proud of me for being so smart. He likes that I'm smart and can do the eighth-grade math workbooks already and that I can read to him from the newspapers he brings. Sometimes, when I've done something that makes him happy, he tells me about the outside. Those are my favorite times. He tells me about catching a frog that was hopping up the steps into his mama's kitchen or pulling weeds all day on a Saturday, and the world outside blooms again just like Mama's magnolias. The world outside is sweet with silky petals that I could stare at all day for being so beautiful, and I wanted to see that world again more than anything until now. He wouldn't be proud of me setting a trap. He'd be angry. And Mama is gone and the part of me that once wanted things is empty, and I don't care if I ever see the sweet, silky outside ever again.

"Next Sunday," he says, stepping up to the chair where I'm sitting. His edges are sharp now. He's real and solid. He runs a hand over my hair and lifts a piece of it between two of his fingers.

My heart, I think, freezes in place. My blood goes still in my veins. I don't blink or breathe. I close my eyes but don't move. I don't turn my head away or pull back. Those things would make him angry. When he drops my hair, I breathe again.

"So long as the weather is good," he says, staring down at his empty fingers and rubbing them together as if he were still holding my hair in them. "Next Sunday, we'll give it another try."

Chapter 31

IMOGENE

Today

Imogene pushes open her bedroom door. Its hinges creak. Mama looks up at Imogene and smiles.

"Look at what I found," Mama says. She hasn't yet changed out of her blue housedress, and a sheer white scarf covers her hair, which still hangs loose.

The boy sits on the edge of the bed, his bare feet dangling but not touching the floor. Mama is sitting next to him, one arm wrapped around his narrow shoulders. With her other hand, she is pushing aside his hair so she can look at the cut he got when his head hit one of the basement stairs. It bled badly, but now that it's stopped, it doesn't look to be too deep. Mama always said cuts to the head were the worst bleeders of all. A snug bandage will take care of it. Probably no need for stitches. Looking first up at Mama, the boy then turns to Imogene and squints though the room is dark. Someone has drawn the curtains.

"The sun was bothering his eyes." Mama strokes the boy's dark hair. "Isn't that right, Christopher? And did you see this, Immy? He got a knock on his noggin."

Imogene is still shaking. It's all that adrenaline working its way out. She steps into the room, squats to the boy's level, and braces herself with one hand to the ground.

"Christopher?" she whispers, afraid to get any closer. "Your name is Christopher?"

He nods.

"And do you remember me? Imogene?"

Again, the boy, Christopher, nods and rests his head against Mama. His color is good and his eyes are only half-open as if he's not yet awake, but he doesn't seem troubled by the quiet ticking of Mama's heart. Instead, he seems comforted by it. Mama smiles at the feel of the boy against her and rests a hand on his cheek. She has realized the same as Imogene. Had Vaughn lived, he would have been the same age as this boy. And seeing Mama with an arm wrapped around the child and a hand to his cheek is like seeing what could have been. Imogene and Russell would have been seeing Vaughn off to kindergarten soon. Russell would've been looking into T-ball because he'd always been a good ball player. They'd have painted Vaughn's room green and marked his height on his bedroom threshold with a permanent marker. It could have been Vaughn sitting next to his grandma, eyes closed, slight smile on his face as he listened to her ticking heart. The same pain in Imogene's gut opens up as when Jo Lynne asked that question . . . what have you done?

"He was worried about getting to school," Mama says, her hand still cradling the boy's cheek. She is at ease with him, not afraid like Imogene. Another way Mama is so much stronger. "Isn't that precious? Told him it was Sunday. No school."

The hair color is the same too. Dark brown, though this boy's hair is straight and pops out in awkward tufts. His mama has likely been cutting it with scissors too dull for the job. Vaughn had soft curls, though he'd have outgrown them by now.

"School?" Imogene asks, pushing herself off the ground. "You were going to school?"

Mama makes a quiet humming sound. "He was worried he'd overslept. He said his head isn't hurting him."

"Which school?" Imogene asks, backing away until she bumps against the doorframe. "Where?"

"Past the cemetery for dead soldiers and the church with two crosses." The boy lifts his eyes to Imogene. "Did Mama come back?"

"The church with two crosses?" Imogene says, ignoring the boy's question and looking to Mama for an answer.

Her mind had been so clear before, just there in the living room, but now the things she's hearing are a jumble of words. She can feel herself squinting, her forehead drawn up tight, as she tries to understand what Mama and the boy are telling her.

"The Episcopal, I figure," Mama says. "You know the one. It's there on Elm. Two pitched roofs. Two crosses."

"You go to school in town?" Imogene says. "Here in Simmons-ville?"

"Where's my mama?" the boy says again, this time looking up at Mama.

"Imogene?" Mama says when she doesn't answer the boy.

Imogene steps into the room again and closes the door to shut out the extra light that is still troubling the boy. She walks slowly toward the bed so she has time to think. Squatting in front of the boy, close enough to touch him this time, she sets the framed photo she picked up in the living room on the bedside table, face-down so the boy won't have to look at Daddy, and stares at his small feet.

"Did your mama take you to school?" Imogene says, resting one hand lightly on the boy's knee. Something inside is beginning to fester and she can't stop her hands from shaking. When he still doesn't answer, she shakes that small knee so he'll look at her. "It's me, Imogene. Remember? Imogene with the red hair? Tell me about school."

Christopher pulls his legs away so his knee slips from Imogene's hands. She's frightened him.

"I think it's time for breakfast," Mama says, tipping her head in the same scolding way she did when, as a child, Imogene acted up in church. "I'll bet Christopher here is hungry. Are you hungry, sweetheart?"

Still pressed up against Mama, Christopher nods.

Standing from the bed, Mama extends a hand to him. "Come with me to the kitchen," she says. "Do you like pancakes?"

Christopher shakes his head. "I want to go back."

"Back where, dear?" Mama says.

When the boy doesn't answer, Mama looks to Imogene still squatted at the side of the bed. Imogene shakes her head in the slightest way, so even though Imogene isn't ready to tell Mama where the boy came from, she'll know he can't go back.

"Mama will come home," the boy says. He slides off the bed and stands before Imogene. "She always comes home. Always. And I have to be there."

"Perhaps you should bring us our breakfast in here," Mama says, lowering herself back onto the mattress and pulling Christopher up next to her. "Let's us stay put. Wait for your mama right here. That'll be fine, won't it?"

Imogene stands, and as she does, the meaning of what the boy has told them is finding its way to solid footing. She should be feeling relief because this means Daddy wasn't holding them down there, the boy and his mama. They were coming and going. But it isn't relief she's feeling, because it was the boy's own mama who was locking him up.

"Do you always go to school?" Imogene asks, careful to speak softly and with a smile on her face, but the anger at this boy's mama has taken root, and the strain of keeping it contained is making her arms go rigid. "Every day?"

The boy doesn't answer and instead takes on that same look he had in the basement. It's a slight tightening of his upper lip as if he's pinning his mouth shut, and he crosses his arms.

"Imogene, that's enough questions," Mama says. "We need a little food in our stomachs. You'll bring us something, please."

"Yes, ma'am."

The basement was the boy's home, and he goes to school. Or he did. Imogene didn't want to believe Jo Lynne when she said that the boy's mother probably locked him up down there, but it would seem she was right. If the mother had no other home, at least the basement was a roof for them, but to lock her boy in and to leave him and to maybe set that fire. That's what Imogene can't make sense of. Not even Jo Lynne, when she asked Imogene . . . what have you done . . . ever truly thought Imogene was the one to blame for what happened to Russell and Vaughn. It was more about Jo Lynne being exhausted by Imogene not doing things the way she ought to.

Imogene got herself pregnant out of wedlock. That was her first mistake. And then she insisted on staying in college even while she was pregnant and even after Vaughn was born and she let babysitters care for him instead of being a proper mama. She left clothes in the dryer to wrinkle, served her husband takeout, dropped her cell phone for no good reason. What have you done? It was a poorly timed question, though that didn't stop it from stinging all these years, because even though Jo Lynne had been talking about a busted cell phone, Imogene knew in her heart that it was her fault Russell and Vaughn died. Perhaps it was this boy's mama's fault too that all these bad things have happened. Imogene had a child, and she let him go. This mother had a child, and she left him. The glimmer of hope Imogene had felt—the belief that she could be strong enough to help this boy when she's been nothing but a disappointment to everyone else—is gone.

Chapter 32

BETH

Before

One week later, on the day we're meant to go outside again, he stomps around the basement, twice tripping on the new carpet squares, and scolds me for not eating. I lie on the sofa, a blanket pulled up around me, and watch him. He digs through the ice chest and counts the cheese sticks and slices of ham. He shakes the cereal box to find it nearly full and waves an unopened loaf of bread in my face.

"You ain't eaten one damn thing," he shouts.

He walks through the rest of the basement. Checks the hamper where I'm supposed to put my dirty laundry. It's empty because I haven't changed my clothes or eaten anything since he told me Mama was gone.

"You stink to high heaven," he says. "You have to wash yourself, comb your hair. Maybe we don't get to go outside today."

I stare at him and say nothing because I don't care. The words he's saying don't mean anything to me. Mama isn't out there anymore, thinking about me or missing me or waiting for me to come back home, and now I don't want anything. I don't even want to live.

He grabs me by the wrist and yanks me from the sofa. Like he did before, he covers my eyes over with a black kerchief. He catches my hair in it when he ties the ends off at the back of my head. It pulls my hair, but I don't cry out or even complain.

"It ain't my fault she's dead," he says as he pulls me up the stairs. I stumble because I can't see. I crack my shin on one of the steps.

Still I don't cry out. "She done it to her own self. But that ain't happening here."

I know a change in the air is coming as he reaches to throw open the door at the top of the stairs. The last time, that change made my legs fold up under me and I screamed and cried because it was too much. I should be scared the same will happen again, but I'm not. The outside doesn't matter to me anymore because Mama isn't in it. But when the door opens, I can't stop myself from inhaling long and slow, can't stop my hands from shaking or my legs from turning watery again. The air is sticky and sugary, like syrup I want to lick from my fingers. I press a hand over my mouth so I won't cry or scream and so he won't grab me up and take me back down again. I do want something, after all. I do want to see outside.

As we walk, our feet hitting the wood planks that are soft and loose underfoot, I count my steps so I'll keep taking them. Three steps forward, left turn, six steps and another door opens.

The air on my face shoves me backward. I stumble and choke, and I begin to cry even though I try not to. He pulls the black kerchief from my eyes as I step through the door. I squint, raise a hand, turn away. It's painful, the sun on my skin and in my eyes, and the outside air makes my stomach swirl. Stumbling down three steps, I squat and hold myself steady with both hands to the ground. It's dizzying, all of it together. A light gust brings with it the smell of winter honeysuckle. I remember them in an instant, like I just yesterday picked the tiny white flowers with Mama and scattered them on the railing outside the front door so we could smell them all day long. Clumps of dirt crumble under my feet. Birds and insects click and sing. Dry grass digs into my hands. When I drop the rest of the way to the ground, light-headed from so much outside, the grass scratches at my cheeks and neck.

He lets me lie there for a time. I press one hand over my mouth to cover up the crying and pull my knees to my chest because something is grinding away on my stomach. The basement is gray and soggy, and down there, I feel nothing. Never quite hungry, never quite thirsty. I never quite felt Mama being dead either, though I didn't know it until now. Everything is more outside and it's painful to be here. I feel what I've missed in a new way. They're close again, the things I've gone without, and I'm reminded of them by the smells and the feel and the sounds. I miss Mama's magnolias and her silky white hair and the tiny perfume bottle she tipped on one finger and the store-bought cookie dough we ate on Saturday nights and the stringy dollar weeds we pulled from around the house. The missing is what grinds on my insides, and now Mama's gone and has left me behind.

Finally, he reaches down and grabs my wrist, the same wrist, and drags me to my feet. I stand without fighting him, already worn down by it all. My arms hang loose at my sides as he wipes dirt and bits of dead grass from my cheeks.

"You get lonely down there?" he asks, looking my face over.

I squint up at him. Even though the sun is low in the sky and there isn't much left of it for the day, it's too much for my eyes. I don't remember the sun being too much before, and I feel the cold now. It makes me shiver as it dries my damp skin.

"I mean it," he says, tilting his face this way and that, trying to make our eyes meet. "I can't hardly think about you, all alone down there. It bother you?"

He's close enough I can smell the smoke on his breath. I didn't used to smell cigarettes on him, and he also smells like Mama's perfume, but not quite. It's some other woman's perfume. Deep creases cut through his thick skin. They fan out from his eyes and the corners of his mouth. Gray hairs sparkle in among the brown. I've smelled him plenty, because you can't stop yourself smelling a person, but this is the most I've looked at him ever.

"I see Imogene with her little boy and he sure does love her."

He stares at me, waiting for me to say something, but I don't. It's like I've lost Mama all over again in a worse way than before. "Guess you loved your mama too. You're lonely now, ain't you?"

I don't know what to say. It should be an easy question to answer . . . am I lonely . . . but part of feeling so sad about Mama being gone is that I've already started to forget her and now I'll never see her again and all those things I've forgotten are lost forever. I didn't realize how much I had already forgotten until I touched the dirt and smelled the outside. I had been mixing up the characters and stories I read about—Laura and Ma and Pa and Mary and their house in the Big Woods—with who Mama really was and what my house really looked like and which road I lived on and the name of the town we sometimes drove to.

Even Imogene had become more real than Mama because he tells me about her and her boy and the man who is her husband. He says Imogene doesn't think he's stupid like most everyone else and I think that's one reason he loves her best. I was beginning to love her best too because she was closer than Mama, and I was not quite so alone when I listened to stories of Imogene changing messy diapers or losing the pacifier yet again or getting spit-up in her long red hair. But now Mama is gone and what I've forgotten is gone too. I am lonely. It's the missing and the forgetting and the loneliness that grind in my stomach. All of them together.

"Guess it's a silly question," he says, looking down at the watch on his wrist and then behind us at the sun. "Course you're lonely. You're alone. But you got to eat, right? You know that. You got to care for yourself."

He says I have five more minutes and then goes on to talk about how much he hates this time of year. The days are so short and he'll sure be happy when the time changes. I don't know about the short days of winter or the longer days of summer, but I nod like I do, and when he points off to the left, I look and listen because I don't want to miss a single thing. I don't want to forget anything else. I want to have much to remember later when I'm alone again in the basement.

"Over there," he says. "Over there is Stone Mountain. You can't see it, but it's there."

I take a step in the direction he's pointing. I know all about Stone Mountain. It's a rocky mound that looks as if the earth has spit out a bit of itself it didn't much like the taste of. Mama and me went there once, and by the time we were done climbing, we were puffing and panting and nowhere close to the top, and Mama said she sure did need to get herself more exercise. Stone Mountain isn't so far from Mama, and pecans grow in Georgia. I was right. Even though Mama is gone, home is still there and I'm not so far away.

"You know Stone Mountain?" he asks, grabbing me by the shoulder and pulling me around to face him.

I shake my head but don't try to talk.

"You sure?" he says. "Because Stone Mountain, it ain't nowhere near your house."

I press my lips tight together because I don't want to say the wrong thing, and then I shrug so he'll think I don't know anything about it.

Later, when I'm alone in the basement, I eat a slice of bread, slowly picking off small bits of it and laying them on my tongue, and think hard about the day Mama and me went to Stone Mountain. And I think of the field outside where he and I stood for exactly twenty minutes. Tall clumps of grass that reached nearly as tall as me lined the flat field, rows and rows that stretched farther than I could see. The grass was brittle and the stalks drooped because it's winter, but not cold winter like Laura has in her stories. It's cold like Georgia cold, and I think in the spring, the clumps will green up and grow taller, tall enough to hide a girl like me. We had the same grass at our house. Tall, feathery pink stalks will shoot up out of the tall clumps when summer comes just like they did back home, and there will be room enough between the clumps for me to run silently and to zigzag this way and that. I did the same with Mama. I would hide, and she would seek. So I know he won't be able to run through the grass like me because he's too wide. If I were to run through those rows and he were to chase after, he wouldn't be able to hear me. But I would hear him.

Part III

Chapter 33

IMOGENE

Today

Imogene walks out of her bedroom, closes the door behind her, leans there, and shuts her eyes. Garland and Jo Lynne were right about the boy and his mama, and that means one less thing to hurt Mama. They were squatters. Daddy had nothing to do with them being in the basement. No one did. Imogene still has no explanation for the wire, though it could have been run long before Christopher and his mama happened along. Or maybe Daddy was trying to help them, though that doesn't sound much like Daddy. Whatever the explanation, the boy and his mama could have left anytime.

Imogene will still have Mama's house to protect and will have to contend with Daddy stealing from the Knights of the Southern Georgia Order and Garland covering it up, and all of that will be trouble enough in the days ahead, but what Imogene's feeling now is anger. What Daddy didn't do, this boy's mama did. She put the locks on the outside of the door, and then the house burned. That's as far as she'll let her thoughts go. But she's also feeling fear. This boy's mama wasn't there for him when he needed her, just like Imogene wasn't there for Vaughn. Exhaustion has left her numb, and she can't look into that boy's eyes when he finds out what his mama did, because the hurt she'll see there will be the same that would have shown in Vaughn's eyes when he realized she wasn't coming at the time he needed her most. She just isn't strong enough.

"Imogene?"

Imogene opens her eyes at the feel of Warren's hand on her arm.

"Is he awake?" he asks.

"His name is Christopher."

For a brief few moments, when she ordered Tim Robithan out of her house and when she woke to find the boy still alive, she thought she was doing something after five long years of doing nothing. She was helping change the course and making things better. She was on track to be the person she'd been before she lost her family. At least she felt a spark of who she'd been—a person who would swim across a lake to find her real daddy or be brave enough to move to Atlanta all by herself to escape a family legacy or keep struggling to make classes and get good grades with an infant at home who kept her up most nights. But that spark is gone and that person is gone, because the boy, Christopher, is alone and will always know his mama left him, and because Imogene did the same to Vaughn. She left him alone. She was wrong to think she could get back to the person she once was. As much as her husband and son are gone, so is the person she was before.

"Imogene," Warren says, his hand tightening around her forearm. "You with me? I need to talk to him."

"He goes to school in town," Imogene says.

"So, he wasn't living in the old house?"

With one good yank, Imogene pulls away.

"Yes, he was," she says, walking down the hallway. "And so was his mama, if you can call her that."

The kitchen is quiet again. The floors and counters shine as if the men were never there, and the smell of all that cleaning has replaced the smell of smoke. Garland and Eddie must have left, and Jo Lynne is out on the porch, talking to someone on her cell phone. Imogene begins flipping open cabinets though she doesn't know what she's looking for. She's angry with a woman she's never met. Imogene loses a child and this woman gets to keep hers, and he loves her, is willing to fight for her, even though she locked him in a basement and left him, what, to die?

"He wants to go back to the house," Imogene says to Warren. "To find her, I guess, and I don't know what to tell him. I can't let him see it all burned down. And Mama, I haven't told her about the house either."

"Can't hide a burned-out house for long," Warren says.

Grabbing a banana from the basket hanging over the sink and a box of granola bars from the top cabinet, she drops them on the kitchen table and sits.

"Jo Lynne was right," she says, resting her elbows on the table. Whatever had been keeping her going—adrenaline, fear, whiskey— is gone. She's exhausted. "It was his mama who was locking him up down there."

"He said that?"

"Not in so many words," Imogene says. "But if he was going to school in town, they were coming and going every day. It was the school over near the Episcopal church. They'll know him there, won't they? Be able to tell us something about him?"

"Did he say if his mother left him like this before?"

"No. But she's left him to go with a man before. He did say that. And that she always came back."

"Then we need to find out who this man is."

Imogene nods.

"So, it wasn't Daddy after all?"

It's Jo Lynne. She's come inside from the porch. She had probably been calling down to her office to talk with them about the boy. She drops her phone in the basket near the sink, tightens the belt on her robe, and smooths the hair around her face.

"You'll call over to the school?" Jo Lynne asks Warren, meaning she was listening to their conversation. "And, Imogene, you'll bring him out? Let me talk to him?"

Imogene closes her eyes and rests her face in her hands. Something has upset her stomach. It might be the burn from too much whiskey and vodka too, or it might be the dread that she is going to be stuck being the person she's been for the last five years. Everything she does, has done for the last several years, is meant to disappoint. And she knows now why she's done it. It isolates her. Little by little, the people who love her can't take any more and then they're gone and there's one less person to care about Imogene, one less person to expect more of her or to encourage her to do the hard work of rebuilding.

"Imogene, are you listening?"

Jo Lynne's arms are crossed, and that one hip of hers is cocked out to the side. As if seeing her reflection in Imogene's eyes, Jo Lynne drops her arms and straightens.

"I'm not letting them take this house," Imogene says. She might not be able to help this boy, because what his mama did can never be undone, and she'll never be able to look into his face once he knows, but she's damn sure going to help Mama. "I'm going to move in here, take care of everything."

Jo Lynne starts to say something, but Warren stops her with a simple glance. They've had occasion to work together over the years and are slipping into what must be a familiar partnership.

"That's for another time," he says. "Jo Lynne has responsibilities to this child. I've let this go on long enough. You need to let her do her work. Can you do that?"

"Yes," Imogene says, pushing away from the table.

"Yes, what?" Jo Lynne says, making it clear she's still angry about Imogene saying she's moving in with Mama.

"Yes, you can talk to him," Imogene says. "He's all yours. His name is Christopher."

It Rises Again

In 1954, *Brown v. Board of Education* overturned state-sponsored segregation. This reversal of the Reconstruction-era practice preceded yet another rise in the Ku Klux Klan in America. In September 1956, the Klan returned to Stone Mountain to host one of its largest rallies in years. In response to the civil rights movement, membership grew to approximately fifty thousand by the mid-1960s. The Klan organized and carried out violent and deadly attacks against civil rights marchers, freedom riders, and other individuals and institutions showing support for the civil rights movement. A 1965 congressional hearing and an FBI investigation contributed to the decline of the Klan, and by the early 1970s, its membership had sunk to one of its lowest levels.

Chapter 34

TILLIE

Today

Tillie parks in the same spot behind his shop that he parked in the night before, snug up against the dumpster, where his car is hidden. He looks up and down the narrow dirt alley. It's quiet because most things are closed on Sunday. The oaks rustle overhead, and somewhere up there, a finch chirps and carries on. From down the alley, someone hollers out to Tillie as he walks toward the shop's back door. It's one of the fellows what work down at the café. He's a scrawny fellow, wearing a white apron around his waist.

"You see it there?" the fellow hollers as he steps out into the alley where he can get a look at Tillie a few shops down. New fellows are always showing up down there. Tillie's friendly with them but can't keep up with their names. "Window there in the back is broke."

Tillie gives the man a wave. "Just kids, I suppose," he says. "But thanks for calling over to the house."

The window that leads into the storage room where Mrs. Tillie keeps her cleaning supplies and extra tables for displaying hasn't just been broken; it's gone altogether. Tillie reaches for the back door but stops and lowers his arm when something crackles under his feet. He glances up at the hole where a window used to be, and sure enough, it's broken glass under his feet. The window was painted shut years ago, and kicking at that broken glass on the ground gets him to thinking that someone must have done the breaking from the inside so they could get out, instead of someone on the outside trying to get in. Again, he reaches for the door, but he's slow about it this time because he's wondering if the door is going to already be unlocked. He pulls on the knob, but the door won't open. He exhales, as if it being locked is a good thing.

Mrs. Tillie's storage room is directly inside the shop, and the door to the small room is open, which it almost always is. Without crossing the threshold, Tillie leans in and takes a look. Rolls of paper towels, bottles of cleaning fluid, buckets, boxes of steel wool, and stacks of rags are all where they should be. The only thing out of place is more glass. There was glass on the ground outside, and there's glass on the ground inside, as if someone came and went out the same window.

Tillie does manage one comforting thought. Both Robert and Tim Robithan are far too big to have climbed in through that window, either coming or going. They'd have been ones to kick in the back door, which Tillie's insurance agent has been telling him for years is little stronger than cardboard.

"Called the police already," Tillie calls out down the narrow hallway that leads to the front of the shop. He stands still, listening. He forgot to turn off the ceiling fan that runs out in the front room. It's out of balance and squeals with each turn of the blades. Other than that, the shop is quiet.

Walking on through the small hallway, which is dark for having no windows, he pushes through a wooden swinging door and steps out into the main showroom. That's what Mrs. Tillie calls it, though Tillie thinks it makes her sound too full of herself.

He'd expected to find tables toppled and books thrown all about. That's what happened last time kids broke in, but if it was Robert or Tim Robithan, or someone doing their bidding, he or she wouldn't care about tossing things around. He or she would go straight for the watches and would be intent on leaving Tillie a message. He remembers that too from his days in the Klan. They like to leave messages. Maybe they'd set a fire so other fellows would be scared too, or maybe they'd . . . and this is where Tillie thinks of what they could do to Mrs. Tillie, and he pinches his eyes closed to chase away the thought.

It's what all the fellows are doing, is what they said to Tillie back then. Just a bunch of us trying to do right by our families. We all get on real good, fellows just like you and me. That's all Tillie had been wanting—to keep his sweet bride safe and to have some other fellows to go fishing with and maybe share a beer with now and again.

Quick as he can, Tillie makes his way through the shop, cracking his shin on a pew Mrs. Tillie pulled out of the old Baptist church out east of town when it shuttered its doors. Stumbling again, but backward this time, he drops down into one of Mrs. Tillie's fiddleback chairs. She'd have his hide for coming down on it so hard, but not even the thought of him having maybe cracked a spindle keeps him from smiling, because he can see the black safe from here, tucked up under the counter and closed tight. First, he'll check to make sure the watches are in there, just to ease his mind, and then he'll give the fiddleback a good cleaning, because he likely smudged it up when he fell, and then he'll see to boarding up that window.

Once behind the counter, Tillie gives the combination lock a few quick spins and the steel door opens. Inside, two watches are wrapped up inside one of Mrs. Tillie's vintage doilies just like she said they would be. Not even daring to touch them, Tillie pushes the door closed and stands. And that's when he sees it. It's hanging right there from the total key on the register. It's a necklace—a light blue moonstone hanging from a silver chain—and while Tillie doesn't know who left it here, he darn sure knows who it belongs to. He pulls out his cell phone, squints hard as he scrolls through the screen, and when he comes to a name that looks pretty close to reading "Imogene," he hits the call button.

Chapter 35

IMOGENE

Today

Imogene stands and pushes her chair under the kitchen table, taking care not to drag the legs over the linoleum.

"I'll send Mama to get herself dressed," she says to Warren and Jo Lynne, "and bring the boy out to get something to eat. Mama doesn't need to know anything about where we found him. And she doesn't need to know about the Knights wanting to take her house either."

Jo Lynne nods. "For now."

"No, not for now," Imogene says. "For always. I'll tell her about the fire, but no one tells her anything about the rest of it. I'm moving in. Mama's not losing her home."

Leaving the food on the table, she walks toward her bedroom but stops and turns when she reaches the hallway.

"Will you know what to say to him?" she says to Jo Lynne. "When he asks about his mama and what will happen next and where he'll go?"

"Yes, Imogene," Jo Lynne says. "I know. It's what I do. Warren and I, we'll both see to taking care of him." And then to Warren, she says, "Would you excuse us for a moment?"

Warren glances at Imogene as if to get her okay. When she nods, he steps out onto the porch and pulls the door closed behind him.

"You understand the kind of trouble this means for Garland, right?" Jo Lynne says, walking close enough to Imogene that she can whisper. "You understand how serious it is, Daddy stealing all that money? And I assume you understand who these men are?"

The sudden memory of Tim Robithan's cologne washing over her followed by the heat of his body and then the feel of his breath on her face causes Imogene to brace herself by placing one foot behind the other.

"If you need money so God-awful bad, why don't you and Garland sell your house and leave Mama's alone?"

Jo Lynne says nothing, and her eyes won't settle on Imogene.

"Oh, I get it," Imogene says. "Mama's the one with equity. Your fancy new house came with a fancy new mortgage, didn't it?"

"Imogene, please. There'll be money left for Mama to get a nice place in town. Something sweet and manageable."

"You know the saddest part of all?" Imogene says, glancing outside to see Warren leaning against the porch railing and talking on his phone. "Mama's been far too good to both you and Eddie over the years, and Lord knows if you asked, she'd probably let you have the place. But I'm not letting that happen. No one is selling Mama's house. And I'm done talking about this."

Jo Lynne finally looks tired. Her hair has wilted where it would usually be curled at its ends, her eyelids hang low, and even the belt around her robe has pulled loose. Normally, Imogene's the cause of Jo Lynne's exhaustion. But not today, or rather Imogene isn't the only one causing it. Garland has gotten himself in a bad way with some very bad men.

Back at her bedroom, the first thing Imogene sees is her bed. The quilt has been smoothed out, the pillows plumped and straightened, and Mama and the boy are gone. Pushing open the door, Imogene takes two quick steps inside. Straightaway, she sees them. They're marching past the foot of the bed, and the boy is quietly counting. He runs his fingers along the oak footboard as if trailing them along an iron fence. When he reaches six, he says turn left and looks up at the ceiling.

"There's the two crosses and the pointed roofs," he says. "Do you see them?"

"Yes, look how shiny," Mama says, holding one of her hands as if the sun is hitting her full in the face. "Now which way?"

The boy points straight ahead. "Four more blocks is four more steps."

Mama counts. One. Two. Three. Four.

"And there." The boy points at the window. "That's Mr. Tillie's store, where Imogene goes."

"How about that, Immy?" Mama says, smiling and clapping.

"Two more blocks is two more steps," the boy says. "And that's where I do school. I need a chair. And a square table. Do you have a chair and square table?"

"Is this how you go to school?" Imogene says. Her voice startles them. In her pocket, her cell phone buzzes. She presses a hand over it but doesn't take it out.

The boy leans into Mama's hip.

"Imogene," Mama says. "You surprised us."

"I'm sorry," Imogene says. "I'm sorry, Christopher. But tell me, please."

"There's not rain, so we walked," the boy says. "If it rains, we can't take outside time."

Again, Imogene's phone starts to vibrate and buzz. This time, she slides it out of her pocket to see who is calling. It's Tillie. She leaves the call to roll to voicemail, and as she tucks the phone back in her front pocket, she says, "Rain?" Her chest begins to lift and lower. She swallows and says it again. "Rain?"

"When water falls from the sky." The boy lets go of Mama and points to the end of the bed. "When there's not rain, we walk past the cemetery where the soldiers is buried. It has the tall fence. It's black and iron. Iron is hard. We walk two more blocks to the church with two crosses and then there's where I do school."

"Was your school there in the basement?" Imogene says, taking care to talk quietly so she doesn't frighten Christopher. She drops onto the edge of the bed. She's said it, and now Mama will know. She's said right out loud that the boy was living in the basement.

The boy says nothing, and instead looks up at Mama as if for an answer.

"Whatever you have to say, little one," Mama says, cupping the boy's cheek and showing no sign she heard Imogene mention the basement, "go on and say it."

"We drive and we walk and we do school at the kitchen table. Except it isn't the kitchen table when we do school. It's my school."

Without looking back at Mama or the boy, Imogene pushes herself off the mattress and walks toward the bedroom door. She moves slowly, her legs weak, and the things around her . . . the pine floors, the wooden credenza inside the door, the light switch on the wall . . . drift in and out of focus.

Placing a hand on the wall when she's near enough to reach it, she says, "Can you wait here with Christopher, Mama?"

If Mama answers, Imogene doesn't hear her. Still bracing herself with a hand to the wall, she turns to face the boy. He sits in the wingback chair now. Mama must have helped him into it. He has turned so his back is to the light that trims the heavy curtains. His eyelids flutter as if his eyes are dry. It's the light. No, it's daylight. He's a person who doesn't know daylight.

Hugging herself with both arms because she's begun to shiver, Imogene closes her eyes and turns away. She thought she'd been wrong about the boy living down there. She thought he hadn't been trapped by locks on the outside of the door and that Daddy had been no part of it. She thought the boy had been coming and going, attending school like every other child, and if he had been locked in down there, it had been his own mama doing it. She thought the mother had been driving him into town and walking with him to school, somehow covering up how they were living. But they were doing school at the kitchen table. That's what the boy said. The walking and driving through town weren't real. The boy squinted at an imaginary sun, ran his fingers along a nonexistent iron fence. It was pretend. All of it.

"Do you know Jo Lynne too?" Imogene says to the boy without looking at him again. This is what Imogene always does, at least it's what she does now. It's who she has become. She knows enough to know she can't do this. She can't be the person this boy needs her to be. "I mean, did you already know Jo Lynne like you already knew me?"

When she hears nothing, she looks back at the boy. He has sunk into the chair. Its broad back is far wider than his narrow shoulders. He isn't afraid to look at Imogene anymore. His eyes are light and trimmed by long dark lashes. They're tired eyes, lined with red, but they're warm too. He puckers his lips as if thinking over what Imogene has asked and then nods. Yes, he already knew about Jo Lynne like he already knew about Imogene.

It was coincidence that Imogene was the one to find the boy. She isn't meant to save him any more than Jo Lynne is. This is no great turning point in Imogene's life, not a moment she will rise to. Whoever told the boy about Imogene told about Jo Lynne too. Imogene can step aside now and let Jo Lynne take over. It's sound reasoning, as sound as she needs, anyway. There's always a way out. She's had to learn that, had to believe that if she were to go on living these past five years. This, whatever it all turns out to be, is too big for Imogene. She can manage taking care of Mama and paying a few bills. How much could the old place really need? But this boy is something different. For him, she can't be the strong one, never really could be. It has always been Jo Lynne.

"I'm going to go get Jo Lynne," Imogene says, resting a hand on the gold doorknob and pulling open the door. "I think we should let her and Christopher have some time together."

"Is he one of Jo Lynne's boys? You dear child."

Out in the hallway, Imogene turns back long enough to nod at Mama, so she'll know that, yes, Christopher is one of Jo Lynne's now. Mama stares at Imogene, waiting for more of an answer. Next to her, the boy rocks from side to side as he slides forward, pushing himself out of the deep chair.

Once standing, the boy says, "But Mama always told me Imogene was the one who would save us."

Chapter 36

BETH

Before

I began to change the day he told me about Stone Mountain being close by and after I felt the sun on my hair and cool dirt under my hands. Even though it's white and not chocolate, I drink the milk he brings me instead of pouring it down the drain. I eat the sliced roast beef and ham so fast he has to bring it twice a week, and I eat eggs too, lots of eggs, because he lets me use the hot plate now. After a time, my stomach stops hurting when I put food in it. My hair stops falling out in my brush and the room stops swirling when I stand too quickly and my lips don't flake and peel anymore. I'm getting stronger, not only my body but my mind too. Mama is only gone because that's what he said. The day we saw those men standing on the courthouse steps, Mama said people like that, people with hate in their hearts, will say anything to scare you because that's the only muscle they have. They fool people into thinking they need protecting. Never believe people with hate in their hearts, she said, so I don't believe him. I don't believe Mama is gone.

I know all about eating good because sometimes Mama would stop eating and she would stop going to work too, and Mr. Williamson would call and leave a message on our phone machine. He'd tell Mama she'd better pull it together because he would hate to fire a single mother. I would take Mama food in her bed, good food like carrots with ranch dressing to dip in and peanut butter sandwiches, until she felt like throwing open the curtains and rejoining the real world. That's how she always said it. I figure this is my time for rejoining the real world.

I also get better at keeping track of Sundays and Wednesdays because I only sleep when I'm supposed to now, and on the days I know he won't come to the house, I walk up and down the stairs even though they creak like they might one day topple over. I walk them not only so I can manage them without making any noise but so I will be stronger. I walk them until I collapse on the hard floors, thankful for once that they are cool. I know about exercise from Mama's doctor. He worked at the clinic where Mama went when she had to get out of bed so the woman wouldn't start visiting us again once a month. He told Mama she needed solid food and a good walk every day. Exercise will heal the soul, he said to Mama, which left me wondering what bad thing had happened to Mama's soul. And after I walk those stairs until I drop to the cold floor, I begin to run them.

I keep getting to go outside for exactly twenty minutes every Sunday, and every time he leads me up the stairs, he ties a kerchief over my eyes. I count our steps and memorize the turns we take and the spots where the floors creak or are uneven. Outside, while he looks at his watch or smokes a cigarette, I look hard at the field of pampas grass that hasn't started to green up yet, but it will when the days stretch out and the air warms. I try to look beyond them, the dry, brittle bunches of grass that grow like rows of wheat, but can't. Off to my left, where I can't quite see it, is Stone Mountain, and to the right, far beyond the side of the house, the land dips and he once told me there is a lake nearby. Maybe we'll go someday, he said. It's nearer to heaven than any other place on earth. We'll go in the morning, just one time, and you'll see how the clouds settle in over it, like smoke almost. Beyond the lake, the land rises again, and above it, I can see the very peak of a chimney. He has also told me there are plenty more books for me if I'm good.

He is happy that I'm eating more and am always awake when he comes and that I talk about my books and listen to his stories. He tells me about his job fixing up the houses that his daddy rents out to the poor folks in the town. He says anybody can take care of numbers and bank accounts. What he does takes real skill, talent even. Craftsmanship, he calls it. He asks me what color I think he should paint a house or what kind of flowers would look best in the window boxes he wants to build for his mama, and he smiles and nods when I tell him what I think.

He likes that I'm studying a math book meant for tenth graders now and that I'm reading science books that are two inches thick. He brings me paper and pencils so I can work my problems, and one Sunday, he brings a small air conditioner that he puts in one of the windows. He uses bolts to make it stay and tells me those bolts are in there for good, no sense trying to pry them loose. I promise I won't try because he says the air conditioner can keep me warm and cool too and make the air not so wet anymore. On another Sunday, he brings needles and different colors of thread and old sheets. One of my books teaches me how to embroider. I practice, and when I'm good enough, I cut out a piece of one of the sheets so it's just the right size and stitch a magnolia like the ones at Mama's house, and now I have a tea towel.

Every time he brings me something new, I tell him thank you, especially for the books, so he'll keep bringing them. My favorites aren't the books about Laura anymore, but I don't tell him that. My favorite is a second-grade science workbook—even though I'm way too old for it—that teaches me about daylight savings time. It's January 17 now, and in March, I'm not exactly sure which day because the workbook is old and tells me the date for a different year, the time will change and there will be an extra hour of light. I know from laying a hand on the stone walls that the nights are cold and the days too, and I can't run in the cold and dark. But my second-grade workbook taught me that autumn is followed by winter and winter by spring.

Even though the books about Laura aren't my favorite anymore, I still remember about Pa and the plans he made. I'm smarter now about the days and times he comes and I know I'm not so far from home. Mama is still out there. I'm sure of that too. He lied to me when he told me Mama was dead because he wants me to need him like Imogene's baby needs her. He talks most about Imogene because I think he wants what she has. But even though I'm certain he lied and that Mama is close, she might not be forever. When the weather is warm and when we have an extra hour, I'll run.

Chapter 37

IMOGENE

Today

Standing on her bedroom threshold, Imogene isn't sure how long since the boy last spoke, telling her that his mama said Imogene was the one who would save them. Imogene. Not Jo Lynne. Not Eddie. Imogene. That's what the boy said, but how much time has passed since he said it?

Beyond the hallway, sunlight spills into the house, but inside Imogene's bedroom, the drawn curtains have made another dark place the boy is being held. And yet he seems content now, as if he's waiting for something or someone, as he stares at Imogene. His pale blue eyes brighten and hold firm, even when Mama rests a hand on his shoulder. The fear he had last night, and of Imogene just moments ago, is gone, or perhaps it has overwhelmed him and he's in some sort of shock. Or perhaps he mistakenly believes what his mama said.

Mama lowers to the boy's level, bracing herself with one hand on the bed. It'll be hard on her knees to be squatting like that. As if she understands what Christopher has said and why he said it, Mama nods and strokes his hair. But she can't possibly understand. She can't understand how the boy already knew about Imogene and Jo Lynne. She must have questions. And still Mama believes the boy and believes that Imogene will be the one to save him. She believes so strongly that she doesn't even ask what he needs saving from. The boy hasn't been going to school in town, hasn't been leaving that basement every day. His mama had built an imaginary world for him. They had pretended to walk through the streets and past the church. Imogene was right after all. The basement was a home with tea towels, a clothesline, and books on a shelf, and the boy lived there a long time. Maybe forever, as far as his life is concerned. And his mama too.

"Jo Lynne is cooking up something for you," Imogene says to Christopher.

"Imogene, didn't you hear him?" Mama says. "This child needs your help."

"Come on with me," Imogene says to Christopher. It's the only thing she can muster. Mama gives Imogene another scolding look. "We'll let you get dressed, Mama."

"But, Imogene," Mama says.

Imogene steps into the hallway to prove to the boy it's safe. She taps a toe on the ground to show it's real and solid and spreads her arms to reassure him there's nothing lurking.

"I'm guessing Garland and Eddie will be back soon," she says to Mama as the boy walks toward the door. "And Warren's here too."

She means to tell Mama she has to keep her distance as long as those fellows are in the house because her beating heart will overwhelm them. But she also means to keep Mama from seeing Imogene pass the boy off to Jo Lynne. Imogene isn't anyone's savior, but she'd just as soon not have Mama see that messy truth splashed about. She should also tell Mama the old house burned and the field too, but it's one more thing she isn't strong enough to do.

Out in the kitchen, Warren has come back inside, and Jo Lynne has cracked open a can of cinnamon rolls, something she'd never serve in her own home because she'd make them from scratch.

"Have a seat, you all," Jo Lynne says, smiling at Christopher but also not making a fuss when he walks into the kitchen. Instead, she behaves as if he has walked into this kitchen and sat at this table every day of his life. She's tightened up her robe and smoothed her hair, and all signs of her exhaustion are gone.

The boy, Christopher, is smaller here in the main of the house. He walks with his head lowered, his hands clasped in front, and his small feet slide forward a half step at a time, as if he's afraid of something falling on top of him. At the table, he stands next to a chair until Imogene pulls it back and motions for him to sit. He squints and dips his head at the sunlight filling the house. Imogene nods at Warren and then points, but he still doesn't understand.

"The drapes, Warren," Jo Lynne says, because she noticed straightaway what was bothering the boy. "Why don't you pull them best you can?"

As Warren walks about the living room and kitchen, drawing the same drapes and lowering the same blinds Imogene had last night when she was afraid of who might still be out there, Imogene sits across from Christopher.

"Go ahead," she says to him, nudging a small glass of juice in his direction. It leaves a water ring on the Formica tabletop. "Orange juice. You like it?"

The boy's back rounds and his shoulders slump forward as he slides a hand across the table and draws a finger across the sweaty glass.

"Probably better wait on that," Jo Lynne says, setting the tray of cinnamon rolls in the hot oven. It's her second batch. The first already rests on a cooling rack near the sink. "Let's get something in that stomach of yours first."

Jo Lynne knows about things like orange juice upsetting an empty stomach and Imogene doesn't. Imogene might know things like that too if she'd been a mother longer. It's another sign she isn't the one meant to save this child.

"Imogene, sweetie." It's Mama, peeking out from the hallway. She'll be looking for any sign of Eddie or Garland because she won't want to cause them distress. Clutching the top of her housedress so it doesn't gap, she leans into the living room and gives a wave.

Imogene stands from the table, and as she passes Christopher, she gives his shoulder a gentle squeeze because that's the kind of thing Jo Lynne would do. "Be right back," she whispers.

"I think you was bringing this to show the boy," Mama says when Imogene reaches the hallway, and she hands Imogene the photo of herself and Daddy when they were younger.

"What is it?" Jo Lynne asks when Imogene slides back into her seat at the kitchen table. Jo Lynne has run a washcloth under warm water and is handing it to Christopher and motioning for him to wipe his face with it. "Make you feel better," she says.

"Picture of Daddy," Imogene says.

Across the table, Christopher is wiping his face with the warm cloth, all the while keeping his eyes on Jo Lynne. She nods and smiles so he'll know he's doing good.

"Do you recognize this man?" Imogene says to Christopher, and she slides the picture across the table.

Walking back into the kitchen after having closed all the window dressings, Warren switches on the radio even though Mama has disappeared into her room, and then he sits next to Imogene. Draping an arm over the back of her chair, he leans across the table to get a look at what Christopher is staring at.

"What's this?" he asks, trying to get a better view of the photo, which is upside down to him, and then he snatches it away. "You can't be showing him that, Imogene."

"Is that him?" she asks Christopher.

Again, she's frightened the boy because she doesn't have Jo Lynne's soothing work voice. She isn't angry with Christopher. She's scared. Scared of finding out what's been done to him. Scared of finding out what's happened to his mother. Scared of how badly this will hurt Mama. Scared that in all of it, she'll be reminded how alone her own son was in the end. But that's not something she can explain to a child.

"It's okay," she says, trying with a quieter, softer tone. "Is that the man from the basement?"

"Stop, Imogene," Warren says. "That's not how we do things."

"The both of you need to stop," Jo Lynne says, sliding a warm roll onto Christopher's plate. She hands him a small tin of frosting, demonstrates how to spread some on his roll, and then hands him a butter knife.

"Christopher?" Imogene says.

"Out, now," Warren says, grabbing Imogene and dragging her from the table.

Imogene yanks away and pushes at him. "Please," she says, squatting so she's looking across the table at Christopher's level. "Tell me. Is that him?"

It isn't much, what Christopher does next. But it's enough. He nods. Imogene looks back at Warren and then up at Jo Lynne. They've seen it too.

"Yes?" Imogene says. "Yes, that's the man?"

Christopher sticks a finger in his mouth, licks it clean, and then stares at it. Jo Lynne gives a nod when he looks up at her, his eyes wide. She knows he's asking if he can do it again, dip that finger in the icing and stick it straight in his mouth. Then he turns to Imogene and again he nods.

"Yes," he says, popping that sticky finger back in his mouth. "That's the man."

Chapter 38

BETH

Before

I see on the newspaper he spreads out on the table that today is daylight savings time day. It's written on the front page. I stare at the date. Down here, one day is exactly like the next. I forget that the world outside has moved on, and I ignore the changes in my body that prove time isn't waiting for me—my hair that hangs to my waist, my legs and arms that have grown longer and thin, the light bulb I can nearly reach without the chair. I've been in the basement for two years.

He says nothing about being glad the sun will shine an extra hour today. I wish he would, because then I'd know for certain it's real. That's how excited I am to see the date and scared all at the same time. Even though I'm looking right at it, looking so hard the thick black letters start to blur, I can hardly believe the day is finally here. But instead of saying anything about spring having finally sprung, he sits at the table and reads quiet to himself, and he didn't bring me any special things today like he usually does. Every once in a while, he lets out a long breath that makes his lips flutter.

When he first told me the days gain an hour, I wondered why I never knew about that when I lived with Mama. How could an hour get added to a day and me not know? But then I read in one of my books that only the clocks change. Spring forward, the science workbook said, alongside a picture of an old-fashioned clock leaping over a row of purple and yellow flowers.

All winter, we have been going outside every Sunday. Some days, the sun has been bright and warm on my skin, but other

Sundays, the sun has been dim and the day cold. As much as I wanted the days to get warmer and longer, I also liked the cold days. While he would set up a folding chair wherever he could find a sliver of sun, I would stand in the coldest, darkest spot I could find. I'd stand where the wind whipped past me, and if he made me wear a coat, I'd leave it open and the hood down. I'd make myself as cold as I could because I could feel the cold. I could also feel the warm when he took me back down into the basement. For a few moments, the only few I'd have all week until I went outside for another twenty minutes, I could be happy to be back inside where I was warm. The tight walls didn't make it hard for me to breathe, and the ceiling didn't hang so low. For those few minutes, I was almost happy. But by the time he would leave me, so would that happy feeling of being warm again.

"What are you smiling about?" he asks me as he folds over his paper and glances at his watch. It's almost five o'clock, and we always wait until five o'clock.

I shrug and say nothing because I can't tell him why I'm smiling, and Mama says I'm the world's worst liar. I can't tell him I'm smiling because it's daylight savings time, and I can't tell him that next Sunday is the day I run.

"Well, I'm guessing I'm going to be the one to wipe that smile off your face," he says, standing and tucking his white shirt into his belt. Sometimes he's still wearing church clothes when he comes here on Sundays, sometimes not. And he smells spicy, like the cologne the men Mama would sometimes bring home wore.

I pull my knees into my chest and rest my chin on top. I think maybe he saw inside me and knows what I was thinking. I lift my head long enough he'll see the smile is already gone from my face.

"It's Imogene's husband," he says. "And boy, too."

Imogene is going to be a lawyer if she ever finishes school over in Milledgeville, and he sometimes says she shouldn't be doing that and should be home with her baby instead, but I think he doesn't like her going to college because he never did. His own daddy doesn't think he's smart. He's told me that before. Sometimes when he's reading the paper to me, he tells me he's smart and God damn anyone who says otherwise. I nod when he says things like that because Mama always said any right-minded person will favor a rose over a cactus. Trick is, make them think you're a rose while all the time being a cactus underneath. Sometimes I pretend Imogene is my sister like Mary is Laura's sister. Imogene is smart and pretty with wild red hair, and when I read the books that were once hers, I pretend I'm smart and pretty too. Being smart and pretty and going off to college to be a lawyer and being a mom makes me think Imogene is a cactus underneath it all too.

"Both of them was killed," he says, popping a piece of gum in his mouth. "Just like that. Truck T-boned them. Right there outside of town. Got family matters to contend with today so can't stay."

"That's okay," I say, hiding my face as best I can. I smell his pepperminty breath.

"But next week," he says, "we'll go for extra long."

Except for Julie Anna and Mama, although I don't believe Mama is really gone, I've never known anyone who died and especially not a baby boy like Imogene's baby boy. His name was Vaughn. I saw his picture once. He had round cheeks and fat legs, and he was hugging Imogene. Her head was thrown back and she was laughing, so mostly, I could only see her red hair. Thinking about Imogene having to go on living without her baby boy makes me think about Mama having to go on living without me. Mama hurting makes me hurt, and I want to run to her as fast as I can so all the hurting will stop.

When he comes on Wednesday, I say I don't feel well so he'll leave me sooner and won't see how I can't hardly sit still for being so nervous about the day I'll finally run. Sunday has never taken so long in getting here, and the waiting and not knowing what will happen has wadded itself up inside me, and I worry it's all going to spill out where he'll see it. He looks sad about me not feeling good. He says, maybe this'll perk you up, and pulls a necklace from his pocket. It has a slender silver chain and a smooth blue stone. He tells me it's a moonstone and that the necklace has been in his family for generations. Family is real important, he says. Nothing more important. He knows that now because Imogene lost hers, and I think it scares him to see what that kind of loss does to someone. I want to ask him if Imogene is going to be all right and will she be able to get up every morning and keep on living, but I don't because I doubt he'll like me caring and worrying about Imogene. He won't understand that I'm really asking if Mama has been able to keep on living without me.

"Wear it every day," he says, dropping the necklace in my hands. "I'm the only family you got now. And this necklace, it'll remind you."

I slip the necklace over my head, lie down, and pull my legs up tight so he'll leave. He wants me to love him like Imogene's baby loved her. I've known that since he first told me about Imogene's baby boy and her husband. He wants a home and a family and even to be smart, all the things Imogene had. Mostly, he wants someone to love him like that little boy loved Imogene.

When the door opens again and a light shines down the stairs, I open my eyes and I think it's finally Sunday. I must have slept right through my alarm that I started setting so I'd never miss doing my chores and marking off the days. I sit up on the sofa where I still do all my sleeping and look at the orange numbers on the clock: 11:53, it reads. But the light I see isn't the light at the bottom of the stairs, it's a flashlight, and I hear two voices. I hear his voice, and I hear a woman too. It isn't Sunday. It's still Saturday night, and he's brought someone with him.

Chapter 39

IMOGENE

Today

Imogene drops back down into her seat at the kitchen table. Next to her, Warren picks up the picture of Daddy, turns it upside down in his lap. Neither of them says anything more because from behind Christopher's back, Jo Lynne is jabbing a finger at them and signaling they better sit themselves down and shut themselves up. Once they're settled, Jo Lynne slips an oven mitt on one hand and takes the second batch of rolls from the oven. Imogene thinks to ask why so much food, but it's always too much food with Jo Lynne. As if he can sense Imogene is about to say something more to the boy, Warren leans over and whispers to her.

"Not another word out of you."

Imogene nudges him away. She knows enough about eyewitness accounts and suspect identification to know she has complicated Warren's job by showing Christopher the picture of Daddy, but she doesn't care. She knows now that Daddy had been keeping Christopher and his mama in that house. And it also means she was right about Tim Robithan and the other Knights being all tied up in this somehow. That fire wasn't an accident either. The Knights probably set it to clean up Daddy's mess, and then they put it out to save a property they felt entitled to. When her phone begins buzzing for the third time, Imogene slips it from her pocket and steps into the living room.

"Hey, Tillie," she says. Back at the table, Christopher has finished his first roll and Jo Lynne is offering him a banana. He shrugs as if she asked him if he's ever eaten one before. "Not a good time. If this is about the watches, Warren's here and I told him already."

"Ain't calling about the watches," Tillie says. "Think this is something you'll want to tend to."

"Can you e-mail me, then?" she says. "Send a picture, whatever information you got? Today really isn't a good day."

"Don't need to send no pictures." On Tillie's end of the line, a loud rattle sounds in the background, most likely him dropping his bundle of keys on the hook on the cash register where he always keeps them.

Imogene takes a few more steps into the living room.

"I really can't do this today," she says, dropping onto the sofa. "And why are you even open on a Sunday?"

She remembers this kind of tired. It's a deep-down tired, so deep her bones ache. She lived this way, day and night, for at least two years after Russell and Vaughn died. She'd been numb for being so tired, for not being able to sleep but not being able to get out of bed either. For not eating, not drinking, not caring or wanting. People didn't know what to say to her during those years. Most settled on giving her a hug, and they lingered as an awkward moment inevitably swelled between them, that moment no words can fill because no words are fitting, and then with a gentle squeeze, maybe to her hand or her shoulder, or maybe cool fingers rested on her cheek, they would walk away.

But after a little time passed, people began to say she could have made no difference. Don't torture yourself with what might have been. She would nod as if they were right. It seemed more polite than telling them how downright cruel they were for saying a mother couldn't help. It seemed more polite than screaming that maybe she couldn't have changed what happened, but at least, if she'd been there, she'd be dead too. Only Mama had known better. God willing, she would say to Imogene, this is the hardest trial that'll ever test you. Your heart'll keep beating; your lungs'll keep on too. And the rest of you will catch up, all in good time.

"I ain't open," Tillie says. "Café at the end of the block called me in about a broke window. Remember that necklace of your mama's?"

"Sure, I remember," Imogene says. "Long since settled."

"Not anymore."

Imogene rests her head against the back of the sofa and stares at Christopher. He is sitting with his hands in his lap while Jo Lynne holds up the banana and shows him how to pull one long slice of peel from it.

"Pardon?" she says. "You're talking about Mama's good necklace?"

"Damned if it didn't turn up hanging from my register this morning. Right there on the total key."

"I don't think so," Imogene says. In the kitchen, Christopher takes the banana from Jo Lynne, and this time, he pulls off a slice of peel. "It's been, what, four years, maybe five since it went missing."

"Maybe so, but it's your mama's necklace I'm looking at."

Mama hadn't been upset about the value of the necklace when it disappeared, not the monetary value anyway, but she'd been frantic to have lost one of her last connections to her mother. It had been her mama's and her mama's before her—a moonstone pendant on a sterling silver chain. She'd been certain she last wore it to Russell and Vaughn's funeral. She remembered for certain, because it was a good long time before she went to pull it out and wear it again. When she did, it was gone. The whole family searched for it, looked under every cushion, behind every dresser. Finding that necklace was the only thing Imogene cared about in the weeks and months after she lost her family.

In the end, everyone figured the necklace was stolen and pawned for cash. Though Imogene wouldn't have admitted it at the time, because even now it sounds pathetic, Mama's missing necklace was mostly why she decided to take up a career rescuing things. She hadn't been able to rescue her family so she had to rescue something else instead.

"You found it in the store?" Imogene leans forward to see Christopher smile and tap his fingers together. He's feeling the stickiness left behind by the banana. That one small thing being enough to make him smile is proof of how little he's had to smile about in his life. Again, Imogene can't let her mind settle on what might have happened to him down in that basement. "You mean someone came in wanting to sell it to you?"

It's familiar, sitting here like this and staring into the kitchen. She did the same just a few hours ago except she'd been staring at Tim Robithan and he'd been staring back and spouting off about Mama's property like it was his own. She had been tired and blurted out something about those watches he'd tried to sell down at Tillie's. She hadn't thought about it at the time, but Tim will know now that they're wise to what he's done and that means he might make his way to Tillie's shop with a mind toward getting those watches back. Sliding forward on her seat, she waves at Warren to get his attention and points at the phone. She covers the receiver and whispers for him to come talk to Tillie.

"Nobody came in selling nothing," Tillie says. "Window back there in the storeroom's been broke, but not a thing missing that I can tell. Was worried them watches were going to be gone, but they ain't. Only thing that ain't right is this necklace of your mama's that's hanging from my register as we speak."

Imogene holds up a single finger to Warren when he joins her in the living room so he'll know she isn't done talking yet.

"I don't understand, Tillie. What do you mean, someone left it?"

"Just that. Broke in and hung it right where I wouldn't miss it."

"Are you all right?" she says. "What did the police say?"

"Well, hell, I'm fine. And the police ain't said nothing. Didn't call them. I'm going to go complaining someone broke in to give me something? Don't make no sense."

Tillie starts to say something else, maybe about the cost of the broken window, but he stops midsentence. In the background, someone is banging on something.

"Hey there, Imogene," he says, coming back on the line. "I'm going to have to call you back."

"Wait," Imogene says. "What is it? Is something wrong?"

Again, Tillie's voice drops. "You say Warren Nowling is there with you?"

"Yes," she says, looking up at Warren. "He's standing right next to me."

"How about the two of you hustle on down here. Natalie Sharon's outside my door, banging to get in, and someone got ahold of her face but good. I'm guessing she's here about them watches, and I'm guessing Tim Robithan ain't far behind."

The banging grows louder, as if Tillie is walking toward it.

"We're coming right now," Imogene says, waving Warren toward the door. "Don't let her in, Tillie. Don't open that door."

Chapter 40

BETH

Before

I'm wearing my fuzzy socks and long sweatpants like I do every night, because even though the air conditioner he put in the window blows warm air too, it's still only March and I get cold at night without them. So when I pull the blanket up to my chin, it's not because I need anything else to keep me warm. I do it so I can hide. The two voices are coming from the top of the stairs, and two voices are scarier than just his one voice.

I know the sound and smell of people getting home late from a night out. I know the clicking of tall, skinny high heels and the smell of smoke and perfume all mixed together, and I know a woman's giggle and a man whispering in her ear in a way that isn't a real whisper. Before Julie Anna started to stay with me on Friday nights, Mama sometimes left me alone when she went out. I'd lie awake in my bed and hope that when Mama finally came home, I'd hear only her voice when she called out to tell me she was back. When the woman started coming once a month to check on us, Mama had to stop leaving me alone because she was afraid of getting in more trouble if the woman found out. She said I might get taken away so I'd better never tell anyone, and I never did but I still got taken away.

A woman's hand is the first thing I see as it slides down the railing. Then a pair of shoes follows, first one tall, skinny heel, then the other. I used to try on Mama's shoes when she was busy putting on her makeup in the bathroom before going out for the night. I'd wobble around in them, thinking my feet would never grow big enough to fit. Sometimes Mama laughed and took my picture. Other times, she hollered at me because I'd ruin them or break an ankle.

"What you got down here?" It's the woman's voice.

The toe of one shoe taps at the wooden stair before pressing down on it, and then the other shoe follows. Behind her, his footsteps are quieter than hers, and that makes me wonder if he's come in the middle of the night before without me knowing.

"Quiet," he says in a whisper that isn't really a whisper.

"What do I got to be quiet for?"

"Just go on."

"You got him?" she says. She's a pair of long, slender legs now.

"I got him fine."

And then I hear a third voice, though it isn't really a voice. It's a tiny chirp, a gurgle maybe. I want to run to my spot under the stairs where I sometimes hid in the beginning. I'd fall asleep under there and wake up on the sofa. But if I tried that now, they'd hear me. Instead, I push myself up and ready my flashlight. I only use it for emergencies now, like when the electricity stops working.

There's more giggling, and the glow from his flashlight bounces around the basement as they near the bottom of the stairs. I blink when it bounces over me, but quick as it does, it's gone and I'm in the dark again. They both stand on the stone floor now, and he hands her something. There's more chirping and gurgling.

"What are you up to?" the woman says as his boots hit the stairs again, but this time, his footsteps aren't light. I wonder if he's going to shut the door now, and if he does, which side of it he will be on.

The woman's head pulls back when the light at the bottom of the stairs pops on. She smiles and turns a shoulder to block the glare. Her hair is straight and dark, almost black, and hangs over her shoulders. She holds something in her arms, and as he comes back down the stairs, she smiles up at him and then looks down on the something. It's a baby. And then she looks at me.

I smile, not because she looks at me but because I think she is Julie Anna. She is small like Julie Anna and slender, though Julie Anna wouldn't wear the thick black lines around her eyes or a skirt that's so short. This woman, girl, is about the same age as Julie Anna too, because her skin is smooth and bright. But while I smile, the woman only stares. When he stops again at the bottom of the steps, she looks back at him, and then her eyes drift around the basement.

"I'm leaving," she says, not looking at him but at me.

"No," he says, resting a hand on her shoulder. "This is what I wanted to show you. Can't just leave."

She waves a hand, shooing him aside. "Get out of my way."

"I figure it could be the four of us," he says, sliding to one side to stop her from reaching the stairs. "You know, you and me, the baby and her."

"What the fuck are you talking about?"

In her arms, the baby starts to cry. She bounces him as she turns in a slow circle to take in the rest of the basement. She isn't Julie Anna. Her voice is nothing like Julie Anna's, and Julie Anna wouldn't say those words.

"She's living here?" the woman says. "You have her locked in here?"

"You and me, we'll get married," he says, stretching out both hands this time. "Like we talked about. Be a family."

"I ain't being a mama to no other kid," the woman says, trying again to reach the stairs, but again, he blocks her path, this time holding up a hand to stop her. "You better move," she says. "Right damn now."

"Tell her," he says, and he must be talking to me. "Tell her this is what you want, to be a family."

I slide lower on the cushions and don't know what to say. I want her to stop yelling because she's holding the baby and maybe something bad will happen and she'll fall.

"Her mama was a drinker," he says, reaching to take the woman by the arms, but she pulls away. "And she's dead now. This girl needs a family. You do too." Then he nods at the baby in the girl's arms. "And he needs a daddy. I can do all that, can take care of all of you."

"Take me home, Eddie, you sick, stupid fuck."

Eddie. That's his name. He's never told me. He said in the beginning I could call him Pa, same name Laura uses for her pa, but I never did. Eddie. His name is Eddie.

"Don't you never call me stupid," he says to the girl.

"I'll call you whatever the hell I want to, you stupid fuck. Getting a family ain't going to make you a man. Ain't going to make no one think any better of you neither. Now, get out of my way."

"Tell her we can be a family," he says, turning to look at me.

I've heard this kind of yelling before, and sometimes it meant Mama got smacked across the face. Now I think this woman might get smacked because his face is turning red and I know being called stupid makes him madder than anything. His own daddy calls him stupid. He tells me that almost every time he reads from the newspaper. See, I follow the news. I know what's what. I ain't stupid. Sick as fuck of people saying I'm too stupid. I nod when he says those things because I see that same red in his face and I know fists sometimes follow that kind of red.

"Tell her I ain't stupid and we can be a family."

The woman tries again to force her way past him, and this time, he pushes her and she almost falls. It's hard to say his name, even in my head, because now he's more like a real person. Eddie, his name is Eddie, has told me many times that his name is one of the biggest names in town, probably in the South, though he never said what that name was. I don't think this woman knows that because she's not talking like Eddie's the biggest man.

"I said get the fuck out of my way," the woman says, leaning forward and shouting the words. Her straight black hair falls along the sides of her face and hangs down over the baby still squirming in her arms. "You're a stupid fuck. Everyone told me so. And I damn sure ain't going to be part of your ready-made family."

"I already have a mama," I say.

The woman swings around like she's going to yell at me too. Instead, she stares. "Where is she?" she says, tossing her head to get the hair out of her eyes. "Your mama. Where is she?"

He takes the stairs two at a time again, but this time, instead of a light turning on, the door slams. I know the sound of the three locks being locked. Sometimes, he only locks one of them. I listen every time because maybe once, he'll forget and not lock any. This time he locks all three.

I've known him for two years, and I know he won't come tomorrow like he always does. I won't get my twenty minutes outside. I won't get to run into the field of pampas grass where he can't see me. I've known him for two years, and I wonder if he'll ever come again. Overhead, his footsteps fade like they always do when he leaves, and then there is silence.

Chapter 41

BETH

Before

The next day, Sunday, when four o'clock comes and goes and Eddie never shows up, Alison shouts at me for being wrong about him always bringing food and drinks and new books on Sundays. That's her name. Alison. Her eyes are wide and her long hair that was like a silky black curtain last night has turned frizzy. She has uneven ends like she cuts it herself. Mama cut her own hair and she was always real careful about uneven ends. Holding Christopher, that's her baby's name, in one arm, Alison begins walking between the kitchen and the sofa, back and forth, looking up the stairs each time she passes. As she walks, Christopher's head flops like I don't think it should be flopping.

"What if he leaves us down here?" she yells. And she says other things. "We'll run out of food. And what about air? Why are you here? What the fuck are you doing here?"

I sit on the sofa, knees pulled up to my chest, and press my hands over my ears, but I can still see Christopher bouncing and flopping. I don't like her asking why I'm here because it's like her saying that I asked to be here. I want to tell her he killed Julie Anna and stole me from my home. I want to tell her this was the day I was supposed to run away and see Mama again but that Alison and her baby ruined it. I should be the one who's mad, not her. I'm smarter now than I was when I tried to trick him with a broken bulb. I'm stronger and smarter and I know Stone Mountain is just outside and there's a lake, a magical lake nearer to heaven than any other place on earth. I want to scream it at her so she'll stop talking and stop walking, but I can't make myself say it out loud. I always thought heaven being just there outside was a sign I'd make it back to Mama one day. She loved God and heaven and singing in the church where we'd see Julie Anna and her parents every Sunday. But I don't tell this girl any of that because some things hurt too much working their way up and out.

"Wednesday," I say, closing my eyes and wishing that was enough to make her go away. "He'll come on Wednesday."

She stops walking. The sudden silence makes me look. She has let one hip fall out to the side so Christopher can rest on it and is staring at me like she doesn't know what Wednesday means. Christopher is staring too, as if he is waiting for me to save him. I know that feeling because I felt it sometimes with Mama. Sometimes I wanted someone to save me too.

"Wednesday," I say, louder this time. "That's his other day for coming."

"How the fuck we know when it's Wednesday?" she says, swings around, and starts walking again. "There's no damn windows." She throws one hand up in the air as if pointing out all the boarded-over windows. "Sure as shit can't tell day from night."

When she turns back my way, I jump from the sofa and reach for Christopher. He isn't crying or squirming, just holding on with his chubby arms and legs, and yet something in his blue eyes is begging me to take him. But Alison's eyes are different. She is breathing heavy, and her eyes look like something inside is about ready to break loose. When she hands Christopher to me, his legs clamp around my waist. He already knows he has to hold on because nobody else is doing it for him.

Three more days pass, and those questions of Alison's play over and over in my head. What if there isn't enough air? Enough food? Enough water? Wednesday comes and goes and Eddie still doesn't come, but Alison doesn't scream at me this time. From the bed where she's been sleeping almost all the time since we knew for sure

Eddie wasn't coming on Sunday, she stares at the steps until four o'clock turns into five and then rolls over.

Now it's Saturday night, and my back hurts from walking with Christopher on my hip. Back and forth, from one side of the basement to the other, I carry him, and if I bounce him just so and let him play with the blue stone that hangs from a chain around my neck, he doesn't cry. Ever since he came here a week ago, I have fed him, changed him the best I can using wadded-up paper towels, read to him, and walked him. I hold him at night, his small head resting where my neck meets my shoulder, and we sleep. When he wakes, I wake, and every day that I hold him, I worry more. My stomach sinks between my hip bones, deeper than it did before, because I'm afraid to eat. I try to, just a piece of bread or a few crackers, but I can't force a bite in my mouth. I worry Alison saying the things she said will make them come true and Eddie might never bring food again and we'll run out of the things Christopher can eat—mashed-up bananas, and carrots I boil on the hot plate until I can mash them too. And crackers. He likes sucking on them until they melt between his fingers.

I try to smile for Christopher whenever I sit down to feed him, because he looks right at me the whole time, and I don't want him seeing what's on the inside of me. I don't want my being scared to make him scared. I could always see the scared on the other side of Mama's eyes, so I think Christopher can see it on the other side of mine too. He's almost one, that's what Alison said. He can sit up on his own and can walk if he's holding my two fingers. His legs are spongy from fat and bow out when he stands, and he squeals at the cold stone on his feet. His tiny ankles wobble on the uneven floors. Even when I'm feeding him and he's happy to have carrots and bananas leaking from his mouth, I don't feel much like smiling. I feel like the basement is sliding deeper and deeper into the earth even though I still see the orange sliver every morning.

I'm already used to going to sleep tired and waking up tired.

After only a few days, I know what Mama meant when she said raising a baby is carrying a whole other life on your back, every day. Mama liked to tell me stories about how it was when I was a baby. She'd stare at pictures in the red photo album that creaked each time she flipped a page and tell about being tired like she never knew a person could be when I was first born. Never done such hard work, she'd say, touching my chin and looking into my face. You're so darn tired you forget the days are ticking by. You forget about things making sense.

Maybe it's the door closing that wakes me. Maybe it's the locks snapping into place. I open my eyes and feel as tired as when I went to sleep, and whatever it is that woke me, it's a normal sort of sound. Christopher is asleep between me and the back of the sofa, where I know he won't fall. My neck and cheek are damp from our being close and his warm breath mixing with mine. And then I remember those sounds aren't normal, not anymore.

I only know Eddie came because he left a box of food on the top stair. Inside are all the things he usually brings plus a can of baby formula and a package of diapers. I drop down on the stair next to the box and cry. I cry because we have food and maybe we aren't sinking into the earth, but I cry too because now I think he plans to keep us all down here. When Alison wakes, I tell her, because I have to, about going outside and the field with grass tall enough to hide us. I didn't tell before because it hurt too bad and I thought we were already sinking, but we aren't, not yet, because Eddie has come back.

I tell her we have to be quiet and good. We have to never yell when we hear him coming, and we have to keep things clean so we don't get critters. Tell him we're a family, you and me and Christopher. I know now that Eddie wanted a family because having a family would make him a man. That's what Alison told me. Everything Eddie does is to please his father and make him proud, and Eddie's father thinks having a family means a man can provide and protect, and a man like that can lead, and more than anything, Eddie wants to lead. So tell him we're already a family, I say to Alison. Tell him we'll be his family. I don't tell about Julie Anna and that Eddie killed her, because already Alison is mostly gone. I need for her to find that spot inside herself that wants things. Do what I say so he'll be happy. If he's happy, he'll take us outside and that will be our chance. Eventually we can run. The tall grass will hide us, and we can find a way out. But as many times as I say it, I'm afraid Alison doesn't really understand.

Chapter 42

IMOGENE

Today

Up ahead, Tillie's shop is quiet and all looks normal for a Sunday morning, except for the broken glass in his door. Imogene stumbles at the weight of Warren's forearm across her chest. She pushes it away, and when she tries to walk in front of him, he grabs the back of her shirt and holds tight. A patrol car is already parked in front of Tillie's, the only car on the block except for the few outside Belle's Café on the corner. Before Imogene and Warren left the house, Warren called in to have an officer respond right away, and that's who is walking toward them.

"Girl's in there," the officer says, jabbing a thumb toward the broken door. "Made this mess when Tillie wouldn't open up for her. Somebody had a time with her face too. Says she fell."

His name is Jacobson. He has thinning brown hair and a large stomach that hangs over his black belt. He's snagged the keys from Imogene's hand a time or two on a Saturday night, and she's seen him down at the lake with Daddy's other men. Even wearing a hood over his face, she'd known him because of his low-hanging belly and the awkward way he rocked from side to side to keep himself moving. Daddy used to like saying they had all kinds among them—police, judges, lawyers, and such—though Jacobson is the only police officer Imogene knows about these days.

"And I'm guessing you don't believe her story," Warren says.

The officer shrugs as if he doesn't much care. "Tillie says she goes with Tim Robithan. He might be inclined to take to a girl's face that way."

Warren glances at Imogene, his brows raised as if the officer's comment is more proof of the danger she brought on herself by tangling with Tim Robithan in her mama's kitchen. And then with a sweeping gesture, he motions for her to walk on inside the shop. He and the officer follow.

Once inside, Warren and the officer study the broken door and Imogene walks on in. Seeing Tillie, she makes her way toward him. He is standing alongside his workbench, and Natalie Sharon sits in his usual chair. The cloth she's holding to her face covers one eye. Though Imogene rarely talks to Natalie beyond a nod hello, they tend to find themselves at the same bar and sitting on similar bar-stools come one in the morning on any given night.

Even though it's chilly outside, Natalie wears a tank top. The slender straps hang loose over the ridges where her collarbone pro-trudes. Her long hair, not quite blond, not quite brown, hangs down around her face and over her shoulders, the tips dark and stiff with dried blood. Her left eye is tearing and red, her top lip is swollen where it has split, and Imogene is guessing whatever is hidden under the cloth she holds over the right side of her face is where the real trouble lies.

"Says it wasn't Tim Robithan what messed up her face," Tillie whispers, juggling a bag of ice that Natalie keeps waving off. "But I already told the officer I figure it sure was. Told him about them watches, too. Wasn't going to, but Natalie started to mouth off about them straightaway."

Imogene nods and glances around the small shop. A light in the back office is on, and someone is banging about.

"That's Mrs. Tillie back there," Tillie says, reassuring Imogene Tim Robithan isn't lurking somewhere in the shop. "She just got here. Drove herself over even though I told her to stay home. And Natalie here, she says Tim didn't give her them watches neither."

"I'm real sorry about all this," Imogene says. "I said something to Tim about the watches this morning. He was at the house. Damn, this is my fault."

She's talking partly to Natalie and partly to Tillie and, truth be told, partly to herself for letting her life get away from her. She sees proof of the mess she's made of herself in the eyes of men like this Officer Jacobson, who's still talking with Warren. Men like him look at her like they know something more about her than they do, like they've boiled her down to the things she can do to them and for them. They look at Natalie Sharon the same. They used to look at Imogene with pity in the early years after Russell and Vaughn died. And then when she started stumbling out of bars with men she scarcely knew, their looks turned to yearning, a clamoring to be the next to have a turn with her, and lately their looks have turned to disgust.

"I wasn't thinking," she says, running her hands through her hair, her fingers catching in the tangles. "Natalie, you especially. I'm real sorry. I sure didn't mean for this to happen, to get you in trouble with Tim."

"Was your daddy," Natalie says. Her face is tiny and she might be beautiful if not for her eyes set too deep in her head. It's like parts of her insides have rotted away, and there's less and less to hold up her outsides.

"I already told you, Natalie," Tillie says. "You lie about Tim beating you, no one is going to believe nothing else you have to say."

Natalie stretches her long, slender fingers as if they're stiff and rolls her head side to side. "I ain't never said Tim didn't beat me. I said I wasn't beat by no one. That's different, you know. Besides, it was her daddy." Natalie points up at Imogene. "And that's the truth."

Up near the front door, Mrs. Tillie, a broom and dustpan in one hand, has joined Warren and the officer. She holds a tissue to her nose with her other hand and is likely crying. The officer takes the broom and dustpan from her as he glances at Natalie. He shakes

his head like Mrs. Tillie's crying is Natalie's fault and gives her a
nod meant to remind her to stay put and keep her mouth shut, a
look he's given Imogene when she's lunged at him while trying to
get her car keys back. As the officer begins sweeping up the glass,
Warren helps Mrs. Tillie to a tufted chair just inside the door. He
squats before her and looks up into her face. He's done the same to
Imogene when she was slumped over a barstool.

"What are you saying about my daddy?" Imogene asks Natalie.

"He give me the watches," Natalie whispers. "That's what I'm
supposed to tell you. Wasn't Tim what give them to me. Was your
daddy. He told me take them down to Augusta. Said they'd have
pawnshops down there, that they'd have the money to buy them.
Said Mr. Tillie wouldn't have no money like that. But your daddy
died and I didn't want to drive so far. Wasn't Tim. That's mostly
what I'm supposed to say."

"You telling me my daddy stole those watches and wanted you
to sell them?"

Tillie sets the bag of ice on the table next to Natalie and guides
Imogene farther into the store, where they're hidden by a shelf
filled with DVR players.

"She says she did the stealing," he says, "but that it was your
daddy's idea. He promised to pay her. Said she could steal them
watches easy seeing as she was at the Robithan house often enough.
Your daddy having money trouble?"

"If Tim didn't do anything, then why did he beat on her like
that?" Imogene says, not answering Tillie's question because she
doesn't want to involve him in the mess Daddy made.

"I'm guessing he must have thought she was telling people he's
the one who stole. Made her come here and say otherwise. Lord, I
hate to think what this girl is in for if Robert Robithan gets word
of this."

"Is he going to help her?" Imogene asks, nodding toward the
officer at the front of the shop.

Tillie shrugs. "Listen, I got to ask. Your daddy, they sure he died of something natural?"

Imogene looks from Natalie to Tillie. "You think . . . ?" She pauses. "No, nothing like that. It was his heart. That's for certain. Nobody did anything to him."

"Just had to ask." Then Tillie pulls Imogene closer as he leans to look around the display. "But listen, them watches ain't why I called." Reaching in his shirt pocket, he pulls out a necklace by its silver chain. "Am I right? It's your mama's?"

Imogene cups her hands, and Tillie drops the necklace into them. The silver chain is dull, but the pale blue moonstone, hardened moonlight so the tale goes, shines and sparkles in the light overhead. Mama had been heartbroken when the necklace disappeared. It had been her only tie to all the Simmons women who came before her. They're the ones who saved us, Mama once said to Imogene, and though Mama didn't say it, Imogene knew she meant those Simmons women, believing like they did and praying like they did to have no sons, saved Imogene and Mama from sinking into all that hate.

"Yes," Imogene says. "It's Mama's, all right. She'll be thrilled to get it back."

"Well then, take it and get on out of here." Tillie presses a hand to her lower back. "You don't need none of whatever is going on here and sure to hell don't need the police getting ahold of your mama's necklace."

"Where did it come from?" Imogene says, slipping the necklace into her front pocket because Tillie is right about it being taken as evidence.

"Seemed strange to me that it showed up at the same time as all this watch nonsense. Asked Natalie already. Says she don't have nothing to do with it."

"You believe her?"

Tillie straightens, lifts his chin, and puckers his lips as if he's thinking. "Told her I have tapes. Didn't seem to trouble her. Figure that means she's telling the truth."

"What did the tapes show?"

"Won't show nothing," Tillie says. "Only one camera." Then he leans out again and nods toward the front of the store. "Pointed there toward the door. Whoever done this with the necklace, they come in through the storeroom. Got a broken-out pane of glass back there too. But Natalie don't know that. Least, I think she don't."

"Imogene." It's Warren's voice. From the sound of it, he's still up near the front of the shop with Mrs. Tillie. "Let's get you on back home."

The Sharons are always in trouble around town. There's a half dozen of them, and they're either speeding, drinking, stealing, or lying, so this isn't anything unusual to Warren. He probably wouldn't even have come down, but instead would have let Jacobson handle it, if Imogene hadn't insisted.

"If the police want to take the watches," Imogene says to Tillie before joining Warren, "you let them. Don't get yourself involved. Sooner they're out of your shop, the better." Then she takes hold of Tillie's forearm. "Promise me, Tillie. You don't want to involve yourself with Tim Robithan. Not Robert Robithan either. I don't want what happened to Natalie over there happening to you or Mrs. Tillie."

Chapter 43

BETH

Before

It's a Wednesday, and I've been in the basement for three years. That's my first thought when footsteps cross overhead. The floorboards creak. Someone is in the house. I haven't thought about Wednesday being Wednesday in almost a year, because ever since he locked Alison in down here, Eddie doesn't come on Wednesdays anymore. Only Sundays, and when he does come, it's only to leave food on the stairs. He never comes down. My hair is longer than it's ever been, and I'm taller than ever too, taller than Alison, who's twenty-one, while I'm only thirteen. My arms and legs are thin and hard now, and I have a waist like Mama said I would get one day. The footsteps grow louder. They stop. The door at the top of the stairs opens and stays open.

I grab Christopher from the floor. He's walking now and rarely stops moving, and his chubby body has begun to turn lean. As his legs clamp on and his sticky fingers reach for my mouth, he doesn't feel soft and spongy like he once did. He makes a cooing sound that I quiet by pressing a finger to his lips. Alison is lying on the bed. She must hear the door too but doesn't move. I'm not sure she can. Holding Christopher close to my chest, I cup his head with one hand so he can hear my beating heart. His silky dark hair has grown long and thickened up in the past year. I used to dream that the door would open and it would be someone other than Eddie, someone who would save us. I try not to think that anymore because it's always Eddie, and when it is, I feel relief mixed with terrible pain. Relief that he hasn't left us and pain that we're still here. But today is Wednesday. He doesn't come on Wednesdays anymore. It could be someone new, and so I can't stop myself from hoping.

For eleven months and two weeks, Eddie has come only on Sunday mornings, always leaving food and diapers on the top step. Last Sunday, I asked Eddie if he would please bring a potty chair because Christopher is nearly out of diapers. He brought two dolls one Sunday, and another he brought a wooden cradle. It fell when he closed the door but didn't break too bad, and he brought a small television set another time. He told me how to hook up the antenna before closing and locking the door. Not long ago, he brought a small refrigerator.

"Where is she?" Eddie hollers down the stairs.

Christopher presses his face into my shoulder at the sound of a man's voice. It washes over me, the relief mixed with pain, but both are quickly replaced by fear. So many Wednesdays have passed without Eddie coming here, and now he has. Something is different. Something has happened to make him come back again, and I'm afraid of what that something is.

"She's sleeping," I say, glancing again at the bed.

"Wake her up."

Bouncing Christopher so he'll not start to cry, I squat next to the bed and look Alison straight on. Her eyes are open, but she doesn't seem to see us.

"You hear me?" he shouts, not moving from the top stair. He'll be listening for Alison, probably wondering if she'll run up the stairs and try to force her way out again. She did that twice, in the first months she was here, and he's ready for her to do it again. He won't know what she's become.

"Yes, I hear you," I say, calling out over my shoulder. Turning back to Alison, I whisper, "Alison, you have to wake up." On my hip, Christopher kicks and leans, mimics me and says wake up, wake up, one of the first phrases he put together, and tries to grab a handful of Alison's hair. "Please, you have to wake up."

Alison wasn't always so lost. During her first few months in the basement, she liked to listen as I read aloud to Christopher from the books about Laura and Pa. I also tried to get her to study the textbooks with me. I loved them, no matter the subject, because they were a reminder that the outside was still there and always would be, and I thought Alison would love that too. But she said no. She only wanted to hear about the outside I remembered. I asked her once to tell me about where she lived before the basement, but she had nothing to say. She had only just moved to Georgia from Alabama when Eddie locked her up. Nothing to tell about Alabama. Nothing to tell about Georgia. Eddie was the best she could find. She had known he was too old, but he talked a big game and she needed a daddy for Christopher. I was pretty sure that meant Christopher's daddy was back in Alabama.

She told me that same day about fellows who talk a big game and how they are always trouble. She also told me about the boy she loved back in Alabama. He was tall and smart and so Goddamn handsome, like a boy in a magazine. I leaned in like she was reading to me from one of my books as she told all about the boy she loved and the way he touched her and peeled away her clothes. She loved him so bad it scared her. That's when her face changed from happy and bright to hard and angry. She was right to be scared, she said, because he ran off on her the second that happened, and she nodded at Christopher.

She asked how old I was and if I had started to bleed. I nodded and told her I already knew about sex because I read a book that told all about it. She said it was good I knew because the subject was bound to come up whether I liked it or not, seeing as how Eddie was a man and I was, well, mostly a woman. Leaning forward, she touched the stone that hung from a chain around my neck. Eddie give you this, didn't he, she asked and nodded like it was another sign of things to come between him and me. And then she said there ain't a book been written that will tell you what you really need to know, and that made her laugh, about the only time she ever laughed. Her laughing made me laugh. And once I started, I couldn't hardly stop. I laughed until my laughing turned to crying. And when my crying faded and the worst feeling I've ever had took over because I remembered what being happy felt like, she asked if Eddie had made a move on me yet. I shook my head and didn't tell her about the time he lifted a strand of my hair and let it slide through his fingers. He will one day, she said. Just remember that him doing something bad don't make you bad. Remember that, and you'll be okay.

I was lonelier after that day because feeling happy again, even for such a short time, had reminded me of all that I had lost. Every day, I became busier with Christopher, and he filled me so full I didn't always notice how lonely I felt, but it was always there, steadily dripping down from overhead. And sometimes, late at night, it would come in a wave that drenched me. The day that I laughed until I cried was my best day and Alison's last good day.

"Please, wake up," I whisper to Alison again and listen hard for any sound that Eddie has started walking down the stairs. "Wake up and be good and maybe we'll get to go outside when Sunday comes."

From the bed she rarely leaves anymore, Alison swings her legs around. I stand and step aside as she sets her feet on the cold floor. The back of her hair is knotted up into a wad because she never brushes it, and she's wearing a thick flannel shirt over a pair of sweatpants. I wash her sometimes when she's sleeping like Mama used to wash the old people, and she doesn't smell so bad anymore. At the sound of Eddie's boots climbing down the first few stairs, her eyes flick in that direction. He's moving slow, feeling out what Alison will do.

"He's coming," I say, still whispering as I bounce Christopher. "He killed Julie Anna, Alison. That's why I'm here. Remember when I told you about Julie Anna?" When Alison first came here,

I told her all about Julie Anna, how her face was always scrubbed clean and that she was smart and would be going to college, but I never told that Eddie killed her. I couldn't tell because saying it made it real. But I have to tell her now so she'll know what Eddie can do, what he might do if we're not good.

"Do you hear me?" I say. I shift Christopher to my other hip in hopes he won't hear me because he's starting to copy the things I say. "He killed her. So be good. Don't yell. And don't run at him."

I've not been so good about keeping things clean since Eddie stopped coming down. I'm always too busy taking care of Christopher, so as Eddie's boots hit the next few stairs, I glance at the kitchen and hope I've left it clean. The canned vegetables he brought last Sunday are still stacked on the kitchen table. We always eat the things that might spoil first, things like eggs, bread, and cheese and the oranges Eddie brings sometimes, and I try to save the things that won't spoil. In Laura's stories, they saved up food for winter, so I save up too. I especially save the things that come in cans, hiding them under the stairs where Alison won't look for them, just in case he ever stops coming and also because Alison eats more than her share. She sleeps and she eats and she stares at the small television that only gets two fuzzy channels. I don't have time to store the cans now. With Christopher still in my arms, I hurry back to the sofa as Eddie reaches the bottom step.

"We go outside today," he says, looking at Christopher but not at me. "Get yourselves together."

In all these months, Eddie has never seen Christopher and he's surprised by how much he's grown. Eddie's changed too. He's bigger in the stomach, and his white shirt pulls tight like the buttons might pop. His cheeks are fuller, and his dark hair is speckled by more gray. As if getting his first good look at me, he drops his head off to one side. I've changed too in the past year. Even though we sometimes saw each other when he was leaving boxes at the top of the stairs, they were quick meetings in dim light.

"Are all of us going?" I say, glancing at Alison, who is still sitting on the edge of the bed, and I hug Christopher tight, which makes him push against me. He was frightened at first, but now he's excited at seeing someone new. He kicks his legs, his signal that he wants down. I wrap a hand around one of his warm feet to calm him.

Eddie nods as he reaches out to touch the tips of Christopher's toes. This makes Christopher go still, and he tucks his face into the spot where one of my shoulders meets my neck. I want to turn away so Eddie can't reach him, but I force myself not to move because it might make Eddie angry if he knows I don't want him touching Christopher, or talking to him or even looking at him. My body is shivering for wanting so badly to pull Christopher away from Eddie and knowing I don't dare. Instead, I hold Christopher tight, our faces pressed together, until Eddie steps past us. And then I exhale.

"You too," he says, meaning Alison though he doesn't look at her. He smells like the outside. It's March again. The magnolias bloom in March. He smells of magnolia blooms and the dirt he's walked through and cigarette-stained fingers, and he fills the basement, making it suddenly too small.

Pushing off the bed, Alison slips her feet into a pair of sneakers that are too big and walks toward the stairs without saying anything. She's hunched over like the weight of her own head and shoulders is too much for her to carry. He tells me don't bother when I go to grab a jacket for Christopher, so I slip on my shoes, and before starting up the stairs, I stuff Christopher's feet into the only pair of shoes he has. Something about this—him coming down here after so long, him saying we're going outside on a Wednesday when it's always been a Sunday, him not looking me in the eye—makes me certain going outside isn't going to be a good thing.

The New Klan

The late 1970s saw another surge in Klan membership. In 1974, a former neo-Nazi organized the Knights of the Ku Klux Klan and began traveling the country to spread the Klan's message of white supremacy. Shunning the title of Grand Wizard for the more mainstream title of national director, the former neo-Nazi wore business suits for public appearances as opposed to the traditional robe and hood. He spoke in an articulate fashion that helped him gain national media coverage, and in a bid to appeal to a broader segment of the population, he attempted to disguise the Klan's radical and hateful views.

Chapter 44

TILLIE

Today

Telling Natalie Sharon to stay put until Officer Jacobson finishes with his phone call and comes back inside, Tillie walks behind the counter and drops the two watches in a small white box. He'll ask Officer Jacobson if he might see Mrs. Tillie home and stand guard over the house after he's taken Natalie to the police station and returned the watches to Robert Robithan. Tillie wants to make sure Robert Robithan knows he had no part of whatever Edison Coulter was up to when he stole them watches, and Officer Jacobson should understand that.

"You're free to leave," the officer says, being careful of the broken glass, leaning inside and looking at Natalie.

Still holding a bag of ice to her right eye, Natalie stares at him but doesn't move.

"She can't leave," Tillie says, holding up the box with the watches. "And you got to return these to Robert. And take Natalie down to the station too."

Officer Jacobson is a good bit younger than Tillie, but still Tillie knows he's one of the Knights, and as such he'll appreciate full well how careful Tillie needs to be.

"Robert said them watches weren't stole," Officer Jacobson says, glancing between Natalie and Tillie. "Said he intends to come by personal to see to them."

"And does that mean he intends to see to her too?" Tillie says.

He's also wondering what Robert might intend for Tillie. After all, Tillie took the watches from Natalie, and he didn't call the police straightaway. None of that will look good to a man like Robert Robithan. In fact, it might look like Tillie was intending to sell those watches and split the money with Edison Coulter.

"If Robert says they weren't stole, then there ain't no crime," the officer says, "and there ain't nothing for me to do here."

"She broke my door," Tillie says. "Ain't you got to take her in for that?"

What Tillie doesn't say, though Jacobson will know Tillie's thinking it, is that Natalie would be safer inside a police station than out on the street.

"Robert said he'd see to that too," the officer says, tipping his hat in Natalie's direction.

Tillie stares at the front door as it falls closed. Robert Robithan was on the other end of that phone call and now he knows Natalie and his watches are here in Tillie's shop, and Tillie too.

"You heard him," Natalie says, walking out from behind Tillie's worktable. She tugs on one corner of her cutoff shorts and slides a finger under the strap hanging off her shoulder, lifting it back where it belongs. "I guess I don't get no money, huh?"

"You can't leave," Tillie says.

"Sure I can," Natalie says. "He said I ain't done nothing wrong."

"You stole from Robert Robithan," Tillie says, setting the box back on the counter. "And he is on his way here right now. He's coming for these watches, and he's coming for you. You're going to have to do as I say, and I don't want no argument."

He'd rather not tell Natalie what she might be facing, but he will if he has to.

The first thing Tillie does is put Natalie and Mrs. Tillie to work filling a suitcase with clothes that'll fit Natalie. Riffling through the racks and picking out clothes for herself and it not mattering how much any of it costs makes Natalie happy, and she forgets for the moment about wanting to go home.

"Pick out some warm things, too," Tillie says, pulling open the front door. "And dishes and such. Pack it all up."

While they're pulling clothes from hangers, Tillie hustles down to the bank at the end of the block and withdraws $800 from the ATM, the most it'll let him take from his account. When he returns, he takes all the cash from the safe and register—another $1,328—and tucks it inside an envelope. Next, he looks up the non-emergency number down to the police station and writes it on a small pad of paper. When Mrs. Tillie hollers that she and Natalie are done, he carries everything they packed up to his car and loads it all in the trunk. Last thing, he opens the car door and motions for Natalie to get in.

"I don't get what's happening." Natalie stares at the open door but doesn't move. Her hair has been combed out and she's wearing a blue dress, both things making her look like the girl she is instead of a grown woman already worn to a nub.

"There's a little over two thousand dollars in there," Tillie says, helping her into the car. She looks straight ahead as if not sure where she is as Tillie hands her the envelope. "That'll tide you over. You get yourself to the interstate and head north. Keep driving until the weather turns colder than you ever felt."

"But I ain't never been in the cold."

"No place is as cold as six feet under," Tillie says.

"I still don't know why I got to go," Natalie says, looking up at Tillie with her one good eye. "Can't I maybe go home instead? It's just watches."

"It ain't just watches, not when they belong to a Robithan," Tillie says. "You can call your mama when you pass Atlanta. But no going home to say good-bye."

Tillie and Mrs. Tillie wait as Natalie pulls away, and once she's gone, they walk back inside the shop, where they both know they're going so they can wait for Robert Robithan to come.

Without saying anything about what might happen next,

Mrs. Tillie puts in a call to the fellow what can board up the broken window and door and then goes to work straightening shelves in the storeroom. Tillie hangs his keys where he always keeps them, sits behind his worktable, but instead of getting to work on a phone, he watches out the front window, and when a red truck rolls past nearly an hour later, he stands. If he's not mistaken, Robert Robithan drives a red truck.

Chapter 45

CHRISTOPHER

Today

I'm alone in my room, but I can hear the grandma and Miss Jo Lynne. When they walk, the floors creak. First they creak loud, but then the creak gets quieter. I think that means they're far away now. Every time one creak ends, I wait, make my hands into fists, and listen for the next. I scoot deep into my chair with wings that almost wrap around me. If I lean a little, the sliver of light doesn't hurt my eyes.

I hear their voices too, so I'm not alone. I don't have to climb stairs here and no one unlocks for me. This door can open, I think, anytime, and that makes my head spin most of all. Open and close. Open and close. The air is full and light, and so much of it all makes me wobbly. I wonder does Imogene or her mama scrape underneath this door so the air keeps moving inside like Mama does to the door at the top of the stairs. Once a month, the first day, Mama uses the straightened-out hanger to poke and scrape under the door so we can keep breathing air.

When I was done eating my banana, Imogene said she had to go away for just a little bit and asked am I okay to stay alone. I said yes, and when she left, I stayed with Miss Jo Lynne and the grandma until my eyes got tired and I went back to the room that they say is mine. Now the room is quiet except I still hear the creaks. My head between my eyes hurts some, and I'm tired like after we have exercise time. This bed is bigger than my basement bed and this pillow is softer. Even though I told Imogene yes, I'm okay to stay alone, I'm afraid she won't come back. My mama was supposed to come back and she never did. Not yet. Before she left, Mama said to be brave like Laura in her books, so that's what I'm trying to do. But I hope I don't have to do it much longer.

I think I slept and now I'm awake again and I hear more footsteps. But these are different footsteps. I know all about the different footsteps people make. I'm hearing footsteps made with big feet, heavy feet, feet that are maybe wearing boots. They're growing louder. Every step is bigger and heavier than the last. I think they're just outside the door that isn't all the way closed when they stop.

Mama always goes up the stairs on Wednesdays. We hear those big footsteps and she knows it's time. She dresses in a white dress on Wednesdays that is thin and hard for her to pull over her head, sits on the bottom step to wait for the clanking of the locks, and then she calls out, I'm coming, and climbs the stairs. I usually only see his boots and the bottom of his pants. They're usually blue, and sometimes he leaves dirt on the stairs that I brush into my hands after he's gone. The last time Mama went, she said she'd be back. She told me to wait at the top of the stairs even though I am never allowed to go there, except I do to get the dirt he leaves behind. But this time was different, she said, and I should wait there on the top step unless I heard big, heavy footsteps. Mama's footsteps aren't heavy. His are.

As I sat at the very top stair, scrunching myself as small as I could so I'd fit and wouldn't fall, I pressed my ear to the door and listened. I listened even though I was scared of hearing those heavy footsteps and even when I got tired of listening and my ear started to hurt and even when my knees wanted to stretch out instead of being scrunched. Mama said that if I heard those footsteps, I should hide under the stairs like Harry from the books did. Hide like Harry until I come back, she said, and be brave. But I didn't want to be brave. I wanted Mama to stay in the basement, but she said this was our chance to get out. I didn't know what out was, and she said it was like where we went on Sundays except much bigger and we'd get to stay all day and all night. We'd get to stay forever.

But Imogene came instead. Mama says Imogene is the one who will save us, but I think maybe Mama is wrong. Imogene isn't quite what Mama said she would be. Imogene's hair is red and filled with curls, so Mama was right about that. But I always thought Imogene would know me because I know her, and I can tell she doesn't. She looks mostly at the ground instead of at me and she picks at her fingernails. Mama calls those bad habits. Mama makes me practice looking people in the eyes. She says that tells people you're strong, honest, and friendly. I shake Mama's hand, say pleased to meet you, and tilt my head so I can look her straight in the eyes. I think Imogene doesn't look in my eyes because maybe she is afraid of me. Mama never said that would happen. She says Imogene might take care of me one day and help me grow up, but she never said Imogene would be afraid of me. When Mama says those things, it scares me and makes me grab on to her hand tight and never want to let go. If Imogene is taking care of me, that will mean Mama isn't, and if Mama isn't, I worry that means something bad has happened to her.

The footsteps haven't moved from outside the door that isn't all the way closed, and I'm starting to get that feeling again, like this outside world is too heavy for me. There's too much. The kitchen floor is shiny and white and makes me pinch my eyes almost all the way closed. There is glass in the windows and not boards, and glass catches the sun and makes it too bright. There are lots of voices here and too many things plugged in that will break the electricity. Too much air. Too much light. Too much to smell and hear and feel and see. Too much of everything. Still sitting in the chair that hugs me with its big wings, I pull my knees to my chest, squeeze them tight, and the door with no locks that Imogene didn't all the way shut slowly opens and the man from the top of the stairs steps into the room and presses a finger to his lips.

"Don't say nothing," he says in a whisper that rattles as it makes its way up his throat and out of his mouth. "Don't say nothing about me, and I'll take you to your mama. You and me, we'll go together, real soon, as soon as it gets dark, and we'll find her. Just so long as you don't say nothing."

Chapter 46

BETH

Before

It's just like the first time Eddie led me outside, only this time I know his name and he doesn't bother tying a dark cloth around my head, or Alison's or Christopher's either. Still, as I hold Christopher tight to my body, pressing my mouth to his ear and whispering that we'll be fine, I feel like I'm walking toward the edge. Christopher must feel it too, the something in the air that is warning us, because he lets me hold him tight even though our skin has turned hot and sticky from us being pressed so close together. Alison walks ahead, her head still hanging as if she's studying the ground, and Eddie nudges me from behind and tells me to hurry it up. I start shaking my head because I don't want to go anymore. I stop and turn so I can tell him, but he gives me another shove.

The kitchen door that leads out the back of the house is already open. It's the only door we ever use, the only door that isn't boarded over. That open door isn't the thing that makes my feet stop. Instead, it's the screen door. Whenever we would push through it on our way outside, back when Eddie still took me outside, it would slap closed behind us. But today, that screen door is standing open and that means someone on the outside is holding it.

Alison doesn't know what I know, so she walks straight through the open doorway. She doesn't look up, isn't frightened, doesn't even seem to know she's outside. It's like someone tipped Alison upside down and emptied her out and now nothing is left inside. She's an empty shell. I stop walking, squeeze Christopher, turn a shoulder so he is as far from that open doorway as I can get him and so I'm between him and it, and I make myself watch. Even from the kitchen, I can smell the fresh air and it's like my lungs haven't filled up, not all the way, since I was last outside. Eddie gives me another shove, but this time, I push back.

"We don't want to," I say.

He takes me by the arm, squeezes, and pulls me along. "Good Lord, it's all you've been asking for."

Alison has reached the bottom step, and through the doorway where the screen still stands open, I see her turn as if she is finally seeing something. She is seeing whoever is holding open the door, but nothing about her changes. She's like that now. If she thinks anything or wants anything, she never says it. She only takes things in but never lets anything out. I stop at the threshold where the outside meets the inside and I make myself look too. It's another man this time. Not a woman like when Alison came. That's all I see. Thick shoulders. Dark hair. A baseball hat like Mama used to wear when we did Sunday yard work. He nods, signaling for me to come on out.

I walk down the three steps, slowly, no quick movements, and lower myself to the ground so Christopher's feet can touch. I shiver to feel the outside air on my skin. The freshness is like a sharp edge after so long inside. Sitting cross-legged, I pull Christopher into my lap. He clings to me, both arms wrapped around my neck, and buries his face in my hair. I pull back to look into his eyes, but they are squinting, nearly closed. It's the sunlight. I hold a hand above them and make a shadow on his face. Over Christopher's shoulder, I see that the new man is watching me. He smiles and tilts his head to see me tending Christopher. I turn away, look straight ahead. Just to the side, where I can see her without turning my head, Alison stands, her arms hanging loose, her face hidden by her black hair. Behind me, a lighter snaps and the smell of cigarette smoke drifts over us, pushing out the light sweetness that hung in the air.

"Hey," the new man calls to me. "How old are you now?"

"Almost fourteen," I say. Christopher lets go of my neck, squirms until he's sitting in my lap, and lets his legs dangle so his toes almost touch the ground. "In a few months, I'll be fourteen."

The air is tightening between all of us, and I'm not sure why. I hug Christopher close and bury my nose in his hair. It smells of shampoo and of the peanut butter he likes to eat on his bananas. I close my eyes so I can pretend it's just him and me out here, but he wiggles loose, lays his top half over one of my legs, and digs a hand into the soft dirt. He holds it up for me to see and then for the new man who is standing behind us to see.

"Dirt," Christopher says, or rather asks.

"Yes, dirt," I whisper.

I've been telling Alison all about the outside in the year since she's been here, not only because she asked but because it kept it real for me. And it's just as I remembered. The pampas grass is tall and greening, and the light is bright, no feel of sunset in the air. I told Alison if we were good, he'd bring us outside again, and the day would come when I could run and be hidden by the tall clumps of grass. I told her about the pathway between the stalks being just big enough for me but too narrow for him. I would get far away and tell everyone about Alison and Christopher. I told her those things when I still thought she'd be Christopher's mama. Now I couldn't leave him, and she couldn't be the one to run. Or maybe she could, but if she did run, I think she'd keep running and forget all about us and never tell anyone anything. One day, when Christopher is old enough to come with me, he and I together will be the ones to run.

I pull Christopher back from where he's doubled over my leg. The footsteps behind us make me turn. They're sudden and kick up bits of gravel. The new man is running toward the grass, and Alison is gone. I didn't hear her move from her spot, but she's disappeared and now she's hidden by the tall grass, slipping between the rows. I start to scramble backward but stop because Eddie is standing behind me. I knock up against his legs. They're firm and don't move.

"Stay put," he says, leaning this way and that to get a look at what's going on. "Don't concern you."

I hear it then, a scream. I press my hands over Christopher's ears. His small fingers grab at my collar as he tries to pull himself closer. We tuck our heads together, and I wait for a second scream because hearing one is too much like Julie Anna's one scream. One scream means it's already over.

Eddie's legs ease away from the back of me. When I look up at him, the last of the sun catches me in the eye. In a few minutes, it'll settle behind the house and we'll be in its shadow. He shrugs.

"Looks like I was wrong," he says, taking in a deep breath through his nose and blowing it out his mouth so his lips flutter. "Girl had been fine if she'd have stayed put. Damn it all."

"What's he done?" I say, not looking up at Eddie anymore but not looking out into the field either.

"You never tried to run," he says. "Always waited for it. But you never did."

I can't let the fear get hold of me, not with Christopher right here in my arms. He'll feel it if I give in, and it'll do something terrible to him. This kind of fear has to leave a mark. Eddie had been watching me all those days when I thought he was watching his cigarette smoke or sitting in the patio chair and reading the newspaper or tipped back, a hat pulled over his eyes, making me think he was asleep. If I would have tried to run, I'd have been the one letting out a single scream. Just like Julie Anna. Just like Alison.

"But why?" I ask. "Why now?"

Eddie shrugs and tips his head toward the field where the man disappeared. "He seen me buying diapers. Didn't like the idea of one of you down here. Sure didn't like the idea of three."

"Who is he?" I ask.

"None of your damn business who he is. Just mind yourself."

I read all about the Klan in one of my history books. Eddie doesn't know about the book, because if he did, I'm sure he'd take it away. I know about the robes and hoods they wear and the crosses they burn and all the people they hate, so many kinds for so many reasons. It makes me wonder who is left that they don't hate. And I know about the many people they killed—shot, bombed, stabbed, hanged, and burned—and all the courts who let them go free. I know Eddie is one of them and that's why he came for Julie Anna. This man, I'm certain, is one of them too. All he needs is a reason to hate Christopher and me and he'll kill us like he has killed Alison.

It's a rustling first, dirt crunching, and then the new man walks out of the grass. He straightens his hat, and as he tucks in the back of his shirt, he stumbles. His chest is pumping up and down, and his eyes are rolling from Eddie to me and back again as if he's dizzy.

"God damn, Eddie," he says. "What the hell do we do now?"

Eddie says nothing, but he's looking down on me and Christopher like he's afraid for us and sorry for us all at the same time. With both arms wrapped around Christopher, I struggle to my feet. I have to do something, and I know what trying to run will get me.

"You don't have to do anything," I say to the new man. "You didn't do nothing wrong. It was Alison's fault. I told her to be good. Been telling her for a whole year. Not your fault she can't listen."

The man is staring at me, the bill of his hat throwing a heavy shadow over his eyes. But even though I can't see them very well,

I can tell they're locked on me now and not rolling from side to side anymore.

"I told her to be good," I say again, because the new man's shoulders are softening as I talk and his breathing is slowing down. "It was her fault. Not yours. Not your fault. I know you're just trying to keep us safe."

I'm making him believe he knows what he's doing. Mama once told me that's mostly what people want, men especially. Don't matter if it's true, just make them believe and they'll be happy. Be a cactus inside but make them think you're a rose.

After a long silence between the three of us, the new man nods. With Eddie close behind, I hurry back inside and down into the basement. I look back once, and the new man is watching us. I know it, and so does Eddie. Christopher and I were moments away from ending up like Alison.

Once Christopher falls asleep, which he does quickly because he's exhausted by the outside, too exhausted even to notice Alison is no longer here in the basement, I work quickly to wash the sheets on the small bed and hang them to dry. Even though Alison mostly never talked, the basement is quieter without her and smaller somehow. I feel bad wanting to wash her away, but those used sheets are like having a dead body down here with us. When I've wrung out and smoothed the last sheet and clipped it tight to the line, I crawl back under the stairs where I know Christopher can't see me and won't hear me, and I cry and shake and scream into a pillow.

The next Wednesday, the new man comes. He brings a pop-up crib. He sets it up, tells me to put Christopher in it. He sits on the stairs while I sing to Christopher and pat his back, and once he's asleep, the new man leads me up the stairs, but instead of taking me outside, he takes me up another set of stairs. He keeps coming, every Wednesday, because he must figure fourteen is old enough. Over and over, I tell him thank you for taking such good care of us and for doing the right thing, and I think my being old enough is the only thing keeping us alive. Alison once told me that Eddie doing something bad didn't make me bad. I think that goes for this new man too. Whatever I have to do, I can do. Because one day, Christopher will be old enough. We'll get another chance, and when we do, we'll run.

Part IV

Chapter 47

BETH

Before

I have hated this room for four years, and yet there is a beauty I always look for when he brings me here. It's the sunlight. The windows here aren't boarded over—no need because they're on the second story—and they're dirty, so the late-day sunlight, as it streams through, is filtered and made soft. The air in here shimmers like no other air I've ever seen. Or can remember. When he fluffs the sheet and kicks off his boots, dust explodes into the air. And as it floats, it catches the light and each tiny speck throws a sparkle. Millions of tiny sparkles that surround me.

This warm light also makes him sleep, and he won't know it, but I've studied him every time he's brought me here. I've watched him like Eddie watched me all those times he took me outside, just waiting for me to run so he could kill me like they killed Alison. Every Wednesday and Sunday, I've made notes about both men that I have hidden in the sofa lining. It's not hate that's driven me, because hate is easy and it's weak. Watching the men gathered on the courthouse steps that long-ago Saturday morning, Mama said hate was all a weak man had and that weak men always fail. I've watched and planned, not to destroy them, because they'll fail at their own hand, but to save us. For four years, I've been readying Christopher and me for the day we could run. And for four years, our lives have followed a routine, and in the routine we were safe. But yesterday, there was a shift. Just like the day Alison died. I felt it in the air that day, and I felt it yesterday. Even though

Christopher isn't yet old enough, our time had come. Today is the day we run.

Eddie was the reason I first knew things had changed. He came on Friday, yesterday, and he never comes on Friday.

"Daddy died," he said, touching my cheek and then trailing his fingers down the thin silver chain that hung from my neck and then down to the blue stone. "Just like that. His heart. Mama's the one with the bad heart. Go figure."

I sat on the floor at his feet while he sat in a chair at the table. I knew it made him feel powerful and smart to look down on me and stroke my hair, and I was strong enough to let him do both. I've learned over the years what Eddie needs, what both of them need, and I've given it to them. I nearly made mistakes in the beginning— my silly plan to trap him with a broken light bulb or to run away during one of our Sunday outings—but I've learned how to be smarter, because once Christopher came, I had to.

"I ain't hardly sorry he's dead," Eddie said, trailing his fingers through my hair. "It's my time now, you know?"

I nodded and smiled as if I were happy for him. Though Eddie never said much about it—some things were meant to be secret, he would say of his family and their business—I think his father was a leader in the Ku Klux Klan. He was one of those men from the history books I read who wore robes and hoods, rode horseback, and carried torches. They were thick books, from high school or maybe even college, and Eddie didn't know what all was written in the pages or I think he wouldn't have brought them. It was always easier to think of those men trapped inside the pages of a book than walking among real people.

"I'm proud of you," I said, reaching out to touch his hand. "You deserve this."

"Where's the boy?" Eddie said, keeping his eyes on me.

At the sound of footsteps on a Friday, I'd sent Christopher under the stairs.

"Boy, come on out," Eddie shouted when I didn't answer him.

He smiled when Christopher first crawled out, but the smile quickly faded and he let out a long breath. Eddie didn't pay Christopher much attention when he was a baby, but now they sometimes kick a ball together on Sundays and he's started bringing Christopher books and treats like he did for me when I was first in the basement. I always thought it was safer to let Eddie think of Christopher as a son, but Eddie's fading smile was another shift I couldn't ignore. I saw the same look on Eddie's face the day they killed Alison. He had looked at Christopher and me on that day, after he knew Alison was dead, let out that same long breath, and was figuring we had to die too.

"Course," he said, "my daddy dying means we're going to have to sell. The land, the whole thing."

He said it as if I should understand. I kept on smiling and nodding because I can do that now. I can feel one thing on the inside—fear, disgust, anger—while showing something else on the outside. It's how I've fooled them both all these years.

"Of course," I said as I brushed Christopher away, sending him back under the stairs. When he was gone, I reached for Eddie's hands. "You can let us go," I whispered. Though I never thought about the possibility of them having to sell, I knew immediately what it meant. "Drive us someplace far away. I don't even care where. I'll never tell. Couldn't even if I wanted to. I don't know your last name. Right? You've never told me. I don't know what town this is. Eddie, please."

He didn't bother with an answer before standing and leaving me, just shook his head. Even if I didn't understand Eddie's reasoning, I did understand in a way that hollowed out my stomach that Eddie's daddy dying and him having to sell this place meant Christopher and I had to die too. And when the man who killed Alison came for me the next day—a Saturday when he's always come on a Wednesday—I knew I was right.

Sometimes, I fall asleep in the warm, shimmering light of the bedroom where he takes me, but not today. Instead, I listen and I watch. Eddie asked me once if I knew the name of the other fellow, the one who comes on Sundays. I lied and told him no, so he believes I don't know his name either. When his breathing slows and lengthens, I roll my head to the side so I can see his face. The silver in the beard he has now sparkles where the sun falls across him. His eyes move from side to side beneath his lids and then stop. He's drifted in the deepest sleep. I know about the different stages from my books. This is the stage I've waited for, the sleep that is hardest to wake from and that will leave him disoriented for a few moments. That's all I will need. A few moments. A head start.

Without moving my body, without even taking a breath that might cause the springs beneath me to creak, I move my head another few inches until I can see the rest of him. His body is still. His arms are crossed over his bare chest. The skin up to his elbows is dark and creased where the sun has beaten on it for years. His chest, where the sun rarely touches, is white and covered by black wiry hair. His thighs, too, are white. All the way down to his ankles. I watch his chest. It moves slowly up and down.

First, I roll onto my side, my head still resting on the flat pillow, and with the open bedroom door in sight, I listen. His breathing is unchanged. He doesn't move. Using only the muscles in my stomach, ones I've worked to strengthen every day by lying on my back and reaching for my toes until I could do it one hundred times without stopping, I lift myself into a sitting position. At the same time, I slide my feet over the side of the bed. I can't help that my body has begun to shake. The room is suddenly cold. The tiny hairs on my arms are stiff. My heart beats faster. My chest lifts and lowers quicker with each breath. I close my eyes, inhale the musty air, and exhale slowly, silently, through my mouth. Straining against my own weight, I pull with my stomach and don't let myself push off the bed with a hand or an elbow. A few more inches and

I'm upright. I stretch until one toe touches the pine floor. When both feet rest on the warm wooden planks, I lean forward and stand.

From the first time he brought me here, I have draped my clothes over the arm of the rocker that sits just inside the door. I didn't think about it that first day but instead did it because Mama taught me clothes don't belong on the floor. We pay good money for clothes and we don't have much good money. That's what she would say. Every Wednesday since, because it always happens on a Wednesday, I've done the same. While I didn't do it that first day with thoughts of running away, I soon did. When eventually I ran, I would be escaping through the bedroom's only door and I'd be able to grab my clothes, a thin cotton nightgown, on the way out.

Touching the stone that hangs around my neck because it makes me think of Imogene, who is strong like the cactus Mama always said I should be, I take a step toward the rocker, not letting myself look down on my own body. I never look. My hip bones shouldn't jut out in the way they do. My skin shouldn't be so pale, almost gray. Though I work to stay strong—running stairs, touching my toes, drinking the milk he brings—my body still reminds me what it lacks. Sunlight and fresh air and a future. I pause with every step and count each floorboard. The third from the bed squeaks. And the fifth. I step over both, pausing to count the long planks again, and yet again, because I can't make a mistake.

At the open door, I use two fingers to grab hold of the thin cotton gown he started asking me to wear the second time he came to fetch me from the basement. It's tight through the shoulders because I've grown since then. I'll wait to slip it on until I reach the bottom of the stairs. But when I tug, a bit of the white lace catches on a rough spot in the rocker's wooden back. I give another tug and it comes loose. The rocker rolls forward, a quarter inch maybe, and back. I don't move. I close my eyes and listen. The rocker goes still again. It's made no noise. He doesn't stir.

Three long steps that I take on my toes lead me from the bedroom to the top of the stairs. I start to reach for the railing as I've done every other time I've climbed down these stairs but pull back because I remember. The brass fittings that anchor the railing to the wall are loose. He mentions it almost every time he trails me up and down the stairs. Got to tighten that up, he'll say, as if we're a normal couple of people. Don't want you taking a tumble. I'm good like that, he sometimes says. Good at taking care of things myself. But I think really he comes for me every week so he can fool himself into believing he's better than he is.

I hate that most, him talking as if I want to be here with him, but I let him do it. I force a smile when he says those things or when he calls me to sit next to him on the bed and pats my knee or kisses me on the cheek as if he's a husband and I'm the wife. He likes me to hold his head in my lap and smooth his hair from his face as he tells me the good things he did that day. I tell him he did real good, not because he asks me to but because I know that's what he needs. Thankfully he never much wants to talk with Christopher. I wouldn't be able to stop myself from saying the wrong thing if he did, wouldn't be able to trap my tongue between my teeth like I sometimes do to stop myself from saying the things I shouldn't say.

Instead of using the railing to steady myself, I drape the cotton gown over my neck, and pressing my shoulders against the wall, I sidestep down the edges of the steps. The edges don't creak or sigh like the centers. Except for the third step from the top. This is the hardest to manage. I bend my knees, make myself low to the ground, lean against the wall, and stretch one bare leg across the loose step and reach for the next. I worried I'd be embarrassed by being naked when this day came, but who would see me except perhaps him? Now, in the moment, I don't have time to feel embarrassed or even sad at what my body has grown into, or rather what it's still struggling to grow into.

When I reach the bottom step, I slip the gown from around my neck so Christopher won't see me naked when I open the basement door for him. I thread my arms through the opening, wiggle my shoulders and tug until it slips over my head, and then yank it down over my thin frame. He's made me wear the same thing for almost four years now, and it barely fits. I never thought I'd be so tall. Mama would be surprised too. You're so thin, she'd say if she could see me now, but my, look how tall.

Hugging myself with both arms, I don't turn to look back up the stairs. Instead, I listen. His feet are bare and so his footsteps won't be heavy, maybe not even very loud. But he won't know to skip over the third and fifth floorboards and he'll grab for the railing when he lunges for the stairs. If he's coming for me, I'll hear him. I told Christopher to be ready and to wait at the locked door as long as he heard no footsteps, no running, no one shouting my name. I smile because the house is quiet and Christopher will be there, waiting, ready to run.

I know my mistake immediately. Because I take a quick, sharp step toward the dining room instead of continuing with my slow, steady steps, I turn the corner too sharp and catch my toe on a splintered piece of the floorboard. I knew it was there. I've seen it just as I've seen and memorized every other splintered or loose board that leads from the basement door to the stairs and beyond to the kitchen door that leads outside. I can't help the cry I let out. I slap a hand over my mouth, but I've done it. I've always known I would only get one chance, but I thought I'd be picking the day. Even though I've been preparing for years, I never thought I'd be forced to run. But now I have, and being forced has made me sloppy.

Something shifts in the air, or maybe I've imagined it. I hold my breath, don't move. If I woke him, he'll be mixed-up in the head as he struggles to shake off his deepest sleep. He'll have opened his eyes, maybe stretched and wiped the sweat from under his chin like he always does. Then he'll roll his head to the side. I usually pretend I'm asleep when he does this because I know he's pretending that I want to be there with him. And then he'll push himself up and the soft yellow light filtering through the dirty windows will clear and he'll know I'm gone. And just as I think it, a floorboard overhead squeals under his weight. I shift direction and run toward the door that leads outside, leaving Christopher behind.

Chapter 48

IMOGENE

Today

Between the time Warren and Imogene leave Tillie's shop and when they pull up outside Mama's house, something has changed for Imogene. It's like a bad taste has settled in her mouth. It's the taste of these last five years, made all the more bitter after the sweetness of that one moment of hope she felt this morning when she woke to find the boy had made it through the night. He had looked at her like she mattered and he needed her and his mama needed her, and that need has to be bigger than Imogene wallowing in her own fear and in her own messed-up life.

As Warren puts his car in park, his phone rings. He rests a hand on Imogene's knee so she won't leave and takes the call. She pushes his hand away but doesn't get out of the car because she wants to hear what he says. Mostly, he listens, and when he hangs up, he tells Imogene what she already figured. There has been no sign of anyone, alive or dead, at the old house or in the burned-out field, and given that Imogene saw no one other than the boy, they won't risk trying to access the basement, at least not for now. Lastly, he tells her they're still checking with all the surrounding hospitals, calling as far as Augusta and Macon.

"I believe him," Imogene says. "The boy, he said his mama always comes back."

The drive ahead that leads to the old house is quiet, no more cars coming and going. The men who had been here looking for Christopher's mama have left or moved on to a wider search.

"Not saying I don't believe him," Warren says. "But think about the timing. Your daddy died, what, on Thursday afternoon? And if we're to believe your daddy was keeping those two, he must have taken the boy's mother Thursday morning at the latest. By lunchtime that same day, he was dead. It's been four days, maybe more, that the boy has been on his own." He starts to reach out again but stops and pulls his hand back. "He's a child. He's scared. No telling what's the truth or what he's been taught to say. That boy's mama, she's either run off or she's dead."

"What if it wasn't just Daddy?" Imogene says, trying to shake off the sight of Natalie Sharon's face. "Someone started that fire. Someone like Tim Robithan."

Warren lets out a long breath. "Lord knows I wish I didn't have to deal with the likes of Tim Robithan, and I believe your daddy owed them a sizeable sum, but doesn't mean they're tangled up with that boy. Doesn't mean they started that fire, either. Hell, they helped put it out."

"Then who?"

"Maybe nobody," Warren says. "You said yourself someone had rigged up the electricity down there. Best guess, boy lit something or left something running that he shouldn't have. I think you're chasing a ghost."

"Garland was covering for Daddy," Imogene says, shaking her head at Warren's theory. "Somehow he was covering up what Daddy was stealing. Tim, the others too I'm guessing, they know that."

"That ain't good news for Garland," Warren says, nodding as if he already suspected as much. "This ain't the kind of thing that's going to court."

"Because the Knights'll take care of it themselves? That what you mean?"

Warren nods. "Like you said, he owed them boys money, enough he was willing to sell off your mama's property. I'd damn sure sell my house and everything in it to make things whole if it was me. But your daddy couldn't do that with a boy and his mama locked up down there. Jesus, I hate to say it, and it's just a theory until we got a body, but that's my guess. He had to clear them out so he could sell."

Imogene pushes open her door and looks up at the house.

"I'll check in with you later," Warren says, popping the car back into drive. "Jo Lynne'll see to the boy, and you ought to think on telling your mama."

"Thanks," she says, sorry now that she shoved him away. "For taking me to Tillie's and all. For being here."

"Imogene," Warren says as she goes to step out of the car, "I ain't trying to take your husband's place."

She settles back in her seat, looks straight ahead. She should tell him she knows that and that the problem isn't him, it's her. It's the guilt of not being in that car with Russell and Vaughn five years ago and of beginning to care for Warren in a way she never thought she'd care for another man, but she can't manage to say any of it.

"I'm just trying to get you in bed is all," he says.

At this, she laughs, grateful he made a joke and saved her from a conversation she isn't ready to have. Thanking him again, she steps out of the car, pushes the door closed, and watches as he drives away. Once his car has disappeared, she turns her face into the wind to clear her hair from her eyes. It's picked up since they left the house, and the sky is dark off to the west. A coolness brushes over her, which means rain is coming.

Inside the kitchen, Jo Lynne has cleaned up all the dishes, and the counters shimmer from the scrub-down she gave them. At the table, Mama is playing a hand of solitaire. It's always been Mama and Jo Lynne's way . . . they can be alongside each other if they're cooking or cleaning or talking about what's needed at the grocery store, but otherwise, they are together in silence. Mama doesn't want to hear the things Jo Lynne thinks or does. Mama's surely like Imogene in that way. Hearing those things makes them real, and that's both sad and frightening. When the door opens, Mama looks up and presses a finger to her lips.

"Our boy is sleeping," she says.

While Jo Lynne is still wearing the robe she wore over last night, Mama has changed clothes and done her hair up. She's curled and back-combed it, more than she usually does, and from the smell of it, she's sprayed it down good with hair spray. She wears a lightweight knit sweater, pink to brighten her face, and she's dabbed gloss on her lips. It's Christopher. He's made her happy. After just a few hours, moments, really, that she's spent with him, he's made Mama happy. It's a reminder that Imogene isn't the only one who lost Russell and Vaughn. Five years, and this is the first time that's occurred to her.

"You should lie down too," Mama says as she meets Imogene at the door and rests a cool hand on her cheek. She trails a finger along the thin scratch on Imogene's face that's nearly faded. "You look tired. Is everything okay?"

Imogene nods. "Do you know about the fire, Mama? Has anyone told you?"

Mama smiles. "Heavens yes. We're not to worry about that. We've got our boy to think about."

"I have smothered chops in the oven and fried corn on the stove," Jo Lynne says, untying an apron from around her waist and draping it over a chair. "Mama's right, you should sleep while the boy's sleeping. Maybe eat something when you get up. Garland'll be back soon. He didn't think we should be staying here alone. And then we'll all go to town in the morning, together."

Imogene holds up a hand to stop Jo Lynne from saying anything more. It's too much to think about just now. Instead, she lets Mama guide her toward the sofa.

"But you're doing okay, Mama?" she says. "Not upset about the old house?"

"That old place won't be missed," Mama says, taking a quilt

from the back of the sofa and draping it over Imogene once she's lain down. "And isn't it nice having a little one in the house again?"

Digging her hand in her front pocket, Imogene pulls out Mama's necklace. "I have something for you," she says, letting it hang from one finger. "Turned up at Tillie's."

"Well, I'll be," Mama says, cupping her hands as Imogene drops the necklace into them. "Would you look at that? This really is a day for miracles."

Jo Lynne tugs on her robe's belt as she leans in to take a look over Mama's shoulder. "Someone tried to sell it at Tillie's?" she asks.

"Something like that," Imogene says.

"I never thought I'd see the day," Mama says, slipping the necklace over her head. She fingers the stone, staring down on it for a few moments before seeming to remember Imogene. "Now, no more out of you. You get some sleep."

Mama is right. Imogene is tired. She'll close her eyes, at least for a bit. Mama is happy now that Christopher is settled and not angry anymore with Imogene for not taking care of him like she should. She even seems to have forgotten about the wire she'd been so intent on having removed. Imogene can take a few moments to rest, and when she wakes, Warren will be back and he'll know what to do next.

Chapter 49

BETH

Before

I always knew, when this day came, I'd have a decision to make. Should I zigzag this way and that, cut a crooked path through the pampas grass tall enough to hide me, or run hard and straight to get as far from the house and from him as possible. As I stumble out the back door, letting the screen slam since I already know he's heard me and is following close behind, I zigzag because I don't want to get too far from the house and Christopher, who is still inside.

Running between the rows, I hold my arms close so I don't stir the thick blades, but they still cut into my shoulders and thighs. A dried, sharp end pokes one eye. I blink to clear it. The pink feathery blooms from last autumn have browned and bits of them scatter. I spit the pieces from my mouth, turn my face to protect my eyes. I always knew I'd be small enough to pass soundlessly between the rows and that he wouldn't, and I had hoped for light to see by, but now, knowing he's right behind me, I am glad darkness is already settling in. The gravel cuts into my bare feet, but I can't feel it. I drive my knees forward, push hard off my right foot to change directions. I run for a few more rows, drive my left foot into the ground, stumble and bite my lip so I won't cry out at the pain when my ankle buckles, and I shoot off in another direction. Already I've lost the house. I was supposed to keep track. Count my steps and turn left first and then right. Left and right so I would always know where I was.

I used to get lost sometimes when I hid from Mama in the

pampas grass that grew behind our house. It was a game we played. I would hide. And Mama would try to find me. I loved it best late in the summer when the feathery pink blooms towered over the field. But sometimes, Mama stopped looking, and I'd sit in the grass, waiting for her and watching those pink, feathery blooms float above me, and maybe I'd fall asleep. When I finally found my way back home, Mama wouldn't remember I had been hiding. She'd kiss me on the cheek and say, time for supper, as if I'd been there all along.

When the screen door flies open again, banging against the side of the house, I drop onto my hind end, pull my knees to my chest, and hug them with both arms. I bury my face and try to quiet my breathing. I hadn't planned for what the running would do to my breath. There is no slap when the screen door closes, so he must have held it and slowly shut it instead of letting it slam. He's wanting to be quiet. I swallow and concentrate on the inhale and the exhale. I knew the fear would change me. It might make me better. It might make me worse. I read about it in one of Imogene's textbooks she used when she was still in college. Now that I'm here, in the middle of it, every part of me is shaking and my breathing and heartbeat won't slow. Hearing would be my best chance. Hearing him before he hears me. But he knows that too. No footsteps cross the worn patch of ground outside the house's back door. He doesn't yell, doesn't order me back inside. He's listening for me just like I'm listening for him.

He'll think I ran toward the main house that is to the west, over what Eddie always called a ridge, but I don't know how far away it is or how to get around the lake, so that was never where I planned to run. Instead, I ran toward Stone Mountain. Somewhere off to the east, just beyond where I can see, it springs out of the horizon. That was always my plan. It was the one place I knew and the thing that could anchor me.

When he shouts my name, barks it out into the field that

stretches farther than I have ever been able to see, I can't stop myself from scrambling backward. I fall into the stand of grass behind
me, struggle to get my feet back on the ground, but each time I try.
to push off the thick, brittle grass, my hands slip and I can't get my
balance. I stop pushing and roll instead of trying to stand. I roll
and then roll again until I land on my hands and knees. I half
crawl, half run deeper into the field, farther from the house. He'll
have heard, and just as I think it, just as I regain my footing and
am moving silently again, the grass behind me begins to rustle.

I take a left and right and another left and I'm running directly
east. I only know because that's where Stone Mountain lies. I drop
to the ground again, tuck myself into the grass. I pull my knees in
close and bury my mouth there to muffle my breathing, but I keep
my eyes open. I've stayed hidden from him long enough that it's
almost dark, and that is protecting me. I was wrong to think I
should run when the days were longer. The dark is more on my side
than his.

It's always been my plan to stay hidden as long as I had to. I've
waited seven years. I can wait seven hours, seven days if I must,
until he gives up and leaves. In the early years, I would have been
alone. And then after Christopher came along, I knew I'd have to
wait until he got older. We started practicing when he was three,
practicing and preparing for this day because I thought he'd be
with me. In between clearing breakfast dishes and taking our pretend walk to school, we would sit together, side by side, our knees
hugged to our chests, our faces tucked down. He was allowed to
hold up one finger to tell me was feeling brave and good. Two fingers would mean he was scared and I would kiss them so he'd be
brave again. That's all. Nothing else. No talking. We couldn't giggle, not even when we practiced. We'd have to be still, like statutes.
I showed him pictures in one of our books. Still like this no matter
what happens or how scared we feel.

He's calling my name now over and over. He's cold, walking

west of the house and away from me, and I can barely hear his voice. That's how Mama and I would play. You're getting colder, I would shout. Or hotter. Hotter. Hottest of all. But he's cold and getting colder. The night air swallows my name as he shouts it. I was wrong. He didn't hear me fall. And then he gets warmer, must be walking down the ridge, back into the field. I squeeze my eyes closed and imagine I'm part of the tall stalks. I know all about them. I've studied pampas grass in a gardening book he once brought. It usually contains itself, won't generally take over. But given the right conditions, it'll spread.

His voice grows louder, and the tall crop of grass that has infested the field rustles as he passes through it. The rustle is distant, like waves far out in the ocean must be. Rolling closer and closer to shore, the rustle grows louder. And now the waves are crashing on the shore. I'm squatted to the ground, am hugging my knees tight. Warmer still and then he's hot.

"Answer me now," he calls out, "or I'll drag the boy out here. And if I drag the boy out, I ain't going to be happy."

Chapter 50

IMOGENE

Today

It's nearly five o'clock when Imogene opens her eyes again. The overcast sky is dimly lit by the faded orange glow of sunset. The house still smells of Jo Lynne's smothered chops, and Imogene realizes straightaway that she skipped lunch.

"You're awake," Jo Lynne says. She and Mama both are sitting at the kitchen table, a deck of cards scattered between them. "I was just heading in to check on Christopher. It's about suppertime."

"Let me go," Imogene says, kicking off the quilt Mama laid over her.

"Warren's been here and gone," Jo Lynne says as Imogene twists from side to side, stretching her back. "Said he'll be back and to tell you he's got nothing new for you."

One look at Jo Lynne reminds Imogene how long it has been since she showered. Jo Lynne wears a pale yellow dress that she wasn't wearing when Imogene first got back from Tillie's shop, and while Imogene's clothes are rumpled and her hair is a wiry tangle of red curls, Jo Lynne is fresh again and somehow rested, though she's probably slept less than Imogene. Garland must have brought her the change of clothes and an overnight bag earlier in the day or maybe while Imogene slept. After checking in on Christopher, Imogene will get cleaned up, eat a decent meal, and give Warren a call.

Christopher's room, that's what it's already become, is darker than the rest of the house, but the small lamp at his bedside has been turned on. It throws a soft glow, making the room warm in a way it never was when it was Imogene's room. Instead of being asleep, Christopher is sitting up in bed and is leaning against the headboard. Somehow, Jo Lynne has already managed to find him new clothes. He wears a loose-fitting blue flannel shirt, rolled up at the sleeves, and a pair of dark jeans. As she walks into the dark room, Mama coming up behind her as she does, Imogene braces herself for his question . . . is my mama back?

"We thought you'd be sleeping, little one," Mama says, lowering herself slowly, softly, onto the edge of the bed.

Christopher leans into the hug Mama gives him, lays his head on her shoulder, and rests a hand on her arm. With two fingers, he begins tapping in time to her heart. Squatting in front of him, where she can rest a hand on his knee, Imogene readies herself to smile for him when he asks about his mama. And he hasn't only lost a mother; he never had a father, not a real one. He and Imogene are alike in that way.

"Is the lake very far?" he asks, his head still resting on Mama's shoulder.

"No," Mama says. "Not far at all."

"Can you point?" he asks.

"You want to go there?" Mama points off to the east. "It's pretty as can be."

Christopher nods and lifts up on his knees so he can face Mama.

Imogene hadn't thought of it before, though Warren likely did. They'll have to consider that Christopher's mama might be at the bottom of the lake.

"It's getting a little late for that," Imogene says. "Can we go another day?"

Christopher doesn't answer Imogene and instead reaches for the necklace hanging around Mama's neck. With two small fingers, he lifts the stone.

"What is it, little one?" Mama asks, glancing at Imogene.

"You found Mama's necklace?" Christopher says.

"Yes," Imogene says. "It's very special and very old."

More than once, Jo Lynne has talked about a child's body knowing long before his mind that he's safe. That's surely why Christopher has slept so long and so soundly. His body knows before his mind. And in that same way, as Christopher continues staring at the necklace, Imogene's body knows something is wrong. It simmers first in her stomach, the knowing, and slowly it spreads.

"How did you know my mama had lost her necklace?"

"Not your mama's necklace," Christopher says. "*My* mama's."

Imogene forces herself to smile. The tightness in her stomach has worked its way into her arms and legs. Her breath is coming faster now.

"You're sure," Imogene says. "Look real close."

Christopher runs one small finger over the stone and nods.

"That's real good," Imogene says, trying not to look at Mama because she'll be wanting Imogene to explain what is going on. "But how about you rest just now? Can you do that for me? I'll sit right here with you and you rest."

As Christopher slides back on the bed, Imogene motions for Mama to turn, and once she's unhooked the clasp, Imogene tucks the necklace back in her front pocket.

Sitting on the edge of the bed, Imogene pulls back the quilt so Christopher can wiggle underneath, and then, in a quiet voice that won't scare him, she says to Mama, "Go get Jo Lynne. Tell her to call Warren and have him come straightaway."

Mama doesn't move and instead stares at Imogene. She wants Imogene to explain, but she can't. She isn't certain what it means, Christopher saying he's seen his mama wearing this necklace, but she needs to tell Warren right away because it might mean Christopher's mama is alive.

"Go, Mama," Imogene says, still in a whisper. "Go now."

In 1981

On a Friday night in Mobile, Alabama, several Klansmen, angered by a jury that had been unable to reach a verdict in the case of a black man accused of murdering a white police officer, armed themselves with a gun and rope and set out to find and kill a black man. Upon discovering a nineteen-year-old black man walking alone, the Klansmen lured him to their car under the guise of asking for directions. They abducted the young man, beat him repeatedly with a tree branch, slit his throat, and hanged him from a tree.

Chapter 51

TILLIE

Today

That is definitely Robert Robithan sitting behind the wheel of the red truck parked just outside Tillie's shop. Glancing behind to make sure Mrs. Tillie is still in the back room and safely out of sight, Tillie walks behind the counter and reaches for the telephone.

Glancing at his watch, Tillie figures Natalie should be getting close to Atlanta by now, where she'll get lost in all that traffic. Keeping an eye on the shop's door, he dials the number he wrote down earlier and tells the officer on the other end that he wants to report a stolen car. He waited until now to give Natalie a head start. He tells the officer the wrong year but the right make and model, mixes up the first three numbers of the license plate with the last three, and instead of calling the car blue, he calls it gray. And as he hangs up, the front door opens.

What Robert first says once he's in the shop, Tillie isn't certain. His heart is pounding, and he's thinking about the doctor what told him to stop eating bacon. The floors rattle with each step Robert takes, and the smell of a sweet cigar fills the shop. Tillie rests one hip against the counter to steady himself.

"Got yourself quite a mess there," Robert says after saying other things Tillie didn't make out, and he nods at the broken front door.

Robert Robithan's face is lined with deep creases from a lifetime of working construction, but in the soft light shining through the front window, he looks like a younger man. Picking up a crystal bowl Mrs. Tillie found at a yard sale, Robert tosses it from hand to hand. It sparkles as it passes through the overhead lights.

"You don't look well," Robert says.

"My car got stole." Tillie forces himself to stand tall. "Right out of my driveway."

The cigar smell is making him dizzy. It's too familiar and is whittling away all the years between what happened then and what's happening now. Robert had said the same to Tillie as he stood holding that fellow's wrist. Hold him tight, Robert said. And then to Tillie, you don't look well.

"Where is she, Tillie?" Robert says. "Been to her house and they ain't seen her."

Tillie knew what helping Natalie might mean for him, but he had hoped it wouldn't mean nothing to Mrs. Tillie. But as Robert toys with the crystal, he is letting Tillie know he can do as he likes with him and Mrs. Tillie too.

"You asking after Mrs. Tillie?" Tillie says. His tongue is swelled up, and talking feels like something he's never done before. "She's there in the back. But I got your watches right here." Tillie nudges the small white box across the counter. "Knew they was yours straightaway."

"Natalie Sharon," Robert says, ignoring everything Tillie told him. "Where is she?"

Another part of Tillie's plan was to have this counter between him and Robert, and he's glad of it now.

"An officer was here," Tillie says. "That Jacobson fellow, he told her to go. Listen, Robert, I don't know what Edison was up to when he stole your watches, but Natalie's just a kid. I knew they was yours the second I seen them. Locked them up tight. Had every intention of giving them back. I wasn't no part of whatever Edison was up to."

Robert sets down Mrs. Tillie's crystal bowl, and in a few long steps, the pine floorboards again rattling under his weight, he stands at the counter. He starts to say something but stops at the sound of heels clicking across the same pine boards.

"Hello there, Robert," Mrs. Tillie says, walking up behind Tillie. "So nice to see you under happier circumstances."

Swatting Tillie on the hind end so he'll move aside, Mrs. Tillie reaches under the counter and pulls out her blue ledger, a large notebook filled with her record keeping.

"And you, Mrs. Tillie." Robert dips his head but keeps his eyes on Tillie.

Mrs. Tillie stands the ledger up on the counter and leans it there. "You'll say hello to Edith for me, won't you? Didn't get a chance to visit much at the funeral."

"Yes, ma'am," Robert says, and dips his head again, a signal he's saying good-bye to Mrs. Tillie. Robert has always had a way of getting folks to do his bidding with nothing more than a nod, and his son can do the same.

"Well, I'll let you gentlemen get back to your visiting," Mrs. Tillie says, and tucking her ledger up under her arm, she turns and walks into the back of the shop again.

"I'm wondering," Robert says once Mrs. Tillie has gone, again ignoring everything Tillie has tried to explain, "if maybe your car wasn't stolen at all. I'm wondering if you give it to Natalie Sharon and maybe she's long gone by now."

Tillie shakes his head. "Officer Jacobson told her to leave. Near an hour ago."

Robert takes another step toward the counter. He's close enough he could reach across and lay a hand on Tillie's chest. But instead of saying anything more, Robert's eyes drop to the register, and the instant they do, Tillie knows he's been caught.

"You say your car was stole?" Robert says.

Tillie nods.

"Stole right out of your driveway?"

"Couldn't believe it myself."

"Must have left your keys inside it, then," Robert says.

Again, Tillie nods, hoping that fellow down to the café doesn't remember seeing Tillie drive up earlier in the day.

"Then what's that there?" Robert Robithan asks, tipping his head at the set of keys hanging from the hook on the side of the register where Tillie always keeps them.

Tillie slides one foot back and then the other. He really doesn't care for himself. It's Mrs. Tillie he worries over. Even if Robert leaves her be, she'll live now with whatever becomes of Tillie and this shop and mostly their home. Robert will tell the fellows to burn it, and probably the shop too. Mrs. Tillie will be left with nothing. Tillie steadies himself with a hand to the counter and starts to let out a breath so he can tell Robert it was all his doing. Mrs. Tillie didn't do nothing. He takes another step, the ground still unsteady underfoot, and then he starts to smile, but he catches himself. He reaches out with one hand and lifts the set of keys.

"These here?" he says. "These here are Mrs. Tillie's keys." Then he flicks the miniature doily Mrs. Tillie hung from her key ring because she was tired of Tillie all the time picking up her set. "Used her keys today. Mine are long gone, I suppose. Like you said, I left them in the car. Been doing it for years. Probably have to get new locks here at the shop else I'll find this place robbed too. Got everything. Shop keys. House keys. Hell, even think they got my safety deposit box key. You suppose a person could get into my safety deposit box?"

Tillie knows he should quit talking. He presses his lips tight together to stop anything more from coming out his mouth and he doesn't move from behind the counter until Robert has left the store and his truck has pulled out of its parking place. Then he drops onto the stool he keeps at the register and closes his eyes. Surely, Robert was angry, though Tillie remembers nothing between looking down on those keys and seeing Robert walk out the door. In the days ahead, Robert might be back with more questions and accusations, but for now those keys have been enough to save Tillie and Mrs. Tillie.

This was Tillie's plan, but in the end, Mrs. Tillie saved it. That's what she was doing when she gathered up the large blue ledger and leaned the tall book on the counter. She always knew, and when she heard Robert Robithan, she knew Tillie's keys were hanging there because they weren't stolen. He took off one key and handed it to Natalie Sharon, and he kept the rest. He kept them and hung them right there on the register where he always did. Behind the cover of that ledger, Mrs. Tillie traded her keys for Tillie's, because Mrs. Tillie always knows.

Chapter 52

BETH

Before

As much as I never wanted to, I had to think about what might happen if I was forced to leave Christopher behind. I knew he'd use him to lure me back, and if he did, I would give in to him. But I never planned for things changing on the outside like they have. If I answer him now, Eddie's daddy will still be dead, and his daddy dying means they have to sell this place and this land. And that means there is nowhere left for Christopher and me. I begged Eddie to let us go, promised to never tell, promised to run far away where no one would know them or us. Begged him over the years too, but the answer has always been no, and that means if we can't be here, we can't be anywhere. We can't go on living. If I answer him now, those things will still be true. My only chance at saving Christopher is to outlast this man. I have to make him think I'm already gone and that I've left Christopher behind so he'll go too.

He continues calling my name and shouting that I better damn well answer him, but he isn't shouting as loudly as he could, and that must mean he's afraid of someone hearing him. I bite the side of my hand so I can't answer when he calls out that he'll damn well kill Christopher if I don't get my ass back inside. I tuck my head and try not to cry because crying won't do me any good.

He's gotten colder again and now I hear nothing and I think my being quiet has worked. I try to figure how long since I last heard him call my name. I worry the rustling in the grass that starts at one end of the field and rolls toward me is him, but maybe it's from the breeze. It doesn't have to be the sound of him passing through the rows, taking long, heavy steps as he gets closer. It's possible he left, and I wouldn't have heard him drive away. I don't know if he parks his car far or close. I didn't hear an engine like I used to hear Mama's engine. I didn't see the glow of headlights like I used to see when Mama came home late. I want to stand and look, but I can't.

I'll count to one thousand, and if I still hear nothing, I'll run back and throw open the door into the kitchen. I'll have to take light steps as I run through the empty, rotting house, maybe even walk instead, because if Christopher hears running, he'll be frightened and hide. He'll do it because that's what I told him to do. I've taught him everything I didn't know when I came to live in the basement and all the things I did know. I've taught him about setting the alarm on the clock every day so he remembers to wake up and marking the days and drawing a calendar. We've studied how many days in each month and how to save food in cans and how never to use the flashlight except in emergencies. If he has to one day, he'll be able to tend himself.

The darkness has settled in my head just like it's settled in the sky. The air is getting cooler. I'm shivering, and it's taking all my energy. I knew I'd have to be careful of that, but I ran when I had to run. I didn't have a jacket to grab, no shoes or boots to pull on my feet. And my knees ache from having squatted for so long, how long I don't know. Not only is the shivering sucking up all my energy, but my legs are too tired to stand and won't carry me far or fast. I knew there would be a pain to holding still for so long. I knew because I have a memory of not being able to move. It was a toolbox in the back of a pickup. And so I practiced for the pain, Christopher and I together did. We sat still as long as we could, not saying a word. But I didn't practice enough.

Dropping back onto my hind end, I let out a sigh because the relief is stronger than I am. I slap a hand over my mouth. He may have heard me, but I couldn't stop myself because it felt so good. I stretch my legs into the path between the clumps of grass, the thick, dry blades scratching my bare feet. I need to keep up my circulation, but I can't stand to do it. I bend my legs and work my knees up and down to get the blood flowing so I'll be ready to run.

I reach one thousand in my counting. He might have left, driven off because he thought I was gone. Or he might be hiding just inside the kitchen door, ready to grab me when I run inside and throw me back down into the basement. I stretch my legs again, work my knees as I prepare them to straighten. I'll stay low as I run from here to the back door. Just in case I'm wrong about him having left, I'll still have the fading light on my side and I'll hide again, crawl through the rows if I have to. Crawl until I'm lost again in this maze. There's nothing I can do, and the darkness won't help me, if he's waiting for me inside the kitchen.

My thighs ache from having squatted for so long, and holding myself half-up and half-down is going to be difficult. I'll straighten my legs but bend at the waist so I'll still be half my size and shorter than the grass. As I'm pushing myself into this posture, the ache in my back springs up, but I can bear that better than trying to force the muscles in my thighs to continue to carry my weight. They've done all they can do.

I make my way to the row of grass that runs along the worn patch of dirt outside the back of the house. No light comes from inside, but the moon is bright enough that I can clearly make out the back door. And then I smell something. It's familiar, like some of those faces I see on the television. It's smoke from a chimney. Mama used to build fires in our fireplace during the coldest months, but not often because the wood was expensive and she wasn't cutting her own. It must be coming from the main house, and that means it isn't so far away.

My legs feel stronger now, and I think they'll work when I need to run. I can see the door to the house and he hasn't shouted out at me and the smoke means we're not far from help. It's adrenaline.

I thought I had run dry, but it's giving me a second chance. Another one of my spelling words. Adrenaline. Being careful not to let my breathing get away from me, I smile. I'm ready to run now and can carry Christopher as far as I have to. And then just as I smelled something I remembered from a long time ago, I hear something too. It's crunching and tiny rocks splattering. It's tires on a gravel road.

"Don't you say a word."

My knees buckle and I'm on the ground again, pressing against the thick blades. They scratch my cheeks and eyelids, stick between my lips. He's close. I hold my breath or, rather, I stop breathing. I don't have time even to take in a lungful of air to tide me over. He must not know how close he is—warm, hot, boiling over—or he'd have grabbed me. Moving slowly, only my head and nothing else, I look up because it sounded as if his voice came from directly overhead. The space above me and as far as I can see is empty, but I'm hemmed in on all sides by the stalks. They tower over me and I don't know where he might be.

"If you can hear me, don't say a word, don't move a Goddamn muscle, or the boy is dead."

I close my eyes, squeeze them as tightly as I can so I won't cry. I squeeze them until they burn because I can't scream.

Headlights come next. They splash across the field and then are gone, and the tires crunching over the dirt and gravel go silent. I can see the east side of the house from where I am, and the faintest yellow glow leaks around that corner. Someone is here. They've parked but they've left their lights on. Maybe it's Eddie and now there will be two of them against the one of me.

Chapter 53

IMOGENE

Today

In the kitchen, Imogene sits and waits for Warren to arrive so she can show him Mama's necklace. She'll have to explain to him that it disappeared four or five years ago and turned up hanging from Tillie's register this morning and that Christopher said he'd seen his mama wearing the very same necklace. It's only been a day since Imogene found Christopher down in that basement, and she has no more answers than when she first carried him up those stairs.

Once Christopher was still and quiet, Imogene crept from the room, and now she sits at the kitchen table and Jo Lynne sits across from her, where she's jotting notes in a small notebook. Mama is dishing up the fried corn and smothered chops that no one ate and putting it all in the refrigerator. The radio sits nearby, drowning out the sound of her heart. Outside, night has settled in early because of the thick clouds that have blown in. The wind has continued to pick up and is catching in the roof vents and making them rattle. Every so often, a bright flash is followed by a low rumble. Imogene pushes away from the table.

"Don't trouble the boy," Jo Lynne says, looking up from her notebook when Imogene starts to stand. "If he wanted to sleep, leave him be. Warren will be here soon enough, and then we'll have to fetch him."

Imogene walks to the door onto the front porch instead, pushes aside the curtains, and looks down the dark drive.

"What do you suppose is taking him so long?" she says, because Warren should be here by now.

"It hasn't been long, Imogene," Jo Lynne says. "Just calm yourself. Might be raining already in town. You know how bad these roads can get."

Sitting back at the kitchen table, Imogene twists her hair at the nape of her neck and then presses her hands on the Formica top in hopes of steadying herself. The picture she showed Christopher earlier in the day, before she and Warren left for Tillie's, is still lying upside down, just as Warren left it. Sliding it toward her, Imogene picks it up. If Christopher was right about the necklace having been the one he'd seen his mama wear, that would be more proof Daddy had been keeping them down in the basement. He had obviously taken the necklace from Mama and given it to Christopher's mama as some sort of gift, and then, all these years later, somehow it turned up at Tillie's. Five years later. Christopher and his mama may have been down in that basement for five years.

But the necklace didn't just turn up. Someone broke into Tillie's and left it there, and it had to have been Christopher's mama. But if she's still out there, why not come for Christopher? Fear. She must think Daddy is still alive and that's why she's afraid. She must think her boy is in danger and she's reaching out to Imogene. Or maybe not. Maybe Imogene has no business trying to figure what any of it means.

Still holding the picture, Imogene stands and walks back to the door, opens it, and steps outside. She moves slowly and quietly as if the hope that Christopher's mama is out there will get frightened away by any sudden movement. The screened enclosure billows, and the rattling vents are louder out here. As if Imogene might find some answer there in her father's eyes, she looks down on the picture. It was taken before Imogene was born. Grandpa Simmons was still living and so Daddy hadn't yet become the one who men traveled the country to meet. Grandpa was still the link to those men who climbed Stone Mountain and lit a cross on fire to reignite the Klan. Studying Daddy's face, Imogene searches for that thing, the one special quality, that would mark him as a man who could do this thing he has done. But all she sees is a handsome man with dark hair and a squared-off jaw.

The something that has been nagging Imogene since Christopher recognized Mama's necklace is growing stronger. It's lifted into her heart, which has begun to beat harder, and it's pressing on her lungs so that each breath comes faster than the last. She throws open the door and runs through the kitchen toward the hallway leading to her room. Jo Lynne startles and jumps to her feet, her chair tipping backward. Mama drops something. Imogene doesn't stop when they call out to her. What is it? What's wrong? Holding tight to the picture frame, she rounds the corner at the end of the hall and throws open her bedroom door. The bed is empty. She stumbles into the room, looks in every corner. She runs back into the hallway, where she pushes past Jo Lynne and Mama, and throws open the bathroom door. It's empty too.

"Imogene," Jo Lynne says. "What in God's name . . ."

Back in Christopher's room, Imogene shoves the picture in Jo Lynne's hands, points for Mama to check the closet, and begins yanking blankets off the mattress, shaking them as if Christopher might be hiding there. Then she drops to her knees and looks under the bed. Nothing. Mama shakes her head. She's found nothing in the closet either. Imogene sits back onto her knees, hands resting on the mattress, and straight ahead she sees it. The curtains are rustling because someone has opened the window and the wind is catching them. She scrambles over the bed, yanks back the heavy drapes. The window is open and the screen is gone.

"Please, Imogene," Mama says, her arms wrapped around herself. Jo Lynne stands next to her, the picture in one hand and her free arm wrapped around Mama's shoulders. "What's going on? Where's Christopher?"

Imogene yanks the picture from Jo Lynne's hands and holds it up to both of them. "Christopher wasn't seeing Daddy in this picture," she says. "He was seeing Eddie."

Chapter 54

BETH

Before

There is silence again, and then someone, probably the same someone who drove up, is stomping through the giant reeds that grow along the west side of the house. I know they're there because I would see them on my Sundays. They grow on the west side, but not the east. Nothing grows on the east side.

His feet begin to shuffle. It's the first I've heard of him since he spoke. He's only a row or two away, and I realize I've made another mistake. I'm upwind, although there was no wind when I first ran. He likes me to wear perfume for him. I have a bottle I keep on the one shelf I have. Every Christmas, since I was fourteen and he decided I was old enough, he's brought me a bottle. Now he might smell it, but his footsteps fade. He's moving away, and I wonder if he's moving toward whoever has come here. I wonder if he or she is in danger like me.

Whoever was stomping through the weeds has stopped, but they haven't left, because the headlights still glow along one side of the house. I don't think it's Eddie because he would call out to Eddie for help. There were a few times over the years when I heard someone on the other side of the boarded-up windows. I always imagined, maybe hoped, it was a person and not some sort of animal, or something much worse. There would be a banging, as if someone were trying to pry off the boards. They likely wouldn't have known they were boarded up on the inside as well. When I was first in the basement, Eddie told me vagrants might happen along, crazy people who'd escaped a hospital. He said they were cold and hungry, mostly hungry. He said those people wouldn't help me because they couldn't even help themselves. Goddamn drain is what they are, he would say, and no telling what they'd do to a little girl, living all by herself in a dark, damp basement. Even though I didn't know what a vagrant was yet—though it would one day be on my spelling list—or why he called them a drain, whenever I heard the banging outside one of the windows, I would turn off my light, sink into the corner of the sofa, and close my eyes until it stopped.

Thinking about crazy people lurking outside the windows, maybe smelling a little girl on the other side, maybe clawing at those boards to dig their way in, was enough to keep me quiet in the beginning, before Christopher came along. I was one person, a child, before Christopher. After, I was another. I was old. Not older, but old. Instantly old. And when that happened, that change in me he surely noticed—the way I carried my shoulders, spoke with my chin high, sometimes buckled my fist—he told me he might be the one banging around. He might be testing us, and if he ever heard me or Christopher, ever heard a single sound or knock or cry for help, he'd take Christopher from me. Christopher changed things in more than one way. Before Christopher, I didn't care about living. I had been willing to give up on my own life. But Eddie knew I would never be willing to give up on Christopher's.

The breeze has grown stronger and smoke still tints the air. I draw my knees close, wrap myself up as best I can for warmth. He is as quiet and as still as me. His footsteps fade until I can't hear them anymore, and now he's somewhere nearer the other side of the house. Him on one corner, me on the other. A stirring in the yellow glow from the headlights is what makes me turn.

A person appears from around the corner and walks along the back of the house. She, I think it's a she, walks quickly as if she knows where she's going. The person goes directly to the back door. The screen squeals like it always does, and as quickly as it slaps closed, another shadow runs from the grass, across the worn patch, and up to the door. It's him. He stands to the side of the door as if ready to run for cover again should the person inside reappear and leans close to the screen but doesn't open it. The shadow of him is larger than the real him I left naked in the bed. Though he's changed over the years, doing things now like rubbing his left knee when he reaches the bottom stair on the days he comes to see me or pressing a hand to his lower back as he stretches and complains, the shadow of him looks large again, as large as the day I first saw him. I don't know how long he stands there, watching, but something happens that makes him turn and walk, not run, back toward the grass.

"Listen to me," he says. It isn't a whisper and it isn't a shout but instead something in between. It's a hiss. "Just go. Run. You do that, the boy'll be fine."

I don't look at him. From where I'm crouched, I make myself as small as I can and tuck my head. It's like it was when I hid from Mama in the pampas grass outside our house. I thought if I couldn't see her, she couldn't see me, and I don't ever want him to see me again. He wants me to leave Christopher behind, and that scares me more even than the thought of him grabbing hold of me and throwing me back in the basement.

As if waiting for me to answer, he pauses. When I don't, he continues. He must be turning his face slowly across the field because some words cut through the night air and are clear, while others are muffled and drop off before they reach me. I want to cover my ears. If I can't hear, he'll be gone and I'll never feel his hands on me again. It will all be gone. But I can't. No matter what I don't hear or see, he will still be there and so will Christopher.

"He'll forget all this. He'll forget you too." Another pause. It's a long pause, so I force myself to look. He has stepped back to the door to take another look inside. He pulls away quickly.

"Run, Bethy," he says, crossing into the middle of the open

patch of ground. "Run away and don't never come back here. Never and I swear I won't harm the boy."

His shadow moves slowly the rest of the way across the worn patch and melts back into the grass, and for the first time since I ran from the house just as dark was settling in, I don't feel fear. If he finds me now, he'll kill me like he killed Alison, but Christopher will live. He understands Christopher is young and can't do him the harm I could or that Alison could have. During all my planning, I made sure Christopher understood the rules. I told him bad things would happen if he ever broke them, bad things like losing outside time on Sundays and frozen waffles for breakfast or even me. It was the most terrible thing I ever did, making him think I might get taken away, but I did it so he'd always listen.

The rules frightened Christopher, but that fear is also what would save him. He'll know he isn't allowed to say the name of the man who comes Sunday and lets us outside for twenty minutes. And I don't think he knows the name of the man who comes on Wednesday. I only know because sometimes Eddie uses it, and when he does, he acts like it was a mistake, but really I think it isn't. Eddie resents him because he works with his head while Eddie works with his back. Christopher can't say my name either. He once asked me who would want to know. Someday, somebody will ask you your mama's name, I told him, but you can't tell. You can never tell. Even then, I knew I'd already be gone when that day came. I never told Christopher my last name. It was instinct. There would come a day that I'd be gone, and if I disappeared, so would all the terrible things that happened. That would make Christopher safe.

The cold has exhausted me, and every muscle aches from having to stay still. Fear was the only thing feeding my adrenaline, and now that it's gone, my arms and legs are empty. They've done all they can do, maybe for forever. I lie on my side on the narrow dirt path that runs between the grass, pull my knees to my chest, and rest my head on the ground. I don't see him anymore. I don't hear him. I breathe the outside air, something I used to dream about. The smell of dirt and the slippery insides of dandelion stems and the magnolias that grew outside Mama's house. Just like breathing in life itself. I tuck my hands under the side of my face, and from there, I watch the back door. Whoever is inside will surely find Christopher unless he hides. Surely he or she will find the basement door, see the locks on the outside of it, have seen the single line of electricity running through one window.

"I'll go," I shout, my face still pressed to the ground. I'm not sure how loudly I say it, or if he heard. "I promise I'll go."

When the screen door closes, I don't see it, but I hear it, and I recognize her straightaway. It must be the hair. It was hidden by something before, a hat probably or a hood. In the dark, I can't make out the color, but the shape of it, full and thick and frizzy in the damp night air, gives her away. Looking from this angle, my head resting on the ground, it makes me dizzy. I think I've fallen asleep and that maybe I'm dreaming. I push myself up, lean on one hand. The swirling in my head settles. I'm not dreaming, though I think the sound of the door closing did wake me. It's Imogene, and Christopher is cradled in her arms. His head is limp against her shoulders. He's asleep, just asleep.

I drop to the ground again. The dirt is cool on my face, but I'm not cold anymore. I draw my hands up under my chin. I want to stay awake until the engine starts and the lights disappear and gravel kicks up again under the tires. My eyelids are heavy. I'll close them for just a moment while I wait for Imogene to make her way back to the front of the house.

Chapter 55

IMOGENE

Today

Leaving Mama and Jo Lynne behind in Christopher's empty room, Imogene runs down the hallway, into the kitchen, and lunges for the sink. Christopher had been seeing Eddie, not Daddy, in that picture. Her stomach spasms, but she's empty inside.

"Imogene." It's Mama. Her warm hands gather Imogene's curls, hold them away from her face. "Imogene, what is it?"

"For goodness' sake," Jo Lynne says, her heels clicking across the linoleum floor and circling Imogene as she hangs over the sink. "You're scaring Mama near to death."

Turning on the cold water, Imogene splashes her face. A towel appears at her side. She grabs it, presses it to her eyes, and stands.

"We need to find Eddie," Imogene says. "Right now."

Jo Lynne gathers Mama again with an arm around her shoulders. "You need to stop this, Imogene. It isn't good for Mama."

"Eddie took Christopher, Mama," Imogene says, talking slowly so she won't frighten her. "We need to find Eddie right now."

"Honey," Mama says, the slightest tilt of a smile catching one corner of her mouth. "Eddie's just outside. Been digging out that wire. Couldn't bring myself to fuss at you for telling him about it. Christopher is probably with him."

Pushing off the counter, Imogene runs out the door and onto the drive because she doesn't believe Mama. It's the necklace Christopher recognized as his mama's and the picture of Daddy looking like Eddie does today. Christopher is in danger. His mama knew it and it's why she broke into Tillie's. She knew the necklace would make its way to Imogene, and she believed Imogene would save them. Rounding the side of the house, she runs up the hill, runs as if she's following the wire, and when another strike of lightning cracks the sky, she sees Eddie's silhouette at the top of the ridge. She calls out to him. A beam of light swings around and catches her in the face.

"Where is he, Eddie?" Imogene squints and holds up a hand to block the light. She continues up the ridge, her ankles buckling on the rough ground and her feet aching because she's left the house with no shoes.

"Immy, darling, you been dipping into my whiskey again?" Eddie says, holding the light under his chin.

"What did you do with Christopher?" she says, reaching the top and staring into Eddie's eyes, the light from beneath making his face glow. "And what of his mama?"

Eddie lowers the light, lets it dangle so it shines on the ground, and his face becomes a shadow. His shoulders and head drop and roll forward. "Immy."

"Tell me."

Eddie's eyes slide to something beyond her shoulder. She turns. Jo Lynne is a few feet away, teetering on her high heels.

"Let's all of us go back inside," Jo Lynne hollers over the wind, and with both hands tries to stop the scarf tied over her head from blowing loose. She teeters a few more steps and reaches for Imogene's hand as if to lead her back inside. "You're getting all kinds of thoughts in your head that don't belong. It's no wonder. All the memories Daddy's funeral must have conjured."

The outermost edges of Eddie's flashlight catch one side of Jo Lynne's face. Long strands of her hair blow across her eyes. Imogene loved her once, wanted to be so like Jo Lynne. Her hair always smooth and shiny. Always smelling of lavender. Always knowing just what to say and how to say it. Jo Lynne saved Imogene, actually saved her from sinking to the bottom of that lake when Imogene wanted so badly to reach her father, even though she already knew the man was gone.

The day a twelve-year-old Imogene learned the truth about her real daddy, she'd heard Mama crying, sobbing really, in a way that made her curl up on her bed and scream into a pillow. It was painful to hear, and with her hands pressed tight over her ears, Imogene crouched in a dark corner of her room. The police came to the house, several cars with flashing blue and red lights. Daddy's men came too. Granddaddy had died by then and Daddy had taken over. Cigar smoke swirled over the kitchen table, heavy boots tracked dirt across Mama's heart pine floors, and fellows were yelling. Doors opened and slammed, radios crackled.

And when everyone finally left, Daddy told Imogene and Jo Lynne and Eddie too that a man had died. When Eddie asked who it was, Daddy said it didn't matter. Ain't nobody going to miss the man. And then he leaned in close and whispered in Imogene's ear . . . Ain't no one going to miss him beside you and your mama.

A woman only cries—curls up and sobs the way Mama did—for a man she loves, and she damn sure doesn't cry like that for one who forced himself on her. That's what Imogene has always been, the result of something nasty and tainted. It made her an easy target for men and women like Edison Coulter. They fed on the likes of her, the likes of anyone they thought was less. Mama had loved the man who Daddy said no one would miss, and that same man was Imogene's real daddy. She had known for certain he was gone the day she trapped herself in the middle of the lake because Edison Coulter had whispered as much in her ear. She didn't know how her real daddy died or why, but she knew he was gone. She lost something else that day too. She lost Jo Lynne.

Jo Lynne would go on to marry Garland and would begin learning to measure and cut and sew the robes and hoods, and

while days and weeks and even months would pass when she lived
what seemed a normal life and would be good at her job and helpful to Mama and even Imogene when she lost Russell and Vaughn,
Jo Lynne's loyalty to the Knights of the Southern Georgia Order
would cast a deep shadow over it all. That day at the lake was the
end of the sister Imogene had once hoped to be like. Imogene
wasn't trying to swim to the other side of the lake that day. She was
trying her best to sink to the bottom.

"You never called Warren, did you?" Imogene says to Jo Lynne.
"You didn't call him. And he's not coming."

Grabbing Imogene's hands, Jo Lynne bows her head and shakes
it slowly side to side.

"I swear I don't know where the boy is," Jo Lynne says, and in
not answering Imogene, she has given her answer. She never called
Warren.

"How long have you been out here?" Imogene says to Eddie.

"Was here when you and Warren left. Hell, you two seen me at
my truck."

"Who else knew about him?" Imogene stares down on Jo Lynne
still holding her hands.

"Better take a look," Eddie says, shining his light toward the
house. Down near the bottom of the rise, Mama is struggling to
make her way up the hill.

"Go back home, Mama," Imogene shouts as loudly as she can.
"Go and call Warren. Tell him to come right away." She hollers
twice before Mama turns around.

"Who else knew Christopher was down in that basement?" Imogene asks once Mama is gone. "Is this why Tim Robithan was at
the house this morning? All those other men?"

"You ain't even told me what's going on, Immy," Eddie says.

"He's gone. Christopher is gone. And one of you two knows
where he is."

"We never intended this," Jo Lynne says, lifting her head. Her face is nothing but dark shadows now and a jumble of hair that's pulled free of her scarf.

"Quiet yourself," Eddie says.

"You made a mistake is all, Eddie," Jo Lynne says, and grabs Imogene's hands again, pulls them close and holds them under her chin. "Just a mistake. We never intended the girl stay down in that basement. I was going to see her to a good home, a better home."

"The girl?" Imogene says. "You mean Christopher's mama?"

"She was young," Jo Lynne says. "We could have found her another home, and she'd have forgotten all about this town. She had a terrible mother. Terrible."

"What do you know about the life she had?" Imogene says.

"I know," Jo Lynne says. "That's all that matters. Her own mother brewed oleander leaves. Was going to drink them. Hell, maybe even have that child drink them."

"She was in your charge?" Imogene says. "She was one of the kids you see to? My God, how old was she? How long was she down there?"

"It was all Eddie's doing," Jo Lynne says.

"You shut your mouth, Jo Lynne," Eddie says.

"I won't. It was your fault. I looked after her some in the beginning. And we'd have cared for that girl just fine until you brought that baby and its mother into it."

"What baby?" Imogene says. "Christopher?"

"Garland knew you couldn't do nothing right," Jo Lynne says. "Daddy knew it. I knew it too. Everyone knew. I should have never sent you to the house that night. Garland should have done it. He'd have never made such a mess of things. You made Daddy ashamed."

"That ain't true," Eddie says.

"What did you do, Jo Lynne?" Imogene asks. "What did you tell Eddie to do?"

Jo Lynne shakes her head and doesn't answer.

"She told me the girl was there house-sitting," Eddie says,

spitting the words in Jo Lynne's face. "It was a Puerto Rican. She was supposed to be alone. I didn't know there was going to be no little girl there."

Imogene remembers when it happened. A young woman was killed while babysitting, and the little girl in her care disappeared. The young woman who died had only been a few years younger than Imogene, and she'd been new to town. There had been brief talk right after the incident that the Knights had been involved because the young woman and her family had been from Puerto Rico. A few months earlier, Tim Robithan and the others had gathered on the courthouse steps and demanded the young woman's father be removed from the college. But the police were quick to squelch that idea, claiming it wasn't the Klan's way, though Imogene had thought it was mostly an attempt to steer the headlines in a different direction. The only real suspect had been the estranged father of the missing little girl, and that's the last Imogene heard of it or can remember.

"That little girl, the one who disappeared, is she Christopher's mama?" Imogene shakes her head, not wanting to work out the ages and years that have passed. "That was eight or ten years ago. Jesus, she was a child."

"Daddy was already talking about it being our time again," Jo Lynne says, not answering Imogene's question. Her eyes are wide and her hair is blowing free across her face. "We were already seeing things change. But it was Timmy Robithan that Daddy was leaning on and making plans with. Chasing that girl and her family out of town, that's all Eddie was meant to do. And then Daddy would've picked Eddie instead of Tim."

"And did Daddy know the two of them were there in the basement?" Imogene asks. "He had to have. How many years. Eight? Ten?"

"Seven," Eddie says. "And he knew."

Chapter 56

BETH

Before

This smell always worries me. I don't like to use the kerosene lantern, not even when we lose electricity. Instead, I use the one flashlight Eddie gave me a long time ago, but because C batteries are expensive and he gets angry when I ask him to buy more, I only use the flashlight for emergencies like when the power goes off and I have to make us something to eat or help Christopher use the bathroom. Even if Christopher cries about being afraid in the dark, I won't use the kerosene lantern because I worry about the fumes. Klan cologne, Eddie used to call it.

I won't light candles either. They eat up oxygen, and after what Alison said, I've always been afraid of too little air. The only ventilation is between the bottom of the door at the top of the stairs and the floor. I check the half-inch gap every month and scrape it with a wire hanger to make sure it's clear. Christopher knows how to light the kerosene lantern, and I've caught him doing it twice. It's the only time I ever spanked him. Fire is a fear even greater than fumes. But that's what I'm smelling now, kerosene. Klan cologne. I open my eyes just a sliver and call his name.

"Christopher," I say as I stretch out a hand. Usually he's lying next to me, tucked inside the curve I make for him when I roll on my side. We fit perfectly, even as he continues to grow. I inhale, thinking I'll smell his warm head. Sweet like shampoo and salty like a little boy's sweat. That salty smell reminds me of playing outside during summer break. Red-cheeked from too much sun. Skin slightly damp, salty if I licked my lips.

A crackling makes me open my eyes. Christopher is a busy sleeper. I ask him sometimes in the morning where he went during the night because his legs sure were busy. I pull out the atlas on those mornings as soon as we sit down for school time, and he points to a spot on the map. I went there, he'll say. Wherever it is, we go to our shelves and look for a book that might tell us about that place. Tokyo is the capital of Japan and eight million people live there. Australia is a continent and a country. There are seven continents. Florida is south of Georgia, and Florida and Georgia are two of fifty United States. Christopher can recite all fifty. He's busy again tonight. He's rolled over onto a newspaper maybe. Eddie used to bring them, but now he says they're full of lies and won't let me read them anymore. Instead, he'll tell me all I need to know. He says the world has taken a mighty fine turn of late. I pat the spot next to me. It calms Christopher to feel my hand on his back.

The smoky smell always gets stronger in the moments after we put out the lantern, but this time the stronger smell lingers. It burns my nose and then the back of my throat. It's the burn that startles me. I sit straight up, reach for Christopher, call his name. But it isn't our small bed beneath me, or the sofa. Christopher isn't next to me. Dirt and grass scratch my calves and feet. I feel it then, something warm on my face. The house, our house, is burning. I squint, hold up a hand. On the second story, a window explodes, and orange and yellow flames shoot into the dark sky. I push off the ground, my knees buckling beneath me. Stumbling backward, half crawling, half walking, I scream for Christopher, but he's not here with me. He's in the basement, where he's waiting for me to open the door for him so we can run. No, Imogene came. Imogene took him away. I had to let him go.

The field is burning too. The clumps of grass, tall blades that grow in thick tufts, are dry and brittle on the inside, like a haystack, Mama would say, because no one ever bothers to cut back the plants in winter. The fire is crawling toward me. Flames are shooting out of the bundles that grow nearest the house. The tops that were once pink, feathery blooms erupt into flames. Sparks flutter overhead, catch a dry, sharp tip, and the grass next to me begins to smolder. Staring at the orange sparks that float like stars, I continue to back away, and still I smell the kerosene. He's doused the house in it, the field too. The smell is heavy enough to burn my eyes. Still stumbling backward, away from the sparks and ash raining all around, I lift the neckline of my cotton gown. It's damp. I press it to my face but turn away when the fumes burn my throat and nose. My skin burns too. My hands and arms. I reach down to rub my legs. It's all over me. He doused the field and the house, and he doused me. While I slept, dreaming I was lying next to Christopher, curled around his small body, him tucked up next to me, he found me and covered me in Klan cologne.

The fire is chasing me now. I spin around, trying to find a path that will lead me away. The smoke is turning everything gray. I have no horizon to guide me, only the thick flames that have taken over the house. But if I know the house is behind me, then a safer place is ahead. I run as best I can in my bare feet. The ground is cold, and sharp rocks cause me to trip and stumble. I need to put distance between me and the flames that are jumping across the field, and as I run, I pull at the white gown that's too tight around my hips and through the shoulders. Yanking out my arms one at a time, I pull it over my head. The thin cotton is wet through and through. The air cools the farther I run, and it soothes my bare skin. I run faster, looking now for water. Someplace to wash my arms and legs and even my face because I taste the bitterness on my lips. Someplace to wring out my gown so I can put it on again.

Eddie is the one who told me about the lake. It's like none other, he said. In the beginning, I believed him. I believed it was a special place, magical even because the fog hung there thicker and lower than any other place, and I hoped to one day see it. But as I grew up, reading books because I had nothing else before Christopher came, I learned the lake wasn't so special. It's all about warmer air meeting cooler air in a low-lying valley. That's what makes fog. The clouds don't hang lower here because this place is nearer to heaven, not like Eddie always said. I'm sorry now that I told Christopher the same story, because this is what he'll think heaven is. But no matter, all Eddie's talk of a lake does mean one is near. We never went there, though I asked more than once. Too close, is all Eddie would say. Too close to the main house, I eventually realized. I need to run back, toward the flames and then across toward the main house. The lake will be there, and on beyond, I think I'll find Christopher.

Chapter 57

IMOGENE

Today

Imogene squats to the ground so she can brace herself with both hands. Too much is coming at her too quickly.

"Both of you be quiet," she says. "Who else knew Christopher and his mama were down there?" When Jo Lynne doesn't answer, Imogene stands and shouts. "Who did you tell?"

"Garland knew," Eddie says.

"Eddie," Jo Lynne shouts.

Imogene looks up at Eddie. He's a dark shadow, his hair catching in the wind, his heavy flannel billowing with each gust.

"And?" she says to Eddie.

"He saw to them on Wednesdays, Immy," Eddie says, shaking his head, slowly at first and then faster. "I ain't never did the things he did."

Jo Lynne lunges for Eddie, catching hold of his forearm and dangling from it. "Don't you say that."

"I ain't never done those things," Eddie says again. "Ain't never hurt the either one of them."

"Shut your mouth," Jo Lynne screams, dropping down onto her knees.

"You knew, didn't you?" Eddie says, shaking his head. "Knew full well what he was doing to that girl?"

Jo Lynne sits back. Her head and shoulders sag as if a weight has settled on her, making clear that, yes, she knew.

"That money," Eddie says, turning from Jo Lynne to Imogene. "It wasn't Daddy what stole it. Was Garland. He stole it, and then went crying to Daddy for help when he couldn't pay it back. The Knights had a lot of cash coming in the last couple of years. God damn, Imogene, money from all over the country. People was finally seeing us for what we are. And then Garland, he took it all. Lost some on a few bad deals. Spent some on you too, didn't he, Jo Lynne? That fancy car of yours, that big house with no kids to fill it. How do you think Garland was making that mortgage?"

"This dress," Imogene says, grabbing hold of the freshly pressed dress Jo Lynne was wearing when Imogene woke up from her nap. "And those clothes Christopher was wearing. Did Garland bring them to the house?"

Jo Lynne, still kneeling next to Eddie, stares up at Imogene and nods.

"And did he see Christopher, talk to him?"

"When you were at Tillie's," Jo Lynne says. "Maybe when you were sleeping too. But I don't know what he said to him."

Christopher's mama was afraid of something. That's why she left the necklace for Imogene to find at Tillie's instead of coming right to the door. She was afraid of something or someone inside the house, someone who could still hurt Christopher. There was a car barreling through a stop sign that Christopher's mama saw coming and she had been trying to stop it.

"You told Garland about Mama's necklace," Imogene says. "You told him Christopher recognized it, didn't you?"

"He said it would tie us to the boy, tie the whole family to what happened." Jo Lynne wipes her eyes with one hand. "But I told him I'd find the boy a new home and then we could sell the place and everything would be fine. Immy, they'll kill Garland for stealing. Do you understand that, really understand? Timmy Robithan as much as told us that."

"After Daddy died," Eddie says, trying to take Imogene's hand but pulling back when she jerks away, "Garland said we could sell the property and get enough money to pay back what he lost. Daddy had already promised the property to Tim just to buy some time, but he couldn't sell what Mama owned. We figured she'd be happy enough to sell and leave the old place once Daddy died."

"So is Christopher's mama dead? Was that the plan? Kill her and then Christopher so you could sell?" Imogene's eyes bounce between the two of them. "Is that what you're telling me?"

"Garland was going to kill her," Eddie says, nodding. "Kill them both if he had to. But Bethy run off before he could do it and then you found the boy. We thought maybe the fire got her, but Garland said no. I don't know where she is, Immy. I swear, I don't know. And I don't know if she's dead or alive."

"Bethy?" Imogene says. "Beth is her name?"

Eddie nods. The glow of the flashlight throws shadows on Eddie's face. His eyes sink deep into their sockets. His cheekbones sit high and protrude. He looks thin, teetering on feeble, a sign of what's ahead for him if he ever grows to be an old man.

"And where is Garland now?" Imogene says, yanking Jo Lynne to her feet. "You called him instead of Warren, didn't you?"

Jo Lynne slowly nods. In the dark, Imogene can't make out any of what her sister is feeling. They've always known what the other is thinking, feeling, though Imogene hasn't been so good at it over the past five years. Jo Lynne didn't just save Imogene that day she nearly drowned; she saved her after Russell and Vaughn died. She was the one who eventually hauled Imogene up and out of the hole she dug for herself, the hole grief dug for her. Even more than Mama, who couldn't hardly get on Imogene even when she was doing her worst, Jo Lynne knew when to stop consoling Imogene and when to start expecting her to live again. And while the dark and hair that's blowing across Jo Lynne's face won't let Imogene see any of what her sister is feeling, she can sense it. As sure as if she could reach out and wrap her fingers around it. Jo Lynne is afraid.

Garland was at the lake that day Imogene nearly drowned. He'd stood on the banks, in the spot where he and Jo Lynne would always go before they were married. It's the spot where the Knights burn their crosses even to this day. Under cover of the pines and along the banks of the lake, they gather because the ground is smooth, almost like a sandy beach, and they believe the lake is nearer to heaven than any other place on earth. And if not for the pines and the low-lying valley, they would almost be able to see Stone Mountain from there. They believe they are laying claim to a world without end because they are closer to it than anyone else. Jo Lynne and Garland picked it because the pines gave good shade, making it cool there even on the hottest, stickiest summer afternoons, and because, one day, God willing, Garland would follow Daddy in a way everyone already knew Eddie never would.

Garland had held a towel for Imogene as she stumbled from the lake, coughing and choking and digging in her ears for earwigs. She'd been crying because as she slipped beneath the water, her real daddy slipped away too, but he didn't come back to the surface with her. He hadn't been evil. Mama had loved him, and now he was gone. Imogene would never know him, and she'd never know what happened to him. Holding his arms open for Imogene, Garland had been smiling as if he understood she needed comforting. He understood she lost something that day and was readying himself to gather Imogene into his arms, but instead, he pulled back when Jo Lynne stepped up to him. Her hair and dress still dripping, black smudges tarnishing the smooth skin under her eyes, one shoe missing, she reached out and slapped him square across his face. Imogene stumbled backward, and Eddie came running and laughing. You okay there, little one, he said to Imogene. Or maybe to Garland.

Eddie laughed harder still to see Garland press a hand over the red swell on his cheek. Garland should have been stronger that day.

That's what angered Jo Lynne. A weak man who stood on the banks didn't fit squarely into her idea of a man, and certainly not into the idea of the man she was to marry. As much as that day ended something for Imogene, it began something for Garland.

Imogene is running downhill toward the lake, tumbling, falling, Eddie and Jo Lynne shouting out to her from behind. Christopher asked Imogene and Mama how far away the lake was. That's where Garland is taking him, and he'll tell Christopher his mama is just there on the other side, just like Eddie told Imogene. Garland will remember that day Imogene nearly drowned, same as Imogene remembers. He'll tell the boy it's a magical lake, and he'll know what a child is willing to do when he, when she, believes in the magic. See it there, he'll say. The other side? It's not so far away. Your mama's waiting for you. Can't you see her smiling and waving? And Christopher will go, a boy who must surely have never stepped foot in a lake or a river or even a swimming pool.

He'll start to walk first and the water will creep higher on his legs, up over his thighs, and when it reaches his waist, he'll find the walking is harder to do. Still he'll continue to drag his feet across the bottom, one step at a time. And Garland will be there right behind him, pushing him along with promises that Mama is waiting just there on the other side. Christopher will keep on because he loves his mama. The water will rise past his chest and reach his shoulders.

Imogene keeps running. The rocks and brittle grass dig into her feet. Her hair blows across her face. She wipes it away, but the wind keeps coming, and the wiry strands stick in her mouth and her eyes. There is no moon, no light to see by. Garland must have opened the bedroom window and called for Christopher to come out. He'll have promised to take Christopher to his mama.

Imogene reaches the pines that shield this side of the lake from the north winds. She pushes off the trunks, bounces from one to the next. The bark cuts into her hands. Her lungs burn. She catches a foot on a root, falls, cries out at the pain that shoots through one knee, pushes herself up and stumbles through dried pine needles and sharp stones, and finally falls to her hands and knees on the smooth spot, smooth as a sandy beach.

Chapter 58

BETH

Before

He drives up in a big black car, and even without seeing his face, I know it's him by the way one boot hits the ground, and then there is a pause before the next boot follows. It's Garland. I'm free now. He will never touch me again, and I can say his name. Garland. He moves slow, as if he has to mull over whatever thing he just did before deciding on what to do next. He tips his head, probably trying to smell the fire, but the wind is carrying the flames and most of the smoke away from the house. Garland is a man always uncertain of what he's doing and it's why he needed me. I made him think I was small so he could feel big. It was the same with Eddie. Mama knew all about being the small one and the one who was trapped and the one no one cared about. Somehow she knew that one day I would be that person too, and she taught me how to fight back. But now Garland is here and Christopher is just inside the house and I don't know what to do next. All my years of planning and practicing, but I never prepared for this.

Other cars have passed by, making me duck my head and pull back into the shadows, but they didn't stop. They drove on through the gate that leads to the house and field that are on fire. But not Garland. Once out of the car, he stands, rests one hand on the car door, seems to look around, though from where I sit on the ground, my body knotted up into a ball to keep myself warm, I still can't make out his face. He pulls off something, a jacket I figure, tosses it back inside the car, and slams the door.

I've been forcing myself to stay here on the ground instead of running to the door. I've known Christopher was here since I ran over the rise and through the gate because three cars are parked outside the house and one of them is green. Eddie once told me Imogene bought a new green car when her other car was destroyed in an accident that also destroyed her family. The moment I saw that car, I wanted to run to the house and pound on the door and tell Imogene about me and Christopher and Alison, but I didn't because I worried Garland was inside and maybe Eddie too. They could hurt Christopher or could take him away from me, or maybe all the people I think should help me won't. Eddie once told me no one would help me and I'd have nowhere to go. He had friends, lots of friends in a town he'd lived in all his life. No one would help me. Except Imogene. But Garland hadn't already been inside, and now he is here and so is Christopher and maybe I've missed my only chance. Christopher is trapped because I was wrong.

The screen slaps shut behind Garland. Stumbling as I force myself to stand, a sign the cold is working on me, I walk around the back of the small building I've been huddled against. It's a shed, maybe, a place where they keep tools. I'm shivering because my gown and hair are still wet, having rinsed the kerosene from both in the lake water, and I have no shoes on my feet. Each step is stiff and slow. Once on the other side, I take a wide loop that keeps me outside the spray of the porch light. I can see the road from here. It's the road to town. Less than two miles straight north. I know it's two miles because Eddie would say he wasn't driving two miles into town just to get a gallon of milk, and I know north because Stone Mountain is east.

The windows in the house are closed so no voices drift outside, but I can see shadows moving about. I drop down alongside Garland's car, using it to hide me from anyone inside who might be looking out, and standing just enough to reach the handle, I fumble with it. I twist it, feel for a button to push, and finally lift and pull. The door opens and a light inside the car pops on. I drop back down to the ground, worried the light will give me away, but the door up at the house doesn't fly open. I grab the jacket he threw into the car before he went inside. It's heavy flannel and smells of smoke. Even before closing the car's door, I thread my arms through the long sleeves and pull the jacket tight around me. Still squatted low to the ground, I close the door and lean against the side of the car.

The sudden warmth makes my body go limp. I pull my knees into my chest and wrap the heavy flannel around my legs. I tuck my feet in tight and lay my head back against the car. Christopher is trapped inside with Garland, maybe Eddie too, and I need to get him out, away from Garland and away from the fire. I'll rest here, just for a moment, and then I'll know what to do next.

When the screen door off the porch squeals again, I open my eyes. I don't know how long I've been sitting here. For a moment, I'm back in the pampas grass and he's just thrown open the screen that sags in its frame, but I'm not in the field and that wasn't the screen door that sags. It was the screen door in the main house. I push off the car and squat, my hands pressed to the ground. His voice is clear now. He's talking to someone who's still inside. I scramble backward and slip around the end of the car where I'm just beyond the reach of the light. Boots hit the wooden porch. The planks creak under his weight. When footsteps hit the gravel, I scoot to the farthest side of the car, and when the driver's-side door opens and the car sinks under his weight, I run for the side of the house.

The bushes here scratch my legs and snag my gown. They're sweet like Mama's magnolias. The smell is subtle, comes and goes quick as a blink, but the memories it gives rise to are sharp. I was a child for such a short time, and even then, Mama needed me more than I needed her, though that's what saved me and Christopher. It made me clever and capable at an age when I shouldn't have been burdened by those things. I want more for Christopher. He should have the joy of being the one who is loved and of believing in goodness for at least a little while.

Shifting my weight from one bare foot to the other, I clench my toes to fight off the numbness and the memories that will do me no good now. I drop down between the bushes that will have only just begun to bloom this early in spring and from here I can see through the back window of his car. There's only one dark shadow, his head and the tops of his two shoulders. He's leaving, and at first I think I'm getting another chance. But that hope fades as quickly as it rises. He could have Christopher with him. He could be sitting in the car and his head wouldn't reach high enough to be seen and maybe he was carried so I didn't hear his smaller footsteps. He'd be asleep and quiet and he could be there in the front seat, and I'd never know it. Christopher knows he can never say Eddie's name. Never. Not even to me. And I've never let him know Garland's name, though he may have heard Eddie say it just like I did. It's been our rule ever since Alison died. No names except your own. Or rather it's been my rule, and I taught it to Christopher from the beginning. If we never said their names, they weren't quite as real.

In the dark field, he promised me he wouldn't hurt Christopher if I ran and never came back, but then he doused me in kerosene, so now he'll think I'm dead. I have nothing. Not even shoes on my feet, and to let him think I am dead is the best I can do for Christopher right now. Until morning, it's the best I can do, but once the sun comes up and he goes to the field, he'll see I'm not there. In the morning, he'll know I'm not dead. He'll drive away now and I'll walk up those same stairs and I'll knock and I'll tell Imogene. I know her though I've never met her. All these years, she's most of what I've had. I knew when her baby died, and I cried with her. We became mothers together, though she won't know that. I'll tell her that Christopher was Alison's first and then he became mine and she'll believe me and I'll be warm at last and I can sleep. I'll wait until he leaves and then I'll go to Imogene and hope she can save us.

I open my eyes and lift my head when the car door opens again. One boot hits the ground and then the other, just like before. I know immediately what has happened.

"You're here," he calls out, though not too loudly because he knows I'm close.

I've made a second mistake.

"I left it for you," he says. Gravel crunches under his boots, growing louder. He's walking this way. "Thought you'd be looking for something warm if you made your way this far."

I hug the jacket. I thought he left it because it smelled of smoke. I should have known he left it to draw me out. It's the cold. It's making me careless.

"Imogene can't help him," he says, still moving this way. His steps are slow, as if he's listening for me between each one. "If that's what you're thinking."

I exhale, don't feel the cold anymore. The shivering has stopped, and my feet are beginning to burn. I rest my head on my knees.

"Only I can help you," he says. "You disappear, and that'll save him. Take yourself and go and I'll leave him to Imogene. She'll care for him. He'll be safe, be just fine."

More footsteps cross the gravel drive, and then the door to the house squeals open and slaps closed again. He's gone back inside. Men have come to put out the fire, and that must mean Garland and Christopher and whoever else is inside are staying. Pulling the jacket tight around me, I draw my knees into my chest and tug at the collar so it'll stand straight around my neck to fend off the cold air. My fingers are stiff and not quite working as they should, and they tangle in the necklace I'm wearing. Eddie gave it to me after Imogene's family died because he was so afraid of never having a family of his own. Alison said he wanted a family to prove he was a man, but I think he wanted people who loved him like Imogene's husband and baby boy surely loved her. I lift the stone, hard and cold even in my numb fingers, that hangs from the chain. It belongs to Imogene's mama, or it once did. I know she likes to garden because Eddie told me. She has a bad heart that stops most people from wanting to be in her company, so she spends long hours alone in her garden. Her plants are behind the house in a spot that gets morning sun and afternoon shade. The shed I was first hiding near will be where she keeps her tools, the rakes and small shovels, and maybe gloves and boots too.

Still holding the necklace, I force myself to stand. I can find those boots if there are any to be found, gloves too, and I can run two miles. I've run stairs every day since Christopher came so I'd be strong. I've run them until I collapsed on the floor, thankful for once it was cold. I can run two miles. I can make it to town. I can find the thrift store because I know it's on Main and I know there is only one and I know the man who runs it is named Tillie and that he keeps an eye out for things reported lost or stolen and that he calls Imogene. Ever since Eddie first told me about the thrift store and Tillie and the work Imogene does, I've imagined it's the same shop Mama and I would visit to buy our secondhand clothes and used plates and silverware. I can run two miles and then Imogene will know I'm here and that Christopher is mine. She'll know the necklace means something, and she'll figure it out. She'll know I'm scared, and she'll know to keep Christopher safe for me.

Chapter 59

IMOGENE

Today

The lake is dark, and just beyond the sandy bank, the wind whips up the water. Imogene listens but hears nothing of Garland or Christopher. No voices, no shouting or crying. She calls out over the wind and the churning water.

"Garland." She lifts onto her knees and screams again. "Christopher, I'm here. It's Imogene." As she walks toward the water, she peels off her shirt and steps out of her jeans that will weigh her down. The day she nearly drowned was the last time she tried to swim. Mama wanted her to take lessons after that day, but Imogene refused. She would always remember the pull of something down below and how easily she had been willing to surrender.

The water rolls first across her feet. It sweeps past her, the cold burning the cuts and welts she must surely have there, climbs higher up the sandy patch of ground, and retreats. Back and forth it rolls, each time reaching higher. She continues to cry out as she walks and then tries to run, driving her knees high so her feet clear the water. The waves break on her thighs and then pull at her waist.

"Christopher," she screams. "Toward me. Pull your arms toward my voice."

The water sprays Imogene's face as she stretches to reach the bottom with her toes. She bounces forward, crying out. Up ahead, the water begins to glow. She turns, coughing and spitting and pulling the hair from her face. It's a set of headlights, shining into the lake. She follows the glow, pulling now with her arms because her feet no longer touch. She lifts and lowers with the water. As it throws her higher, she kicks and pulls to ride it to the highest spot, and for a moment, she sees it. A head maybe, a set of shoulders, but then she's down again, coughing and spitting. She struggles to stay in the light's path because the wind and the water are pushing her off course.

Jo Lynne was never an athlete in school. Imogene was the one who played volleyball and basketball and ran track every spring. But as a swimmer, Jo Lynne was always graceful and strong. Even before Imogene sees her, she knows it's Jo Lynne swimming this way, her arms cutting through the water, her kicking feet powering her through the wind and waves. She glides past Imogene, slicing the cone of light as she swims closer to the middle of the lake, where Imogene always imagined her real daddy was waiting just beyond. Imogene reaches with her arms and kicks toward Jo Lynne's wake, fights the pull of the wind to stay in the light's center, kicks to keep her head above water, and continues to scream for Christopher to swim toward her voice.

Pull with your arms. Kick with your feet. Trust yourself. Look at the bottom and pull and kick. Imogene forces her face into the water, feeling it again, the pull of something from down below, something that was hoping for her that day when she was twelve and now is hoping for Christopher. And then a thought. She could be wrong. Garland may have taken Christopher someplace else, and now she's trapped here in the middle of the lake. She tucks her head, causing her body to flatten out and ride on top of the water, reaches with her arms, one after the other, and struggles to keep her kick below the waves. When she needs a breath, she lifts her head, and each time, her feet begin to sink as she does. And each time, she screams Christopher's name.

Chapter 60

CHRISTOPHER

Today

The man drags me through the water, one arm looped around my chest. I'm on my back but can't keep my legs from falling. He's pulling us with one hand that reaches out and digs down into the water over and over. I'm crying now because I don't believe Mama is here, but I don't want him to know because that will make him angry and he might let me go. Mama always said to never make him angry. She told me to talk like I'm a rose, sweet and flowery, to men like this, but to be a cactus inside. The cactus will always survive.

The water fills my mouth and I cough and I try to spit it out. We're lost in the darkness. My skin feels rubbery for being so cold, and my feet drag behind me and are falling toward the black bottom. When we started walking, the water barely touching our toes, he said the water's deep and asked did I know what deep was. I said no, and he said that's how far the water will cover you over if you don't stay with me. You can't breathe underwater. You know that, right? So hold on tight.

When he came for me, I was waiting. He didn't tell me when he'd come but he said we'd go when it turned dark and he'd knock on the window and I would know it was him. So even though it wasn't all the way dark, when I heard the tapping, just like he said I would, I pushed up on the window like he showed me and he tore the screen. When I crawled out, I fell on my knees and tried to tell him that I saw Mama's necklace, but he told me to be quiet. His voice made me cry just like I'm crying now, and I tried to make myself stop. Play the silent game, Mama would say when I felt like crying and knew I shouldn't. Buckle your mouth up and twist a lock, and she'd use two fingers to twist a lock on my mouth that wasn't really there. But I couldn't stop myself from crying because when I fell, I put a tear in my new pants and a red scrape on one knee and I wanted to see Mama's necklace again. I tried to walk fast like he wanted me to, but I couldn't because I didn't know where to look. I never knew how big the outside was even though Mama told me. Bigger than you can see, Mama would say. Bigger than your arms can stretch or your voice can carry.

It was dark when we started walking but not so dark as it is now. I never saw a dark sky before, and I hoped to see stars that glittered up there. Mama told me all about the stars and planets and the moon, and sometimes we would turn off the big light and shine the little light through a box poked full of holes. Tiny specks of light danced on the ceiling, and Mama said that's what stars are like. Except this sky was dark and there was lots of wind that blew my hair, and there was wet rain, too, on my face. All of that together made me cold as I walked with the man, and Mama would be angry because I took outside without a coat. We never took outside time without a coat because you just never knew. I was happy when the man stopped walking and pulling on me and handed me a coat he brought special for me. He held it while I slipped my arms in each hole. It was puffy and I was warm when he took my hand and said, this way. He said to leave the coat on all the way into the water. It'll keep you warm.

After I put the coat on, the man smiled and asked me, did I know about the lake, about it being a magical place? I nodded because Mama told me heaven was there at the lake and it was just waiting for us every day we took outside time. We would soak it up because that's where hope was and happiness and all kind of loving, and I knew that's where Mama would be.

The man stops digging in the water when a cloudy light stretches

out over us. I can see the water now, except it's black and everything
is black and we're still lost. Maybe there isn't a bottom under all this
water. Maybe the water goes on forever and Mama is lost in it just
like we're lost. I try to look for her in the smoky yellow light, but
the water sprays my eyes and runs up my nose and I can't make it
stop. The water is picking us up and pulling us back down, over and
over, but mostly it's pulling us down, and I spit more of it out of my
mouth. I never knew water would pull with all its might to drag me
down to a black bottom I can't see. Mama always said I was full of
might—that means strength, that means you're mighty—but the
water is mightier than me or the man. We're bobbing straight up
and down now. I think I hear a voice. It's a yelling voice but the
water is louder than anyone can yell, and then his arm begins to
loosen around my chest and then it's gone. I kick my feet, reach for
him. My coat, my new special coat to keep me warm, is heavy and
pulls me, and the water pulls me. I can't say his name, am never
allowed to say his name, but I do.

"Mr. Garland," I cry, and I cough because the water spills into
my mouth. "Mr. Garland."

But he's gone. And the black water has hold of me now. I slap
with my arms but they don't much move because my coat is too
heavy for me. You're getting too big, Mama would say as she
climbed the stairs with me on her back. It made her stronger to
have me as extra on her back. Up and down she would go, only
carrying me on the way up, and I would go down on my bottom,
and when I got older, I would hold the railing and walk by myself.
Now my coat is too big and I'm not strong enough.

Another arm digs down into the water and wraps around my
chest. I think it's an arm. I'm lifted and I suck in air but I suck in
water too. More coughing. More spitting. The arm isn't big like
Mr. Garland's and not as strong. It's Miss Jo Lynne. I remember
her from the kitchen. Miss Jo Lynne with the sweet frosting. She's
telling me lay your head on the water, press your belly button to the

sky. But the bottom is still grabbing at my feet and legs and pulling hard and we go under and back up again. Miss Jo Lynne coughs like me. She wraps her arms around me and tugs at my coat. She cries out, screams I think because the zipper won't unzip. We practiced zippers, Mama and me. Zippers and shoelaces. Miss Jo Lynne is crying and screaming right in my ear and telling me to take it off. Take it off.

She's kicking now and the land is getting closer. We're not going toward Mama anymore. My heavy coat pulls at me and Miss Jo Lynne is crying as she kicks us toward the sandy spot where the trees don't grow. Someone is calling for me. I think it's Mama again and I kick and twist but the hands hold tight. I spit water and shake my head because it's in my eyes. I hear my name again. Someone is screaming for me. Someone who knows me. It's Imogene with the red, wiry hair. I see her. I kick and reach because that's what she's telling me to do, but my heavy coat is pulling at me. Imogene is screaming my name. Miss Jo Lynne's hands are gone and Imogene hooks an arm around me like Mama would do when she toted me to bed. I'll carry you like a sack of taters, Mama would say. Imogene is spitting and coughing and the land is getting closer. Now she's screaming for Miss Jo Lynne. Come back, she's screaming as she digs in the water. And then I feel it under my toes, the sandy ground. We fall on it, Imogene and me, and we lie there breathing, and I think Mama is gone.

Chapter 61

BETH

Earlier today

I can feel that it's almost morning. It's the time people most slip through the cracks. The seam between day and night or night and day. There's a sogginess to the air. Sometimes I'd wake and Mama wouldn't be home, and I'd find her on the porch, asleep in a chair. Her hair would be damp from the heavy, wet air, her clothes limp like they just came from the washer. I'd shake her and she'd come inside. I can feel that moment of touching Mama's warm shoulder and of wanting to cry because I didn't know why Mama was so unhappy that she'd sprinkle oleander leaves in a cup of hot water or drink whiskey until it killed her. I can feel it so hard, that moment of waking Mama and knowing she was broken inside, that it's weighing me down, and even though it's almost light, I have to walk on the road where the walking is easier because I'm just that tired.

Later today, after the air has dried out, someone will see the broken window in the back of the thrift shop. I know for certain Tillie will find the necklace I left, but I can't know for certain he will call Imogene, though I believe he will because I know he loves her. Imogene was married to Tillie's son, and Imogene's baby boy was his grandson. Everything Imogene lost, Tillie lost too. I know he loves her, and I believe he will help. Eddie knows everyone in town, that's what he's told me all these years. And the people he knows will protect him and not care about a person like me. But I know all about Tillie because I know all about Imogene, and that's why Tillie is the one person who might care about a person like me. He's the one person who might help me.

Eddie gave me the necklace the day he asked did I want to be a family, a real family. I kept it and wore it, not so we'd be a family but because the necklace was a way of being close to Imogene and her mama before her and hers before her. Imogene was strong enough to survive having a different daddy and a family who died, so I could be strong too. Other than Christopher, Imogene is the only other person I've really known all these years, though she hasn't known me. Her life is really the only one I've lived.

When Imogene's little baby and her husband died, I believe Eddie was scared, maybe more scared than he'd ever been in his life, that he'd die too and never have a family of his own. He'd be a man who left nothing behind but hate. I'd read everything I could ever find about the Ku Klux Klan in all the books Eddie brought me over the years, even read once about the man who I believe was Eddie's great-great-grandfather. Eddie would be no different from all the men I saw in all the black-and-white pictures I found in those books. He'd be nothing but a tattered robe and limp hood and would never be remembered. I think Eddie knew that too, and that's mostly why he always talked about Imogene. In the beginning, I thought it was because she had it worse than him. But I was wrong. He talked mostly of her, because even though she eventually lost it all, for at least a time, she had everything. She is strong in a real sort of way, isn't always afraid. She is a cactus who doesn't much bother trying to look like a rose.

I know that sound. It's like childhood sneaking up on me. It's tires on a gravel road. I think of Ellie and Fran. They'll be big as me now. I imagine they're still riding on that bus to Macon for the field trip. They're sipping sweet tea from a can and their heads are tipped together and they're telling stories about the day they'll finally see me again. They'll tell me all about the things I've missed, the names of every teacher and the jobs they had each summer and what color they painted their bedrooms. I can't remember their last names anymore, but I think I'll know them when I see them. I think they'll know me too.

Yes, that's childhood sneaking up on me.

Every night during the warm months of spring, Mama and I would sit on the porch and wait for that first white, velvety magnolia bloom to show itself. When the bushes finally bloomed, those were the happiest weeks, at least for Mama. We'd sit in the plastic chairs she called lawn furniture, close our eyes, and breathe in that scent. I would sip powdered lemonade that made my lips pucker, and Mama'd sip whiskey on ice. Breathe it in good, Mama would say of the sweet scent, 'cause it ain't going to last.

I always knew Mama was thinking about something other than magnolias when she breathed in those flowers. She was thinking about something that had already come and gone, like a time before I was born. Lord, how I wish I could grow up all over again, she'd sometimes say. Mama saying things like that would make my insides ache and even leave me crying because the days and weeks wouldn't stop passing by, not for anybody, and one day I'd be sorry my sweet youth was gone. But I had Mama for a while, and I had Christopher too. Nothing lasts forever, that's what Mama always said on those nights we sat in the plastic furniture, as if breathing in the scent of those flowers was like breathing in life itself.

The tires are inching forward now, and behind me, the sun is up. It's warm on the top of my head. I pull the jacket I'm still wearing tight around my shoulders. It's his jacket, heavy flannel. My lids flutter from the glare bouncing off the white gravel. The road is rough under my feet because I never found the grandma's gardening boots, but it's good to feel the tiny stones and the soft, dry dirt between my toes. It's something real after so much of nothing for so many years. So simple and so beautiful. The engine is rattling too. One ankle wobbles, and I stumble. I right myself and keep walking. This is the way back to the house where Christopher will be sleeping. Soon enough, Tillie will see the broken window. He'll call Imogene.

The tires have stopped moving. They're quiet. I walk through patches of shade that bounce across the road—the sun shining through the branches that shift overhead with the wind. Leaves rustle. Something creaks. A door opening, I think. And it slams closed. He's brought the smell of fire with him. It reaches me before he does.

As I continue to walk, I can't feel my feet. In Mama's front yard, the grass weaved itself between my toes and up around my ankles and rooted me to that spot. I couldn't move that day, couldn't run. And I can't run now. The seam between night and day has passed. Imogene will know what the necklace means. She loved her boy like I love Christopher and she'll want to save him because she couldn't save her own son. No one will want it more. No one but me.

I don't scream like Alison or Julie Anna. Not even as he grabs my shoulders and yanks off the jacket I'm still wearing, his jacket. Not even as I'm pulled from my feet, off the road, and down into the wet, grass ditch and into the trees where the ground is covered with brittle pine needles. Not even as the sunlight is blocked and the air turns cool. I don't scream.

Even Now

In August 2017, Unite the Right organized a rally in Charlottesville, Virginia. During the two-day event, 250 participants, which included white supremacists, white nationalists, and Klan members, carried torches, firearms, clubs, Confederate flags, and various Nazi symbols in their efforts to unite the various hate groups and protest the removal of a Confederate statue. Significant violence occurred when the white supremacists met with counterprotesters. At approximately 1:45 P.M. on August 12, a self-proclaimed white supremacist drove his car into a crowd and killed a thirty-two-year-old counterprotester and injured nineteen others. The perpetrator of these crimes was ultimately convicted of, among other things, first-degree murder. Shifting remarks from the forty-fifth president of the United States, which included a hesitance to condemn the hate groups by name while instead choosing to cast blame on both sides, were met with great criticism. In the days that followed, the president insisted there were "fine people on both sides." White supremacists, associated with various groups, openly praised the president's seeming reluctance to specifically name them or hold them accountable.

Chapter 62

TILLIE

Today

Tillie opens up the shop later than usual. He tapes on OPEN sign on the plywood that now covers the broken glass in his front door, sweeps the yellow pollen from the sidewalk, and unlocks the register. Mrs. Tillie didn't come in this morning. Tillie will tell folks she isn't feeling well. You know, he'll say, we've been fighting what ails her for ages. They'll be headed to the Coulter place once Imogene calls them to say come on over. She's tangled in a worse mess than Tillie. Jo Lynne is dead, Eddie's sitting in a cell, and Garland ain't been seen since last night. Imogene said she'd explain but not just yet, so Tillie's waiting for her call. After years of hoping the Knights of the Southern Georgia Order were behind them, he and Mrs. Tillie are back to being as fearful as they were the day Tillie first left them.

Robert took his watches when he left the shop, and Tillie called out after him that he didn't have nothing to do with Edison Coulter stealing them and that he didn't have no idea where Natalie Sharon made off to. Only time will tell if Robert believes him. So far, there have been no reports of Tillie's car being spotted, but just as he is thinking it and hoping Natalie Sharon is well beyond Tennessee by now, a blue sedan pulls to a stop outside the front door and Detective Warren Nowling steps out.

"I hear your car's been stolen," the detective says. His eyes are red and his lids are hanging too low.

"And I hear you got a hell of a mess there at the Coulter place," Tillie says, nodding that, yes, his car's been stolen. "Don't know nothing about Natalie Sharon, if that's what you're asking."

"I'm guessing Natalie is safer with me not knowing," Warren says. "So, no, ain't here about her. Here to ask a favor of you, Mr. Tillerson."

"Happy to help if I can."

"The pines, can you take me?"

Tillie starts to ask what Warren means by the pines but stops because if Warren is asking about that place, he has good reason, and Tillie's so damn tired of hiding.

"Who you expecting to find out there?" Tillie asks, afraid he's thinking he'll find Natalie.

"Got a missing woman on my hands. Not expecting to find her there, but fearing I might."

"We'll need to head south," Tillie says, locking the shop behind them and hoping like hell they don't find Natalie.

The two men don't say much during the drive. Warren sometimes goes with Imogene, though Mrs. Tillie says a person could hardly call it that, and so Tillie isn't sure what he thinks of the man and his intentions. Still, Tillie owes it to Imogene to help him. She's going through some kind of terrible mess, and if this fellow means anything to her, she'll be leaning on him. It's time she leans on someone other than Tillie.

"How long's it been?" Warren asks as he slows and parks where Tillie tells him to. He knows Tillie was once part of the Klan, and it's why he asked for Tillie's help finding the pines.

"Forty years," Tillie says.

"Never had call to go looking for this place since I've been in town," Warren says. "When's the last time someone turned up out here?"

As far as Tillie knows, it's been fifteen years, but he doesn't tell Warren that. Maybe he should, and then Warren could tell Imogene the truth about what happened to her real daddy. Tillie sure never could. He doesn't tell about the young fellow who died here forty years ago either. Instead, he shrugs. "Really couldn't say."

The road has brought them around to the south side of the river. This is where the thick clay of north Georgia gives way to sand. The hickories on the north side grow tall and have a wide green canopy that can't be beat for its yellow coloring come fall. But here on the south side, the pines crowd together, and their long needles litter the ground at the base of their trunks. To the north, the land is higher and it falls here to the lower ground of the south and the river falls with it. It's as if the whole of Georgia split in two right here just outside of Simmonsville.

"How far?" Warren says. He has to holler because the fall of the water is loud this close to the river.

Tillie points to a spot he remembers better than he'd have thought he would. It doesn't look so different from when he was last here, what with all the trees being of the slow-growing sort. While the path is mostly gone, he still knows the way. Giving Warren a wave, Tillie leads him straight into a thick mess of pines. They stand close together like maybe they're all waiting on something.

Tillie never thought much about the noise of the water falling from the north down into the south, but it's loud and it never stops. As he and Warren walk, the noise grows because they're following the river and walking closer to that split that causes the fall. Tillie never realized it before. He's tried not to think about this place since he was last here, though he sometimes wakes and feels as if he's been trapped in the middle of that mess of pines, unable to find his way out. The fellows always came to this place because the noise was good cover. No matter how loud a man screamed, no one would ever hear him over the fast-running water.

Just up ahead, the pines will stand aside. They'll give way to an open patch where the wire grass takes over. When Tillie reaches that spot, where he feels like he's crossing over a threshold, he stops.

Back then, all them forty years ago, it had been a windy day.

Tillie remembers because he'd been standing right alongside Robert Robithan as his wife told them the story. The three of them stood on the sidewalk not far from Tillie's shop when she pointed across the street with one hand and used the other to hold her hair from being blown across her face.

"He was right there," Edith Robithan said. "Just before you got here, he whistled at me. Heard it clear as a bell."

She had to speak up for the wind blowing like it was. Tillie stood with one hand to the top of his head to hold his hat on. He should have asked how she could hear a whistle from across the street when he couldn't hardly hear her talking right next to him, but he didn't. Neither did Robert Robithan. Neither did the other two fellows who had walked up and joined them.

Tillie's first mistake had been leaving his shop when he saw Robert and Edith out on the sidewalk, Edith looking upset. His second, and biggest, and the one he'd always regret, was not asking how Edith heard such a thing over all that wind. Beyond that, there are parts Tillie can't remember, though he knows he did them. And there's parts he'll never forget. The feel of that young fellow's leg next to Tillie's as they sat together in the back of Robert Robithan's car. The crease in his shirtsleeve where his mama must have run an iron over it. The way the fellow turned toward Tillie and started to smile because he knew Tillie from his shop and how the smile quickly faded. But the thing Tillie will most remember is the look of fear in that fellow's eyes, and how that look turned so quick to acceptance and then sorrow, real sorrow, because that young fellow had always thought better of people. But he also wasn't surprised to have been so wrong. That's mostly what Tillie lives with now—knowing his face was the last thing that young fellow seen.

"I ain't going no farther," Tillie hollers.

Warren steps up alongside him and starts to ask why, but then he sees enough, same as Tillie.

"Jesus Christ." Warren pulls out his phone and starts running into the clearing.

Strung up between the lone two pines, feet tied together and a six-and-a-half-inch fixed-blade knife sticking out of his chest, is Garland Hix.

Chapter 63

IMOGENE

Today

Imogene pours Tillie a cup of coffee and sits across from him at the kitchen table. A plate of buttermilk biscuits sits between them. They're leftovers from what Jo Lynne made the morning after the fire. She added black pepper and bacon to them, and the kitchen still smells of both. Grated frozen butter was her secret, but even knowing that and doing the same—freezing a stick of butter and grating it into the flour—Imogene could never get as good a make on her biscuits. Imogene knows enough about grief to know the pain around losing her sister and the anger she feels toward her will take a good long time to work themselves out. Mama says they'll see to giving Jo Lynne and Garland a proper burial, but it's not going to be at Riverside Baptist.

In the living room, Mama and Mrs. Tillie sit on the sofa with Christopher nestled between them. The sunglasses Christopher is wearing were Mama's idea and belong to her. They're too big for his face and keep slipping down his nose, but they've stopped him from squinting and complaining of a headache. The doctor said after a little time, his eyes would adjust, and other than that and needing some of Mama's good cooking and a whole lot of TLC, he was fit and fine to go. Already Mama and Mrs. Tillie have taught him the rules of Go Fish. The colorful deck of cards is spread across the coffee table between the three of them, and so far, Mama's ticking heart isn't causing anyone any trouble.

"What have you told him?" Tillie asks, glancing at the three of them.

"Not much. Just that they're looking real hard for his mama."

Imogene stretches a hand across the table and squeezes Tillie's. He looks tired. She forgets his age sometimes and tends to see the Tillie he'd been when she and Russell were kids, running through the shop.

"Well, here's what I'm adding to your plate," Tillie says, scooting so his back is to the living room. "The Robithans, all them fellows in fact, they say the watches weren't stole. Say it was a misunderstanding."

"They're covering up for Daddy?" Imogene says, glancing at the window when she thinks she hears a car.

"They ain't covering up for nobody but their own," Tillie says. "They're saying no one was stealing, and there ain't no debt either."

Imogene lets out a long breath and pushes away from the table to get a better look outside. She's tired of thinking about Robithans and watches and unpaid debts. Warren said he'd be by again as soon as he had more news, and that's what she cares about because she's hoping for news of Christopher's mama. When Warren stopped by earlier, he told them about Garland being found strung up between the pines. Imogene had stared up at him as he spoke and had not one feeling for Garland. All she could think was that at least Jo Lynne didn't have to live through this and that maybe the young woman, Beth, would know she was safe and could come home to Christopher now. As if seeing the thought in Imogene's eyes, Warren shook his head and said they hadn't yet found the woman Eddie first told them was named Beth.

Since being taken into custody, everything Eddie has told them fits with Beth having been the little girl who disappeared that night several years ago. Eddie also confessed to having killed the babysitter, a young Puerto Rican woman name Julia Marianna Perez. He said they wanted real Americans teaching Americans and that he went there that night to scare her and her family out of town.

"On top of everything else," Imogene had asked, "does he really believe that?"

"I'm guessing the facts of geography don't much matter to those fellows," Warren had said.

When Warren's car doesn't appear in the drive, Imogene scoots back up to the kitchen table. She glances over at Mama and Christopher. As much as Mama is tending Christopher, he's tending her too. It'll be Christopher, not Imogene, who gets Mama through the difficult days ahead. If she's feeling the loss of Jo Lynne and Garland yet, or that Eddie will spend his life in prison, she isn't showing it. Maybe Mama has been living her whole life knowing Jo Lynne and Eddie would come to a terrible end. Maybe she's been preparing and grieving since they were children and first slipped a hood over their heads.

"So, that's the end of it, then," Imogene says. "No debt. No missing watches. We don't have to worry about them coming after Mama's house."

Tillie shakes his head. "No, Imogene, it ain't the end of it. They're saying them things because without a debt, there ain't no reason they would kill Garland. No motive, no crime. They're saying it to cover for themselves."

"You're giving them too much credit."

"No, I ain't." Tillie lowers his voice and leans over the table. "I'm going to tell you something, and Goddamn it, you're going to listen to me. There ain't a doubt in this world Timmy Robithan drove that knife into Garland's chest, and he done it because Garland stole near a quarter million dollars. Don't you think them boys will stop wanting their money because Garland is dead."

"Tillie, I have too much to think about right now. Let's leave it to another day."

Tillie stands and jerks a thumb toward the door so Imogene will follow him. Outside, the sun is full in the sky and the air is still cool. The hint of smoke hanging over the house is a reminder that everything really happened. Once on the porch, Tillie pulls the door closed.

"You know I was one of them once," Tillie says.

Imogene nods, motioning for Tillie to keep his voice down. She's already worried about Mama and she doesn't need anything else troubling her. She most certainly doesn't need to hear talk of the Klan.

"And you think I got out to tend to Mrs. Tillie, don't you?"

"None of that matters," Imogene says. The history here at this house and the grounds around it is too heavy, and it feels as if by talking about it, they're feeding it.

"It does matter," Tillie says. He rubs his eyes and takes a deep breath. "I didn't get out because of Mrs. Tillie's health, and I'm ashamed as I can be that I used her that way. Ashamed in a way I can never fix, because Russell died believing that's the only reason I broke with them fellows. Probably died believing I'd still be one of them if it weren't for his mama's poor health."

"He never thought that of you," Imogene says. "Please stop." She wants to get back in the house because even knowing Christopher is just inside isn't enough. She wants him with her. She wants to hear every word he says and to be looking down on him every time he wakes. She wants to bend the facts of what he's been through to protect him even though she can't do such a thing. She wants to keep him safe.

"I got out," Tilly says, "because I stood under those pines south of town and held a young boy's arm while Robert Robithan spit in his face and jammed a knife in his heart. I stood there, felt the pain shoot through that child's body, and I didn't do nothing but run. I was a Goddamned coward. So I damn well know what them men can do, and don't you think they wouldn't do the same to you."

"I understand, okay, just stop. You need to calm down."

Tillie pulls a kerchief from his front pocket and lowers himself onto the chair where Daddy used to sit most nights. He blots his forehead and upper lip.

"They did the same to your daddy, too," he says, lifting his eyes to look her straight on. "Your real daddy, I mean."

Imogene turns away and crosses her arms. When they first stepped onto the porch, she felt it coming and now it's here.

"You already knew, didn't you?" Tillie says. "I'll be damned. Guess I should have realized. You even come to me and Mrs. Tillie at the time and told us about the police at your house. Course you knew."

"Edison wanted him dead." Imogene glances back at Tillie. She's never said it out loud, probably because that would have made it harder to deny. "Didn't he? And Tim Robithan did it."

That night at the lake, when Imogene almost drowned herself, she'd known her real daddy was dead and that Mama had loved him. She knew because of the way Mama cried. Imogene knew, and she wanted to die too. It was part of the gift of being young and the curse too, because for that one day at least, she knew the truth and was brave enough to believe it or naïve enough or even foolish enough. But then the truth got clouded over by her having to live in a house with Edison Coulter. If she was going to do that, she couldn't believe her real daddy was dead, because then she'd have to believe the rest—that the Klan had killed him. Tim Robithan killed her real daddy, and Edison Coulter ordered him to do it.

"And that's why Timmy is where he is today," Tillie says. "He done Edison a favor, and Edison returned it. But that ain't why I'm telling you these things, and it sure ain't to hurt you. I want you to understand why your mama stayed here with Edison. Lottie has always known full well the kind of trouble the two of you could end up in if she crossed Edison. She understood in a way I'm afraid you still don't. She stayed to keep you safe."

Imogene's always wondered why Mama stayed, though she couldn't bring herself to ask. No matter how gently she might have posed the questions, there'd have been accusation in it. Mama had been protecting Imogene, simple as that, because like Tillie, Mama fully understood the danger of that kind of hate.

"I didn't want you ever doubting your mama like I fear Russell must have doubted me."

Imogene pushes off the railing at the sound of tires on the gravel drive. "Hand to God, Tillie. I never once heard Russell have a single doubt about you. Not once."

Warren's car pulls up and stops in the drive.

"You go on," Tillie says, pushing himself out of his chair. He pauses long enough to smooth his hair, something he must still do for Mrs. Tillie. "Ask your mama; she'll tell you about your daddy. He was a redhead too."

Waiting until the door has closed behind Tillie, Imogene walks from the porch and meets Warren on the drive. The pecan trees north of the house will have to be trimmed soon, their branches close to clipping the top of the gardening shed, and Mama will be wanting to lay down fertilizer by the end of the month. Every Thanksgiving, they make Mama's praline pecan cakes for the neighbors, and this year will be no different. Imogene will see to that.

"We found her," Warren says, and because of the way he takes Imogene's hands, not worried about her yanking away from him, she already knows the young girl is dead.

He goes on to tell Imogene that the girl, Bethany Jane Liddell, was found dragged back up into the trees not too far from the house. His best guess—Garland killed her while Jo Lynne was serving biscuits and gravy to the Klan in Mama's kitchen and the fire was barely out at the old place. He figures Garland wanted to kill both Bethany and Christopher to sever any ties to him.

"Probably was holding out hope he could still get your mama to sell the place and take care of his debts."

"This whole time," Imogene says. "Even before Tillie could find the necklace she left for him in his shop. She's been gone."

Warren also tells her that the young girl, Bethany Jane, wasn't Christopher's real mama. Imogene already knew that, though she hadn't told Warren. It was something Eddie said, or maybe it was Jo Lynne when they were all up on the ridge. She can't remember what it was, but it had rooted itself and she was afraid of what it might mean. Christopher might have a family out there who would want him and Imogene would have to let him go. She nods and runs her thumbs over the backs of Warren's hands. She'll have to tell Christopher that his mama is dead, and she'll have to be strong enough to see the look in his eyes when she does. She'll have to be strong enough to see Vaughn in those eyes and not turn away. She'll have to be strong enough to keep holding on.

"Eddie won't tell us anything about Christopher's real mother, not even her name. Says Garland killed her and doesn't know where the body might be. Killed her because she tried to run. I figure he won't tell because he wants Christopher here with you."

Imogene nods and turns to go, but Warren holds tight to her hands.

"I'm still worried about that money," he says, tilting his head so he can look down into her eyes. "They'll keep coming until they get what they're owed. Men who'll do what I seen done to Garland, they'll keep coming. What your daddy was hoping to get for those watches, that wasn't even going to put a dent in what Garland needed to pay back."

"You know what's almost funny?" Imogene asks, ignoring what Warren said. "I remember Edison having a fit when he realized the house, this whole place, was in Mama's name alone. Granddaddy had to explain to him twice how it was best to only have her name on the deed so it couldn't get seized in a lawsuit. Not even sure if that's true. But instead of Mama protecting it from some lawsuit, she's kept the Klan from getting hold of it. That's almost funny, isn't it?" She pauses and looks up at Warren. "Now Mama is the last Simmons who will ever own this place. And I can guarantee you'll never see another Knight on this property."

"Please, Imogene," he says. "You and your mama really need to think of leaving here. Your mama owns this place, you're right about that. And it's hers to sell. So sell it and move on. Natalie Sharon, she's gone, and you can bet it's because she's afraid, and that was over a couple of watches."

The hardest part for Imogene has always been imagining the final moments of her son's life when he realized she wasn't there and that she wasn't coming. Did he miss her, wonder why she wasn't sitting alongside him in the back seat like she should have been, almost always was. Worst of all, was he frightened? She hadn't been there for either him or Russell because she'd stayed home to get caught up on the laundry. Daddy had told her she was no kind of wife or mother. You got no food in the house. Dishes is piled in your sink. That child ain't had a haircut. You ain't no kind of wife or mother.

And so when Russell and Vaughn went to the park to ride the swings, Imogene stayed home to do the things Daddy said needed doing. If she hadn't been folding the laundry and chatting with Jo Lynne about something she can no longer remember, could she have seen the truck coming up from the right? Could she have seen that it wasn't going to stop and warned Russell in time? Every day, for the past five years, those last few final moments have unraveled in exactly the same way and so the ending has never changed. And every day, for the past five years, she has hated Daddy because everything he was, every belief he held, destroyed her life when she lived instead of died. Destroyed it until now.

"Christopher is staying, yes?" Imogene asks.

"Do my best to keep him here with you," Warren says. "Don't have a hope in hell of finding out if he has any family out there.

But please, think about what I said. You all need to think about leaving here."

Sometime in the days after the accident that killed Vaughn and Russell, Warren told Imogene that her son's and husband's final moments were really final seconds, split seconds, because it had happened that fast. There was no time for fear or suffering. That's all she's ever had to hope for. Warren told her Vaughn and Russell were gone instantly, both of them were. But maybe Warren only said that to spare her. She knows him well enough now to know he's kind like that.

"Come on inside," Imogene says, leading Warren toward the house. "Mama's cooking."

There will come a day when a new family moves into the simple farmhouse that doesn't look much like what people imagine of a plantation home. They'll scrape and paint the clapboard siding, marvel at the tall baseboards they're certain are original, and think the worn patches in the pine floors are authentic and quaint. And maybe they'll learn that the Klan once gathered alongside the lake just east of their new home. Maybe they'll occasionally feel the chill of the history that hangs over the house, though they'll never quite understand that, while those men no longer march past, dressed in their robes and hoods and carrying torches, they're still out there, just underfoot. The town, Imogene hopes, will never forget that the hate is still simmering and that it can rise again. If they're never gone too long from remembering, they'll always be ready. Mama and Imogene will be staying in the house for now, for as long as Mama wants. This house, this land, will never again be a foothold for the Knights of the Southern Georgia Order.

ACKNOWLEDGMENTS

My thanks to the many fine people at Dutton who supported this novel. Thank you to Christine Ball for her many years of commitment to my work, and to Maya Ziv for her guidance, enthusiasm, and keen eye. Thank you also to Emily Canders, Madeline Newquist, and Elina Vaysbeyn for their professionalism and for taking such great care of this novel. And much appreciation to Jenny Bent of the Bent Agency for her many years of guidance and support and for the late-night tweets that made me laugh. I would also like to thank James Sewell for his insight and Brenda Kocher for sharing some of her knowledge with me over a few cups of coffee. I am especially grateful to Brenda and Tibet, as are many in our community, for the important work they do. And thanks to Stacy, Kim, and Karina for their ongoing support and friendship, and thanks to Roy Peter Clark for sharing his journalist's eye. I've also been thinking lately about several of the writing friends I first met many years ago. While we may only see each other online occasionally these days, my thanks to Adam, Lisa, Scotti, Michael, Chris, and Angela.

Lastly, thank you to William, my first reader, and to Andrew and Savanna, who haven't read my work but who are always eager to discuss a story line and make a suggestion or two.

ABOUT THE AUTHOR

Lori Roy is the author of *Bent Road,* winner of the Edgar Award for Best First Novel; *Until She Comes Home,* finalist for the Edgar Award for Best Novel; *Let Me Die in His Footsteps,* winner of the Edgar Award for Best Novel; and, most recently, *The Disappearing.* She lives in St. Petersburg, Florida, with her family.